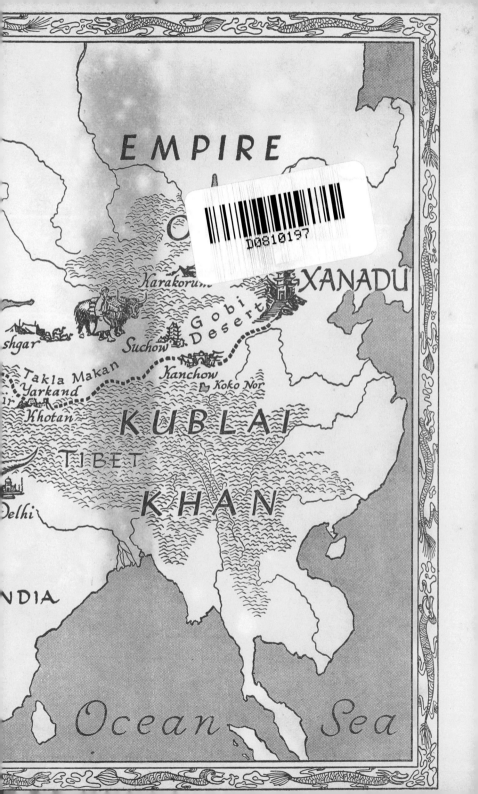

CARAVAN TO XANADU

CARAVAN TO XANADU

A Novel of MARCO POLO

EDISON MARSHALL

FARRAR, STRAUS and YOUNG

New York

TO AGNES

CONTENTS

Prologue

PROLOGUE

WHEN MARCO POLO, A FAMOUS TRAVELER AND NOBLE CITIZEN of Venice, had come to ripe years and pleasant fortunes, he was summoned to the ducal palace and honorably received by the Doge, Pietro Gradenigo.

"I have just read a manuscript describing the lands and peoples visited in your travels," the Doge remarked, "and I had a curiosity to look into your face."

"I thank your Grace," Marco Polo replied with a courtly manner, "and I hope my humble recital gave you pleasure."

"It did indeed, as well as instruction. Thereby I learned of the customs and commerce, climate and politics, of many kingdoms and cities that I didn't know existed under the sun. I took pleasure in reading of the wondrous sights, such as broad seas, cloud-capped mountains, deserts, palaces, and wonders past counting that you beheld, and of the soul-stirring sounds, such as the voices of demons amid the barren sands and the blare of trumpets and cymbals of mighty kings as they rode forth to battle, which you heard with your own ears. I took note of the sweet perfumes that came to your nostrils, as well as the grievous stinks, and of the exquisite viands and heavenly wines that pleased your palate. I marveled over the furs, silks, gold, and jewels that passed through your hands. But I couldn't share with you these rare and enthralling experiences, because you did not give me leave."

Marco Polo gazed half in bewilderment, half in consternation, into the Doge's countenance, which was half clouded, half lighted, by a faint smile.

"Your Grace, I'm not sure that I understand you," Marco said.

"You didn't make me your companion, Marco Polo. It was as though you didn't trust me to share your joys and sorrows, victories and defeats, let alone the more delicate sensations of your body and soul. Indeed, you didn't even let me see your face."

"It's the face of an aging and tired traveler——" Marco Polo began, in his perplexity catching at the straw.

"It was not so when the great journey began or even when it ended," the Doge broke in. "Even now, your brow is high and noble, your eyes are sparkling with the zest of life, your nose is long and strong and fit to follow through the world, your mouth at once delicate and firm. Your body is sturdy and retains vestiges of youthful grace. Marco Polo, are you a merchant before you are a man? I don't believe it. Did no poetic feelings rise in your soul when you gazed upon rivers so great that in comparison with them the Po is no more than a mountain brook? Weren't you frightened of the dangers along the road? Did not many times your life hang by a hair?"

"Truly it did, but——"

"Did you sometimes laugh? Did you never weep? Did no fires kindle your liver when you gazed upon the beautiful maidens of the Kashmir?"

"I conceive you now, your Grace. Since the scenes themselves were so strange and new to my fellow citizens, I thought best to describe them as mundanely as possible, for credence' sake. And while a great many remarkable adventures were inherent to my journey, I thought that their narration would bring upon me the charge of self-glorification, and thus make suspect the whole writing."

"Seen in that light, Messer Polo, your restraint was wise. The ignorant, the narrow-minded, and the crass are by nature skeptical, as well as stone-blind to the poetic turns of Fate. Still, I hope you will have leisure and inclination to essay another account of your great emprise, to be circulated only among the nobility, the gentry, and others of equal education and imagination. With them you may dare be honest. You may prove to us, even at this late day, that the world is more wide and wonderful than our fireside dreams envision, and that it's still the oyster of the brave and resolute man.

"Marco Polo, you trusted in the old gods, the gods of Reward and Retribution, or you would have never set sail for Cathay," the Doge went on, his eyes alight. "Tell us the fate of those who defy those gods! You sought Adventure, knowing she would yield to your rough wooing. Tell us of the bed you made with her, and what children were born. Reveal your secrets, Marco, my friend and fellow citizen! Lay bare your heart."

BOOK ONE

CHAPTER 1

THE OLD ARAB

I AM MARCO POLO, A VENETIAN. ALTHOUGH THERE HAVE BEEN other appendages to my name at various times, some of no small honor, thus I declare myself before the world and history, my name and my degree.

I declare too, with the same largeness, that there is no city in the world like my native city. When I was twelve years old—old enough to marvel over my father's and mother's and my own conjunction in this happy spot—I went alone into San Marco's church, walked with bent head lest my eyes be dazzled or made proud by its manifold glories, and on my knees gave humble thanks for the great boon. And on this occasion I did not slip a petition or two into the offering. Although my heart was ever bursting with desires, many of them springing from great needs, by the strong grip of my will I muted every one.

In my inward heart, Venice was something more than the wondrous city of my nativity. All men knew she was the Bride of the Sea—made so by a mystic bond of which the ceremonies of Ascension Day were only the acknowledgment—and I, a boy of twelve, largely undistinguishable from a thousand urchins along the lagoon, held her to be my foster father and mother. My earthly father had sailed away before I was born, and I had never laid eyes on him. My own beautiful mother had died before I could talk plain, when only with my hungry lips and arms could I tell her of my love. Would then the Sea's Bride, ever gay and tender, deny my plea made with tear-filled eyes between sleep and waking in the full black tide of night, such a scene of advent as most mortals visit sometimes in their lives?

I did not find the answer until another midnight, when at risk of a public flogging, if not a burning, I mounted all four of the great bronze horses brought from over the sea when Venice was newborn, and which stand on the outer gallery of the church—I believed what came into my heart that night. I still believe that some mystic relationship between the spirit of the city and my spirit—if it were only a lad's love born of loneliness—shaped in no small part my future fate.

Why not begin my chronicle with an event of that same year?

I was well grown for my age, with the big hands and feet that foretell large stature among men, and if I were ever noticed in a crowd of boys, it was because of the peculiarity of blue eyes going with black lashes, eyebrows, and hair and olive skin. Of themselves they were no novelty. Blonds were seen every minute or two on the Rialto. Still, they were not as common as in Genoa. I suppose the reason was that the latter city lies in the shadow of mountains, while our merry, highborn lady plays in the sun.

In Venice, even rainy days are gay. On the day in question, the sky was bright as a steel mirror brought from Damascus. But it was not in respect to the warm weather that I wore a flimsy shirt and tattered breeches and no more. The poor rig spared my better turnout, itself no fine array God wot, in fact hand-me-downs from my cousin Leo. Besides, in the part of the city for which I was bound, rags that could not hide purses were healthier than robes, less conspicuous, and lighter to run in. It was a part of the city that I greatly loved—it was my college, which I would not swap for Padua—and when I went there I shed all vestiges of respectability along with my cares.

By the da Lorenzo canal, a high-smelling backwater of the lagoon, I joined four of my playmates on a mighty voyage. Our argosy was only a big skiff owned by the fisherman father of one of our crew, and our adventure was to go as near as we dared to a very strange ship newly come to anchor. She had only threescore oars, but very tall masts. While she could not run as fast as our centipede galleys when the wind failed her, when it blew fair I thought she could outfly them as an albatross does a gull. Her wings were folded now, but they must be as big as an albatross's in proportion to her body, longer and sharper than any vessel's I had ever seen.

"Now what do you reckon she is?" asked Felix the fisherman's son, my best friend. We were resting on our oars a cable's length distant.

"She's a vile Infidel, and you can lay to that," another answered.

"I'll tell you what she is. She's a zebec." And my authoritative tone did not betray the wildness of my guess.

"How did you know?" one awed fellow asked.

"My papa and my uncle fought with them in the Sea of Marmara. They're the swift war galleys of Algiers."

Just then a black-bearded man on the deck, with a naked waist and a great, hooked sword, saw us and shouted something in an unknown tongue. At once a half-dozen of his fellows came pouring from the castle—tall, brown, some half naked and others fantastically dressed—yelling and gesticulating with what seemed extreme fierceness. My companions were so frightened that they were snatching up their oars, intending to run before the ravening crew launched their longboat.

I was somewhat less frightened, less because of a bolder heart than because of a cooler head. These bearded sunburned sailors were the wildest I ever saw loose on a ship deck, but I had seen men of their dress and complexion chained together after galley fights on the eastern seas. I could not believe that they had brought their war vessel into the lagoon without the consent of the harbor master, or would dare shed Christian blood in sight of the Lion of San Marco. Their shouts sounded more frantic than ferocious, and their beckonings might indicate distress.

"I don't think they'll hurt us," I told my mates. "Let's go up——"

"And have 'em snatch us aboard and clap us in irons?" one of them screeched, desperately plying his oar.

"They'll whack off our stones and sell us for harem slaves," added Felix, the lively witted fisherman's son.

One of the turbaned crew was holding up a small, bright object that I took for a silver coin, meanwhile clapping his other hand on his heart. This did not cinch my decision as much as a passion that had mastered me before—extreme curiosity. I had more of it than any boy I played with. I would take greater hazards to have it gratified.

"If you won't come alongside, I'll swim for it," I said.

My friends looked glum and Felix shook his head.

"I'd go with you, Marco, if this was my boat," he told me. "But it's my father's boat."

At that I slipped overboard into what I thought would be warm water. It seemed to have chilled as by some treason of nature. Only devilish pride, for which more sinners have died than saints have for piety, kept me stroking. The ship began to loom high and sinister. My heart lay so heavy it was a wonder I did not sink. Saracens were notorious slave-catchers—bold as sharks—and it was told on the Rialto that they performed Satanic ceremonies with Christian children. . . .

Yet my leaden arms kept flailing, and suddenly I became aware of a splendid victory.

With joyful faces, two of the Infidels threw down a rope ladder. Others held out hands to give me a lift—all were exclaiming pleasure and praise. One cried "Bravo!" quite like a Venetian, strutting the accomplishment before his fellows. This last touch of nature did more to reassure me than all the rest.

When I had soared over the rail, the men gathered about me, their faces sober now, while their leader tried to tell me something. I could not understand a word of the heathen lingo, but he shouted and sweated like a Christian; and when he was struck by an idea and beckoned me to follow him down a dim hatch, I did so without much fear. He led me into an incense-scented room lighted by an oil lamp. I became aware of a great heap of multi-colored rugs, and then of a human form. The flickering light revealed a brown, bony face, snowy eyebrows and beard, and white raiment.

"Mustapha Sheik?" my guide called in a reverent tone.

"Yea, Kemal Capudan," the old man answered feebly.

After a brief conversation, the lamp was brought so that the gaffer could see me better. Thereby I discovered the most wonderful face that my eyes had ever lighted on, though I could not tell where its wonder lay. Although he wore no gold or jewels and his garments appeared to be white cotton and the only indication of luxury in the room was his heap of rugs, I believed that he was as great a lord as the Doge of Venice.

"So you've come to help me," he said in my native tongue. "What's your name?"

"It's Marco Polo, your Honor."

"Your speech is not in accord with your habit. Of that, I must know more later. Marco, we're anchored here by the sufferance of the harbor master, under orders that no man leave the vessel until certain papers are issued by the Council. Meanwhile I have come down with an old sickness, and without my medicine—our store of it was stolen at Malta—my good mariners are afraid I may succumb. I will not, but almost wish I might, so great is my pain."

"If you'll tell me what it is and give me the money, I'll get you some."

"We call it bhang, or hashish, and savants know it as Indian hemp. But I fear it will be hard to find in Venice."

It was then that I thanked my patron saint and namesake, San Marco, for knowing so well the city that he guards. Among my favorite resorts were the apothecary shops, with their strange wares. Now and again I had eked out pocket money by selling toads, snails, glowworms, and snake eyes, and even more gruesome objects.

"Doubt not I can find you some, your Honor," I told him.

The piece of gold that he handed me was not as beautiful in my sight as his brightening face. The quest of the medicine became a glorious emprise. The fleet pike would be hard put to it to beat me back to the boat.

2

Returning to the zebec with the medicine in my pocket, I had no lack of stout henchmen. They rowed our four-oared argosy under the very sail of the Infidel and watched with round eyes what seemed the adventure's end. Eager hands reached down. To the hand I took for the captain's I entrusted the potion; when I showed him six silver grossi I had received in change, his jubilant cry of "Backsheesh!" told me I could keep them. This was a word known to every lad frequenting the quays, an importation from Egypt and the Levantine coast meaning "commission" or "gift."

My companions were thrilled enough by the rich gift, but I had them tarry awhile in the hope of some greater happening. My reward was the return of the swarthy captain to the deck and a glorious halloo across the water. At my answering shout, he pointed to the sun. Three times he swept his arm westward to indicate the passage of three days—common sign language among the polyglot people of the port—then beckoned from me to the ship. My comrades looked at me as though I had come in to a fortune.

At dawn of the fourth day a bumboat captain who claimed to know Arabic brought me alongside the zebec. After a little wait, the ship's longboat bore Mustapha Sheik to Spinalunga Island across the bay, where I witnessed a strange scene of farewell. While he stood tall in a white robe of mourning, flanked on each side by a servant, one after another of his followers bowed down before him, weeping. It was not hard to guess that he was going into exile for the remainder of his days. No doubt he had been banished from Islam, and the zebec had ventured our waters solely to transport him here. If Spinalunga were his chosen instead of enforced abode, I thought it a good choice: the Venetian Jews dwelt here by law, among them many patriarchs whose noble faces resembled his, and who could be his friends.

Truly I should have wondered at his journeying westward instead of eastward from his native deserts. The answer lay, as time revealed, in his curiosity regarding Western Europe and what he called its waking from a long sleep. He thought that the last years of his life could be spent more interestingly in Venice than in any other city available to him.

I helped his servants install him and his goods in a small but worthy house facing the lagoon, and ran some of his errands. He gave me golden Torpini dates, rarely seen in Venice, pomegranates, and melons, and told me I could come another day. On that day I was allowed to look at some of his treasures—books with bejeweled covers, illuminated scrolls, and instruments that I thought must be for alchemy but instead were for studying the stars. These things fascinated me, suggesting distant lands and mysterious lore, but no more than the old man himself with his wonderful lean face and living eyes. I kept coming back. I was always sure of his welcome and the visits were exciting in ways I could not name.

He was never loath to put down his manuscripts or lay aside his calculations to answer my questions, and the day came soon that he questioned me carefully as to my history. I told him that my father, Nicolo Polo, had departed for Constantinople with his elder brother Maffeo about six months before my birth. According to their letters to their half-sister Flora, they had lived in the Venetian quarter there for six years, buying and selling goods. Then they had gone to Sudak in the Crimea, and on eastward to a city called Bolgary, where they were living the last my aunt had heard.

"Bolgary?" Mustapha Sheik echoed in a wondering tone.

"It's on a river called the Volga."

"Well I know. Marco, that's a very long way. Have you any notion how long?"

"Not a very clear notion."

"By crow flight I would guess it as close to two thousand miles. But men may not follow the flight of the crows, and by caravan road the distance is nearer three thousand miles. Do your father and uncle have to go that far—amid such ready dangers—to make their fortunes?"

"According to the last letter, they found their way homeward blocked by warring tribesmen and were making for another city named Bukhara."

Mustapha looked more thoughtful than before. "Has your father sent abundant moneys for your support?" he asked.

"He hasn't sent any. We supposed he wasn't able to do so with safety. My aunt Flora's husband, Uncle Zane, looks out for me some. He expects to be repaid with interest when my father comes home rich."

"Your father could have sent money, if he knew the means. There are Jews in every city as far as Bukhara who'll warrant the payment of moneys by fellow Jews in any other city, and their only fee is its use in the periods between. But I suppose your father wouldn't trust them. Has he promised to recompense your uncle?"

"No, your Honor, he's never mentioned it."

"What has he written you on the subject?"

"I've never heard from him."

"Never? Then surely he has sent you greetings in his letters to your uncle and aunt."

"He has sent greetings to their son Leo, but has never mentioned me."

"Perhaps he doesn't know that his wife bore him a son."

"Uncle Zane has referred to me in several letters—asking what to do for me. My father never replies."

"Your uncle Zane must love you, to continue with your care——"

"He doesn't love me and Aunt Flora cares very little about me. They give all their love to Leo. Uncle Zane has no money except what came with Aunt Flora, and the Polo name still carries too much weight with him for him to turn me out. But I cost him almost nothing and I'm away all day."

"That affords you time to come here, for which I'm glad." Mustapha Sheik had me bring him a cup containing a liquor of bhang, sipped from it, and set it aside. In reply to his further questions I told him that my mother had been above my father in name and had brought him a fair dower, most of which he had taken with him to Constantinople. She had died of fever when I was not quite four years old. Her maiden name was Lucia Carpini and she had come from Perugia, between Florence and Rome.

Something I had said had aroused the old Arab's intense interest. I could not see it in his face but felt it in his silence and stillness.

"Marco, do you remember her fairly well?" he asked.

"I remember loving her beyond all the world, and thinking that the world had ended when she died."

"Did she ever speak—or did you ever hear—of Friar Johannes Carpini? He too came from near Perugia."

"I think—I'm almost sure—that he was my mother's uncle." Then there came a mild aching above my eyebrows that I had felt a hundred times before. Trying to bring some vague, very early memories into focus always brought the pain, and often the mere thinking of my mother.

"That valiant old man went farther than Bukhara. It's to him that we owe final proof of the most important political fact of our century."

"Political" was a big word for a boy of twelve, but I would not let him know it. "What is it, Mustapha Sheik?"

"Of course you've heard of Prester John, whom folk believe to be the greatest of Christian kings, ruling half the world."[1]

"I've heard that he's king of seventy-two kings, and is waited on by seven of them at a time. When he goes to war, thirteen crosses twenty feet high, made of solid gold and jewels, are carried before him, each guarded by ten thousand horsemen and a hundred thousand footmen. In front of his palace is a mirror two hundred feet tall——"

"The more learned in Europe know now that he doesn't exist. If he's not made up out of whole cloth, he was a minor king in Africa, and a Coptic Christian. But the most learned—a handful of geographers at the universities of Islam and Christendom—know of a real wonder hardly less than this imaginary one. They found it out from the journal of old Johannes Carpini."

"Is it a secret?" I asked. "If it's not, I entreat you to tell me."

"The greatest secrets in the world are open to those who'll listen and believe. I think your own mother could have told you this one, if Friar Johannes was indeed her uncle. There was a real king, Kuyuk Khan, greater and richer than legend makes Prester John. He was followed by Mangu Khan, and now by Kublai Khan. Kublai has no magic mirror and no giant crosses precede him into battle, but fully a thousand kings, great and small, pay tribute to his throne. His treasures are beyond counting. His empire is many times larger than that of Rome in all her glory. His subjects number Allah alone knows how many hundred million. He's greater than all the kings in Europe rolled together—and yet no European has ever seen his face."

"It may be my father will see him." And my neck prickled fiercely.

"It could well be. And for that glory, he may be blinded, or be killed, or bring home such riches that the very Doge would seem a beggar in comparison."

"How far is Bukhara from the kingdom of Kublai Khan?"

"It's within his kingdom, yet perhaps three thousand miles from his capital."

"If my father doesn't go there in five years, I'll get there first."

Mustapha Sheik beckoned me to him, put his hand on my forehead, and looked deeply into my eyes.

"Do you love your father?" he asked quietly.

"No, I hate him."

"Because he abandoned you?"

"I don't care about that. But it is well to know how he made my mother cry."

"If his goal is the Court of Kublai Khan—and it may be, if he talked to the old friar—you can never catch up with him now. It would be five years or so before you could even start."

"I'll catch up with him, before I'm through, and go beyond him."

"For the reason you just gave?"

"There's another reason, if I could just remember what it was. It was something Mama told me the night before she died." Suddenly the ache over my eyes almost burst my forehead. "It had something to do with two fires——"

The pain dimmed and the intense strain in Mustapha's face slowly faded away.

"Five years," he said quietly. "They are very few compared with mine, and you mustn't grow impatient. If Nicolo Polo becomes the first Venetian to prostrate himself before Kublai Khan, his son Marco may be the first to stand at Kublai's side."

3

On my next visit, Mustapha Sheik showed me a curious object for measuring the height of a heavenly body above the horizon. It was called an astrolabe and was of ancient invention, although its use had been largely forgotten in Europe.

"From the roof tops of Medina the stars are most beautiful and bright," he told me in explaining his possession of the instrument. "I longed to know them better, and to know their orbits and their influence on human affairs. To this end I studied what we call *al jabr*, a branch of mathematics wherein symbols such as *x* and *y* substitute for quantities, and the chords of circles as expounded by my great countryman, al-Battani. With the help of such sciences, and the simple device that you see, used in connection with the Toledo tables prepared by Arabian scholars, I could compute almost the exact place in the heavens that any wandering star would occupy at any given moment of the year."

Since I had never heard of these sciences, his meaning was over my head, but it was as though I jumped like a dog and snatched it like a bone. There was something in his voice and presence that made me listen not just with my ears, but with my whole body.

"Then a great fact dawned on me," Mustapha went on. "Men know the heavens better than they know the earth. So I turned to the science of geography, for which my groundwork in astronomy had prepared me. But for any larger grasp of the subject, I must know the discoveries of great travelers, living and dead. And they have been my study for many years."

"Could I study them too?" I burst out. "Then when the time comes——"

"When the time comes! What would we do without that promise, that hope? Come just after sunrise, when I have prayed, every day for seven days. Then we will see."

After that week of testing, he told me to come when I pleased and stay away when I pleased. I was not to forsake my companions or to skimp my sport, or to neglect the bright school of the quays and canals for the sake of his dim chambers. The upshot of it was that I came almost every day. The only reason that I knew was that I could not stay away. Usually I stayed four or five hours, and every minute of it was like following an unknown path through a breathlessly silent woods.

"*Salem alicum* (Peace be between us), my son Marco," the old man greeted me on a summer day of our second year's friendship.

"*Alicum salem* (There be peace between us), Mustapha Sheik!" I replied with punctilio.

The salutations were heard every day on the Lido, but not so some other expressions as we conversed. The truth was, we were talking in simplified Arabic. It seemed that I had picked it up from him almost unawares, as I might catch lice from a street mate; actually, as I now perceived, he had slipped it on my tongue like a lozenge. Now he served me a sticky sweet, most pleasing to the palate, golden dates stuffed with bitter almonds, and a sherbet of some sort, highly spiced and filling the room with sweet scent.

"What news of the Rialto?" he asked, when I had eaten my fill and more.

"A Genoese spy was found in a closet, cavesdropping on the Council, and beheaded in the Piazzetta," I reported. "Two triremes of Luciano Veniero arrived last night, one from Jaffa, laden with gums and spices, and the other from Tarsus with a cargo of fair-haired slaves."

"Ah, that reminds me," Mustapha Sheik broke in. "I know you

did not fail to notice the red-sailed merchantman with the high castle. What did you make of her?"

"Doubtless she was from England, laden with Cornish tin. One of her blond boatmen cried out on San Giorgio the patron saint of his nation, and I saw Sebastian Cussi, who buys tin for the Arsenal, making toward her in his pigeon-breasted gondola."

"Truly her master used tin for ballast, but he also brought raw wool, salt meat, and timber. And what, think you, will he take in trade?"

"Why, if he's wise, he'll take weapons, and iron to make 'em—swords, spears, pikes, and halberts—and shields and armor. For his nation's divided against itself, and King Henry fights his own lords."

"The Jews tell me that peace will come before summer's end, and they're better prophets than the astrologers. I think the ship had best take glass to repair what's broken, and wine to pledge new friendships, and finery for the newly rich."

I would soon not be hearing such things from his lips, I was thinking. Mustapha's lowered eyebrows formed a white bar as he peered at me.

"Has your uncle said any more about bonding you to the iron-master?" he asked.

"He's made up his mind to it, the day after my fourteenth birth-day. He didn't tell me so, but my cousin Leo wouldn't miss the chance."

"Then he must be convinced, at last, that Nicolo will either never return or will come back a beggar. Marco, what we need is time——"

We had talked thus before. What made this conversation memorable was its interruption by a shout from the canal. We went to the door to find Pietro, a gondolier of my good acquaintance, stopping at our wharf with a fine swirl.

"Did you hear of Messer Veniero's ragusey making port from Jaffa?" he called.

"Of course. What of it?"

"When the clerks unrolled a bale of carpets from Tabriz, there was a letter in 'em, addressed to your aunt Flora. They think it's from your Pa amongst the Infidel."

The letter was being taken to my uncle's house, which for lack of any other I called home. It beat me there by about five minutes, but my aunt was so dithered by the sight of it—not three months since she had said Mass for her brothers' souls—that she had not yet found the courage to open it. This she did featly at sight of me. Perhaps it contained news of a legacy.

It did not, or any other benison to me. I had not deigned to expect it. And in my heart was another thing, grown there since the last letter from Nicolo Polo, seemingly hard as a rock and like a rock foundation to a new structure of manhood. I did not want a message from him and would be weakened by it had it come. What I had hoped for was a boast of wealth whereby my uncle and aunt, mistaking me for his future heir, would provide for me better and leave me free from bondage.

The letter declared that he and his brother Maffeo had dwelt in the Tatar city of Bukhara nearly three years. Meanwhile the wars waged across their homeward paths had spread and fiercened, so they had decided to move on eastward, perhaps even as far as the Ocean Sea, in search of a roundabout but safer route to Venice. Many of their trading ventures had failed, whereby they found themselves in reduced fortunes. And this was the upshot of their hopeful voyage to Constantinople nigh twelve (at this writing) years before—separation from their loved ones and, unless their saints befriended them, death in an alien land.

I did not believe a word of it, but my uncle Zane did so, and found a moral to his liking. His dull, run-of-the-mill face flushed with self-righteousness.

"Well, Marco, after hearing this, I take it you won't be so eager to go gallivanting on the seven seas."

"It's bad news, your Honor, truly."

"I'll hazard you'll be glad to follow some other occupation, and with no more talk."

When the moon had set—a favorite meeting time for the old astronomer and his chela—I told Mustapha the letter's contents. He sat for a while clutching his bearded chin; then he came out on the roof top with me and began pointing out stars for me to name. I did not miss many, since he picked the largest and most beautiful. These were about thirty out of three thousand.

"They're all you'll ever need for taking bearings," he told me. "But my son, you could never win by running away to sea. Your brain must be as stocked with knowledge as your purse is stuffed with gold. The longer you follow, the less fit you are to lead—I want you trained for leadership before you leave my door. That will take, at the least, three years more."

"Master, I want to adventure to the Court of Kublai Khan, not become a munshi in a school."

"How will you go about winning his favor, which is the road to power and a key to his vaults?"

"Tell me, master."

"Remember, he's not only a mighty but a great king. Every word that has trickled out tells us that. All day and night he drives to extend and strengthen and prosper his prodigious empire—whereby he enhances his own godlike power."

"Then he'll want to know all the West can teach him that's any good."

"You asked me what you need, and I'll tell you. It won't pleasure you to hear it, but I'll trow you'll not give up. You know a deal about ships and markets, and something about stuffs. You've picked that up on the Rialto and the quays. You've read widely for your years in books useful to you, and I've taught you useful things. But what do you know of the science of war, as the great captains wrote it down? Are you yourself skilled with any weapon, wherewith to win the respect of your followers or save your own life? Since you could walk you've watched the glass blowers, the shipbuilders, and the armor makers; now you should learn some of the bedrock principles behind their skill."

"I'll do my best, if I can get out of going to work for the iron-master. And there might be a way to do it."

"Marco, you are almost a young Arab, when it comes to craft——"

"If another letter would come, hinting of my father's soon return heavy with gold as an English hooker with tin, and I was to be his heir, my uncle Zane would seat me ahead of his own son."

"And now you're wondering if I'm a good forger?" The black eyes glistened, to my great joy. "I confess to it, having had to change some books to better sense. But someday Nicolo Polo might find out the cheat."

"What matter if he does? He won't love me any less or leave me any poorer than before."

"A new letter would be hard to believe on the heels of this one. Still, the idea's right, if the method's wrong. Do you think you could get hands on the present letter, deliver it to me for a night's keeping, and return it to your uncle's cabinet without his ever discovering the theft?"

"Why, 'twould be child's play!"

"So was a Mongol lad's hiding himself when his kinsman came to kill him. His name was Genghis, and out of it came terrible things. Then essay it, child, and take pains that you're not caught."

It was a good thing that I heeded him. The trick looked so easy as to need no forethought, and only at the last minute did I provide a spare exit from my uncle's chamber, in case my plans went wrong. The balcony door, left open on such sultry nights, gave me easy entrance, and the watch lamp enough light. My uncle and aunt, naked in the bed, slept the sleep not of the just but of the good digesters, and despite their meanness looked as innocent as two white, fat pigs. I found the parchment in the top drawer of his escritoire, and I was making toward the balcony when a great gust of wind slammed shut the portal. Being warped by the rain, it could not be opened without kicks and blows and accompanying squeaks and groans.

My kinfolk wakened and carried on a brief, half-witted conversation about the weather. If they had had enough assiduity to arise and see about it, they would have caught me, not red-handed but red-faced, crouching behind the footboard. As it was, their mumblings died away, and I made my exit through an adjoining chamber whose inner bolt I had taken pains to slide. It would be a lesson to me in double safe-guarding for the rest of my life.

Mustapha Sheik mixed sal ammoniac with water, doctored the parchment,[2] and schooled me in my part. I replaced it without mishap, and the sport began after the morning prayers.

"Uncle Zane, have you still got the letter from my father?" I asked, so gleeful over the game that I had no fear of giving it away, and hence could play it well.

"I haven't got around to burning it," he answered grumpily.

"Did you notice if it had a small ink blot about the middle of the parchment toward the left-hand side?"

"No, and why should I?"

"Yesterday I listened to some sailors drinking in an inn, and one of them, who had been to Aleppo, told how the learned priests of St. Thomas write to one another in secret. He said the sign that the parchment contained hidden writing was an ink blot, its position on the page being a cipher too. If it was at the top, what they called the brain, the letter concerned scholarly matters to be read at leisure. If it was on the left side, called the heart, it dealt with loved ones. If on the right side, called the hand, it dealt with war. And if at the bottom, called the feet, it was a most urgent message, which the receiver must discover and answer in dire haste."

"I trow 'twas a sailor's yarn. How could a parchment contain hidden writing? Perhaps if it were split, then glued together——"

"It's worked by some kind of enchantment, borrowed from Prester John." The mere mention of this name, one to conjure with these hundred years, softened my uncle's brain. "And when the parchment is heated, the invisible writing stands forth as boldly as though inscribed in India ink."

"I never heard the like!"

"My lord, now Marco speaks of it, I do believe there is a blot of ink on Nicolo's letter," my aunt broke in. "I noticed it, thinking that his hand might be palsied. By your leave, I'll fetch it."

"Do so, wife, and let's dispose of this hocus-pocus once and for all."

My aunt's hand shook a little as she handed him the parchment. There was a small blot on the left-hand side, as I had noticed and remembered on first reading. My uncle prided himself on being a Doubting Thomas, but he was patently shaken.

"No doubt a coincidence, but an odd 'n, I do confess," he remarked. "Now we'll apply heat, as the sailor fellow said—go the whole hog, say I, in any venture—but if secret writing appears on the page, I'll eat my surcoat. Amelia, bring flame to a candle." This last was to a serving wench, whose eyes were bulging.

My uncle began passing the parchment over the flame as though toasting a herring. We could see how debonair he was—a man of the world who could relish a bit of nonsense—and he had a joke ready to crack as he turned up the heated side. Instead he wellnigh dropped the page.

"Great Beelzebub!" he burst out.

"What is it, my lord?" my aunt cried, and Amelia was crossing herself fast as if scratching fleas.

"There's writing here, I tell you. It's come out on the parchment like the handwriting on the wall. No doubt it's the Devil's work—it was fire, the Devil's own element, that brought it out—but if holy priests can use it for their communings, so can our dear brother. Let me toast it a bit more."

Meanwhile I did not grin even into my sleeve. Although Mustapha Sheik had explained the whole process, insisting it was no more magical than boiling an egg, still the sweat came out on me at sight of the writing, and chills ran down my spine. And now my uncle was able to read it, penned by Mustapha in a good imitation of my father's hand. This he did between gasps, reading it in a quaking voice.

While it was a deal less sensational than I had wished—Mustapha Sheik had told me that credibility was the very soul of cunning—truly it caused great stir:

> My dear sister Flora,
>   Be not saddened by the outward seeming. The truth is, I have prospered too greatly to dare risk the telling save in this secret way. Pray for my return, and expect the prayer to come true within four years. In the meanwhile, bid my son Marco, whom I have never seen, prepare himself for the place he must fill as my heir and successor.
>   May your saints protect you from all ill, and may you show yourself worthy by a pious life and by ceaseless love and obedience to your good husband.
>   Nicolo Polo

This last greasing had gone against my grain, but now I rejoiced at Mustapha's wisdom. Of all largess, flattery was the cheapest and the most effectual, he said; and to scorn its employment in a good cause was a sign of either dim wits or of hidden shames. Also, the wise conqueror never took the last crust. One's words to eat is not a dainty dish, and if my uncle gagged too painfully, he might make us trouble.

The trick succeeded so well that it scared me a little, lest it be used as balance against a later failure. My aunt moved me to a better room and my uncle bought me finer raiment. He would have engaged a good tutor for me if I had not proposed that I find my own at half the cost to him. The money went for books, some lessons of great use to a traveler, and a fine English bow such as had set Saracen teeth achatter in the Crusades. It was six and a half feet long, beautifully shaped of yew, and the weight to draw it into a full, beautiful, deep crescent was fifty pounds.

So I passed from primary school to college.

CHAPTER 2

THE YOUNG FATHER

MEANWHILE I PASSED MY FIFTEENTH BIRTHDAY AND MY SIXTY-eighth inch. I weighed one and a half quintal, as we weigh fish, and was shooting up and filling out to the dismay of my mother's tirewoman, who let out my clothes, and to the consternation of my cousin Leo, who feared I would outspan him at this rate. Going on sixteen, I must soon present new evidence of my father's prosperity, my uncle making many countings of the moneys he had spent on me. By now it would be an easy thing to go to sea. Any galley captain who saw me shoot a bow would gladly hire me as a castle guard, not so much for my hits as for the doleful misses of most archers, and because I was quick. But in all likelihood this would still be a fatal thing as far as my ambitions were concerned.

Late in the month of May, I was watching the unloading of a wondrous cargo from Alexandria. Besides the more common riches of the Orient—bales of carpet, bolts of cloth, chests of spices, and stacks of sandalwood—there were live peacocks for the gardens of great villas on the mainland, pet monkeys for children and harlots, snakes for apothecaries, and talking and singing birds. I hardly noticed a dirty bireme docking an arrow cast distant. A ship's clerk told me it hailed from Acre with a cargo of dressed leather. When two gentlemen disembarked and walked by, I gave them my second-best attention, and intended to make it short.

Instead I began to regard them with growing curiosity. They boasted very little gold and no jewels at all and were dressed very plainly compared to the dizened roosters I most admired, although the cloth was black velvet of no mean price. Their faces were more tanned and weathered than those of most rich merchants, who lie in their cabins in rough weather and sit under pavilions in good. But these were faces to mark and remember long.

The older had a long nose, a square jaw, and wide, thin, straight lips, all suggesting severity. His hair and beard were a sandy red, and his eyes blue. The younger face was as handsome, in a manly way, as any I had ever seen. The eyes were large and brilliant, of hazel color I thought, the nose high-bridged as a Spanish duke's and finely chiseled, the mouth at once strong and voluptuous. He wore no beard, only a fine brown mustache. With this quite noble countenance and high-held head went a large, fine body of impressive stature and native grace. It did not surprise me that the handful of ladies accompanying their lords or fathers in visiting the ships put on their prettiest airs, while the bawds and serving wenches gazed wistfully.

Behind the younger man walked a youth of about fourteen and a younger boy, both handsome and elegantly dressed. Since he looked far too young to be their father, I took it that they were sons of the older gentleman.

Although their differences were more conspicuous than their similarities, I could not doubt that the two men were brothers. Their eyes, though different in size and brilliance, were set exactly alike, and there was no gaiety in either pair. Instead there was a firmness or an imperiousness such as I had rarely seen.

Intent on their business, they did not return my glance, and soon disappeared in the crowd. I tried to pay them no more mind, only to yield at last to overweening curiosity. When a Dalmatian pikeman disembarked from the same ship and swaggered off toward a wine shop, I accosted him.

"Friend, will you tell me who were the two gentlemen in black velvet?" I asked. "I think I've seen them somewhere before."

"Why, they're Venetian merchants, brothers to each other, returning home after a long journey."

"How long a journey? I've heard of some that lasted five years." And I had not given my heart leave to beat so fast.

"I didn't hear 'em say, but they've been to countries so far away you've never heard their names."

Not long ago I would not have missed this chance to boast. "I've heard of Armenia and Persia—and a city named Bukhara."

"Why, they're just a stone's throw compared to where those gentlemen came from, and it's called the Celestial Kingdom of Cathay. Their name is Crispi—Giovanni and Roderico Crispi— and if you ask 'em, they'll give you a monkey without any tail."

With a droll look and a rolling walk, the Dalmatian went on his way.

I went home and began to wait. A good part of the waiting I spent in my chamber, shaping and fledging arrows, and in this I could take pride; but no small part of it I stood at a casement watching the entrance ways. I was fifteen and a half. Youths of like tender age had commanded galleys in bloody strife at sea. They had no fathers or mothers when the great catapults began to hurl quarter-ton stones. They stood or fell by their own manhood.

Several festooned gondolas passed our door. There was many a flurry of people on the bridge, but not two tall travelers, in black velvet, with their attendants. The long day died; twilight gave way to night; I supped, lay down, listened, and at last slept. My reason told me that the travelers' names were Giovanni and Roderico Crispi. But in my dreams I wept. . . .

"Master Marco, you're white in the face," said an old charwench who had served my mother. "I fear that one of those tall ships you love has brought you the plague."

"I'm plagued if I know," I answered, laughing like a loon.

But the sand ran on in the glass. A servant maid had turned it twice, thrice, four times, since the Angelus. She was very Cronus, I thought, he who had castrated his father and eaten his sons so he could never be overthrown. The shadow of the style moved across the sundial, and beneath it, deep-carven in the stone, was this terrible legend:

Every hour wounds. The last hour kills.

We sat down to our big, rich midday meal. I could not eat, but I showed a bright face when the porter blew his horn. There were visitors at the door. I felt nothing more in my heart and instead was rallying all my physical and mental forces, exactly, it seemed, as I did when I drew my longbow for a difficult shot. I was almost pleasantly conscious of coolness and steadiness.

"They are Venetian merchants, newly returned from the East, with their attendants, and they seek admittance to your Honor's presence," the servant said.

"Why, you may show them in, and welcome," replied my uncle Zane. For the merchants of Venice were her true lords.

They came in, the older leading the way, and as he passed the threshold I saw that he did not fill the doorway as did the younger. Their eyes were set alike and both had an imperious look, but the older man's, although less bright, were not as cold. He was the more rugged-looking, but not the strongest. Their surcoats and leg gear were dark-blue velvet; and in addition they wore mantles of ceremony, lined with red silk and fastened at the throat with gold chains. Most of their train remained in the anteroom, but the two handsome youths, richly and elegantly dressed, followed them still.

"Welcome, my lords, to my humble abode, and will you honor me by sitting at my board?" quoth my uncle Zane.

"Why now, we'll not sit yet," answered the younger brother with great courtesy, "but we may beg to do so, when we're sure of our welcome. Zane—and I address you so by right—do you know me?"

I did not know him. He had addressed my uncle by right, he said, but there seemed to be something wrong. I had thought about it a hundred times since yesterday. I had always understood that Nicolo Polo, my father, was the younger brother of Maffeo Polo. Actually I could not remember being told so and very easily could have got the wrong impression when a little child and carried it all these years. That was the way of it, surely— because the younger of these two brothers was not old enough to have a son fifteen and a half, and hardly sons fourteen and twelve. In that case, it stood to reason that the older, plainer, less arresting man was Nicolo Polo.

He was the better man in the way of goodness than the younger man. He could have darkened my mother's ways but not cracked her heart. He could have neglected me from sheer unwillingness to bear responsibility for me, not ignored me on purpose. If he were my father, not the other, I would be happier . . . and safer. . . .

"Why, there's something familiar in your face——" So spoke Zane, my uncle, and now there was a pallor in his own face and a tremor in his voice.

The taller, youthful brother turned to my Aunt Flora.

"Lady, have I no resemblance to someone you knew?"

"Oh, you have," she answered, so white and faint that I thought she might swoon, "but I dare not speak——"

"Be bold. If you miscall me, I'll not be offended."

"If you are who I think you are, you were barely eighteen when you left here, sixteen years ago. It would be no wonder that you've changed greatly. But you"—and my aunt turned to the older brother—"you will I address with a bold heart. Of you, I'm almost sure."

"Who am I, Flora?"

"By blessed Jesus, who died for me, I believe you're my brother Maffeo, as though risen from the grave."

"And who stands beside me?"

"It must be Nicolo—and it is!"

2

I had been going on fifteen, but suddenly I had become a full man.

I looked upon my father. The air in the room seemed to have become crystalline as after a rain. At the moment he was being greeted by the embracings and tears of his long-lost sister, while his long-lost son looked on. It was like him to return the greetings with great warmth, for no fish was he, instead a full-blooded, passionate, and strong man. More than that, he was a magnificent man.

"And this fine youth is our nephew and your dear son," my uncle Maffeo exclaimed as he greeted Leo.

"He's asked about you almost daily, it seemed to me, and longed for your return," Uncle Zane replied. But he looked at Nicolo, not Maffeo. He was not one to mistake the buttered side of his bread.

"Why, Nicolo, he was only a toddler when we left here, but now he's of an age to return with us," Maffeo went on when both had greeted my smirking cousin.

"It's a pity we can't take him," Nicolo replied, settling that matter once and for all. "Now I have a surprise for you, my dear kinsmen!"

With a proud expression, my father turned to the two splendid youths behind him. "Maffeo!" he called. "Andrea! Come forth and embrace your aunt whom you've never seen."

I had been waiting, with a queer, cold patience, for the pair to be presented. Until the last second I had maintained the possibility that my uncle Maffeo might do the presenting. The handsome boys resembled him at least as much as I resembled my sire.

"Nicolo, you don't mean——" my aunt gasped.

"I do, and they're my legitimate sons. When news came of poor Lucia's death, I took another wife, the daughter of a noble Venetian, Angelo Trevisen, dwelling in Constantinople."

You took her in a hurry, Papa, by the look of things.

"Oh, I can hardly believe it," my aunt cried, when she had kissed them both. "They're so tall and fine."

"About eleven and ten, but well grown for their years, I grant you." My father beamed on them.

"I suppose I shouldn't be surprised. You've been gone over sixteen years."

So he had—leaving Venice six months before I was born. And time dries all wounds, my aunt should have added to smooth everything over. And we all knew that my mother had been dead nearly twelve years, so who could find fault with the widower's having a son of eleven? Actually the fine fellow was at least thirteen, but what did it matter? Perhaps he had divorced my mother *in absentia* and had had plenty of time.

"Now I've lost Felicia as well," my father went on. "It was well that I had my boys—and my great ventures with Maffeo—to help heal the wound."

My father's voice became resonant and he was deeply moved.

"And you've traveled to the ends of the earth!" my uncle Zane exclaimed.

"To the very kingdom of Cathay on the shores of the Ocean Sea! Zane—Flora—neither of you can dream what we've seen! And I must tell you now—in our first hour together—that in just a little while we must go again. Such we have promised the King—Kublai Khan we call him—the greatest king on the earth."

"He's made us the bearer of great tidings to his Holiness the Pope," Maffeo explained when my father paused. "He entreats him to send one hundred priests, learned men and pious, to his Court, there to instruct and baptize the heathen hosts—and we, Nicolo and I, are to lead them there.[3] I want you to be the first to know of the great honor paid us, and anyway, it can't be kept secret any longer."

"Not only honor," my father added. "The one of us whom he favors most will be made his viceroy—virtually the king—of a realm as great as France, to have and hold its revenues for five years. The other will sit on his Council for the same period. Then we'll both return to Venice, rich beyond the dreams of avarice."

This was the news I was waiting for. It was natural enough for my father to reveal it in the first half-hour of his own and Maffeo's return. It was the meat of the coconut, as Mustapha used to say.

The news itself was of such prodigious moment in my fate that I did not instantly perceive a strange fact of its transmission. I had not merely overheard it, as seemed the case with the previous announcements; I had been included in the audience. Perhaps he had become conscious of my presence without realizing or even suspecting who I was. It might be so, but I did not believe it. Instead I believed that the news was for my ears more than any, and in this degree he had acknowledged me at last.

At that instant, Aunt Flora took notice of me too. Perhaps she had never forgotten I was here, but one shock after another had caused her to neglect me until now. The immediate stimulus was some echo of the silent communication between my father and me. She stiffened and changed color.

"I'll leave my boys here, with allowances for their care and schooling," my father was saying. "Then when the new Pope is elected——"

Aunt Flora gave forth a gasp so deep it sounded like a sob. "Nicolo!"

"What is it, Flora?"

"You haven't spoken to Marco!"

She spoke rapidly in an excited tone. That caused the slow voicing and quiet of his reply to be all the more marked.

"No doubt you mean this young man." And very slowly he turned and looked me in the face.

"Don't you know who he is? Blessed Jesus, forgive my sin!"

"If he's the one of whom you have written me—you call him Marco Polo—I know only too well who he is."

"Oh God, there's some awful mistake. He's your son. Nicolo, he's your firstborn, by your wife Lucia. Your own begotten——"

"I regret to tell you, Flora, that Lucia bore me no son. *De mortuis nil nisi bonum*—yet I must speak."

"Jesus, mercy!"

"If this is Lucia's son, which I have no doubt, he's the son of her lover, one Antonello, a wandering jongleur from Perugia. Only for the sake of her fame have I suffered him to bear my name."[4]

3

The great consternation created in our company by my father's words caused a long, heavy, almost breathless silence. I was deeply grateful for it, because it gave me time to rally my faculties and act. The action was in my head, but it was no less positive than many by my hands, and hardly less violent. I forced my thoughts through a welter of hopes and fears, weaknesses and strengths, to a sure conclusion. I was quite certain that I need never question it in the future.

Certainly to us, and perhaps to himself as well, my father, Nicolo Polo, had told a black lie.

My father's gaze was fixed on my face. I did not return it—my instinct was to refrain from any act of defiance. He was red in the face, his stunned hearers white. The silence stretched for second after second and I wondered if I would be the one to break it. I did not wish to and looked to my aunt Flora.

She remained aghast, but out of the corner of my eye I saw a sudden darkening of the dull-white face of my uncle Zane.

"*God's wounds!*" he burst forth like a thunderclap.

"Oh, my lord!" cried his wife.

"What's this you're saying?" Zane persisted, turning with great energy to my father. "That Marco's your wife's bastard? Then what of the message you sent him in the secret writing?"

A perverse impulse to laugh aloud swept me from head to heel, but I contained it, and only a gasp came out.

"What secret writing?" my father demanded in a loud voice.

"In your last letter to Flora. You spoke of your dear son Marco—how you'd make him your heir——"

"By my saints, we've all been bitten by tarantulas! I sent no secret writing. Would I endow the living monument, the very witness, to Lucia's infidelity and my own pain?"

"Then it was the Devil's work. It was a wicked enchantment, to ruin me, worked with the Devil's fire. Flora swore to the hand-writing. On the strength of it I've spent God knows how many lire on Marco's care."

"Was it signed and sealed before an officer of the Court?"

"No it wasn't, and why should I expect it to be, when 'twas sent from some heathen land? You'd never told us of his bastardy. You let us go on thinking he was your own——"

"When I left here—and it was the cause of my leaving—I couldn't bring myself to tell anyone of the disgrace. I was not even sure that Lucia was with child—she swore she wasn't. After I had gone, I dared not write the truth, for only a fraction of my letters reached you—most of them were rifled and no doubt read by rogues and rival merchants."

"That may be, but I'll have my money back, fair weather or foul."

"Uncle Zane, I'll pay you every dinero," I said.

My voice was more firm than I dared hope. To my surprise, it worked another silence, not as explosive as the other, but more strained. Aunt Flora looked deeply distressed and my father tense. There was malice in Leo's eyes. He was not sure that the secret writing was the Devil's work.

"I'll fetch the letter, Papa, if you'll give me leave," he said.

"I think that would be best," my father said gravely.

In a moment it was in his hands. He looked at it with knitted brows, then called for a lighted candle. After he had toasted it a moment, he examined it carefully, reread the doctored writing, and put it down.

"It's not the Devil's work," he told Zane. "Only a clever trick."

"Who's the trickster? By heaven, he should hang!"

"It's someone who's acquainted with alchemy—Arabian, most likely—or who knows someone of that ilk."

"Uncle Nicolo, Marco has been seen hundreds of times at the house of an old Arab in Spinalunga," spoke up my cousin Leo.

"Then I don't think we need search much further for the forger. However, I am seeing the offense in a little different light than at first. The truth is—and I admit it freely—I've not dealt altogether fairly with Lucia's son Marco. The sin was wholly on her head, not in the least on his, yet it has been visited upon him in no small measure."

"I'm not sure that I follow you, Brother Nicolo," said my uncle Zane. His polite tone did not mean that he had forgotten the small sum I had bilked him of, rather that he remembered the vast sum to accrue to my father from his coming venture.

"Pardon me a moment. Marco, did your mother confess to you, before she died, that you weren't my son? Did she boast of it, I'd better say? 'Tis true you were hardly four years old, still it's possible that you'd remember."

"No, your Honor, she didn't."

"And the notion never entered your head?"

"No, sir. How could it?"

"Then of course you were puzzled and hurt that I made no mention of you in my letters. Finally you succumbed to temptation to forge a mention, for your pride's sake——"

"Not only for pride's sake," my uncle Zane broke in, "but for silver grossi spent on his back and belly."

"I'm myself partly at fault for not making the situation clear both to him and to you," my father admitted handsomely. "I'll demand no punishment for the forgery, and I'll go further than that. We're taught to return good for evil. Before I leave, I'll try to find a place for Marco in the establishment of some merchant. I think it won't be difficult, if I throw business his way."

My father had spoken firmly and with quite a manner. Even when quoting the great Christian maxim, not a trace of butter greased his tongue. He was so great an adversary that I marveled he should be one at all—what was there about me, a youth not yet sixteen, to attract his zealous attention? Since eagles do not hawk at flies, obviously it was the fruit of some old passion, and hence, of course, a weakness. But he would need a hundred weaknesses to reduce him to my fair match—or I must gain a hundred strengths.

"I'll let it go at that, on the condition Marco pays me back out of his wages," Uncle Zane replied. "Half of 'em to hand till the debt's paid! Otherwise I'll cry the cheat myself."

"There's still another condition." My father turned to me. "You may no longer call yourself Marco Polo. You may take the name Marco Antonello——"

"I'll not do that until the bastardy's proved," I broke in, greatly flurried within to be contesting him this soon, but surprisingly steady without.

This shot told far beyond my excited expectations. For an instant I thought I saw real hate gleaming in his eyes. It was not easy for him to control his countenance and then his voice.

"You'd best not doubt my word, young man," he said.

"Either my doubting it or my believing it won't change the law. The law is that if I was born while you and my mother were still married—and had opportunities to cohabit—I'm to be considered legitimate until proven otherwise. Any lawyer in Venice will tell you that."

He had not expected me to know that point of law. Actually I took no great pride in it, since copulation is such a fascinating subject to youths of my age that we become remarkably well informed as to all its ramifications. What should make me justly proud was remembering it in this tight moment and making good use of it.

"I don't believe I'll have any trouble with the law. And if you're thinking that you may come into a large sum of money by denying the truth, you're fated for a disappointment. This letter states that Maffeo and I had lost a great part of our capital. A good portion of the rest was stolen from us by fire-worshipers who attacked us on the homeward journey and who would have killed us except for the golden tablet given us as safe-conduct by Kublai Khan. This the villains dared not touch, but they took the jewels he had given us, and all the money except what we had hidden in a bucket of camel's milk. The remainder we have paid to money-lenders to take up the bond on my father's house in San Felice."

He was interrupted by an anguished grunt from my uncle Zane. Then he went on with lordly calm.

"It's true that our prospects are bright for a great coup, but it won't be realized for many years. So, to make it short, Marco—for I've already wasted too much time—I advise you to accept what I'm willing to do for you, and be grateful."

"You said a post of profit with a favored merchant if I'll forswear you as my father."

"It amounts to that."

"I'll not give up my honored name unless you prove me a bastard. But I'll address you as Signor Polo and renounce all claim on you for support or patrimony if you'll grant one plea."

"I'll hear it, for what it's worth."

"You said that you and your brother Maffeo are returning to the Court of Kublai Khan with one hundred learned priests. Give me a place in the company."

The proposal amazed him. The slight widening of his eyes indicated it had affected his superstitions in a way to dismay him too. But as his intelligence took hold, I thought he was glad I had made it. He was going to enjoy its rebuffing.

"You're about sixteen, aren't you?" Signor Polo said thoughtfully. "In my youth, that counted as a full man. But have you served an apprenticeship with any merchant?"

"No."

"Have you ever been out of sight of the towers of Venice?"

"No, Signor."

"Even if I would permit an unlearned and unexperienced young man to burden the company, where would you find the money to pay your way?"

"I'd go as an attendant on one of the holy fathers."

"The journey of the fathers will of course be financed by Holy Church. Perhaps a few curates will accompany them, if the wherewithal can be found for ship and caravan transport, but what menial service they require will be furnished by the masters from stage to stage of the journey; and the luxury of attendants is not in keeping with their calling, as well you know. Anyway, I wouldn't let any person claiming relationship to me or to my late wife work his way with us—a matter of what the Orient knows as *izzat*. In plain words, if you went with us, someone would have to pay your way."

"If I can pay my own way, and I agree to renounce all claim on your estate, will you let me go?"

Signor Nicolo Polo could hardly hide his smile. "Traveling in good array, so as not to lose face for the company before the heathen?"

"Yes, Signor."

"Let us all understand your proposal, Marco, to avoid future argument. By Venetian law, you reached the age of discretion when you were fifteen, and we are dealing before witnesses. Your agreement to renounce claim to my estate is given for my consent to join our party at your own expense. If you're not able to find the necessary funds, it is not my lookout, and your renunciation still stands."

I felt a dull pain across my forehead just above my eyebrows. If I could only remember a scene of just before dawn, as I stood by

my mother's bedside, and her frail hand enfolded mine and the
lamplight guttered . . .

"You're asking a good deal, Nicolo, of Lucia's son," Aunt Flora
broke in.

"He's no kin of yours, my sister, or of mine. And he aspires to go
to Cathay."

"Will you give me till vespers tomorrow, that I may pray to my
saints for guidance?" I asked.

"I'll not refuse you that."

"And I think you should tell how great a sum he would have
to raise," Aunt Flora prompted.

"He hasn't asked me. I dare say he trusts that the pot at rainbow's end will hold enough."

"I do ask you, Signor Polo," rose a taut, nerve-rasped, stubborn
voice I hardly knew for my own.

"Then I'll answer, although I fear it may shake your ambition.
In round figures, say three thousand lire—a thousand pieces of
gold."

4

Signor Polo began to tell the others of his and Maffeo's journey
to the Court of Kublai Khan. I listened long enough to gather one
fact of great bearing on my own problem. The two travelers could
not have gained that star-far place except for the lucky chance of
falling in with one of the Khan's ambassadors, returning to his
master after carrying out a mission to Kublai's brother, a subject
king in Tatary. Nor could they have made the return journey
except with the safe-conduct of the golden tablet bearing Kublai's
seal. They were not protected from savage tribes outside of the
Khan's law; yet without the talisman their hope of retracing their
steps would be an empty dream.

I went to my room and called Rosa, once my mother's tirewoman. She gazed at me with frightened eyes.

"What do ye want, Master Marco?" she asked in a quavering
tone.

"Only to talk to you a while."

"I thought ye might, after you'd seen the master, tall and alive.
But I daren't stay but a minute or two. Let me be changing your
sheets, for Jesu knows they need it."

"You never told me there was trouble between Signor Nicolo
and my mother."

"That I didn't. I thought both of 'em were gone——"

"Do you know that he's accused her of wantonness with a low-born lover, and me the fruit of it?"

"Too well I know it. I heard him make the same charge when you were in the womb."

"How much of the charge was true? And I charge you to speak truth."

"You are Nicolo's son. My lady vowed it, her hand in mine, before Our Lady. Antonello the jongleur had gone to Florence a good year before your birth. What had been between them before then, no soul on earth may say. Antonello was the son of my lady's nurse, and they played together as children, and mayhap they discovered each other, with no harm done, as children will. He came to Venice with his troop, and sought out my lady, and she admitted him to her bower now and again, while her lord was trading in Trieste. Her lord, I said. So she confessed him, here below. But she would not confess him her Lord above. And that was what he craved, in his blasphemous, miscreant heart. For a while he was master of her body, but by blessed Jesu, he never won her soul."

"You said that no one living could declare her innocence or guilt. Is Antonello dead?"

"Sixteen years ago."

"Was he older than Signor Nicolo?"

"At least a year younger. My lady was fourteen when she wedded, and her lord seventeen. But God did not let her conceive till she was full fifteen."

"Then Antonello died young!"

I was watching Rosa's eyes. They wavered, then returned to mine.

"It's hard to live on with your guts pulled out, and cut in four."

"Who did it, I wonder?"

"Save your wonder for a two-headed calf! A young merchant, trading in Rimini, cried him for a thief. When the watch searched him, they found the merchant's purse. Antonello swore that he had borrowed it for legerdemain from a merrymaker the night past and that the gentleman had disappeared before he returned it. But who would believe such a fantastic story?"

"Was the crier Nicolo Polo?"

"No, it was Maffeo Polo. And if the merrymaker were Nicolo, he had made full merry. He'd proved the gentleman from first to last. He hadn't sullied his hands or steel in base blood. One must cross swords with an equal invading his bed, but a rat's death isn't good enough for one who brings lice. If the court knew naught of this, they knew that jongleurs were lewd, lawless fellows who needed lessons. Antonello was hanged, cut down while still alive, and quartered."

"Signor Polo must have loved my mother with great passion."

"He hated her with the black hate of Hell."

"Why?"

"Because she was above him when she became his bride, and he couldn't bring her down. It was no good to whip her, because she wouldn't weep. It was no balm to sport with trulls or even highborn ladies, for he knew not one could hold a rushlight to her, and worse than that, she rejoiced at their serving in her stead."

"She did weep. I heard her."

"Sometimes tears ran down her long cheeks, but I was within sound of her voice day and night, and only once did I hear her weep aloud. That was when she had news of Antonello's death. His slayer didn't hear her, for he stayed in Rimini for her lover's drawing and quartering, then took ship for Constantinople. The master would have given his soul to have heard her, but, glory to sweet Jesu! he never did, and I would die in slow fire before I told him of it, and if you should tell him, may your soul be saved for my lady's sake but your living body crisp and blacken in slow fire!"

"Be still! As I hope to see salvation, I never will!"

Only my own vehemence caused me to realize hers. As she had talked, she had shaken and smoothed my bolster, spread sheets, and emptied pots; and because my pitch of feeling had mounted beside hers—like a flute in tune with a lyre—I had remained unaware of the steep climb. I had thought Rosa had much phlegm and little bile, but now I had never seen such eyes in a human head.

Suddenly she sighed. "I would you could have heard her, Marco, for your soul's sake. But you couldn't have, because you were not yet born."

"I was in the womb, and I heard her through its walls."

"Mayhap you did! Mayhap you are only mad!"

"But I can't remember what she told me the night before she died. For good or evil, I charge you to tell me."

"I can't tell you because I don't know."

"Then you lied when you said you were always within sound of her voice, and for that you need a flogging."

"I didn't lie. My lady made no sound at all for three days before she died. But I wasn't always in sight of her hands, and perhaps they gave you some signal."

The pressure of pain grew across my forehead until it seemed my eyes would burst out.

"There were two candles burning . . ."

"That is so."

"She had me put them both on her bedstand."

"Yes, yes, I found them there."

"She took a piece of white leather—perhaps it was a parchment —from a hiding place and held it in the flame, but it did not burn."

"Jesu, have mercy!"

"Was it a letter that the Devil wouldn't let her destroy? Did he draw the yellow teeth of his very element, so she might die with sin upon her soul? Or did her saints make cold the flame, to save her from doing evil?"

"Don't think about that now. Leave that for the priests to settle, when you've recalled it all. What happened next? You'll foul the chain of memory if you don't haul——"

"I don't know what happened next. It's faded out." The pain too had dimmed away.

Rosa wiped her face. "Someday it will come," she prophesied.

"It might have come just now, if you'd told me the truth from first to last."

"May my soul perish——"

"You said you didn't know if Antonello was my mother's lover, but later on, when your caution was lost in heat, you called him just that."

"The wish was father to the thought, Marco my child. It may be that my lady never lay in the embrace of love, only of hate. When death called her to his cold bed ere she was twenty, she might never have known a bed warmed by a sweetheart's passion. So I wish she'd broken her vow to rejoice her soul in Heaven and to torment Nicolo's dreams. Would not her saints save her from the wrath? Aye, if they too had dwelt in mortal flesh and knew its yearnings. If atonement must still be made, I take it on my soul."

Her weak voice rang. I looked to her scrawny form, her breasts that were ever dry and now were wasted too, her anxious old-maid countenance, and these were all transfigured by her one great love. Perhaps it was the love of a grown-up child for a doll that broke, with no warmer, better doll to come and comfort her, the story ended as complete as though the child herself had died.

I will live on in your stead, Rosa. I'll be your lover, yourself, and your child. Doubt not I will be your avenger.

"You'd be better off if Antonello, not Nicolo, had been your father," Rosa went on. "Poor as he was, lowborn, not even handsome, his seed would have been blessed."

"I don't doubt it, but I thank God for my evil begetting."

I did not finish, just then, what I was about to say. It came to me it would have no validity until I had said something else in another place. Until then, I would have nothing to lose but wind. I had posted no bond to forfeit if I broke faith. A gauge had been thrown, which I had neither yielded nor picked up. I could not run with the hare and hunt with the hounds.

So I left her and went back to the dining hall. The strong, pure, marine light burst through the casements facing the lagoon and shone on Signor Nicolo Polo and my kinsmen seated at the board. Nicolo's face was flushed with wine and glory; he was a full-blooded man. The others were hanging on his words.

"May I speak, your Honor?" I asked, when my entrance caused him to fall silent.

"You have my leave," he answered like a king. Before many years, he meant to be a very king in Cathay.

"I've been thinking over the proposal that you made me." And I could not keep my voice from shaking.

"Thinking over it? You said you'd pray over it."

"I have, your Honor." For my last words, Rosa bearing witness, were in thanks to God.

"Let's see if I remember it exactly," Nicolo continued. "If I don't, one of these witnesses will correct me. I promised you a place in our company adventuring to the Court of Kublai Khan provided you journey in honorable array at your expense, and here and now renounce all claims to my estate."

"Those were the very terms, or I'll eat my shoon," said Uncle Zane.

"And now you've come to tell me that since the world knows you as the son of Nicolo Polo, and the burden of proof of your bastardy is upon me, a bird in the hand is worth two in the bush, and you'll stay in Venice."

Many men, waiting for an outcome, will betray what they hope for by prophesying just the opposite. Perhaps it is by way of placating the gods of evil fortune. Only very clever or bold ones will give voice to their desire, in the way of either suggestion or intimidation. Nicolo Polo was both clever and bold. I was quite sure that during my absence he had thought over his proposal to me and every dictate of his reason had made him hope that I would accept it. It was a thousand-to-one wager that I could not raise three thousand lire, and my renunciation of claim upon him would be a happy riddance.

He had spoken in a rich voice, almost jokingly, as though to save my face in defeat, smiling the while, causing the others to appreciate his charm. Only I saw him suck a quick mouthful of air when he had finished. All I knew was that whatever he wanted in the way of my answer he wanted very much.

"I'm going to continue to believe I'm your son," I said, frightened half out of my wits lest I play mouse to his cat.

"I don't blame you. Besides that, one thousand pieces of gold don't grow on every bush. But I'll trim that figure a little, Marco, if your heart's set on it. Show me eight hundred pieces of the yellow stuff, and I'll make you welcome."

His tone was good-humored. His eyes were intensely bright, perhaps with excitement but more likely with mirth. My heart faltered and my bones unbraced. Yet I heard myself speaking.

"I'm grateful for your generosity, and I accept your offer."

My uncle's warm and almost jolly look remained unchanged, but if my saints stood by me, it was frozen on his face.

"You fool!" broke in my cousin Leo.

"Shut your mouth!" came Uncle Zane's vehement cry.

Signor Nicolo Polo turned his usual calm countenance toward his sister Flora.

"I can't say that I'm surprised, but you must be."

"What do you mean, Nicolo?" she gasped.

"I think you've remained doubtful of my charge that Marco was Lucia's son by a lowborn lover. I had remained doubtful that he himself didn't know it, though I'd been willing to give him the benefit of the doubt. Now it's proved that he does know it. That was my purpose in making the proposal, although I regret the trickery. Would he renounce a heritage as my son unless he knew well he was not my son, and that I could prove it? He saw he had nothing to lose, and if some merchant would lend him one thousand pieces of gold, everything to gain."

"I follow your reasoning closely, Nicolo, yet I don't want to believe that Lucia——"

"Don't believe it, Aunt Flora," I cried, the outburst saving me from crying in another fashion. "It's because I'm his son that I can go to the Court of Kublai Khan."

And this was what I had been about to tell Rosa. Next to Nicolo, she was the one most entitled to hear it. But I had only an inkling of its meaning.

CHAPTER 3

THE LEPER

HOW COULD I GO ABOUT RAISING ONE THOUSAND GOLD BEZANTS? It was not as hard a task as raising a sunken ship out of the sea, or as easy as to raise the Devil out of Hell—it would require amazing luck, but not a miracle. My best chance, I thought, was to find a speculator who would hazard twelve hundred or so— the difference to be spent in trade goods—on the long shot of a twentyfold return. The Polo name was well regarded on the Rialto. Should Nicolo succeed in taking it from me, I would still be half a gentleman, because my mother's family, the Carpini of Perugia, were impoverished but noble—indeed they outranked the Polos several steps. I knew some tricks that might impress a potential investor with sporting tastes—some of them of real value in navigation, others of an alchemical sort, such as invisible writing, which Venetians would think just the thing for swindling uncouth heathen, but which actually were better known in Islam than in Christendom. As for my age, most scions of merchant families made their first ventures at sixteen.

Much and perhaps all depended on my allowance of time. In this regard, I had one great stroke of luck—the appointment of one hundred learned priests to follow the Polo brothers to Cathay must await the election of a new Pope to succeed Clement IV. If this were not delayed, it was still unthinkable that the vast business of their assemblage and dispatch could be completed this year, so Nicolo had set next spring as a starting date.

The news of the brothers' return caused a great flurry on the Rialto. They were received by the Doge, who professed more than a passing interest in the enterprise, and they dealt with Papal Legates and other great folk, who promised their support of the great mission when the throne of San Pietro was again filled. Meanwhile the pair had moved into the Casa Polo, the mansion where I was born. Hence came worthies and adventurers of all sorts, every one itching for Oriental treasure; and my uncle Zane and his son Leo buzzed about like bluebottle flies around a dunghill.

Yet I was soon impressed by a momentous fact. This flurry was like choppy waves on the lagoon rather than rolling billows. The Venetian people did not begin to grasp the significance of what Nicolo and Maffeo had done. I could hardly believe it of my gay, bright-eyed, quick-minded fellow citizens, and even Mustapha Sheik could not explain it fully. It appeared that their horizon spread no further than Denmark to the north, Portugal to the west, the High Altai to the south, and the eastern shores of the Caspian to the east. Beyond this was Vagueness washed by the Ocean Sea. Regardless of all reports to the contrary, they chose to believe that the remainder of the land was ruled by a stupendous Christian monarch, Prester John. If Nicolo and Maffeo had brought back chests of jewels as big as walnuts, the toe of a roc, a live unicorn, and a monkey without a tail, they would have rocked the town. But they had nothing to show but a bag or two of coins and a quaint-looking gold tablet bearing outlandish marks.

Not that our business men disbelieved the story—or so they proclaimed. It could be true as Gospel for all they knew. Polo was a good name, and some fishermen off Brindisi had seen a mermaid only a month before. But with bandits on land and pirates at sea, tempests, rocks, jerry-built boats, import duties, wages out of sight, and the Genoese bastards to top off all the rest, their policy was to retrench rather than expand. For their part, and not to mince the matter, any merchant who sent a bottom beyond Alexandria or the Crimea should wear a cockscomb.

In one part of my mind and heart, more passionate and less logical than the rest, I rejoiced at this dubiosity. I did not want any rush to join the venture, lest I lose out on its great prize or be left behind. But always I fetched up against the adamant fact that the fewer folk who became aroused, the less my chance of finding a financier.

Mustapha Sheik had given me quarters in his house to be closer to the moneylenders of Spinalunga. Actually, the Jews were far more likely to risk capital in an enterprise of this kind than the Christians—I did not know why, unless they were more cosmopolitan in outlook and more learned. I began going to them, and in almost every case was cordially received and eagerly heard. Most were reluctant to refuse outright and several delayed the decision; yet with the passing weeks I found not one who would risk one hundred bezants, let alone a thousand. One of the major reasons was the revival of the Saracen power after its late defeat—they feared that Constantinople and even Jerusalem might be retaken. Another argument gave proof of the Jews' grasp of Oriental affairs, but this was no comfort to me—that there was a great deal of rivalry between the descendants of Genghis Khan for the overlordship, and this might break into open war.[5] A third difficulty, and perhaps the greatest, proved that the Jews were equally informed on the keyhole chitchat of Venice. Why did not my own father and uncle pay my way, or advance me the moneys out of my patrimony?

The moon did not cease her waxing and waning, the whole host of stars moved a little with the seasons, and the planets seemed to wander where they listed, although their courses were as inexorably fixed as the very sun's. I could hardly believe that half a year had passed since my father's return—and afterwhile, a full year. On the day of his return, I had known myself for a man. After sixteen, I walked and talked so that no one doubted it. Another summer's end found me seventeen and no nearer Cathay than the last summer; but neither, thank God, was my sire.

The Legates were uncommonly slow at electing a new Pope. The Polo brothers worried over their repute with Kublai Khan; he might easily be led to think them scoundrelly adventurers who had had no intention of obeying his sublime commands. This anxiety preyed upon them all the more in the gathering quiet of the Casa Polo. The portico no longer swarmed with would-be wanderers to the world's end. Captains of galleys had stopped vying with one another in offering their services, and the Doge had graver business on his mind. The return of the two travelers from very Cathay had begun to look like a nine-day wonder. When they passed a knot of merchants on the Rialto, sometimes there was elbowing, and even winks, behind their backs. But if sometimes Maffeo turned and looked, Nicolo never did.

Fall winds blew and bit, and the wild geese returned. The brothers determined to set forth in mid-April, new Pope or no. Meanwhile my doors of hope were closing one by one. Only one, always the widest and the brightest, still stood wide.

"Marco my son, how much would you risk for a thousand pieces of gold?" asked Mustapha Sheik when the mid-March morning sun burst through the casement glass and ensilvered his long beard.

"I'd lay my life on the toss of a coin and grievous sin on my soul," I answered.

"The risk to your skin is not that heavy in the venture I'm thinking of, but it's far from light and my belly faints at the thought. There are those who'd say your soul's risk would be even greater, but with all due respect to Christian dogma, I think it will come through unscathed. And for the love of Allah, don't hang on my words as though they were a life line thrown to you in a sinking ship. If you don't get to go with the Polo brothers, what will you do?"

"I'll take service with a merchant, the best I can get, and wait till my ship comes in."

"Will your heart be broken?"

"No, only cracked a little." But my errant Adam's apple bobbed up and down.

"Do you know that if I had the gold, I'd put it in your hands, not to spare you a cracked heart, but as an offering to Allah—God, you say—for my sins?"

"I don't ken you, master."

"Why should you? It's a matter between Him and me. It's the light I see, which may be a will-o'-the-wisp, yet I must believe it for my soul's sake. I want you to go, Marco Polo. To that end, I'll lend you a hundred bezants, which will pay what you owe to your uncle Zane and furnish you for the thing I have in mind. You can repay the sum, if the chance comes, to the School of Averroës in Morocco."

"If I live long enough, I will."

"I've been pondering the matter since leaf fall. A month ago, you could as well pine for a roc's egg, as did Aladdin's bride, as for help from me. A fortnight past, I saw hope glimmering dimly at the bottom of the well, but I had no bucket to go down. As late as a week ago, the difficulties of the venture loomed so great, and the danger so deadly, that I couldn't bring myself to broach the matter to you. Now one of the dragons guarding the treasure has been given a bone to gnaw. Even so, many dragons remain, and perhaps the treasure itself is as visionary as the pot of gold at the rainbow's end."

Mustapha Sheik spoke calmly, as was his wont. But his eyes, so black in contrast with his beard, glimmered like jet.

"*Bismillah!*" I cried, like a good Moslem.

"In the city of Medina I knew slightly a merchant of the common name of Haran-din. He had become rich by buying and selling slaves. On one of his voyages he was captured by a Venetian and himself sold as a galley slave. Being much too old for the labor, he expected to be thrown to the sharks within a twelve month, but no such mercy was vouchsafed him. Within two moons a patch of skin on his hand showed silvery as the moon. So he was delivered from his bench and put in the lazar house of Chioggia. In a few weeks more, perhaps in a few days, he will be freed from there also, by a more kind delivery, but one he won't welcome in that place."

"Death?" I asked.

"Truly. But he doesn't want to meet him there. He wants the appointment to be in Zara, on the shores of Hungary, across the Adriatic from Rimini."

"Why there, Mustapha Sheik?"

He was always patient with my questions. "Because in Zara there is a Mohammedan mosque containing a relic from Mecca. You may ask how it comes there, in a Christian state. Because Stephen, the king, wedded a Cuman woman, whose people swore to become Christians, but who are half Mohammedans, half pagans. When those leaning toward Allah desired to raise a temple, he gave them leave. Haran-din prays that he may kiss this relic, a stone fixed in the walls, which once lay upon the Hill of Mercy, and which touched the Prophet's foot when he shouted 'Labbeyka!' unto God. And he sent me word that whoever brings him forth into the light and bears him to Zara and enables him to kiss the stone before he dies, him he will make his heir."

"I wish you'd told me sooner, Mustapha Sheik. Now the time grows short."

"It would have grown long if you had undertaken the venture even a week ago. A warden, Captain Vico, knew that Haran-din had secret wealth, but it was useless to torture him because the malady was so far advanced that he could no longer feel pain, and that is the nature of this most strange and awful affliction. He knew too that Haran-din had conspired to escape, whereby to dispose of his treasure, so he laid a cunning trap to kill anyone who stole his way to the prison bars. But Haran-din gave him a jewel that a certain Jew had kept for him, wherefor this Vico promised, on the forfeit of his soul to be burned by demons through eternity if he breaks faith, to leave open an outer gate at such a time as to circumvent the outer guard. Thus only the inner guard will remain to be eluded, which Haran-din declares would not be difficult for a resolute, resourceful, and cunning man."

"If so, why doesn't the warden arrange for a confederate to deliver Haran-din and so share in the reward?"

"Because Haran-din will trust only another Mohammedan or a Jew, with whom Captain Vico has no dealings and whom he himself would not trust."

"Why won't Haran-din trust a Christian?"

"Because he believes that a good Christian would free him from the lazar house only to let him die in some odor of sanctity, in a last attempt to save his soul, and the common run of Christians would not dare touch his leprous hand."

"Am I neither one?" I asked with a grin.

"You're a most mongrel mixture of good and bad, to my soul's joy."

"Do you think he'll trust me?"

"I'll put a mark on your hand that he will trust."

"And I must touch Haran-din's hand?"

"You must clasp it, for the way is long and dim, and he is nigh blind. You may cover it with a cloth, but that will only assuage your horror of it, not reduce the danger of contagion."

"I'll defy the inner guard with a merry heart, as well as other perils of the way, but that danger chills me to the marrow of my bones."

"I too am chilled to the dried hollow of my old bones, but take comfort in the belief—well-nigh the knowledge—that the dreadful chance is far less than most Christians believe, and for this one exposure would hardly be one in ten."

As I heard the thrilling words there had been visions before my eyes, and these had half eclipsed my view of the speaker's face. It came clear to me now, and suddenly my joy in him clutched at my heart like the deep-toned wondrous music of San Marco. He was very old, I thought, and his beard was as white as the snow that sometimes blows on the northeast wind off the Julian Alps. The bald spot on his crown was hidden under a black cap, but his head was like an old crag half covered with snowdrift. While the parchment of his face was rich with secret writing, its drawn look now, and the strange brilliance of his eyes, told me that he had just fought a grievous battle—and he had won. But I dared not speak of it yet.

"One in ten!" I cried. "Why, that's nothing."

He shook his head as though his voice had failed him, and tears stood in his eyes.

"Even if it turns out rainbow gold, I'll not be sorry I chased it at that rate," I said quickly.

"I don't think it is. Unless his malady has deranged his mind— and one of its most awful attributes is enduring sanity to the very last—he wouldn't lie to me who has broken bread with him, and eaten salt. He writes me that he has one jewel left. It was paid him on an old debt a year ago, and put in the charge of a certain Jew dwelling in Spinalunga. It is a pearl among pearls, he told me, and if it were shown to a connoisseur buying for a king, it should bring one thousand bezants, if not more."

I thought for a time that I could get out of asking him my final question, since it would hurt his thin old throat to answer it. It was forced upon me because we loved each other.

"Mustapha Sheik, why do you tell me of this, knowing that if I win my prize or lose my life, we will be parted?"

"What choice do I have, Marco? Have you forgotten how you came on our ship? My mariners told you I was sick—you saw the terror in their faces, and for all you knew I was stricken with the Black Death—yet you went into my darkened cabin and ministered to me."

"But I didn't come for that. I wish I had, but I came only— I don't know why I came!"

"I think I know what compulsion brought you there, and I wouldn't have it changed. It's the same that will help to bring you to the earth's ends, if you live. Yet you ministered to an old and ailing Infidel. Now the wheel has turned full circle, and you must do so once more, and as a beginning, not an end. It is like the repetition, in reverse, of a figure in a wondrous weaving. And the weaver is Fate."

2

Mustapha Sheik furnished me with a carefully drawn plan of the lazar house at Chioggia, showing its doors, stairways, guardrooms, and corridors, and approaches from both canals and alleys. Its legend contained instruction in the times and procedures of mounting and changing watch, the casting of food into the cells, the passage of the dung cart through the halls, and the midnight carry-out of corpses. It had been prepared by a Jewish architect before he died of jail fever, and I thought that if his ghost still haunted the fetid halls, he would be glad of its employment in this need.

Although Mustapha had doctored my father's letter and tutored me in the wile, stratagems were foreign to his nature. His life had been one long honoring Truth, and he could not readily twist it even in good cause. My mind was far more devious, and in that way—although I was still too close to the woods to see the trees— typically Venetian. Venice was one great countinghouse. For a quick profit, we would sell a throne in Heaven or buy a gridiron in Hell. It was I, not he, who thought of the device that might earn the victory.

The odds in my favor might be two to one, good enough for an adventurer of my age. But not so for this desert man who had lived to be old. He made me go over the scheme piece by piece, forward and backward and inside out, to find its weaknesses. His quiet questions as to what I would do in such and such a case prepared me for the trial. At last it was as though I were clad in armor.

Two mornings later I was at the fish dock at sunrise, watching the smacks come in under gay-hued sails. Fisherfolk are happy folk wherever you find them, living exciting lives and dying quick deaths, daring and debonair; and these, being Venetians besides, could not endure a moment's drabness even on a darkling sea in storm. When visitors remarked on the blazing red or burning orange of their sails, their gay reply was that they wished to be seen a bit farther than they could be smelled. When my head ached over the hardest problem of the whole venture—where to find a lieutenant equal to the challenge—this valiance caught my eyes like a beacon fire.

The sail cloth was no more gorgeous than the cargoes. Some of the decks were banked with shining tunny, opalescent dolphin, or rainbow-hued wrasse. Others, boarded high, held sardines as numberless as silver coins in the treasure vault of a Sultan. Herring, sea bream, and sole mixed with red mullet, and pop-eyed cod consorted with angelfish to catch the sun.

It was not long before the boat I was waiting for came in with a load of blue-silver mackerel, the finest in our waters. There was no finer boat in our fishing fleet than this, bravely named *Grazia da San Pietro*. Always she skipped along with a great air, partly to please the tall young man at the steering oar. He was brown-skinned, black-eyed, limber as a roebuck, quick as a chamois.

"God be with you, Felix!" I called.

Although we had not sailed together for a good while now, we retained kindly feelings toward each other. However, we had found these hard to express. Our occasional meetings brought forth the usual routine questions and stock answers, a lewd anecdote or two, promises to frolic soon, and a noisy, fast farewell. In truth our roads had forked sharply soon after Mustapha Sheik had become my guide and master.

"Good day to you, Marco, and what are you doing in this hell of smells? I thought you'd be in a countinghouse, sniffing frankincense and myrrh."

"I want to talk to you, when you've the leisure."

Leaving the slippery chores to his crew, he followed me into an ale booth. When we had drunk, I reminded him of our brave voyage to Mustapha's zebec, five years before.

"Do you remember what booty we bore off?" I asked.

"As though it were yesterday. We had six grossi change from the gold piece after you'd brought the drug, and we spent it on sweetmeats."

"How would you like to help another sick man and win one hundred lire for yourself and the same for your crew?"

So I told him of my plan, omitting only the amount of the prize that I hoped to win. Truly I need not have taken the latter precaution; one hundred lire loomed large in his sight, and he never questioned my right to a lion's share. This was all the more surprising to me, considering that he seemed better fitted to lead the enterprise than I was.

I looked at him in sudden and sharp envy. Physical grace in man and perhaps in woman is not merely a matter of harmony with time and event; it is also an awareness of surplus strength. While I had been learning, he had been living. It was more true that he had learned by living, while I had lived to learn. He had discovered the secrets of the fish, whereby they could not escape his net. Very rarely could the weather take him by surprise; it could not help signaling its intentions to his trained eyes. These last had been keened by the daily sharpening of use. His ears were two sleepless watchdogs and the sea their sounding board. His nose was a wonderful thing, an ineffable gift of God, for thereby he found a thousand interests and excitements. Whether on land or on water he was poised, alert, cool, confident, and well oriented. Attacking or attacked, he was a formidable adversary, a trained fighter.

I saw him clearly, and the shadow that he cast across my mind. Apart from his hate, Nicolo Polo was well briefed in not wanting to make me a member of the company adventuring to Cathay. If I could pay my way he would suffer me to do so; he had persuaded himself that I could not earn it. I was not enough like Felix.

"I'll have a go at it with you," Felix told me. "But don't ask me to touch a leper. It would make me puke."

An hour short of midnight, Felix's crew rowed the *Grazia da San Pietro* into the canal that approached the lazar house from the lagoon. My outer clothes, although worn thin, and bought cheap, looked finer than any I had ever worn, fit for a patrician's son. Underneath were the gay-colored shirt and hard-woven woolen breeches favored by fishermen. After bathing with oil and soap until, he said, he smelled sweet as the Doge's bride, Felix had similar garments next to his skin and a gondolier's habit without. We left the ship in the shadow of a little-used bridge, climbed onto the bank, and at the next bridge hailed a vacant gondola. While I hung back in the gloom, Felix spoke the first lines of our play.

"My master will pay double for your boat," he told the gondolier, "but only under specified conditions."

"I'll hear 'em and decide," the fellow answered grumpily.

"He's a young nobleman, as you can well suppose, and he'll meet tonight a young wife of—let us say someone of a station equal to his own. He wishes me to conduct them for a matter of two hours while you take your ease in an inn. So to attract no attention, I have put off my master's livery and donned the habit of a public gondolier, but it was one that I wore before I entered his service, and you need have no fear for your craft, for he'll pay for every speck of paint I knock from her fat sides."

Already Felix had exceeded his instructions. The matter was the same, but couched in livelier language. Indeed he imitated perfectly a high-spirited rascally servingman of a lecherous young lord. I was afraid that the show was too good for the boat owner to believe.

At least the man was no kill-joy. Like a true Venetian, he entered into the game.

"A young nobleman, say you! I've had an old nobleman, a member of the Council if you must know, board me unmasked with the wedded daughter of a princely house. Wild horses couldn't drag from me what happened thereafter, but if I were one to gossip——"

He paused, as though in fair play.

"God knows an oyster is a public crier compared to you, and

my master trusts you further than his own grandma," Felix cried, rising to the occasion. "It's his sensibilities, not his reputation, that demand the privacy. If you won't respect them, say so, and I'll look elsewhere."

"I'm a man of sensibilities myself."

I waited Felix's reply with as much pleasant expectancy as the gondolier. Fishermen are famed both as delightful liars and as skilled at repartee.

"Then you'll sympathize with my master? You know the sort that must break their bladders before they find ease in an open boat. He'll turn his back on his best friend even in the wildwood, and as for sitting next to a lady in a public jakes, why, he'd sink through the boards. When he's frolicking with a light-o'-love, the squeak of a mouse will unman him. So you can imagine that with arms laden with forbidden fruit and a stranger behind his table——"

"Say no more, my friend. Only pay me in advance, with an extra grosso to spend in entertainment while I wait, and leave my mother—for she bears me as tenderly as my dam once did—moored under San Paolo's bridge."

3

It was a pleasant beginning for our adventure, and, we trusted, a good omen. But our cheer began to pall as we drew near the fortresslike pile that housed the living dead. Truly Venice was famed for the good health of its citizenry, doubtless by the blessing of San Marco, yet there were enough lazars of all sorts to pack it full as a dunghill is with worms. It stood in a gloomy backwater among towers fending off the sun; its stones were gray with cold slime; silt and seaweed fouled its doorways. Every window was barred, and all were dark except those of the guardrooms, which were bright enough for a gala night. The air became tainted an arrow cast distant. As we drew nearer a company of rats swam in a V-shape pack across our bows, climbed onto a dock, and vanished in a crack in the wall. There were at least fifty of the loathsome beasts following a captain as big as a half-grown cat, and I wondered to what feast they had been summoned.

We tied the gondola to a piling where I had seen others of its like in the last few days, and where presumably it would attract no attention. Then, lowering our caps and pulling up our neckcloths, we made our way to a recess near the iron gate known as

Dead Man's Portal, where a rushlight flickered and cast a rigadoon of shadows. This gate should open about midnight to let the outer guard bear the day's accumulation of corpses to the charnel boats, from which they were thrown into a mass grave. Ordinarily the door would be locked behind them by Messer Vico, the junior warden, and opened only for their readmittance. Since we had sent him a prearranged signal, we could expect him to omit the precaution tonight as though by a fault of memory. The dead had to be identified by a town watchman at the end of the alley, prayed over, and shrouded before being stowed on the boats, so we could count on at least a half an hour to effect Haran-din's rescue.

My wait very soon grew chill. Since the night was warm, I could only attribute this fact to cold sweat. To try to conceal it from Felix, I kept up a pretense of gay whisperings, but apparently he saw through it, or perhaps was himself under more strain than his debonair manner revealed. In any case he brought forth a leathern flask containing a pint of strong wine, which we shared with great pleasure.

We were enjoying its warmth when we were given a great scare as well. An officer of some kind, bearing a pike, emerged from the shadows and came toward us along the moonlit quay. If we ran the day was lost; if he found us and raised an outcry, our fix would be even worse; if he attacked us there might be an added load for the charnel boat. Our best hope was that he would pass by without seeing us. And it seemed to be winning when he stopped, held his weapon ready, and spoke in low tones.

"I'd a notion I'd find you here."

"Who are you, friend?" I asked.

"Captain Vico, the junior warden. I received the signal, and thought I'd take a look at you, and if you appeared a gentleman, I'd lend you a hand."

I knew the smell of this full well, and it was greasy.

"When are you going to unlock the door?" I asked with growing boldness. I did not know its source or whether it was quite real. Anyway, it had an instantaneous effect on Messer Vico.

"The bolt's slid already, but the coast's not clear until the guards bring out the stuff."

"You've a ring of keys on your belt. Does one of them unlock the Infidel's cell?"

"No, signor, only the keys of the outer rooms. But the lock will be easy to break, and you'll have plenty of time, some of which is by my special provision."

His low voice had become gleeful in an obnoxious way. It was like the happy croak of vultures as they hop toward carrion. I did not want to ask him how he had lengthened the time, but saw no way to dodge it.

"How did you work it, Captain?"

"In a way you'd never think of. Last night I had the kitchen knaves fix a mess of kale, green and half-cooked. Maybe you know it will burst your belly with colic, and flux you worse than spoiled fish. I don't mean you, your Honor. I mean them who has to eat it, when they've nothing else."

"I see."

"I gave it to half a dozen wretches with one foot and four toes in the grave. Old folk wasting away still crave their victuals—some of 'em more than blacksmiths—but they wouldn't have touched the stuff if I hadn't sanded their mush for two days running. Would you call that slipshod work, young sir, or would you call it fore-sight?"

"I don't know what to call it till I know your purpose."

"You haven't guessed it yet? When a body's tottering on the brink, a breath o' wind sends him over."

"They died?"

"Whist!"

Messer Vico had cocked his head to listen to a grating sound from the iron gate. As it swung open, he stood forth as though to oversee the proceeding. Two by two came the burly guards, each pair carrying a bier on which lay a naked corpse. Somehow I had thought they would all be old men, but what I took for a beardless gaffer with frail limbs showed in the rushlight as a wasted crone. Then I saw a male child among the number and then a fair-haired damsel—newly wedded, perhaps, or a virgin bride of Death.

"Ain't that the wench who came to nurse her father, and wouldn't pay your rent for a soft, warm bed?" Captain Vico called jovially to one of her pallbearers.

"The very one," the bravo answered. "Instead she warmed her-self catching fever, which was hot enough, and now she's gone to join him in a hard, cold bed."

I thought the pale parade would never end. It did, though, at last—when I had counted nine. Behind them marched six idle guardsmen of a full squad of twenty-four. The shapes faded into the darkness; and the noise of jests and laughter and complaints over shirking fair shares of the load grew faint and indistinguish-able. There was still a flickering half-circle of shadows before the rushlight, but done was the awful dance of jumping jacks on the wet stone.

Captain Vico returned to us with a proud smile.

"Wait a minute more in case one of 'em glances back," he advised. "You've time to take your time, as you plainly see."

"There are more than usual?" I asked. My voice sounded strained.

"Several more. But I reckoned there might be." The side of his face drew—I saw it in the deep, cold gloom, and I could guess that it indicated a long, knowing wink.

"Six more?"

The question caused Felix to look at me in a startled way.

Captain Vico shook his head. "Sometimes they've got more life in them than you reckon, but there were three that got here sooner than they would have, including one that I had least counted on."

"The old woman?"

"We'd better get on the move——" Felix broke in.

"Why, you've time to sit and play a game of chess. Young gentleman, how did you know it was her?"

"I saw you look surprised as they brought her out."

"You've sharp eyes, and no mistake! Them old women are the greatest lingerers in the house. Well, it turned out you didn't need the extra ones, but many a night there's only two or three, and I've seen the night when we drew a blank. My only aim was to help you win, and I had no notion of asking a share in the prize. But if you've thirty lire handy——"

I did have, and I had considered handing them to him. Instead my hand found other work to do, it seemed on its own volition. I had been hating the creature with a swiftly expanding hate, and suddenly he fell down. I had hardly heard the thud of my fist against his cheekbone—perhaps I had aimed at the eye that had winked—before I hated myself for the reckless act. Quite possibly it would wreck our scheme.

"Devils in hell!" Felix broke out in a low-voiced violence. "Do you want to hang us all?"

"I'm sorry——"

Felix jerked a cloth from around his neck and a cord from his pocket. "See, he's coming to already," he grumbled as he crouched with busy hands beside the fallen man. "For the love of God, Marco, the next time you hit a man, hit him in the jaw."

With unbelievable swiftness he fixed a gag in the warden's mouth and tied his wrists and ankles. Thrusting him into the darkest part of the recess, we dashed for the iron gate. It opened readily and Felix led the way into the dim hall. Soon we both stopped, sickened by the foul air and appalled by the gloom. Here and there a low-burning lamp was bracketed to the wall, but these only caused deeps and shallows of darkness that bewildered the mind. There were black openings that might be corridors, gratings, and barred doors.

"Which way?" Felix whispered.

I could not tell him, but by standing still and shutting fear out of my heart, I looked at the map that Mustapha Sheik had furnished me. I did not do so with my hands and outward eyes, but inside my head where I had stored it, line by line, and with the eyes of the mind. This was the thing I could do, the part I was good for. I was not a good captain but I would make an excellent councilor. . . .

In a moment I knew which one of the black holes to make for. Beyond was a door, as sure as the devil, and a steep stairway. . . . At its head opened a long hall; with the flickering light it seemed a mile long. Through this gloom we sped, I counting eleven cells. At the twelfth we stopped.

"Haran-din?" I called into its fetid dark.

"*Shair Allah* (The justice of God)!"

Under my surcoat was an iron bar. I took it out and thrust it through the ring of the big padlock and began to pry. There was no result but a grating noise and then a clang as the iron slipped and struck the cell door. With a grunt of disgust, Felix took it out of my hands. He placed it carefully, his elbow came down against the powerful upward twist of his forearm, and the lock broke off.

My eyes had grown accustomed to the gloom and I feared to turn them on the inmate of the cell. Many a leper becomes a living carcass, half dismembered. Haran-din had the white form of the disease, so that most of his skin was silvery-looking, picking up the vestiges of light so that it appeared to have a phosphorescent glow. He was naked except for a breachclout and a round cap.

"Come quickly," I murmured in the silence.

It seemed that he too should be able to see in the pale dark, so long had it been his medium. Instead he groped his way toward the door. I was reaching to help him when he gave forth a wail like some strange swamp fowl. Out of the gloom rose a fast football of stone. I had hardly time to turn when three keepers, carrying pointed sticks, burst out of a black passage.

A few seconds ago, Felix and I had been taut as harpstrings with force we could not free. There had been nothing to spend it on after the lock broke; the action of the adventure had been reduced to a snail's pace. Suddenly we were in a swirl of violence. The guards flung themselves on us, their weapons raised to strike us.

They would have done better to employ them as spears. The most likely reason they did not was a humanly interesting one to be considered only in peaceful leisure. These fellows were not knights, to level lances at the foe, but base keepers of half-dead folk. They used their sticks to prod with through the bars, whereby they were greatly feared and hated, terrible weapons indeed to the poor wretches who could only grunt and shriek and beg for mercy. In truth they were like the forks employed by demons in Hell, for there too the damned are bound in iron and cannot fight back. But well the villains knew that Felix and I differed greatly from their usual prey. Losing faith in their sticking and stabbing, they hoisted them like clubs.

Before their wielders could strike us, we were at grips with them. They were three to our two, but whatever terror was in me was transmuted first to excitement, then to fierce joy. Perhaps I realized it was not a fight to the death. If they carried daggers they did not draw them, partly perhaps because they took me for a nobleman whose kniving would be avenged inside or outside the law, mainly for care of their own skins.

While Felix held his own against two of the wretches, I grappled with the other. We had been fighting an endless time, it seemed, before I dared believe I was his master, and at that instant events took a new turn. More likely not twenty seconds had gone by since the attack began, but these were so furious that none of the three guardsmen had breath to call for help. Suddenly one of Felix's pair broke from his grasp and went sprinting down the hall.

"Help! Help!" he shouted at the top of his voice.

Then for the first time I saw what a wolf in strength and swiftness Felix was. I had better compare him to some splendid denizen of the deep, such as a great gleaming swordfish whose shadow in the water is the nightmare of the sharks, and which causes their teeth to chatter like castanets. For in battling the sea and its creatures, these graces had come upon him. The giant threshing tunny had taught him nimbleness, and the writhing tentacles of the octopus had proved the strength of his hands.

Although the second man tried to hold him, Felix flung him

from him in one wrench, then darted in pursuit of the runaway.
I trow he was not two ticks of a clock behind him at the start, and
although they vanished almost instantly in the shadows, I had no
trouble following the race. The volume of the quarry's shouts for
help had not begun to reduce when they suddenly stopped.

Yet a heavy trouble began to lie on my exultant spirit. What
was the good of winning the brabble if we lost the prize? The
turmoil had slacked off, with Felix's man groaning and clutching
his knee, and my fellow panting and grunting, although not strug-
gling very hard, in my grasp. And in this quiet I could vision the
half-score or so stout watchmen in various parts of the building
having heard the shouts, and rushing to their fellows' help. The
wonder was that they had not already appeared.

"Get away as fast as you can!" I shouted to Haran-din in his
native tongue. "The outer gate's unlocked."

"Nay, I can't keep my course in the murky gloom," he answered
calmly.

"Try it anyway, for the love of God! The alarm's raised now,
and the pack will be upon us——"

"I think not. The watchmen doze at their posts, and they'll pay
no mind to calls for help. Why, the halls ring with them day and
night as some poor soul is prodded or beaten, or belike is devil-
ridden."

Although I could hardly believe the more hopeful words, the
rest that he spoke had curious results. Pinning my man down with
one arm and one knee, I struck him in the face with my free fist.
It was a short blow, but the hardest I had ever dealt, and I aimed
it where Felix had bade me, at his jawbone. A marvel to me was
the way he wilted. It was a lesson in human vulnerability I would
not soon forget.

Just then Felix appeared, dragging by the collar the fellow he
had chased. He too was hors de combat, and his capturer lost no
time in heaving him into an empty cell whose door stood ajar. It
came to me that one of the nine corpses on their way to the
Potter's Field had been found here tonight, and its heaving-out
had left the cage for our convenience, and that the new-freed soul
that had lately dwelt in the cankered flesh made merry on its
flight to Heaven over the upshot. Swearing by San Pietro, the
patron of fishermen, Felix seized my sleeping beauty by the scruff
of the neck and dropped him beside his own. When the last of
the three, awake but harmless, had joined his mates, my copemate
shut the door and shot the padlock.

He was more than my copemate, I thought, half in warmheart-edness I could not stay, half in a great dismay. He had proved himself the captain of the venture.

Meanwhile I had got my hand on Haran-din's arm and was tugging him out of the cell. God knew I could hardly bear to touch the silver skin, and to grasp it tightly was unspeakably worse, because there was no firm flesh inside, only a moving jelly. Still, I did not let go. Sick in the belly, faint in the heart, I led him up the hall, down the steep stairs, through the anterooms. It was a thing I could do, and I did it. Although it was not of the splendid order of the things Felix could do, I felt fierce pride.

Our pace seemed no faster than a turtle's as it makes across hot sand toward the cool sea. I dared not tug too hard on Haran-din's arm, lest it pull out of its socket. Felix, pacing ahead of us only to turn back and wait our crawl, begged and cursed in vain. We could hurry no more than the black oxen of Time. Even so, the star of the gateway grew and brightened.

At last we passed through it, and the still-tainted air that Haran-din breathed must have seemed as sweet as the perfume of Paradise to a hero newly slain for Allah's glory.

4

I got my Infidel into the gondola and Felix pushed off. No longer did we look the part of a Venetian lordling and his rascal—our faces, hands, and garments were smeared with jail filth—nor smell it either, unless I missed my guess. So there was nothing to stop us from heaving together on the oar. Truly our fat duck cut the water on the way to the rendezvous. Her owner, the voluble gondolier, had never raced her so fast to get to a fire.

When we came up to the *Grazia da San Pietro*, not one of her crew would lay hand on the lazar. Only by help of a rope passed around his waist was I able to hoist him aboard. My first thought was to leave the gondola adrift, but since our course lay toward San Paolo's bridge, I decided to tow her for a little so the stink would get out of her and her jocund owner could retrieve her before he cast too many curses on our heads. She slowed our passage only a minute or two before I cut her loose. Now the breeze would ground her within a cable's length of her destination.

I got two pieces of worn sail out of a cubby. One I spread on the hard boards for Haran-din to lie on; with the other I covered his pale, wasted form. It was a poor bed at best, I thought; but perhaps he could not feel its hardness beneath his rotted bones. If he needed no covering against the cool breeze and the cold splashings, at least it shielded him from our sight. But perhaps he was as insensible to this as to the rest, and the mercy was wholly ours.

As I thought of this, a sudden weakness came upon me, and I leaned against the rail, my eyes streaming tears. At last I must lean over, ghastly sick. Still I did not seem lowered in the estimation of the oarsmen, rough, lewd, hard-bitten fellows though they were. Not one of them glanced at me; instead they talked quietly to one another above their stroke.

The ship sped, and soon we were well away. The moon set, and still no bell towers clanged an alarm, and only owls and bats could find us in this close dark. Surely we could rest our fears till sunrise provided the rowers did not rest their arms; and by then I hoped we would be seven leagues out on the Adriatic—perhaps much farther if Neptune gave us a fair wind and tide. If so, we would be out of danger except for provost galleys set on our track. Since there was no indication that our means of flight had been discovered, we had every prospect of a clean escape.

No great danger lay in Captain Vico. He had not seen my face and had laid himself open to a beheading on the charge of receiving bribes. The guards we had laid out had had only dim looks at us in the fetid gloom.

The ebb tide had turned back soon after our setting forth, and now before a southeast wind was making into the Gulf of Venice with far more power than usual. And this was the wind we had most hoped to be spared, since it was directly contrary to our course. It was rising a little with the tide. While there was not the slightest sign of a brewing gale, our rowers were hard put to it to make headway. This would have roweled our nerves even on a lawful journey, with no gnashing of teeth behind us. Our destination, Zara, lay nearly sixty leagues beyond Chioggia—two days' sail in the best of weathers. Now, as the dawn cracked, we had barely cleared the shoals off the mouth of the Adige.

I had hoped we would be a speck in the great glittering blue of the Adriatic long before this, instead of, as Felix put it, two shouts and a halloo from port.

"There's a ship on our larboard stern," I told him.

He peered a good ten seconds. "I don't make her out," he answered. "Are you sure she's not a low-hanging skean of mist?"

"I'm sure. And her course is due east."

Felix looked flabbergasted. "What kind of eyes have you, to make out a sail I can't?"

Well, Mustapha Sheik had told me they were the sharpest he had ever seen on man, woman, or child.

"She's close-reefed," I told him, trying to get back part of the capital I had lost tonight. "From her lines, I'd call her a bireme."

Meanwhile the light was clearing with that glorious rush of first spring dawns. Felix flung salt water from a draw bucket into his eyes, then rinsed it out with fresh water.

"I can see her now," he told me. "But I couldn't if you hadn't showed me where to look."

"I doubt if she can see us. We're against the shore and she's against the morning. If you hug a little more on a south'ard course we may give her the slip."

He called orders to that effect. Meanwhile I got a spying tube— a hollow stick which, pressed against the eye socket and peered through, cut off all dazzling light and usually assisted vision.

"She's a bireme of about forty benches," I reported. That meant twenty on a side, each with two oarsmen. "Her high castle and long beak show she's a fighter. If she isn't a marine provost I'll eat her pennant."

"What would she be doing out here this time of day?" Felix asked, wide-eyed.

"She might be attending to her duty, chasing rovers and smugglers. On the other hand she might be looking for a heathen smuggled out of a lazar house."

"By our Blessèd Mary, if someone saw us get off the gondola, our heads'll roll in the Piazzetta before another tide!"

"That's a lot of trouble for the state to go to for one Infidel leper," I told my comrade when my head had cleared. "Still there's no proof we've been seen. The provost marshal's first thought would be that his own tribe stole him, on a holy venture, so he'd send out a galley to look for a zebec or a dhow. However, for lack of either, she might search every boat that journeys east."

"She's changed her course more southerly, and she'll be sure to see us when the sunrise lights our oar blades."

"Then we'd better be afishing, like honest men."

So we heaved our two-hundred-pound hook to anchor in twenty fathoms. Two fellows ran out a short net as though to make a trial cast. Felix and I had already shelled the outer garments concealing our fishers' dress, and with a grim look, he rolled up the foul rigs, fastened the bundle to a net weight, and tossed it overboard. The rest of us watched what might be a sea-dragon with eighty legs, who might come fishing for us.

From the hump on the dragon's back there rose what looked like three stiff hairs. The number increased to a thick patch as more and more spyers mounted the galley's castle.

"She's seen us, but she's keeping her course," Felix muttered.

"Keep praying to San Pietro! If her master is an easy-going lubber, he'll pass us by, but if he's a veteran of Trepani——"

Then the color ran out of Felix's face like red wine from a broken glass.

"God in Heaven, she's veering this way!"

My face blanched the like, if the cold sweat beading there was any sign. My terror was quite likely greater because it spread further—it gave me eyes to see not only our arrest and ironing, but our behanding at Santa Croce, our dragging to the Piazzetta on the tails of horses, and our beheading between the pillars.[6] If our lifting of Haran-din would be counted only theft of first offense, we would get off with a flogging and being branded on the hand. But the same eyes searched desperately for hope, and for this—in my great need—they turned cold and sharp.

"We'd better cut the anchor rope and run for it," Felix gasped. "There's a little mist blowing and if it thickens, maybe we'll fade out."

That would betray our guilt, and the chance of hiding did not seem one in ten. Still, we must be ready to run if we were not able to gull the galley captain into letting us pass.

"Call to the fishers to haul in, but free the fish under water, so they won't gleam in the sun."

"That'll take time. What's the sense of it? Why not let the net go?"

"To make it look like a water haul, so we'll have an excuse to change grounds."

But this could be our last trick. If the galley veered to intercept us, there was no risk too desperate to run.

Five minutes crawled away before the net was stowed and the dinghy made fast. Although the galley's oarsmen were stroking at half-speed—as if she were making toward us only for lack of a better object—she loomed larger and looked fiercer than before. Truly she had not gained three cable lengths against the brisk wind and heavy tide, and was still a good league distant.

Felix ordered oars out. I had thought to request an easy gait, so as not to show fear, but thereby I would show fear of his refusal, which was enough to make him refuse in his present quandary. So with a faintness of heart concealed in a strong voice, I made it my command.

Then we watched like wild geese watching a distant fowler. Every rower's head was turned at exactly the same angle as he bent to his oar. The shape that the galley showed us shortened with terrible slowness. She might be only giving a little way to the head wind. . . . Suddenly I scorned such wishwash, and knew well we were under chase.

"Now is the time for speed," I told Felix.

But before he could give the command to the cockswain, there rose from the deck a wild, frantic cry.

"Wait, wait, for the love of God!"

All hands heard terror in the yell, but only I understood the language, and I could not begin to see its sense. If there had been a mist cloud on the water big enough to hide a rowboat I would have paid it no attention. Instead the sun was sucking up what little haze there was, the only clouds were scattered and bright, and there was no sign anywhere but of fair weather. It looked to be foul enough for us, after two or so hours' run at desperate speed. I believed it would take a miracle to deliver us from capture, and why should we expect it? We were serving a foul Infidel against the Christian law. In spite of Haran-din's pitifulness, no reasonable man would believe in the saint's intervention in his behalf.

"Bid the men keep the same stroke for a moment more," I told Felix.

I saw no revolt in his face and instead the dim glimmer of a hope. Perhaps he thought this silvery Infidel might work a charm.

"What is it?" I asked Haran-din. "Speak quickly!"

"Is a provost galley bearing down on us? I think the rowers said so."

"Yes, and we must run."

"What good to run with twelve legs against a hundred? Can't you hide me?"

"There's no hope of that."

"Then show mercy in Allah's name, and don't let them take me alive!"

Hearing that, my heart banged my rib bones.

"Do you mean, Haran-din, that you want us to throw you overboard?"

"What is the good of that? I'll float, and they'll see me shining like a fish, and pick me up, and bear me back to my cell! Don't you know my bones are eaten away and my flesh is all dry rot, light as cork?"

Horror came down upon me like a cold fog.

"Won't you drown?" I cried.

"No, I can't drown!" he yelled. "If I breathe water instead of air, still I'll live. That is the way of us lepers—we can't die by our own hands—it's the curse of Allah, the great, the glorious! You must kill me before you cast me forth. And even then they'll take up my body and bury it in filth."

I had run to Haran-din's side to help save his breath, and now Felix ran to me.

"What does he want?"

"He wants me to put my dagger through his heart."

Haran-din caught the word "dagger" and raised a long wail.

"Fool, that won't kill me," he howled. "A thousand daggers of pain and woe have pierced me in vain. You must beat me to death with clubs. Make sure that no breath of life remains before you cast me forth. Don't cut off my head, because it will be lost, and belike it must search forever for my trunk, and then I can't ever feast in Paradise!"

I looked up from the terrible face to the remorseless foe. So long a time had passed with me kneeling here that I expected to see her looming above our mast. Instead she was still no longer than my finger. Where she had been three miles away, now she was two miles, six cable lengths. Her oarsmen maintained their same steady pace.

"Will you help me kill him?" I asked my comrade.

"No. I can't touch him. I'll be hanged first."

"Hearken, young noblemen!" Haran-din broke in. And now the horror that had engrossed me let go its icy grip, because the frenzy of his face and voice had given way to calm. He spoke in a low, even tone. I held my breath lest I miss one word. My skin crept in wonder.

"My great countryman, Mustapha Sheik, sent me your name, and I have put it in a parchment as your reward," he told me. "If the Christians take me away alive, I charge you to burn it in Mustapha's sight, or your hands that have touched me will rot away. So if you would have my jewel, my treasure, my white pearl worthy of a king's throne, wield your club manfully, and with a right good will!"

White-faced, Felix plucked at my sleeve. "Are you going to kill him, Marco?"

"Yes," I answered. "Be still."

"I'll wait, but don't take too long. You must drop him over the starboard rail while the rowers screen you."

"And for your comfort, Christian, know that I'm content to die here in the sun," Haran-din went on. "It is written that those who fall on the road to Mecca come to the same glory as those who live to shout '*Labbeyka*' on the Hill of Mercy. It is clean here, and warm. And—and though they find and carry away my body and feed it to swine, still my pearl in your hand will not lose its luster, although it will win you only half the glory that I wished for you."

"What must I do—what must happen—for me to win it all?"

"By great cunning, save my body from their evil hands."

I looked around as in a daze, intending to speak to Felix of this strange thing. Then my eyes fell on a common thing and my hair rustled up on my head.

"Tell the rowers to ship their oars and drift to a stop," I ordered.

His eyes round as doubloons, he obeyed.

"Let half the rowers stand by the capstan, to screen what I must do."

"What are you going to do?"

"Will you help me? If you will, it will take half the sin off my soul and mayhap we'll both be saved."

"I can't lay hand on the leper for good or ill."

"This is for good. I declare it before God or may He strike me dead! Get me three fathoms of rope, the strongest aboard."

Felix uncoiled the inch-thick yellow serpent. It was made of new hemp and would hold a boat of this size in a heavy gale. When Felix had cut off twenty feet, the boat's forward drift had checked and she had begun to lurch sideways in the wind.

"Haran-din, will you walk with me once more?" I asked.

"Yes, my son. Wherever you lead me."

I took his arm and raised him to his feet and led him toward the bow. Without my asking, some of the rowers walked opposite him, screening him from the eyes of watchers on the approaching galley. Truly he did not need this shield, because distance hid him still, and they were careful not to touch him.

It was then that Haran-din guessed my intention. A last terror came into his face, dreadful to behold, but I thought it changed to glory and his half-blind eyes caught fire.

"Allah! Allah! Allah!"

I think it was only a second later that all my comrades made a like discovery in the same stopped breath. Only one of them spoke —a bow oarsman, new to the sea, crying "Mother of God!"—but there rose a sound like a long sigh, and every man stood still.

I began to fix the rope. As it looped about Haran-din's shoulder, he freed his arm, brought forth a folded parchment that he had concealed under his tight-fitting cap, and handed it to me. Then he stood deathly still. I pocketed the parchment and went on with my work. Round and round went the rope, knot after knot I tied, until the rotted body could not possibly fall from the arms of its protector until it was utterly dissolved.

"Will any of you help me heave?" I asked, when all was ready.

No man spoke or moved. The only sound was the lapping of water against the drifting ship, and the shrill of the wind.

"Forgive us, comrade," Felix said. "We can't help you."

It came to me then that I did not need them. Alone I lifted the great iron anchor with its strange rider. For a second I rested it on the edge of the bow.

"Farewell, Infidel," I said. "May you find bliss in Paradise!"

"Farewell, Christian. May God be merciful to you in Hell!" Then his voice rose in a wild triumphant shout that rang through the heavens.

"*Labbeyka! Labbeyka! Allah akbar!*"

I thrust lightly against the iron. It fell with a great splash. Out ran the anchor rope with a rattling rumble—ten, twenty, thirty fathoms. It slacked, and I fixed the pin. The ship drifted half her length, then heaved in vain.

"He'll lie quietly while the galley captain's looking us over," I told Felix in a queer, thin, shaking voice. "Then we'll cut the rope and leave him to Allah's mercy."

"Why, 'tis Heaven's mercy too," Felix answered in almost the same tone. Then it deepened with resurgent power. "Fishers, spread your nets!"

CHAPTER 4

THE PEARL

NOT ONCE ON OUR HOMEWARD SAIL DID I GLANCE AT MY parchment. Mostly, no doubt, this was to help keep the secret from Felix and his crew, but partly it was to maintain our fellowship as long as possible. The business of a great jewel's paying my way to Cathay would sever us soon enough. I need not deal with it here, on the sunny deck. I almost wished we could stay together always.

I paid Felix and his crew out of the hundred bezants Mustapha Sheik had lent me. We made our farewells and I went my way to Mustapha. Then in his presence I broke the seal of the parchment.

It read, in the best Venetian language:

To Simon ben Reuben
By the Sign of the White Stag
San Stefano's Gate
Greetings
When this parchment comes to your hands, count me among the dead.

I bid you deliver without cost to the bearer, Marco Polo of San Felice, the jewel I have put in your keeping according to the laws of your tribe.

I charge you to give him the very jewel brought from the Western Sea, a precious and most beautiful pearl. It is so fine that I have given it a name which, translated into his tongue, is Admirable. Does it not deserve the name? It is a female pearl, more soft, light, white, and lustrous than the male pearls, which are harder and redder, and Allah knows it is most admirable, which its name means.

All who have seen it admire it. But do not covet it, Simon ben Reuben, first because it is against the commandment that your God Jehovah gave unto Moses, and second because I gave you moneys to keep it safe for me.

If the pearl be broken, woe unto you, Simon ben Reuben, and to all your posterity.

Put it in the hands of the aforesaid Marco, as I bade you, for he has won it by a certain service; and he is to have it without charge or claim by you. Truly it is worthy to adorn the throne of a king, but do not lay covetous hands upon it, in the name of your father Abraham. It is my treasure, my gem, my greatest joy, my flawless pearl of pearls. But deliver it to Marco Polo, in the name of Allah.

Haran-din

Mustapha Sheik, wearing a long black surcoat and a high fur cap, went with me to claim my reward. In a high house, shabby without but elegant within, we were shown into a kind of office, where there was a long table with benches, pens and inkhorns and scrolls, lamps, forceps, and scales of different sizes, one of which was the most delicate instrument I had ever seen, capable of weighing a third of a carat, or approximately one grain. "Shall I let the parchment out of my hands until the jewel is delivered to me?" I whispered to Mustapha while we were waiting.

"Shall Simon ben Reuben let the jewel out of his hands until the parchment is delivered to him? Business would be done slowly at that rate. You may examine one and he the other. He'll not make way with the paper. Even if he were a scoundrel he wouldn't dare, knowing not how many folk have seen it. I've known Simon slightly many years. His word is better than his bond, because he himself must guard the honor of the first while the law enforces the second according only to what is written down. But since the Christians claim the right to drive them from their precincts, Jews return the compliment by driving hard bargains. With the more noble Jews, this does not permit dissembling and sharp practice. Others draw the line only at outright lies. No few will steal and shed blood—the same as no few Christians."

In a moment a grizzled gaffer, thin and frail-looking, and wearing a gaberdine and a skullcap, came through the door. Behind him strode a handsome bold-looking Jew of about twenty-five, with large flashing gray eyes and a fine black beard, and in much finer garb. I had often seen the latter on the Rialto and knew him for Saul ben Simon—that is, the son of Simon—a moneylender for the jewelry trade. He stood back modestly while his father greeted Mustapha Sheik. It almost brought tears to my eyes to see those two old men, both aliens in Venice, both exiles from their ancestral deserts, touch hands to heart and forehead and bow so nobly.

Simon introduced his son to Mustapha. I thought that Saul might not pay proper respect to the old Arab and was as fixed for anger as tinder for lighting. On the contrary, he evinced what I could not doubt was sincere reverence. It was in greeting me—after his father had received me most cordially—that I detected

barely veiled contempt. Possibly he had heard of my disinherit-
ance by my father, a dreadful disgrace in Jewish eyes, made worse
by my being his oldest son. Perhaps he looked down on all Christians.

"It's my father's birthday," Saul told Mustapha Sheik, "and if
you have business with him, I pray to stand in his stead."

"My young friend Marco Polo has business with him," Mustapha
answered, "and I doubt not he'll accept you as his voice."

I handed Saul the paper. He read it without the twitch of an
eyebrow.

"I fear, noble youth, that Haran-din's brain has become maggoty
from his malady," he said slowly and calmly. "He made a disposition of the pearl years ago."

I did not fly into rage. I ached to, it seemed, but dared not.
Whether by the guidance of my saints, or by some inward monitor,
I strove to keep my head as clear as when computing the course
of planets under Mustapha's tutoring.

"So?" I answered, marking time.

"He gave us a paper, saying that at his death we were to sell the
pearl, and devote the funds to certain uses pleasing to Allah, his
God," Saul went on. "It was the finer pearl of two—the less fine
we delivered only a few days ago to another party——"

"Marco, he refers to the gentleman who left the gate open,"
Mustapha told me in Arabic. But I knew by the gleam in his eyes
that he was merely waiting, as I was, to hear what Saul had to say,
and that he had no intention of yielding our prize without a last-
ditch fight.

Perhaps Saul knew it too.

"Truly, it would take a Daniel to sit upon this case," Saul went
on, smiling with great charm, "and since none's about, let's judge
it for ourselves."

"Pray instruct us," I said.

Saul looked up with a startled look, as well he might. One of
Mustapha's maxims was that there was no tool in all controversy
as potent as courtesy. He had said that it not only shields its user's
passions and intentions, but suggests power. Evidently it had become pounded into my head, because I had employed it without
thinking.

"That I can't do, so I suggest we put our heads together. Mark
you, he begins the document by his injunction to count him as
one of the dead. In that case, isn't it my father's bounden duty to
sell the jewel as he had previously enjoined him? Doesn't this end

the business? But reading on, I see that our supposedly dead man has changed his mind, which according to a fundamental principle of Christian, Arabic, and Mosaic law, is *ex delicto*. Who ever heard of a will written by a ghost, in contradiction to his living will, coming to probate?"

"I relish your wit, Saul ben Simon," Mustapha Sheik intoned.

"But may a man declare his own death?" Saul asked me, stroking his beard. "No, it takes an officer of the Crown. Therefore, let's take the stand that Haran-din was a living man when he penned these lines, and they constitute a revocation of his previous testament. Thus I've no choice but to deliver a pearl to his creditor herein named."

"Excuse me, your Honor," Mustapha broke in when I was breathless with relief. "Not *a* pearl, but *the* pearl."

"I stand corrected, and before we go any further, let us all be satisfied as to the particular pearl involved. Is that agreeable to all?" And he looked with a bright smile first to Mustapha, then to me.

When we had both responded, Saul unlocked and opened a heavy wooden door. Revealed was a kind of inner closet, made of polished wood and banded with iron. A heavy brass lock of a style I had never seen gave to the turn of a delicate ivory key, and a portal half a foot thick swung wide. From this he took a foot-square box of wrought iron, which sprang open without a visible key. His strong hairy hands went into the box and brought forth a small ivory cabinet. Smiling, he took out a pearl of the size of my thumbnail and put it in my hand.

Of the thousands of pearls I had seen in and about the ships, this was one of the finest. Its shape was spherical, its skin was of very delicate texture and utterly flawless, and its orient, as the pearl dealers say, could hardly be surpassed. Although I had never heard of a "male" and "female" classification of pearls, the terms were commonly used in regard to turquoises, and I thought that describing this pearl as female was very apt. It was so white as to be almost translucent, and its iridescence was so soft that I thought of it as comparable to the radiation of the flesh of a modest virgin.

However, it was not as large as I expected and I could not believe it would bring more than six hundred pieces of gold.

"Noble youth, will you show the pearl to my father and ask him to identify it?" Saul asked.

I did so. Simon ben Reuben took the jewel in his long, thin fingers, held it close to his velvety old eyes, and returned it to me.

"This is the larger and finer of two pearls put in my charge by Haran-din," he answered in his soft voice. "The other was disposed of some days ago according to his instruction."

I handed the pearl to Mustapha Sheik. He gave it a quick inspection, then spoke in a tone of deep anxiety.

"Saul ben Simon, this pearl is not worth a thousand bezants."

"I never maintained that it was."

"But Haran-din did so, and in writing. He was not one to lie to me or to be deceived. Why, half that amount would be a fair price in the jewel mart."

"Saul"—and it was Simon's deep, soft voice—"hand me the parchment."

"It's some other writing that Mustapha refers to, my father. This one mentions no sum."

"I'll read it, just the same."

Again Saul's face was still as a stone, and it seemed to me he stood as still as one while Simon's eyes moved down the page. He handed it back without comment.

"I would take a chance on it at a higher sum," Saul remarked.

"How much higher?"

"Substantially so. What if I lose on it? My father and I have done good business with the Mohammedans, and Haran-din's soul might be troubled if he's promised something he can't deliver. Let us subtract the amount of my estimation from yours and divide the remainder. I'll pay seven hundred and fifty."

"That's very generous, Saul ben Simon," Mustapha said with a deep breath.

"Shall I accept it, master?" I asked.

Mustapha Sheik hesitated longer than I expected. His lips had moved to say yes when the patriarch spoke again.

"Saul, my son, I am struck with the international character of this dealing. Haran-din was a Mussulman, so is Mustapha Sheik, you and I are Jews, and Marco Polo is a Christian."

"It is true, my father."

"Mohammedans are like us Jews in being aliens in Venice. They are not spat upon, as we are, but they are hated greatly. Yet Mustapha arranged for a Christian to serve his tribesman Haran-din in his need—a service so great that Haran-din thought to reward him with a thousand pieces of gold."

Saul had turned so white that his black beard looked false.

"My father, shall I buy back this pearl with a thousand gold pieces?"

"Paying twice its worth? What kind of business is that?"

"I would have his name and acknowledged satisfaction on this document."

"Saul, my son, I fear you have committed the very sin against which the letter warns, and coveted a jewel that's not yours."

"What would you have me do?"

"I would have you hold from taking advantage of the unintentional ambiguity of a letter written in terror and the shadow of death. I would bid you not fail the trust Haran-din placed in us, to read between the lines of his letter."

"You've shamed me, O Father, before a Christian."

"You have shamed both of us, and our nation. Now send for the pearl whose name is Miranda, meaning Admirable."

2

Mustapha moved closer to me and spoke in an undertone.

"I should have anticipated this development," he said. "Haran-din dealt in slaves, supplying the shahs and sultans of the Transcaucasus. Many traders owed him moneys or goods when he was captured, and like good Mussulmans have paid the debts since. Also, I was quite sure there was no such thing as a female or a male pearl."

I could not reply nor would I let the others see me watching the door, so I turned my back on it and gazed through a barred casement into a flower garden. When I heard it open, I turned slowly, and my first sensation was of surprise.

I expected to see a very fine Circassian. These bright blondes from the Caucasus brought the highest prices of any girls sold in Venice, and were used almost altogether as concubines. A good many belonged to the Greek Church, but had been forced to renounce Christianity so they could be bought and sold by Christians—a queer way to beat the devil around the bush. Quite often the girls forswore themselves willingly, to have a better life. One glance, however, proved my guess wrong. Her face and form had not the Circassian molding, her hair was of different dress, and instead of a bright blonde, she was a pale blonde.

By now I was sharply alert, hard to fool. I was surprised by her appearance, but not with pleasure; considering the lengths Saul had gone to keep her, I had expected a great treat for my eyes. Instead they took in a rather odd-looking—as far as their experience went—blonde young girl. At most I would call her pretty. I could not think of her as either beautiful or gorgeous.

She might be as tall as most Circassians—perhaps as much as four inches over five feet, far taller than most Venetian girls—but she did not look it, because of her slight figure. Circassians had voluptuous figures—big white round breasts, round white arms, and boldly curved thighs. They looked at you and took your breath. This girl did not weigh much more than a hundred pounds. Her hair, instead of a bright gold, was about the color of wheat straw. She wore it in two long plaits that looked like new hemp ropes. Her eyebrows and long eyelashes were the same pale color and not very noticeable in this light, but to do her justice—and I was hunting hungrily for her every asset—they drew the attention more and more as you looked at her. Her eyes, very long for their width and set wide apart, appeared to be rather darker than I would expect to go with her pale tints—I thought that they were light brown.

The faces of Circassian and Greek girls, generally golden-haired or redheads, are almost always long and markedly aquiline with thin, high Roman noses and strong chins. Miranda's face was rather short, and in profile appeared somewhat incurved. I could call it that. An artist about to paint her picture, and keeping his heart cold until he could draft the outlines of her face, would note that her forehead was high, curved, and set forward, her cheekbones were delicate but prominent, the bridge of her nose was slightly concave rather than convex, her upper lip short and deeply incurved, and her chin nicely fitted to the swift slope of her jaws. No doubt that kind of analysis would aid his brush. Warming to his work, he would observe that her forehead was very pure and white, and her nose the most beautiful he had ever seen.

I had never seen a beautiful nose before. Some with very high bridges had been noble-looking on highborn men and on old ladies, but on most people's faces and on pretty girls especially, the less you need observe them, the better. Going children one better, noses should be neither seen nor heard. I could not imagine why this one was beautiful, unless it had to do with its delicacy.

The general effect was not at all spectacular. It was of wistfulness and shyness and very-youngness. However, I kept finding aspects of her face and body that quickened my thoughts and feelings. The spare flesh over her facial bones was delicately molded, and under the eyes had a lustrous appearance. Her mouth had a property that is supposed to be common but which really is rather rare. I, like I am sure almost every lover of woman, wanted to kiss it. It was not voluptuous or very full or very beautiful, and its little smile was somehow sad, yet I felt that to kiss it would be an experience of great beauty and bliss.

Quite possibly Saul had kissed it. This was not a certainty—merchant citizens of Venice had found they must never underestimate the steadfastness of a Jew in keeping patriarchal law—and the Jews of Christendom rarely owned or dealt in slaves, although girls of their own nation were bonded servants in their houses and, in many cases, virtually concubines. However, Saul certainly craved to do so, and as tricky a man as he might find a lawful loophole to keep her for his own. If so, I was sure he would pay more for her than I could get from any slave dealer in the city.

Too well I remembered a saying of their trade: "Unlike a diamond, which can be weighed and graded, unlike a rug, whose stitches can be reckoned, unlike a horse, which can be put through paces, a two-legged filly is worth no more nor less than some fool will pay."

As I was thinking this, the maiden stood there in the kind of long sleeveless smock in which slave girls were usually offered for sale. Her eyes were cast down, her hands were folded on her breast, the lamplight glossed her pale-gold plaits and her small bare arms. And I found it best not to look at her as I schemed the best way of turning her into gold. This was not from any wanting her myself. It was a feeling, very hard to pin down, of self-distaste, almost of self-disgust. It was as though I were committing some vulgarism in the presence of great folk.

"What do you think of her, Marco Polo?" Saul asked. His voice betrayed a good deal of anxiety, but whether for me to rejoice or be disappointed in her I could not guess.

"I take it she is the 'pearl' that Haran-din calls Miranda," I answered, to gain a little more time.

"You heard my father order her summoning."

"Haran-din valued her at a thousand pieces of gold. That is a large sum for any slave girl."

"I agree with you."

"I've the right to ask for proof that she's the one, but I don't think it will be necessary if you'll answer a few questions. How old is she?"

Saul turned to the maiden. "Miranda, tell this young man how old you are."

She raised her eyes to gaze straight into mine. "Signor, I am sixteen."

Thinking hard of what I would realize from her, I heard this with dismay. Virgin slave girls intended for concubines were in good demand at twelve, higher-priced at thirteen, and at their prime at fourteen. After that age they declined rapidly in value: I had never heard of a virgin of sixteen bringing a thousand pieces of gold. My comfort was that she did not look it, and no doubt I could make her conceal the fact.

"Where did she come from?" I asked Saul.

"A countryman of Haran-din's, owing him a debt, brought her here not quite a year ago. He didn't say where he'd got her."

"Is she some fashion of Greek? I can't remember seeing her like."

"Why don't you ask her?"

"Miranda, to what nation do you belong?"

"I belong to no nation. I am a slave."

"Were you born a slave?"

She raised her head and lifted her eyes. "No, signor, I was born free."

"In what country?"

"On an island in the North. I doubt if you ever heard of it."

"What's its name?"

"Albion."

"The name means White Land. Is it a large island?"

"It's somewhat larger than the Rialto."

"What country is it near? Are all the people blond like you? What is their religion? Who is the king, and what's the name of his capital? Don't be so short-spoken. Speak out."

"Lord, I remember none of those things."

"How old were you when you left there?"

"I don't remember that either. I was sick—and found myself on a slave ship. What happened before then could have happened to some other girl, as far as I recall."

"Then how did you know you're sixteen years old?"

"I've a feeling that I am. But I will be any age you tell me."

"Saul, has Miranda told you anything of her history?"

"No, and if you question her too closely she begins to lie. You ought to hear some of her stories—an imp gets into each of her eyes and she makes them up as she goes along. I think she was sold into slavery not long before she was put into our charge—she certainly knew very little about it. At that time she could speak not a word of Venetian. But she knew a few words of Arabic, and she let slip to one of the handmaids that she had been in Malaga."

This last was the Saracen city on the Spanish coast and the busiest slave market west of Constantinople.

Saul spoke in an irritated tone. When she paid no attention to him or to me, only stood there with her hands folded and her eyes cast down, I felt annoyance growing into ire. I was not at all sure that her wistful look was not put on. I was positive she would not bring more than five hundred pieces of gold.

"She hasn't learned her duty as a slave even now," I remarked. "Perhaps if you'd given her a good dose of birch oil, she could talk better."

"Did you hear that, Miranda? He meant you should have a good whipping, and I'd have been tempted to give it to you, if my revered father would stand for it."

"And well he shouldn't!" Mustapha cried in a booming voice. "The idea of laying a lash on the lovely child! Marco, I'm ashamed of you. And pray what would you two strict disciplinarians expect of a delicate maiden snatched or sold into slavery? The shock was enough to erase all the tablets of her memory."

The girl's eyes widened and she turned, white in the face, to Simon ben Reuben.

"Lord, have I leave to speak to the venerable Arab?"

"Of course, my dear."

At that she ran to the bench where Mustapha sat and bowed low before him, her ten fingers touching her forehead. The latter was an Arabic gesture of obeisance and entreaty. I had seen Mustapha's servant give it on rare occasions.

"What is it, little lovely one?" Mustapha asked.

"The patriarch can't keep me. It's in a paper that he must sell me—he's told me so. Will you buy me, O Sheik? I'll serve you, body and soul, as long as we both live."

"I cannot, young Moon of Beauty—Moon of Ramadan! Even if I had enough gold, I have sworn unto Allah never to own another slave. That my countrymen deal in them you know too well. Saul spoke of your knowing a few Arabic words—you have just made an Arabic obeisance. It's come to me, in great pain, that it was an Arab—likely a Saracen from Malaga—to whom you first went into slavery."

Her eyes became so bright that I expected her tears to flow. Instead she gave him a fleeting smile.

"That is true."

"Did he buy you, or——"

"I pray you don't be troubled by it. It's as though it happened to another girl, one I hardly knew."

"I didn't know that our zebecs sailed as far as your island." She caught her breath, and panic seemed about to seize her. Then the gentleness in Mustapha's face and voice reassured her.

"Then you know our island!"

"I've never been there, my darling, but I guessed it first from your appearance, and then very soon you confirmed my guess. If you want to keep it a secret, you mustn't use a certain name in front of those who know Pliny and are disciples of Ptolemy."

I had read Ptolemy with great care, and now recalled his speaking of Albion. I would have to ask Mustapha. . . .

"Will you promise not to tell anyone?" the girl asked.

"If you wish it kept a secret, it must be for some good reason, and I won't tell a soul, even your new master."

"My new master? I thought I was only being looked at——"

"There he stands—my chela, I wish I could say my son in blood, Marco Polo. He has title to you from Haran-din."

Miranda turned slowly, a sheen of excitement in her eyes.

"You are Marco Polo?"

"Yes."

"I've heard the patriarch speak of Nicolo Polo, the great traveler——"

"That's my father."

"Are you a merchant?"

"Remember your manners, child," Simon ben Reuben broke in in a gentle voice.

"I entreat you to forgive my forwardness, but will you answer one more question?" the girl persisted.

"You may ask it, and I'll see."

"Is it your intention to sell me, or to keep me?"

"Excuse her presumption, Christian youth, for she has not been long a slave, and even a dog would ask that of a new master, if he could."

"My father's always making excuses for her," Saul broke in, half sulkily.

"Since the patriarch speaks for you, I'll answer you," I said. "I intend to sell you to the first buyer who'll pay a fair price."

"And what will I do without her bright eyes and shining hair?" the old man went on. "Saul, have my handmaiden bring Rebecca's old lute. The young merchant will be pleased that she's so accomplished, and I yearn to hear her once more before she goes."

"I doubt not Signor Polo is in haste to take her away."

"Have you time to hear her play and sing, young signor? Saul only pretends not to care for it. I know from his face that he likes it very well."

At my assent, the lute was sent for. It was proper for a slave musician to ask her master what song he preferred, or at least get his consent to her own choosing, but Miranda did not observe the amenity.

"I'll give you 'Young Rob o' the Tower,'" she told the old man, as though she were a princess instead of a slave.

"Oh yes." And then in a proud tone to Mustapha, "This is a song Miranda learned from an old minstrel, and has translated into the Venetian tongue."

Miranda struck a deep, soft note and began to sing in a minor key. These were the words of her song:

> Beggarman O beggarman, out on the lea,
> Did you pass a bold knight of high chivalry?
> I gave him a kiss, I gave him a flower,
> For he's my true lover, Young Rob o' the Tower.

> Fair maiden, I passed him, and bright was his shield,
> And mighty his motto, *The Foeman Shall Yield!*
> But cold will grow kisses, and wilt will a flower,
> So wait not too long for Lord Rob o' the Tower.

> Sailorman O sailorman, home from the sea,
> Did you pass a bold knight of great gallantry?
> When Saracen's spy him in coverts they'll cower,
> For he's my true lover, Young Rob o' the Tower.

> Fair maiden, I passed him on tall horse-of-tree,
> And loud roared the tempest, and louder laughed he.
> And mirth it hath healing and prayer it hath power,
> So break not your heart for Lord Rob o' the Tower.

> Pikeman O pikeman, red from the fray,
> Did you pass a bold knight in battle to-day?
> He promised to wed, I gave him a flower,
> O fetch him to me, my Young Rob o' the Tower.

> I fear he'll not wed you, fair maiden of Devon,
> He died in the battle and rode on to Heaven;
> And gifts that you gave him in sweet unbless'd hour
> Will fetch you to Fire, not to Rob o' the Tower.

3

I listened and looked at her, and never before had my eyes and ears so joined as though to create a new sense. Her voice was low and sweet, and I saw it shaped in her small, lustrous throat. The melody was a lovely thing, soft and sorrowful, and I thought it accompanied a loveliness in her mouth and eyes I had not seen before, and a loveliness of hands moving in stately measures.

I wondered if she had given a flower to some lover, whereby she had fetched up in slavery. . . . But I must be jealous only for my thousand pieces of gold.

"I know now what land she came from," I told Mustapha in Arabic. "She lied when she said it was a little island."

"She said it was bigger than the Rialto, and it is."

"Did you believe her when she said she had forgotten——?"

"She wants to forget, I think. And as the song said truly, 'Mirth it hath healing and prayer it hath power.' Be kind to her, Marco my son."

The entertainment was over. Apparently it had pleased Mustapha and Simon more than Saul and me; perhaps this was because they were both old men with not much to win or lose from life, and hence they could devote their ears and eyes without prejudice. Perhaps they were more moved by youth and loveliness than in the days when they could possess it themselves, and it was possible that, having more experience, they recognized worth and rareness that we young men missed. They were exulting together, their eyes moist with emotion.

Saul was waiting for me to announce our departure with my property. He was trying, not too successfully, to resign himself to it. I did not go yet; there were two matters on my mind that I felt compelled to settle before we left. One of them, involving the law, could cause a great deal of trouble if what I feared was true; yet I thought best to confront the danger now.

"Miranda, are you a Christian?" I asked. It was an unlawful act for a Venetian Christian to own Christian slaves.

The girl looked me calmly in the eyes.

"No, master. When I was in Malaga, I renounced Christianity and took Allah for my God."

I was quite sure this was a downright lie, but I heard it with vast relief. Afterward it seemed to me that I had taken a heavy and foolish risk in asking her the question in front of witnesses.

If she had answered yes, what action could I have taken? As it was, my title to her had become almost unassailable.

The other matter was simply one of good business. Both Jews would count me a fool if I did not pursue it; if they were remiss, they might be subject to suit. My undoubted reluctance to broach it made me angry with myself—certainly I was not going to renounce my rights, and perhaps be cheated, because of a wistful face and a kind of grace.

"The parchment describes the jewel as flawless," I remarked, glancing over the writing. "I suppose he meant that just as a perfect pearl is of beautiful shape and unmarred skin, the maiden's form is without fault and she has no hidden canker or witch's mark."

"That was Haran-din's statement," Saul answered irritably. "We don't have to warrant it. All we must do is deliver on his order the chattel he put in our care. As for any disfigurements, you can look for them in privacy as soon as you get to your lodgings—as I don't doubt you will."

"Your latter remark is uncalled for, Saul my son," the patriarch chided him.

"I'll grant that point," I said. "But there's another that involves your care of her. The parchment reads, 'If the pearl be broken, woe unto you.'"

"We guarded her as well as we could," said Saul, "but that's a danger from which a legion of dragons couldn't guarantee to protect her. I trust that the goods are undamaged. If otherwise, I express the wish that no charge be made against me personally, directly or indirectly. She was put in my father's charge. Such a reflection on my honor I'd be bound to avenge."

He had tried to cheat me less than an hour before. But there was no doubt now that he meant every word he said, although for a Jew to take up arms against a Christian would condemn him to death by torture.

"Master, I beg leave to speak," Miranda broke in.

"It's granted."

"I swear by Blessèd Jesus——"

"That oath has no warranty unless made by a Christian."

"I swear by Allah, the great, the glorious, that I'm a virgin."

"I will consider it established. Saul, you evinced awhile ago a desire to keep her. I'll ask if you'd like to buy her."

The room became exceedingly still. Saul tried in vain to control his countenance. He was deeply shaken.

"As a matter of curiosity only," he said, "what price are you asking?"

"A thousand gold bezants."

"It's far too much. Since we're used to having her here, and would miss her singing and the like, I might be persuaded——" He paused, and he could not keep his eyes from wandering to his father's face.

"My son, is there no balm in Gilead?" the old man asked solemnly.

"I only meant——"

"Better the sight of the eyes than wandering of desire."

"I entreat your forgiveness."

A moment later, the patriarch called me to him and began to ask me kindly, civil questions about my conditions and ambitions, such as an old man may properly put to a young one. I had a hard time answering them, because Saul and Miranda were talking in low tones halfway across the room. I was trying to separate their voices from Simon's to hear what they said.

At first they seemed to be speaking sorrowfully of their parting. The maiden's eyes were big and I could not doubt that she felt a deep affection for the handsome young Jew, if not ardent love or carnal passion. Although I believed her claim to virginity in the narrow meaning of the word, the two could have very easily indulged in dalliance, and the mere thought enraged me. I repeated to myself that I was not going to be taken in by her touching appearance and manner, combined with some other quality I could not identify. Beneath these she could be lascivious as a witch child. Perhaps because my senses were sharpened by suspicion or I strained harder than before, I began to catch their words.

"I'm sorry that you were shamed in front of your father and the old Arab," she was saying. "I wouldn't worry about the opinions of the young slave trader."

"The young slave trader is now your master. He can sell you to a baboon who has enough gold to buy you. If you'd confided in me, maybe I could have saved you."

"I told you it was impossible. But I want you to tell the patriarch what your motives were in trying to keep me here."

"Even if it was hopeless, as you say, I could have done better for you than this. I could have sold you to Paulos Angelos this very morning, if you'd let me. Haran-din became officially dead when he was taken from the lazar house, and our first order from him would have held in court. But no, Paulos's promise that you'd become the favorite of a Thessalian duke didn't move you. Yet you sang your prettiest for a Venetian bravo."

"Why do you call him that?"

"I grant he's gentle-born, but you can see he's of a violent, ruthless nature. Obviously he led the party that delivered Haran-din from the lazar house——"

Miranda gave me a covert glance. "Are you going to turn him in?"

"You know I can't, even if I wished to. Haran-din was my father's client and Mustapha Sheik his friend. But I probably was mistaken in one thing I told you about him." Saul's voice grew somber. "He'll probably not sell you. He'll keep you a few years for his own plaything, and then sell you for a field worker. That will be the end."

I had heard the talk unmoved, contemptuous, not really trying to understand. My attitude was that they knew I was listening, although of course they did not. Then I saw what shook me more than I wanted to confess. As Saul turned away, his eyes brimmed with tears.

A moment later Miranda was kneeling before Simon ben Reuben, her eyes wide but dry. Christian children in Venice were rarely taught to kneel to their parents or to anyone except princes or priests; I thought she was observing a Jewish custom. The patriarch raised her up, kissed her between the eyes, and spoke to her in his low, old, yet deep, rich voice.

"I wish I could set you free and adopt you into my nation, but that's beyond my power. But I'll entreat Jehovah to guard your ways, and I'll give you what we call a mezusah, a little gold shell containing our God's promises to us, which we hang on our doorpost. Wear it on a cord over your heart. It's not a good-luck charm or a talisman of any sort. It's only a symbol of my own faith, wherewith I bless you. For I've learned to love you, my child. And to whatever faith that has brought you to this pass, I know that you'll be true."

CHAPTER 5

THE CHALLENGE

IN A MOMENT I HAD THE SLAVE GIRL STOWED ABOARD OUR GONDOLA. She was my property now, by the law of Venice; my power over her was virtually as complete as a farmer over his oxen; the clothes in a box she carried were as much mine as those on her back. But I wanted something more than Venetian law standing behind a parchment given me by an Arab leper to attest my ownership. The fact was, which I was most anxious to conceal both from her and from Mustapha Dey, I could not yet believe in it.

Believing a thing and believing *in* a thing are two different things. The first could be a mere cold receptivity of mind, while the second was an activating force. It came to me that I would have trouble looking on any human being as my sheer chattel, and there was something about Miranda that defeated the attempt. Although I disliked and in some fashion dreaded the inquiry, I began to seek the reason.

It lay partly in her appearance. She did not have any of the familiar aspects of a slave. The state of slavery is the most abject in all the world—a free beggar's is kingly in comparison, a chained beast's is higher, because he doesn't know the meaning of the word. I was used to seeing it manifested in various forms. New-caught slaves from the outlands were usually wild-eyed and defiant or dazed with shock or in terror dreadful to see. Well-fed, well-clothed house slaves imitated their masters and even outdid them in arrogant manners. Most of the girls on sale for the usual use had the manner of young whores—this well-known fact applied to virgins as young as twelve. Only partly was it by the instruction of the merchants. They had perceived beforehand, during the dressing and grooming period, that they were in deadly competition with one another to attract rich buyers.

Miranda gave none of these signs. There was no strain in her face, and only what seemed an echo of sorrow. She was watching the scenes on the bank, and her passiveness did not suggest inertness so much as poise. Most slave girls smile too brightly, flash their eyes too much. She talked to Mustapha gravely, her face lighting sometimes. Once she laughed gaily at one of his jokes, but she was not trying to make any sort of impression on either of us. I felt that she was fully aware of her beauty—more so than I, perhaps—and that awareness, to the degree of using it in her need, had affected the thing itself—made it more quiet and more telling. Perhaps I could not doubt it any more. It was not an adornment to her. She was composed of it.

All this seemed to amount to one simple thing—she did not perceive herself as a slave.

This fact disturbed me so greatly that the disturbance felt like anger. I could not wait to impress her condition upon her. Until she realized it, I did not think she would be marketable for anything like the sum I needed. Most concubine-seekers did not want grave girls whose lives turned inward; they wanted bright, vivacious girls who strove to please. Her quietude would be mistaken for sulkiness. Only merchants dealing in rarities would bid for her, and at prices low enough to compensate for their risk.

I saw a chance for my first stroke when Mustapha spoke to me in Arabic.

"Marco my son, you may have to hold her some weeks before you can make proper disposition of her," he said, unable to conceal his anxiety. "Selling her is a dreadful thing to contemplate. At least you must deal only with the most honorable and humanitarian traders."

"I must sell her within a fortnight," I answered. "If she tries hard enough, she can please her master and have a good life. She's intelligent and accomplished and her face could be quite beautiful if she'd brighten it up."

"Could be? It is! I hold her one of the most beautiful maidens I've ever seen." Mustapha Sheik tugged at his beard. "And what provision can we make for her creature comforts while she's with us?"

"Why, we don't need to make any. Simon and his family spoiled her, but the sooner she discovers she's a slave, the better for her, so she'll make an effort to please. As for food, she can have our leavings."

"I wouldn't hear of it, Marco. Nor do I think it wise to have her share with Hosain and Dasa." These were Mustapha's body servants. "No, it would be most unwise. Hosain is young and lusty and like so many Arabs, lacks self-control. She must have a place at our table."

"Sooner or later she must learn——"

"She'll drink no bitter cup within my house, if I can spare her! The child has had more than life's fair share already, and how many more troubles to come? For that little while, her beauty will grace our board. It will be like sunlight through a casement of stained glass in the bleak of winter."

"If it pleases you," I answered, impressed by his nobility as much as touched by his childish ardor.

"And what shall we provide her in the way of a couch?" Mustapha asked.

"She can make her bed on the floor of my room. There are plenty of carpets."

Mustapha Sheik made no immediate reply. I had a hard time remaining silent when I saw the real distress in his face, but my heart had strangely hardened. . . .

"Marco my son, I consider that most unwise. If you are going to sell this maiden, not keep her for your own, you must protect her against yourself as well as from others. Thereby she will bring a far better price and be in higher repute with her purchaser."

"She'll take no harm from me. I'll warrant that."

"An angel incarnate couldn't warrant it. For a young, lusty man to sleep in the same room with a pretty unkindred maiden is to challenge Kismet. If she is already in his temporal power, as in this case, Kismet would decline the challenge as unworthy of his steel."

I had never known Mustapha to employ in a light way the name of Allah or of Mohammed. Usually he spoke of Kismet no more solemnly than most Christians speak of Fate. However, there was an earnestness in his eyes at odds with his humor.

2

Hosain, Mustapha's servant, carried Miranda's box to a dressing room adjoining mine. A freeman, he could be expected to resent waiting on a slave, but he added to the cheerful service an eloquent salaam. Possibly he mistook her for tonight's concubine of his master's ward; in any case, this was not the way to put her in her place. I decided to start her schooling as we were waiting for dinner to be served. I was determined not to be moved by her wistful smile and childish grace.

"The venerable Arab, my host, Mustapha Sheik, is so lost in his studies of the stars that he grows careless of the proprieties of this world," I began.

The statement was far from true. Mustapha grew careless of the conventions, but he was a strict observer of what he believed were the real proprieties.

The girl gave lively attention to my words but showed no flattering interest in me.

"Oh, I think he's a wonderful old man!" she cried.

"He asked me to give you leave to eat at his table for the short time you're here. Of course I offered no objection."

"He's very kind."

"It's strange that you could take to any Arab when you've been owned by Arabs."

"They're a different class entirely. Do you suppose he'll talk to me about the stars?"

"I've known him to talk with slaves as cordially as with great folk."

"There was a great scholar in my own country who did the same." Her eyes softened from the memory. Then, returning to the here and now: "Try to get him to, will you, master? I'll eat only half as much, if that will be a saving to you."

"I bid you eat your fill. You're already too thin to bring a top price in the market."

If Mustapha had heard me, he would have rebuked me for what he would consider harshness to a helpless child. She struck me as being far less childish and better able to help herself than she appeared. Still, I did not quite penetrate my own motives. Perhaps I wanted to outdo her idea of me as a crass young merchant.

Our ivory and rosewood table, about a foot high, was the finest piece of furniture the house boasted. Miranda regarded it with delighted surprise and took childish pleasure in sitting on a floor cushion, persuading me that she had seen nothing of Saracen life but ships' holds and slave pens. I half expected Mustapha to be lost in thought and forget her existence. Instead he was inspired to a brilliant, thrilling discourse. I wanted to observe her table manners, but she had none. Her food got to her mouth so neatly and deftly that I was startled when her plate was empty. She caught my eye, rubbed her stomach, and gave me a triumphant smile.

The excitement of her coming soon put Mustapha to bed with one of his brow-splitting headaches. His servants fixed bhang for him—all they could do—and went out. When she and I were left alone, she was not a whit abashed. After walking about to inspect the various objects in the room—considered bad manners among Venetian great folk—she took a seat near the window where she could watch the boats and the sea birds on the bay.

Meanwhile I was pondering how she had become a slave in the

first place. Her appearance and ways denied that she was born one. Since she was neither stately nor haughty, yet well mannered, I took it that she might be the daughter of a franklin, a bailiff, a clerk, or even a poor knight. It was barely possible that she was the daughter of a shipmaster and had been captured by Saracens while accompanying him on a journey.

"Is the country you came from—Albion, you call it—a desert country?" I asked.

"It's the most wonderful green land on earth!" she burst out.

"Is it a long way from here?"

Her eyes changed expression. "Halfway across the world."

Then, out of a clear sky, I asked, "Is Henry a good king?"

The bolt struck true. She could not hide her consternation. "I never mentioned our king's name."

"Surely you're not too ignorant to know it. Have you ever seen the beautiful Eleanor of Castile, his son Edward's wife?"

"Then the old man told you, in spite of his promise!"

"To put an end to a game not worth playing, you told me yourself. Very soon after you mentioned Albion, I remembered it was a Greek name for Britain. The song you sang was patently English. It even mentioned Devon, the province where we buy most of our tin."

"I forgot you were a merchant."

"Why do you try to hide it, Miranda? Were you trying to flee England when you were captured, and are afraid you'll be brought back?"

Of course I knew that this was not the explanation and it was hardly out of my mouth when I conceived a far more likely one. It was that her father had sold her into slavery, a common event throughout Europe. If she had loved him greatly, she might go to these lengths to conceal the fact. Her sense of measureless disgrace could easily make her wish to forget her past life.

I decided not to taunt her with the fact. I, too, had been strangely dealt with by my father. However, the fellow feeling made me all the more resolved to bring her to heel.

"I don't remember," she answered sullenly.

"Your future master won't care where you've come from if you can make his days happy and his nights blissful. Have you any accomplishments other than music?"

"I can weave well, and sew a fine seam."

"Do you know how to dress your hair other than as ropes, redden your lips, and whiten your skin?"

"The first two I can do, but no one can whiten snow."

"Let me see this snow. All of it. If it's lustrous, I'll ask more for you and presumably you'll have a richer master. If it's scrofulous, I'll be lucky to sell you for a dairymaid."

"I'd rather you'd sell me for a dairymaid than any other office. I can milk well and kine like me and stand for me."

"I wish to survey your form, so I may have a better notion of your value. Remove your garments straightway, and let your hair flow free."

"Lord, speak truly to your slave! Is your purpose to sell me, or to keep me for your own pleasure?"

"I told you my purpose."

"Do you swear to it by your saints?"

"By my very namesake, San Marco!"

"Then I entreat you to reconsider your command."

"Why should I?"

"It isn't well for your purpose and profit."

"I'll be the judge of that. Besides, every possible buyer will demand the same survey while I stand by. Would he buy a pig in a poke?"

"When a buyer surveys me, your mind will be on gold, and each will be seeking the advantage of the other. Now the day dies and you and I are alone except for a sleeper in another room, and the light through the casement makes for lechery——"

"What do you know of lechery, unless Saul taught you?"

"I know nothing, but my woman's instinct warns me."

"Your woman's instinct is a small thing compared with a thousand pieces of gold. Obey my order swiftly, and when you're ready for my inspection, say so."

I opened a scroll and looked at the illumined script. It was a piece of histrionics, but I needed every diversion I could find. Not once did I glance sideways at a growing whiteness, blurred now and then with pale gold. The minutes crept away. A repeated pale gleaming was Miranda's arm as she combed her hair. This went on a long time, then a white-and-gold shape moved about at the edge of my vision.

At last came a clear, low voice.

"I'm ready, master, for your inspection."

My first thought was that Miranda had spared no pains in setting herself off. This was before my eyes cleared to behold her. For her seat she had chosen a massively carved chest of ebony that happened to stand in front of a blood-red tapestry. . . . But-

ter wouldn't melt in her mouth, but this proved the minx she was.
. . . But the thought ran out and I began to behold some sort of
valor, even of nobility, in the act.

Her beauty was not breath-taking so much as touching. She sat
with one knee raised a little and turned away from me, her hands
in her lap, her pale tresses flowing over one white shoulder and
screening a white breast that I deduced was round, young, nymph-
like, and tipped with rose. Her eyes, golden-brown in this light,
neither sought nor avoided mine—it was as though she were alone,
lost in girlish thoughts. Her face, unique in subtle ways among all
I had ever seen, was in repose, her smile was childlike and pensive.
The evening light from a casement at one side ignited a still,
steady, unflickering, cool flame in the deep spate of pale-gold
hair, and that was only one of its gracings.

My temples throbbed and the scales fell from my eyes. No
longer could I perceive Miranda as a chattel to sell and forget.
She was a lovely maiden of great grace and quiet beauty, beauty
that pertained to both mind and body, beauty that could touch
the heart even as it enflamed the passions.

No more could I count these days with her as a pleasant wayside
adventure as I made for my main goal. Unless I was as steadfast
in my course as the eastern stars to guide me, I might never set
sail.

3

On the opposite shoulder from the one hidden in flaxen hair
there was a lovely highlight. Its delicate molding was thus revealed, and traced in shadow was the collarbone, such a beautiful
feature in young girls, leading to the unprotected hollow of her
throat. The profile of her head and body on the exposed side was
sharp against the scarlet tapestry behind it, and the long line,
sweeping inward at the waist, out and down the long, slender
thigh, and curving over the knee to the tapered ankle, might recall
the first beauty that Adam ever dreamed when he wakened from
his slumbers on the sixth-day afternoon, and Eve sat waiting for
him, her whiteness so empassioning and so perishable against the
riotous flowers. Until then he had been a clod.

Her eyes widened a little as I rose and slowly came toward her.

"You can see me better at a distance, master," she told me.

"That's for me to judge."

"If you're satisfied, I'll dress."

"I'm not nearly satisfied. Now you may stand, Miranda of England."

I said this last, it seemed, because of her whiteness, always associated in the Latin mind with the Angles and the Saxons. Its effect on her was as though I had touched her with a whip. She rose instantly, faced me squarely, and dropped her arms to her side.

"Come forward a little," I ordered.

"I beg you to remember——"

"I want you to stand in better light."

Now she stood in the full flood, yet she was not as exposed as a moment before, because the expression on her face served as a veil. Rather it was an absence of expression, a complete stillness, as though she were no longer a person, only a carnal form. It seemed as though she had drawn miles away.

I could not accept the defeat and came close to her. I touched her chin and drew my hand down the side of her throat and along her shoulder.

"It seems smooth enough to satisfy most buyers," I said.

"You're taking advantage of me, master," she said, her low voice lending great dignity to the words. "It's unknightly."

"I'm not a knight. I'm a merchant. I hope to be a great traveler." But saying this last weakened me for holding to my rights. It was as though I had spoken to an equal, not my slave, and it became harder to treat her as a slave. Perhaps I had invoked the best side of me.

"I too would like to be a great traveler," she said quietly.

"Some of the merchants take their concubines with them on their long journeys. I hope such a one will buy you."

"Hear me, my lord. I make you three prayers, and if one of them is answered I'll bless you by Saint George, no small prince in Heaven. One of them is to keep me for your own. If that's your wish, I stand here waiting your pleasure. One is to sell me to a buyer who'll prize my virginity and let me aspire to such honor and happiness as a concubine may win. The last is to do with me as you will, then sell me not for a concubine, but for a dairymaid, as you yourself said, or a vineyard or field worker. Some honest farmer may buy me and I may live in the sun."

"That last is fool's talk. What would you be worth on a farm? You would break like glass——"

"In that you're wrong. I am of slight build but I am not a weakling. There was no maiden in—no matter where—who could ride as long and as well. In one month I could earn my bread and in three I would match my day's work against any wench of the homestead."

The eagerness of her voice and face told me that she spoke truth—she would choose the rough, active life, in which slaves were the most free, over the bird-cage luxuries of concubinage in some Christian palace or Infidel harem. Before that, and for as long as I desired, I could have her for my own. As I stood in reverie, the warm glowings throughout my body leaped to flame. The sight of her grave, full lips caused mine to draw with an almost painful rigor; there was dull pain across my brows; my hands tingled and throbbed.

I had experienced only the sudden lusts of young manhood and their rude satisfyings. They had been like hunger for meat many times magnified. I had never realized the exquisite torment of desire, the word itself meaning an unearthly thing, something visited upon us from a star. I had not known that she was in the world.

She stood waiting, breathing slowly and deeply. Her eyes looked almost black between their long, dense lashes. She was white except for a flush on her cheekbones, and sweat beaded her white brow. Unconsciously her hands had opened, not inviting the clasp of mine, but ready for them, equal to them. There was a half-smile on her lips like some ancient enigma.

"I can't keep you for my own," I told her in a tone of voice heard in the market. "I must raise money for a long journey. Neither can I have you for a time and then sell you for what you'll bring. It wouldn't be enough for my needs. Instead I must dispose of you at once, before you are damaged, to some rich man who wants you for his concubine, and will pay well. Now you may put on your shift."

I was watching her closely as she did so, but saw no admission of defeat.

"I'm already damaged, master," she said quickly.

"I don't believe you. You swore before your saints that you're a virgin."

"What is an oath to a slave?"

"By that test, you're not a slave?"

"Remember what is written between the columns on the Rialto: *Let the trade be fair*. Didn't you demand, in the Jew's house, that I be free from mark or canker? A pearl without flaw?"

"Yes."

"What if now you find that's not true? Will you take me back there and ask for a pearl out of the sea? Or will you keep me for your own, as a lapidary might keep for his own wearing a jewel that he knows is flawed, and yet of great luster?"

"I don't know until I see the fault."

She returned to her seat, crossed her legs at the knee, and held up her right foot so that I could see its bottom. Full on the sole there was a dreadful mark. It was in the shape of a crescent, at least two inches in span, blood-red, and deep in the flesh. It had been burned there with a red-hot iron.

"No one will see it," I said quickly.

"Likely not while I'm being offered for sale, and perhaps not the first time my lord takes me to his couch. But sooner or later, when he plays with me, or wakes me with tickling, won't he discover the flaw? What bold paramour has not kissed the little feet he loves?"

"He'll discover it, surely."

"And see, it's no common scar, but truly a brand. No Saracen trader would put it on me to mar my value—plainly it marks me as some jealous Saracen's handmaiden. Won't the haughty Christian lord who buys me curse you for a swindling knave?"

"What will I care? I'll be far away."

"The brand is a terrible one," she went on after a little thought, "but it doesn't lame me in the least."

"I can see that."

"You've heard me sing and play a lute, but you haven't seen me dance while others play."

"You'd dance beautifully, I know."

"Better yet, I can walk as well and as far as a gypsy woman. Being light of weight in proportion to my strength, I could keep pace with the other marchers in a caravan. No place on a camel need be kept for me except when we must race, thus leaving more room for goods."

"I'm glad to hear it. Many a merchant likes to take his favorite concubine when he sets forth on a long journey."

"Master, if you'll keep me, I'll take you on a more wonderful journey than to the Court of Kublai Khan."

"That's the talk of a liar, a fool, or a witch."

"I'm no one of the three. If you don't keep me, you'll never know what I am. We'll travel far together. You'll come to great riches and honors—I swear it by Saint George. In due course we'll come to the destination you desire. And this first setting forth, now, before darkness falls, will requite you for the gold you've lost."

"You speak too knowingly for an innocent maiden, and you speak too well."

"I'm pleading for my very soul. My body can live on in the place you plan for me, but I fear my soul will die. As for my speaking out of my heart, remember, I'm not a frivolous Venetian girl, kissed by the sun. I came from a cool, windy island in the North Sea, its beauty all the greater for its half-veiling in mist, and its sons and daughters are of the same stuff as Richard the Lion-Hearted."

"Still I'll sell you to the firstcomer for a thousand pieces of gold."

"The firstcomer might not buy me!"

"I'll sell you within the fortnight to the Prince of Darkness rather than miss the journey to Cathay. Now dress, covering yourself well, even your slim little arms, so I may not think of them so much as around my neck. And since you're strong by your own boast, you'll need no help in moving your bed to the anteroom."

"So I'm not to sleep in your chamber?"

"I can resist temptation, but why put myself to the trial? There will be trials enough on the caravan road to Cathay."

4

I shared my supper of cold fish and barley cakes with my new slave. Also she drank a fair half of a flask of good, cheap red Apulia wine; and since wine was a rarity in England all except with the rich and was forbidden in Islam, I expected it to affect her strongly. All it did was paint her cheeks a little, and light her eyes.

"Why should I succumb to Italian wine?" she demanded when I called attention to her fortitude. "I was raised on stout English ale!"

I worked late and slept hard. Morning brought a short, stout, sallow-skinned fellow with jackdaw eyes and a greasy skin whom I took for a ship's cook until he stated his business. He wished to know whether I meant to keep or to sell a certain property that I had procured yesterday at the house of a rich Jew.

"I mean to sell her. Do you know who might like to buy her?"

"Not I, but my master might, if the price is in reason. He's had an eye out for her for a good while, as he'd tell you himself. But if you'll excuse me, young gentleman, are you sure your title's good? It's not a common thing for a man of your years to have a slave girl worth five hundred pieces of gold."

"This girl is worth a thousand. I have a rich father, as you no doubt know, and this is my first venture. Simon ben Reuben will vouch for my title. Who is your master, if you care to tell me? Is it Franco Adriani?"

"How did you guess it?"

"I've heard he had a taste for novelty, and he was the first lord I meant to approach."

Franco Adriani's name was known wherever beautiful girls were sold into slavery. Born of a rich, ancient, noble house, he had only this one passion and pursuit. The Circassian beauties vied with one another to take his eye. He kept what amounted to a harem, and if no favorite reigned for very long, he was generous with the whole flock, and his castoffs often became the wives of his henchmen.

I need not bring Miranda to his palace for his inspection; he would come here. This was in accord with his practice, to attract as little attention as possible to his purchases. By the same token he avoided lowering either the pride or the price of the many aspirants who failed. When the hour drew near for his arrival, I ordered Miranda to bathe, perfume, and array herself to the best advantage. I was more curt with her than her forlorn look deserved, why I did not know.

Franco's famed gondola, decorated with silver mermaids sporting in a green sea, stopped at our landing. Our prestige with our neighbors immediately rose. In deep distress, Mustapha retired to his cell and bolted the door. Small, with prematurely gray hair and a fine, high nose, our visitor had many a mark of the patrician, none of the satyr. I had heard demimondaines call him beautiful, and truly they did not miss it far. The molding of his face was delicate, his skin had a girlish freshness, his eyes were unusually large and clear, and only his mouth affected me adversely, being babylike.

First he paid due honor to my name and to this house. He was a great admirer of Nicolo Polo, the great traveler; he was gratified that his native city had become the haven of the famed Arabian scholar, Mustapha Sheik! Now might he have the pleasure of beholding my slave girl, Miranda?

When I rang the bell, the girl entered and stood with lowered head. I could see no rebelliousness in her face, although she appeared pale and her eyes were quiet under the pale-gold arches of her brows.

"Face me, Miranda," my lord ordered.

Miranda looked him calmly in the eyes.

"An odd type, truly, yet engaging," he said to me. "Where did she come from?"

"That, your Honor, is a trade secret. Too many like her in the market might mar her uniqueness and hence her value."

"Then I'll wager she's from the north shore of the Aegean Sea. There are a good many pale blondes in ancient Thrace, although redheads are more common, and since she's not a Christian——" Franco Adriani paused politely.

"So she avers."

"Then I venture she belonged to the Cult of Dionysus, still obtaining there. Its members have shut themselves off from modern culture and their licentious religion and life have made for a singularly delicate beauty of face and form. I've no doubt that Nicolo Polo picked her up for a song on his homeward journey from the Far Levant, and this is your first venture in the trade. Now bid her take off her clothes."

I did so. She bowed her head as in obedience and started to leave the room, then her eyes met mine in an unmistakable signal to follow her. There was something in her face that frightened me into compliance.

When I had made a lame excuse to the nobleman, I found Miranda standing by the casement, very pale now, her head still high, and tears gleaming between her long flaxen lashes.

"Master, I beg you not to sell me to this lord," she said in tones of quiet desperation.

I shook my head.

"Give me this one reprieve," she went on. "I'll smile on every other buyer who comes here."

"No other buyer will pay the price I'm asking. I'm almost sure of that. Your delicate beauty wouldn't appeal to most rich men seeking concubines. He may not want you, but if he does, I refuse your plea."

"Do you know who owns the lazar house at Chioggia?"

"The City-State of Venice, I suppose. And what has that to do——"

"No, it's been obtained by patent by a rich kinsman of the Doge, one who buys jewels from Simon ben Reuben. Simon doesn't know it, but I do—I found it out from his gondolier, who saw me and asked me to run away with him. I wish now that I had. So I tell you this, in sadness, but by Saint Michael and Saint George, it's true. If you sell me to this nobleman, you'll not live long to enjoy your thousand pieces of gold."

"What do you mean to do?"

"I'll get word to him, unless I die first, that you're the one who delivered Haran-din. When will you visit the Court of Kublai Khan? Not before you've visited the headsman on the Piazzetta."

I had no choice but to believe her.

Now the door was closing between her and me. I was going into the presence of the nobleman with no idea what to offer him in the way of apology or excuse. I could think of none he could not see through—and his fury might go to terrifying lengths.

But he did not look up as the door closed, causing my head to cool. It came to me that if this were a weakness on his part—the attempt to hide his anxiety—it called attention to his strength.

Perhaps it was the strength of the Devil in him that made him go to these lengths to satisfy his lusts; perhaps the lusts themselves were in his brain more than in his slight, delicate body; in any case, he was a high nobleman of Venice.

"Your Honor, the slave girl Miranda has entreated me not to sell her to you, and I entreat your pardon for causing you a visit here in vain."

His only response for some long-drawn seconds was a slight rise of color.

"Is it your intention to keep her for yourself?" he asked presently.

"No, my lord. It is rather that she hopes for a different kind of life than she would have in your Honor's house."

"If the question is a proper one, what objection does she find to my ménage?"

"I think she considers it too tame. She is a member of some Germanic tribe and wants an active life."

"I can't exactly blame her for that. After all, if female slaves weren't human beings, I doubt if they would interest me in the ways they do. If there is blame, it seems to me to lie on you. You did, indeed, give me a fool's errand."

"Again I crave your pardon. I would have gone ahead with the sale except for her threat to bring about my death. I've reasons to believe she would try it, and would probably succeed."

He stood in thought a few seconds, then smothered what I felt sure was a false yawn.

"I won't ask you those reasons. I'll remark that my admiration for the maiden has increased greatly, and if she will consent to become my concubine, I'll pay you my top price of three thousand lire—a thousand gold bezants. As for your yielding to her in fear of your neck, it was at least human. And I am obliged to you for not offering me some asinine excuse."

I bowed low. He nodded his head in reply and departed. Deeply depressed rather than angry, I roamed about a few minutes, then went to find Miranda. She was lying on her bed, her eyes red and her face tear-stained. As she started to spring up I bade her lie still.

"I told my lord that if I sold you to him, you'd have me killed," I said. "So he's gone."

"I've shamed you in front of him?"

"It would seem so."

"Why don't you take a stick and beat me? By every law of slavehood, I deserve it."

"Because if I again saw your naked back, I'd lust for you."

"What of it? You would control it as you did before. And if beating me would rid you of your anger toward me, I'd gladly stand the pain. I can hardly bear for you to hate me, master."

"I don't believe I understand that."

"Whom do I have besides you? Simon and his son are gone— the old Arab is lost in his readings. My father and mother and my sisters and brother and the rest of my people are far away, where I will never lay eyes on them again. Only in dreams can I see their faces. I can't hear their voices save in dreams."

"I'm only your owner——"

"What else has a dog?"

I could not refrain from stepping close to her, bending down, and kissing her childish lips. Perhaps I did not try. It seemed that I was moved only by pity for her, but that was a cheat. Another passion had lain in wait for my first unguarded moment, and it blazed up like Greek fire. Her soft, warm, delicious mouth should have invoked a tenderness in me; instead I devoured it while my hands, rude as a Tatar's, ravished her body. Then her gaze arrested mine. It was not pleading and it was not afraid, but it was sorrowful and strange. For the space of only one caught breath it made me pause. She saw no remorse in my face, but shame was there, and it was as though she leaped to my help.

With one strong upsurge, almost unbelievable in so slight a form, she broke my grasp upon her and thrust me back. Then, turning on her side so I could not see her face, she cried like a broken-hearted child.

"I should have let you go on," she wailed. "I should have torn my own clothes to give you way. Then you'd have to keep me—and I would be saved."

CHAPTER 6

TEMPTATION OF BEAUTY

WHEN THE MORNING BROKE I DRESSED IN MY BEST ATTIRE AND called at the principal slave markets of the city. To the merchants, I advertised a virgin slave girl of great beauty, accomplished in music, dancing, and household arts, and priced at one thousand bezants. Although I was in no way bound to do so, myself having solved the easy puzzle, I did not reveal that she was an English girl, and gave out that she was a Germanic heathen from the great forest lands beyond the Oder River. My hearers were glad enough to let it go at that—too close inquiry into a slave's origins often disclosed connections with Christianity embarrassing to buyer and seller alike. Actually, her secrecy troubled me more than I could justify to myself, as though it were of ominous cause.

Most of the traders threw up their hands at my price. Didn't I know that this was their selling, not their buying, price for the most precious Circassians? So many blonde girls were being brought in from the mountains of Greater Armenia that the market was in danger of a glut! I would have thought this was mainly haggle if they had hastened to look at the property. As it was, no principal merchant and only half a dozen agents appeared in the course of the week.

During these inspections, Miranda's behavior seemed above reproach. She stood with bowed head, answering the buyer's questions in a low voice and with modest mien. It was their strange manner toward her that caused my anxiety. Every one took a cursory look at Miranda's face, appeared cold to it, then kept glancing back. They appeared puzzled and quite strongly affected by it, with the one odd consequence of putting on their best manners. But they did not ask her to disrobe nor did they show any real eagerness to buy her.

A fine-looking Moor, buying for the Bey of Tripoli, heard of

Miranda through some gossip, looked at her shyly, and offered six hundred bezants. I thought he could be persuaded to pay a good deal more, but for two reasons I did not now encourage him to do so. One of them was that I was no longer pressed for time. The rumor that a new Pope would be elected soon had caused the Polo brothers to delay their sailing at least an additional fortnight, by which time I hoped to see some competitive bidding. The other reason did no credit to a slave dealer with bounding ambition. If she were bought by a Moorish prince, she would certainly go into purdah—behind the harem curtain out of the world—and her least dream of freedom had better die to start with. The truth was that the English loved freedom with a passionate love.

There came to my mind a name Saul ben Simon had mentioned—Paulos Angelos. He had wanted to buy Miranda for a Thessalian duke, but she had balked. Inquiry revealed that he was a quiet-appearing Greek who supplied a few Saracens with fair-haired slaves, but whose main traffic was with the Christian noblemen and rich merchants in Eastern Europe. He was at present in Genoa, but I left word for him to call on me as soon as he returned.

About the twentieth night since Miranda's arrival was a summer night. Although the month was still April, the soft breeze was the fag end of a hot wind off the Libyan desert, tired now from its journey across the Ionian Sea. I wakened sweating, and a flood of pale silver drew me to the window. The moon in the fullness of her reign was huge, gold-tinted, rising with great splendor over Homer's wine-dark sea. The common run of stars dared not show themselves, but a few great lords of the host, of ancient right and glory, gleamed in their far-flung strongholds; and certain gods and goddesses who had lost their earth domains, such as fiery Mars, serene Venus, and august Jupiter, blazed their wandering way through the purple deeps.

How many mortal eyes looked up, wide with wonder, over this vast earth! On how many populous lands undreamed of in our geography did the stars look down!

Mustapha Sheik was a disciple of Ptolemy, the great Alexandrian of eleven hundred years before, who in turn had developed the theories of Eratosthenes, the ancient Greek who had proved, to Mustapha's satisfaction, that the world was a sphere twenty thousand miles in circumference.[7] Ptolemy's great book almost forgotten in Europe and banned by the Church, had been translated into Arabic about the time of Harun al-Rashid; known as the *Almagest*, it ranked with the sacred Koran in the old man's sight.

The way that ships went down and came up from the sea, and the shape of what must be the shadow of the world thrown sometimes on the moon, had convinced all thoughtful people that the world was spherical. Still, I was not able to grasp it—the idea of us humans walking about on the outside like a bee on a thrown ball even when the sphere was upside down addled my head. Although I had scoffed volubly at the vulgar view of the world's being a disk, in the center of which lay the continent islands, surrounded by the Ocean Sea, truly it seemed the more reasonable of the two. Even so, I had come to realize a fact still barely glimpsed by many learned doctors of Padua—that the habitable world was many times as wide as exploration had shown.

Nicolo and Maffeo Polo's journey had been up and down, around and about, yet they had dared estimate the crow-flight distance from Venice to Kublai Khan's Court at six thousand miles. Great God, that was close to ten times the straight shoot to very England! To contemplate such a journey almost unjointed my backbone with ice-cold thrills.

My wild hopes and fears were interrupted by soft sounds in the anteroom to Mustapha's chamber. Miranda had been wakened by the close warmth and was tiptoeing about, causing me to thrill with guilty excitement. Listening as sharply as a wolf and with wolfish wickedness, I perceived that she had gone to a narrow casement through which Mustapha often gazed to wonder and puzzle over that most constant of all the heavenly host, Polaris, the North Star.

Imagining her there, gazing toward England, redeemed me. My heart warmed, I made my stealthy way into the passage, where, by drawing a curtain, I had clear sight of her in the flooding moonlight. She was wearing a knee-length shift ghostly in the silver luminance. In all the windows of the moon's gazing there was no other shape so lovely and so wistful. Of all the beautiful textures on which the bright beams fell, the silks and satins of night-frolicking lords and ladies, the plumage of birds, and the deep soft fur of sables in the cold forest, none was as beautiful as her flaxen hair.

I called her name softly, so as not to frighten her. She turned and looked at me and I had a sense almost of enchantment.

"Would you like to be steering by those stars on the northward course?" I asked.

She shook her head. "I've come too far and seen too much ever to go back."

"Even in England can you find the North Star by the pointers in the Great Bear?"

"The Great Bear? Do you mean Charlemagne's Wagon? We children used to call it the Big Dipper. Long ago."

"It's a clear and wonderful night, Miranda. Would you like to go boating?"

She hesitated, a faint and dreamy smile curling her lips.

"I would like to," she answered at last, "and if it's my fate, I will."

"What do you mean by that?"

"I'll be like the Mussulmans from now on—the bravest of them. I'll fight for what I want, but whether I win or lose, I'll look my fate in the face."

I had her put on a cloak over her bare arms and unstockinged legs in case we were seen by ramblers. Then we crept away to a light gondola belonging to a rich neighbor and free to our use. I at the long oar, she seated queenly in the cabin, we slid across the silver sheen of the lagoon.

If we were looking for privacy, it was everywhere. The curfew had rung long since, the watch kept to the alleys and the canals, and the ships slept at their anchor ropes like tethered camels on the desert. When I dropped my iron in five fathoms, we could expect a mermaid to come alongside sooner than a mortal and all sight of our boat was lost in shimmering moonlight. I came and sat beside my English girl.

"It was a short journey," she remarked.

"That's because you didn't pull an oar."

"It may save you from going on a much longer journey."

"Is it your fate to say that?"

"I said it, so it must be. I wouldn't think that Fate would bother about little things, but perhaps she must. I said it to be fair with you. The moonlight—and the silence—and you and I away from everyone might make you forget what's best for you. Or what you think is best for you."

"What do you think?"

"It would be best for you to take me and keep me."

"How would I get to the Court of Kublai Khan?"

"We would get there somehow."

"We? I can't believe it. What's the next best thing?"

"To take me, keep me a while, and then sell me for a dairymaid as I told you."

"What's the advantage of that? I couldn't sell you for half what I need."

"Perhaps your greatest need is for me. I feel in my bones that's true. And if you sell me for a farm wench, you may be able to buy me back when you find out the truth. Maybe I'll have had a stable-boy lover, or even the householder, but they won't have hurt me any. If I disappear in a great house, you can never find me again. If you could, perhaps we would both be so ashamed——"

"I don't understand you, Miranda."

"Why should you, Marco?"

"Who ever heard of a slave calling her master by his Christian name?"

"You've made free with my lips and tongue. Mine can at least make free with your Christian name."

"Why shouldn't I understand you? Women are known to be of more shallow mind——"

She laughed loudly and heartily and had to wipe her eyes.

"Besides that," I went on, "I'm not sure you're not a downright liar."

"What lies have I told?"

"It was at least an evasion when you said your native island was somewhat larger than the Rialto."

I could see no advantage, and perhaps some disadvantage, in thus prompting her to talk about her home and childhood, yet I could not resist doing so.

"It wasn't as big an evasion as you think. My home was an island separated by a narrow strait from the English coast. It's not as cold as most of England. It almost never snows there. Many birds stay all winter. The water is quite warm."

"Are the people mostly fair—like you?"

"They were originally Jutes—a very blond people from what is now Denmark. But we're all English now, even the dark Cornish."

"In what kind of house did you live?"

"A small house—compared to my cousins' by the brook. It's a long way from here—and the years are long. The girl who lived there—the one you asked about—must have died and been buried at sea."

"I take you in her stead—my slave girl Miranda. And since I took a great risk in obtaining you, it may be I'll enjoy you as much as I can, short of marring your value."

Except for a slight lowering of her head, she made no answer.

"I bid you lie across my lap, your breast against mine."

The awkwardness of her arriving at the position, if it were not pretense, indicated that it was new to her. I remarked as much.

"It's quite new, my lord," she told me when she was settled.

"I would have thought the swains in England would have taught it to you."

"They were great hobbledehoys smelling of beef and mutton, not subtle Venetians. Sometimes they caught me, but a little wriggling set me free. Sometimes we played kiss-in-the-ring and sometimes I gave one of them a kiss under the mistletoe. But my grandam kept watch of me when we went into the woods amaying."

The trouble with me was, I could see her in those woods. She was thirteen or fourteen, her movements still a little childlike, her eyes busy with flowers, her hands quick to pick them, her basket already brimming. Before that, I could see her at grave play with a doll, or eating with her spoon, or in rosy sleep. She had a little bed, and a roof over her head against the rain. There were people around her, some of whom had loved her greatly, although there was one who loved gold more. It was one whom she trusted to protect her against all enemies. She did not know of his great passion or, more likely, some great need. Perhaps his dearest dream hung on the obtainance of five hundred pieces of gold.

Strange men came to the door. They looked at her and signs passed between them and her father. She was not afraid, only a little uneasy. Then there came a night that he took her with him out into the darkened harbor. They were making for a boat with lateen sails. . . .

I must stop these flights of fancy. I had the strange feeling that they were more dangerous to me than her perfumed body in my arms.

2

"There's something I should tell you, before we kiss," I said.

"Yes, lord." Miranda leaned back a little, as though to give my words her full attention.

"A famed slave dealer who's been out of the city is returning tomorrow. I think he'll want to look at you on the following day." She nodded her head slightly. "I think you've seen him at least once. He's a Greek by the name of Paulos Angelos."

"I did see him, and I was wondering when I'd see him again. I noticed that you marked his name when Saul mentioned it."

"Saul said you managed to prevent his buying you."

"I won't again. If I'm to become a rich man's plaything, I'd rather have him place me—that is the word used—than any other merchant. I think he takes more pains to satisfy his clients than any other. The more satisfied my owner is with me, the better I'll be treated."

"Under those conditions, perhaps we'd better not kiss at all."

"It's for you to say, my lord."

"You know nothing of love-making, do you?"

"Only what I've heard—and what you've already shown me."

"Do you think some slight knowledge might be an advantage to you, when you go on sale?"

"I don't read your riddle."

"Your great innocence, showing in your face, gives the impression of coldness. I think if you were once awakened to the ecstasies of love, that would not be true. There's no doubt that such a wakening changes the expression on a maiden's face. I'm sure the merchants would pay more for you—they have a sixth sense, you know—and you would be more responsive to young, virile buyers who come to look at you."

"It's a very good argument, Marco. But isn't the wish father to the thought?"

"It may be. If so, why shouldn't I act on the wish itself? I have a feeling you'll soon be gone. I would like to have something to remember you by—and what could be as sweet as a night of love? Since I'll be on guard against it, no harm will be done."

"It's in your charge, Marco my master."

The use of both addresses thrilled me. They seemed to mean that tonight I could be both her lover and her lord. But since the moon, the tide, the gentle ripples, and all the rhythms of the night were unhurried, I could afford to stay still awhile, just to look at her. I had never known joy of exactly this kind and degree.

Her beauty was such strange beauty to us brunet dwellers on the Mediterranean shores. I had seen young girls from the Piemonte with slight bodies, spare, lovely molding of flesh over delicate bones, and with almost these same tints of hair, eyes, and skin—still, they had not looked like Miranda. Not to cool my head so much as to prolong this introduction to the feast, I tried to measure her uniqueness and guess at the explanation.

Her general type was no doubt more common in England than

Temptation of Beauty 99

in the other Northern realms. Mustapha had told me that the blood of the English people had been richly mixed. The blond and dark strains of ancient Britain had been well stirred before the Romans came; later the golden Angles and Saxons and the red Jutes and Danes had been baked in the pie; and only two centuries ago came the Normans, who were none else than Northmen settled and interbred with the more ancient dwellers of Northern Gaul. But above and beyond all this was the reflection in her face and form of a unique self; and I dreamed that a strange fate had brought it to flower. It was a flower of different loveliness than any I had ever seen. Its seed had not fallen in the garden of its ancestral kind but had been blown upon rough ground. I thought of it as having the beauty of a lone star on a lonesome night.

Adoration of it caused me to remove her cloak and unlace the strings at her throat so that I could slip her shift down from her shoulders and expose her bosom. I made her help me pull off my shirt so that my chest was likewise bare. For a while I was entranced by the sight alone of her milk-white skin against mine more dark, the small steep hills barely touching my chest as I held her out a little for my wonder-struck viewing, the narrow shoulders almost straight from the slim base of her throat, their joining with her arms, and her small, luminous head with its beautiful face all revealed by the glimmering moon. If ever eyes were charmed, they were mine.

I drew her closer to me and held her in my arms. I could not compare my joy to the joy taken by a connoisseur in a wonderful jewel, because jewels were not warm. I had known my big chest as an abode of emotion—the place where the breath stopped at times, or was wildly drawn, and the heart fainted, swelled, ached, thumped—but not as a seat of sensation. Now her slightest movement against it thrilled it through and through. Her young breasts became taut and their slight yielding against hard bone and muscle gave me exquisite pleasure that only a clod would not perceive and love. Her nipples drew erect and firm as her breathing brushed them a little back and forth, and their slow, involuntary caressing of my chest became a sensation almost too exquisite to endure.

Her lips had parted a little in her happiness, and I bent and kissed them. She was quietly happy, it seemed; I was wildly so. But this difference between us became a cloud in my own high sky. It was of the thin but shadow-casting stuff that jealousy is made of; and there is no bliss so unstable as that of carnal love, which can change a man in one moment from his best to his most base.

"Did you take pleasure in my kiss?" I asked.

"Be still."

I could not heed her. I owned her body and mind. I was jealous because I did not own her soul.

"I bid you tell me."

Very slowly she drew back.

"Why not? Swains and maidens have taken pleasure in the like since time began, and older folk as well. Your lips are firm but not rough and you smell clean. What more can a slave girl ask?"

"Are you happy to be here, or do you wish to go back?"

"I'm happy to be here. Your caresses are sweet and I hope you'll give me more, for what have I to lose? If I were a free girl and you an English swain whom I favored, I wouldn't tell you so, at least in this free way. I'd say and do only enough to make you persist. So it would seem that slavery has freed my tongue at least—but it's not true. The truth is, I'm not free to be silent. I must answer my master's questions and tell the secrets that are a woman's right and strength."

"Tonight will you treat me as though you're free? Give what you like, withhold as much as you please?"

"It's impossible, and anyway you've no right to ask it. The people at home have a saying—a very old one—that fits the case. You can't have your cates and eat them too." Cates were sugared breads made in England.

"Do you mean that if I take your favors, you can't give them?"

"A slave has none to give. They are already forfeit."

Straightway I was delivered from an evil as though I had prayed, and my heart leaped in joy. I kissed her soft lips again with intense pleasure, but I did not ask her to reciprocate or to make any kind of an answer. Perhaps she took this for the kind of fairness that English people like, and wanted to reward it. At least the lingering tension went out of her body as it nestled against mine.

As I fed with deepening hunger at her warming mouth, she was being instructed by another master. Her lips rounded out with the surge of her own blood, and the changes in her glowing eyes revealed the ebb and flow of her maiden passion. And I, a liberal Venetian, would teach her the arts of love.

"I didn't know that wooers——" she began when she had held her breath a long time.

"Don't English swains woo their sweethearts in that way?" I asked.

"No, they are too bashful. And it's a good thing they don't, because a peasant youth might prevail over a daughter of the manor."

I had thought for a moment that she was jesting and this might change the scene. Truly she was not guilty even of a childish artifice. The magic grew apace. Soon I had lowered her shift until its top was around her waist, and the tapered slimness there caused it to hang loose in enthralling invitation.

"Wait, my lord," she said, holding my hand.

"If you like."

"Perhaps you can do all you desire, but I'll not be the same."

"I spoke of that, and allowed for it," I said.

"Will you be the same? I ask the question in my need."

"Do you mean that we may fall in love with each other?"

"If we did, what would happen?"

"I'd leave you your virginity—as it's counted in the market place —and sell you for a thousand pieces of gold."

She let go of my hand. "I suppose that's all I need to know."

"Didn't you know it before? I thought I'd told you. If not in those same words——"

"You did tell me, but tonight I'd begun to doubt it. I thought it would not be easy for you to let me go. You seemed so happy in making me happy."

"Since I've already given my heart, it must be the imitation of love. Still, I'll act as though it were real as long as the game lasts. Let your robe fall."

"Why not? I must do so for any buyer in the market. What may a slave expect but imitation love—imitation life?"

For the first time in my hearing her voice was slavelike, and so was the expression on her face. With downcast eyes and mechanical motions she slipped off the garment and hung it over the gunwale. To do this last she emerged from the partial shadow of the canopy into the moonlight.

Then a change came over her, arresting my attention. It was the effect of some swift revival of her spirit, but what had caused it I did not know. Perhaps the change was merely the sight of her body, pearllike in hue almost to the semblance of iridescence, slight, beautifully feminine, but intimating a kind of strength no man can attain or understand. She did not withdraw into the shadow: I thought she was too proud. Her head raised, her face lifted, her eyes seemed to be seeking some beacon in the sky. "I told you I'm a good walker," she said quietly. "I didn't tell you I'm a good swimmer, too. I wouldn't be here if I weren't." She turned to me, unashamed of either me or herself. "Follow me, Marco. Keep pace with me if you can. The imitation of love is only lust, and we'll drown it in the sea."

3

In Miranda's manifold aspects of beauty, there was none more telling than these glimpses of her whiteness in the dark, moonlit sea. At her strokes its sheen broke into myriad gleamings. She swam as serenely as a heron flies.

I could not remember when I could not swim. My mates had played in and out of the canals as children in dry-land cities play in and out of the streets. Stronger of limb, I could easily overtake her present gait, but I wondered if I could keep pace with her in a long jaunt. I was a splasher and a thruster, while she appeared to insinuate herself through the heavy water with mermaid ease. For the moment I did not accept her challenge and kept to her silver wake. Her rhythmic movements delighted my eyes.

Gaining slowly, I drew within ten feet of her. Then I became aware of a little something wrong, a flaw in the perfection of the adventure, which I had not yet identified. It was a common experience with me to feel a fall of spirits before discovering its cause. Suddenly my gaze riveted on Miranda's right foot. I saw clearly now what I had seen inattentively for several seconds—a black mark on the white sole. It was of crescent shape and in better light would be blood-red.

Stroking a little faster, I slowly gained until I came abreast of my companion. Thus she had ceased to be my slave in a single moment in this still dim world of moonlight and wide waters; and her half-glimpsed nakedness did not mean what it had meant before. I had thought to forget the dreadful mark, but instead it wrought upon me with greater force; it too had a different meaning for me, deeper and more portentous. It took the center of my mind. I began to perceive that it was the central fact of the present situation; because of it, this was not merely a moonlight adventure, but what I believed was a stroke of fate. The journey was not an aimless one—Miranda and I were bound for somewhere.

My mind and heart open to mystery, no longer afraid to confess it, I caught the signal of Fate in the shriek of a sea gull. It was not a common sound at this late hour and I searched for the bird in the dim sky, wondering at its trouble. I did not find it, but I found a shadow on the water some fifty fathoms distant. Emerging from reverie, I recognized it as an islet, not more than two acres in extent, known to shipping by the unromantic name of Sea Pig's Wallow. Sea pigs were of course porpoise; perhaps a dying porpoise had been stranded in a shoal here before the land rose. This could have happened a century ago; the silt from the rivers built slowly but surely, and the very Rialto was its handiwork. Sea Pig's Wallow was a mile or so off the ship lanes, and since it appeared to be only a reed bank common along these shores, it was as forsaken by human kind as a barren reef in mid-ocean. But if gulls were nesting there—which I now believed—it must have solid ground.

"Let's try to land," I said.

She did not reply at once, only swam toward the islet. When the water shoaled to waist-deep she found firm footing on the weedy bottom and turned and faced me.

"Is that a command?" she asked.

"No. You can take it as a request."

"We're already hidden from the world, and there we can't hide from each other."

"I don't want to any more."

"Then what will we find there, Marco?"

"Maybe I'll find truth. That's what I want—and need. Until I do, I can't set a course."

"The truth of—what?"

"Who you are. Why you are a slave. What the brand is that you wear."

"I told you those were my secrets——"

"I want to know them. I think it is for your good as well as mine."

"There are no buyers here—and I am naked."

"That will help me to find the truth. I can never find it by hiding from temptation. Are you afraid?"

"No. I once was brought onto a ship deck nearly naked. I was afraid then, and with full cause, and after that——"

She stopped because her throat filled, but she continued to look at me with tear-filled eyes.

"Do you want me to promise——?"

"No. I'll ask for nothing that's not my due as a slave. It was the agreement I made."

I led the way to a beach of well-packed silt; then there was knee-high grass as soft as meadow clover. Gulls rose in pale flocks, shrieking their protests at our invasion. Miranda followed me, glimmering in the moonlight.

"Sit down, Miranda," I instructed her.

She bowed her head and obeyed. I sat within a few feet of her. Almost at once the gulls began to settle. Their harsh complaints died away, and soft squeakings, as of many knives being whetted, made a continuous murmur all over the island.

"What island did you come from, Miranda?"

"Will you never tell anyone as long as I'm a slave? Otherwise I can't remember."

"I swear it by San Marco. I think I know the answer this far. The Isle of Wight."

"I didn't tell you, did I? I have such strange dreams——"

"What you said would give a clue to anyone who had studied geography. The people there were Jutes originally, it is warmer than most of England, snow is almost unknown, and birds stay all year. But the strait isn't very narrow; in fact it's broad enough for Wight to be a real island instead of part of the mainland cut off by a salt creek. Since you don't look like a daughter of any Englishman I've seen, that helped me guess."

"It's the most beautiful island in the world, I truly believe. You should see the sea cliffs and the Four Needles—they are limestone towers—with the gales buffeting them."

The moon showed me a slight change in her face. I thought that her eyes were glowing and her smile was wistful. Anyway, she was more beautiful than before—but that was always true.

"Why did you leave there, Miranda?"

"It would be very hard to tell you, Marco."

"I want you to try. The guess I made may not be right."

"Your other guess was right. Perhaps this one is."

"I hope it isn't. I thought that your father—perhaps your step-father or someone not so close to you—had sold you into slavery."

"Then why should I keep secret my name and abode and all the rest?"

"Because you were ashamed."

"You guessed wrong, master."

"Will you tell me the truth of it? The whole truth?"

"I'll try. No one in Christendom knows it, and until now no Christian has cared. I didn't tell Simon or Saul because they would have wanted to act on it through the English Jews. They would have used persuasions hard for me to resist. I want to tell you, although it's harder than you can believe, partly because I shut it away from myself—buried it in a grave. It's quite true that when I was reminded of it, it seemed to have happened to someone else, not to me. But tonight something more has happened. I don't fully know what it is—partly it was being in your arms in the boat— and now this, our coming out of the water onto this little island, with no thought of being ashamed. I think that the imitation of love has been drowned in the sea."

"I think real love has taken its place," I answered.

"It will die too soon to be real. But for this hour it's taken us out of the world and somehow away from evil. Yes, I can tell you, and I thank my saints, and forgive me if I cry."

"Begin at the beginning."

"My name is Marian Redvers. My father is Sir Hugh Redvers, and his grandfather was the younger son of Richard de Redvers, to whom the first Henry gave the island and great Castlebrook. Isabella de Fortibus, who holds it now, is my cousin and god-mother. But the manor that my father held in fief was not large, and when he bore arms against the King under Simon de Mont-fort's banner it was revoked by royal command. Since he was attainted for fighting on after Evesham, the lands were not re-turned in the Baron's Peace, and he had only enough gold to clothe his back and obtain for my brother Godfrey an esquireship to the Earl of Devon. So I had no dower, and I loved my father and my brother beyond all counting."

That was simple enough, I was thinking; there was nothing amazing about it. Not very rich knights were continually losing their all in their liege lords' quarrels; little maids commonly gave immeasurable love to their fathers and brothers. But my heart raced and I was breathless with suspense.

"My mother's sister was married to a French merchant of Bayonne," Miranda went on. "She invited me to come and live with her, promising I would make a good marriage. The ship was attacked by Saracen pirates in the Bay of Biscay, and was rammed and sunk. A few sailors were picked up, but no other passengers. I was saved because I could swim well and had thrown off almost all my clothes. I was taken to Malaga and sold to an Arab who owed money to Haran-din. And if you're satisfied, we'll swim back to the boat."

"Don't lose heart, Miranda, or faith."

"You can sell me and forget me more easily——"

"That's my part. Your part is to speak on."

"When the pirates brought me aboard their boat, they looked at me and thought I was too skinny to bring very much in the slave market—they themselves liked plump girls. But one of their number believed I was of high birth, so they decided to hold me for ransom."

She stopped and her throat worked. I saw it in the moonlight.

"Go on, Miranda," I said.

"You can guess it now."

"I want you to tell me. I guessed so wrong before."

"There's very little more. They asked me my father's name and abode, and I wouldn't tell them."

"Why not?" But I knew too well. I only wanted to hear her way of telling me.

"My father was descended from Richard de Redvers, lord of the Isle of Wight, who had fought bravely for Henry I and won his love and favor. My brother was the last of the true de Redvers blood and should have been lord of Castlebrook and Wight—and he will be someday. And both were worthy of my love. Both would have beggared themselves to save my virginity from the Infidel."

"Now that's plain enough," I said, looking at Miranda while she looked away across the glimmering waters. "But the Saracens wouldn't take kindly to your closed lips."

"No, they didn't."

"So they tried to open them with iron."

"Not in my mouth. This iron would have burned it. If they couldn't get ransom, they must get what they could for me in the slave market. They tried where the burn wouldn't show when I stood on the block."

"You were all alone on their ship?"

"The English sailors were in irons below the deck. They kept shouting 'Saint George! Saint George!' to encourage me. The whipper couldn't stop them."

"None of the sailors knew your name or where you came from?"

"Not one. I was so glad. I think the least of them would have died rather than tell if I'd asked it. The English are hard and cruel but they can hold a course."

"Why did the Saracens stop?" I knew this, too.

"They believed that they would only disfigure me for nothing."

"Were they right or wrong?"

"I can't tell. My prayers were answered and I was spared. It's been more than a year now. My father and brother have said Mass for my soul and never doubt that I was lost at sea."

"How do you know?"

"I have dreamed it many a night and it came to me truly just tonight, when I heard the swans flying north. That was what wakened me and brought me to the window. They were going to England."

Although I had been awake and at the window, I had not heard the swans. Perhaps Miranda had heard their wild, strange singing only in her dreams. That would not impugn its being a sign.

"You didn't mention your mother."

"I lost her, as you did yours, when I was little. She'll weep in Heaven at my becoming a slave, but she'll know——"

Miranda turned her face from me, but not in time to hide the tears flooding her eyes. As I came to her to kiss them away, she sprang up and ran down to the beach and into the still water. There came back to me her voice, low-pitched, lovely, and strange in the whist of the night.

"Forgive me for crying. This was a bridal night—and it's over."

CHAPTER 7

THE PARCHMENT

SOON AFTER SUNRISE I ROSE, PUT ON MY OLDEST CLOTHES, AND went to a gardener's market not far from the house of my uncle Zane. It had been Rosa's custom to visit it twice weekly as long as I could remember, always at the same hour, and I doubted greatly that she would fail the rendezvous today.

Presently I saw her, a basket on her arm. She was wearing the habit of a tirewoman that my mother had given her instead of the coarse smock of a charwench, her present office; although it was almost as faded and worn as her own face, it was still her pride when she ventured abroad. I caught her eye and led her to a near-by bridge. She sat down on the edge, shelling a mess of dry beans. I lounged beside her, as might a nephew who had come up in the world of late, although not very far.

"I didn't expect to see you again, young master," said she.

"I'm not your young master any more, Aunt Rosa."

"You were once, so you'll always be. I hold with things as they were long past, not as they are now."

"Why didn't you expect to see me? Not here, I grant, but in my uncle's house?"

"Your cousin Leo, he heard how you've tried to borrow from the Jews, and how you failed. He told Signor Nicolo of it, and foretold you'd be gone from the city on the day that Nicolo and his brother Maffeo set sail."

"What would cause me to be gone?"

"Don't you know? It was plain enough to Leo and his sire, for they're a knowing pair. How could you stay for shame? Where was the thousand pieces of gold you said you'd have, to pay your fare? But you'd come back, they said, when folk forgot, and say nothing more of it."

"What did my aunt Flora say to that?"

"She reckoned it was true, but still she was amazed that you'd sent the fifty gold pieces to settle your debt."

"Did you hear this with your own ears, or was it repeated to you?"

"I heard with my own ears, when Signor Nicolo and Maffeo came with their trains to break Lenten fast on Easter Eve."

"What comments did Nicolo make? But I dare say you've forgotten——" I spoke in an easy voice.

"Forget, would I? Aye, I will, when Antonello's ghost forgets the merrymaker who lent him a purse. Nicolo said nothing, pro or con, as to your being ashamed. But he asked a dozen questions as to the money worth of the old Arab, your master. Was Signor Zane certain of what he'd told him before? Did the hundred bezants he'd lent you exhaust his credit with the moneylenders, and all he had left was his allowance from the Emir of Medina? Signor Zane swore to it by half a score of saints and the bones of God. He thumped the table till his wine spilled and I feared the glass would break. Then Signor Nicolo bade him calm himself—after all, it was no great matter, he was merely curious as to the prospects of the fine young man known as his son. And there was no scoffing in his eyes, only a white light."

"It was strange he would talk so boldly in your hearing."

"What did he care for churchyard meat like me? My head had been addled since my lady died—the serving wench Amelia had heard Signor Zane tell him so over their wine cups on the day of Nicolo's return. Aye, on that very day Signor Nicolo asked about his lady's tirewoman Rosa, whom he'd not forgot in all those years! Shouldn't I be proud?"

Her gaunt thumb pressed against a dry bean pod. It popped like a burning cane and the beans shot six fathoms across the water.

"Surpassing proud," I said.

"Yet it proved not half my glory! In his last visit, the one I spoke of just now, he sought me out!"

"You mean he summoned you into his presence."

"Nay, I do not—may my tongue wither if I lie. When he saw me scouring the threshold stone he came and spoke to me. Was I not old Rosa? How did I fare? He would buy me an unguent for my lame bones. And how long since I'd visited the grave of my dear mistress?"

"What then?"

"I answered him as well as he could expect of one whose head is addled, and wondrous patient he was with me, I'll be bound. He spoke of this and that, for me to remember, and then he questioned me about my lady's last sickness. Did she leave any letters for him? But no doubt she left one for her son Marco? Perhaps she gave the lad something to keep until he was grown up. It might be a parcel of some sort, or a bottle, and it may be that she had got it from her uncle, Friar Johannes de Carpini."

A dull ache spread across my forehead.

"What else did he say?" I asked. "Try to remember every word."

"He asked if she said anything about a salamander."

"What was the sense of that? A salamander's a reptile that's supposed to be able to live in fire, but Mustapha denies it."

"Could old Rosa—but I was young then—have stolen the parcel and kept it all these years? If so, I had better tell him and save a whipping. For my mistress had something hidden, and I knew it. I had best pull my wits together to remember. Then when my head shook as though with palsy, and I looked upon him with empty eyes, he struck me hard in the side with his scabbard."

"Why, that's a trifle!"

"Nay, it was not, because of what he cried. 'Why don't you weep at that, you maggot-headed hag?' For my eyes were dry as bones. 'Why, you didn't hurt me a whit,' I told him, as near as I could the way my lady said it. Then his eyes went dark as though he gazed into Hell. 'Don't repeat a word of what I've told you,' he said to me when the spell passed off, 'or I'll have you shut up in a madhouse where you'll learn what whipping means.' And with that he went his way."

His way was toward the Court of Kublai Khan. He would be setting sail in a week, perhaps, certainly within the month. Rosa's way was down to death, and she would take it soon. One could scarcely imagine a less important event in the sight of the world. A poisoned pigeon falling dead in the Rialto would cause more comment. That would be the end of my mother, too. An under-kingship in Cathay would be balm to Nicolo's feelings and he would forget her dry eyes and strange smile. He would have several queens, a drove of concubines, and a galaxy of handmaid-ens. He would no longer remember Lucia's relief when he tupped trulls or won fine ladies' favors.

What of it? No one lived forever. . . .

"I have two questions to ask you, then I'll go," I said.

"Aye, Master Marco."

"In what room of the Casa Polo did my mother die? It seems to me it was up the stairs—along a corridor to the right—through an archway——"

"Why, what's happened to my wits? Now I think of it, Signor Nicolo asked me the same question!"

"Did you tell him?"

"I couldn't recall, just then, but I've been thinking on it since, and 'twas the room next to the balcony, o'erhanging the water keep."

"He'll search them all. And now try to remember this. A year before Nicolo returned, Dame Muccini, who lived across the canal, lost a gold cross once worn by Saint Agnes, with an amethyst in the center. Her tirewoman Carlotta told you of it, and of its find-ing."

"That she did!"

"It seems you told me she consulted a witch——"

"Aye, the Black Woman of Martyrs' Walk. She told the lady to look behind a mirror in her chamber, and there she found the relic hanging on a nail, where she herself had hidden it when afeared of robbers. I didn't know witchcraft would work on a holy emblem, but it seems it did."

I took leave of the beldame, quite sure I would see her again, then made for Martyrs' Walk. Dame Muccini had gone to her saints and quite likely the witch to the Devil; if I did find her, I would throw away a lira on a fool's errand. The neighborhood proved to be a poor one, inhabited mainly by leather workers.

And when a Negress came to the door of the house pointed out to me, I could hardly bring myself to state my errand.

She was not black but a deep, rich brown, and I had never seen a woman past forty who looked less like a witch. Nearly six feet tall, burly but not fat, each breast big enough to nourish triplets and her arms strong enough to defend them from an ogre, she appeared to be a combination of motherliness and happy childishness. Her eyes were round and a little popped. Her mouth was big and could not help smiling.

"Are you known as the Black Woman of Martyrs' Walk?"

"Why yes, some call me that!" she replied eagerly.

"I hear that you're a fortuneteller."

"Whoever told you that, young gentleman, missed it a mile! I never told a fortune in my whole life."

"Aren't you a seeress of some kind?"

"That I'm not! If you'd ask me whom you'll wed, I'd have no more notion than a bedpost. But sometimes I can help folk with their troubles. Maybe it's to find something they've lost, or to make up a quarrel with a friend or a sweetheart, or to get over a hate, or a sorrow, or a shame."

"Then who's your master? It couldn't be the Devil——"

The woman laughed like a peal of gongs.

"I should say he's not! I don't have ought to do with him. But they say I can cast out a devil, sometimes, if he's not bored in too deep. A maid who mewed all the while like a cat, and another who shamed herself before folk, and a youth who dressed himself in women's clothes—all these stopped their strange ways, and became like other folk, when I'd ministered unto them."

"Is it a laying on of hands?"

"In a way of speaking."

"In whose name?"

"In no one's name, your Honor. I'd be afeared to claim to speak or act in some holy name. What I say is just what a mother would tell her child when she finds out his trouble."

"Where did you learn your art, if that's what you call it?" Since she was so cheery and forthright I did not miss the chance to question her.

"My master bought me for a concubine when I was fourteen. He was a doctor in a great school in Alexandria. He said that madness was not caused either by devils or the moon, but by the evil of a body's soul fighting the good. This he'd learned from a pale-brown bearded man dressed in white, with a red mark on his forehead. I've forgotten his name—could it be Swami?—but he came from beyond the deserts under the rising sun. And it was he who taught my master to turn grown-up folk into children."

"God forbid!" And the sweat came out on me in cold beads.

"It was only for a few minutes and did no harm. The brown man said that many in his own country had that power, and while some were wise doctors, some were tricksters and mountebanks.[8] Because my master had me hold the mirror or the ink bowl that he used—he told me I made the sick people feel at ease—I watched him do it a hundred times. When he grew old and feeble, I did it in his place—not nearly so well, but well enough to help folk with troubles that a black woman could understand. I earned enough silver to buy his bread and wine. When he died, he left a paper setting me free. I became the woman of a Maltese sponge fisher and followed him to Venice. Now he too is dead."

"How did your master use the mirror or the ink bowl—or are you forbidden to tell?"

"The sick one looked into it at my master's bidding. That was all. A candle flame does just as well. If I knew the whys and wherefores, I would tell you, but I don't. Now tell me your trouble. If I think I can help you, I'll say so—otherwise I'll not try. If I do try, you'll tell me if I've succeeded. If I have, give me your blessing and a silver coin. If I haven't, give me your blessing only. You can be sure I'll not harm you."

There were few things in this world that I was as sure of.

"My trouble is to remember something from long ago."

"Why do you squint your eyes when you say that?"

"Because even to speak of it causes a pain across my eyebrows." Then I went on with blunt words, a way of talking that might be compared to a way of walking when a resolute man goes to a hard, unwelcome task. "I was about four years old. My mother was sick unto death. She had me bring two candles to her bedside. She brought forth from some hiding place what I thought was a parchment, and I think it was pale brown from age. She had me do something more with the candles, but I can't think——"

I had to stop and catch my breath, lest my brow split apart from pain.

"There, there," the woman said, stroking my forehead with her big, pink-palmed hand. "No haste, young master. Tell Cleo what the trouble is, and she'll try to help you."

"Cleo?" And the pain mysteriously dimmed.

" 'Twas my master's name for me, short for a great Egyptian queen whose name I forget. 'Twas in the way of a joke."

"She brought the parchment to the flame," I said. "I thought she meant to burn it up. I guess it was moldy from age—it didn't catch fire or even smoke. Then she put it where she'd got it. Then . . . then . . . *she touched her finger to her lips*——"

This last I got out in a desperate burst, and I would not have wondered if blood had spurted from my ears.

"She wanted you to have the parchment, didn't she?" the woman said, a wonderful tenderness in her face.

"Of course."

"You think it was her will, or a deed to riches?"

"No."

"You never found it, and you want to know where it is?"

"Yes."

"Answer one question, to let me see if maybe I can help you. I'll keep my hand on your forehead to save you part of the pain."

"Ask it," I said with dread.

"Did you see where your mother hid it, and forget, or did you never know?"

I tried to remember. The dull ache over my eyebrows tried to grow to bone-cracking agony, but the strong hand held it back. Then it ran to the back of my head, like an imp of Hell. My brain was cracking like a dropped melon. . . .

"*Yes!*" I shouted. "*I saw her!*"

"That's all, young master," I heard Cleo's soft voice, now speaking in a minor key, and with a kind of lovely sadness that most tender women sometimes employ to children sick or in pain. "It won't hurt any more. And maybe Cleo can tell you where the parchment is."

She had me lie down on a worn and shabby couch. Then she got a candle and started to light it with flint and tinder.

"Must you use a candle, Cleo?" I asked.

"Why, no——"

"I wish you'd not, if there's any other way. I keep seeing those two candles."

"I should have known it!" She paused and glanced around the room. "Do you see the little hole in the curtain that gleams like a star?"

The hole in the black cloth was no bigger than a pinhead, but the noonday light beyond made it diamond-bright.

"Like the North Star," I answered without thinking. The North Star is not nearly as bright as dazzling Sirius.

"Just look at it steadily, my son. Does it tire your eyes a little? But I'll stroke your temples and you won't get a headache. . . . There. . . . I think you may want to go to sleep. . . . Do you feel a little sleepy, young master? I believe you do. I believe your eyelids are drooping and you can hardly keep them open. . . . All is all right. . . . You may sleep if you like. . . . Yes, go to sleep. . . . Sleep, my son. . . . Sleep . . . sleep. . . ."

My thoughts began to straggle and I felt myself falling into warm, pleasant, peaceful sleep. A strong, warm hand continued to stroke my head and neck, and I felt safe under it, and free of all trouble and pain. . . . A voice on which I set great store, one that would never guide me wrongly, sounded in my drowsy ears. . . . Time ran on.

"Young master!"

It was a cheerful voice now, and quite strong. My brain caught at pleasant wakings long and long ago, but the memory failed before I could seize it. I wakened to find Cleo looking into my face, a smile on hers. Instantly I knew where I was and on what business I had come. . . . Yet I wished I could have slept on. . . .

"Did you have a pleasant nap, your Honor?" the woman asked.

"Most pleasant, thank you."

With that polite response, I became more sharply alert. Cleo was smiling, but her face was beaded with sweat and her eyes were big and troubled. She made her voice sound cheerful by a none too easy effort.

"I take it you weren't able to help me," I said. I meant less than that, and more.

"I found out what you wanted to know," she answered, the forced cheer gone from her voice. Her eyes were cast down.

"Tell me, please."

"Your mother had you get the two candles and put them side by side, only a palm apart. She took the parchment out of an iron pipe just outside her window that draws rainwater from the roof and flushes it into the reservoir below. It was rolled into a cylinder. She unrolled it and held it between the two candle flames. The flames licked it but didn't burn it. She whispered something you couldn't hear, but her gesture told you that the parchment was for you and you must not tell anyone. Then she rolled it again and put it back in the pipe."

I heard her and thought upon her words without a trace of pain.

"It must have flushed out years ago. . . . No, the end of the pipe turns a little—if the cylinder kept its shape, water could pour through it . . . but it would surely rot away."

"If it was of common parchment, yes."

"By what wonder of wonders did you find out all this?"

"It was no great wonder. You remembered and told me."

"Talking in my sleep?"

"You were between sleep and waking."

"And you gave me no drug?"

"No, and you would have told me more than that, if I'd asked you."

"I'll go and look for the parchment. I don't expect to find it, but it won't trouble me any more. Here's a lira grossa."

"I can't take it, young master!" To my amazement her eyes filled with tears.

"Why not?"

"I want you to give it to some beggar on the street, and tell him to say a prayer for the Black Woman of Martyrs' Walk."

"You've earned it. Why won't you take it?"

"I may have helped you, but I'm afraid I've hurt you, and maybe I've killed you. It may be I've led you a step down toward Hell. Good fights with Evil in every soul, my master told me, but in your soul the battle is most dire."

"How do you know? Tell me, if you will and if you can."

"I heard wings of angels and whipping pinions of fiends."

I considered how to go about looking in the water pipe by my mother's death room. The insistence of my reason that it would be a fool's errand must not and would not reduce the energy of my effort or the risk I was willing to run. I could not go nor could I stay until I knew.

This was the best chamber in the Casa Polo, so nine chances out of ten it was occupied by Nicolo. If he thought it was haunted by my mother's ghost, he would be more likely rather than less likely to choose it. Surely he would want her to see the beautiful young girls who shared his bed, for if once she would have joyfully yielded them her place, thirteen years in a cold and rainwashed cell would teach her to envy them. He would leave a watch light burning when he entertained them, so her ghostly eyes could behold their frolickings, and he would fancy her in the doorway, her phantom ears hearkening to their cries of passion and whisperings of love. . . . I had better stick to my business. If Nicolo did not occupy the chamber, his brother Maffeo did so. And to climb the steep wall by rope or ladder and gain the balcony without waking him was out of the question.

If I could catch the brothers away from home, it would be difficult to guard against their unexpected return. Meanwhile I could very easily trip over one of Nicolo's sons or a house wench. Obviously, the best time for the raid was when the family was assembled at meat, with a good share of the servants in attendance. If I provided some sight of interest, they would watch through the glass, and chambermaids would hang out the upper windows. Serenaders would cost only a silver lira. For two lire there could be duetists accompanied by a string quartet.

Then a thought came creeping out of my brain like a little gray, venomous snake and caused my eyes to sink into my head. For three lire I could provide a troop of jongleurs.

Would Nicolo go where he could not see and watch them? Not he, not Nicolo, not that lordly man who meant to be a king in Cathay!

It did not take me long to learn that three companies were at present in Venice, one of them down-at-heels. This last I followed and watched—a better lot than I had supposed. Their songs and tricks were a little too witty, not quite coarse enough, to please the street crowds. Their master was a juggling clown. He had a sallow nondescript face except for a nose like a Spanish duke's. I marked the inn where he and his troop put up, and when he washed off his paint, I met him in the courtyard.

"What is your name, friend?" I began.

"Gregorini is good enough for the time and place."

"Did you ever hear of Antonello, a jongleur from Perugia, who tossed his last ball eighteen years ago?"

"He said he was from Rome," the clown answered. "It sounded better."

"Then you did know him." The back of my neck prickled.

"All of us know one another, well, not well, or scarcely, depending on one another's prosperity. Even the dancing bears would have claimed to know Antonello if they could speak. He was the best of us all."

"He was? How wonderful!"

Gregorini looked at me sharply. "Are you his son?" he guessed, the wildest guess I had ever heard a man make.

"I don't think so. But I think he was my mother's lover."

"He was the best of our trade in Italy, one of the five best in all

Europe. Sometimes a householder gave him wine with his own hand."

"Was he your friend?"

The clown's great black eyes wheeled slowly to mine.

"In the name of Thespis, he was."

"Perhaps he boasted to you of bedding a highborn lady named Lucia. I hope he did bed her, and I wouldn't blame him for the boast."

"He never told me of it, but there was some such thing in his life. As you no doubt know, he was killed by a highborn hater."

"That hater lives in Venice. I think he hates all jongleurs. I want you and your company to appear before his house at sundown tomorrow, and put on your best show. If you could call yourself Antonello the Younger, it would help out my jest."

"It's no jest, my friend. I see that in your face. As for my being Antonello the Younger, that's easy. I've a dozen different names, here and about. It's a common thing for obscure actors to call themselves after famous ones who've gone before. We would cry ourselves down the canal as Antonello's Troop. But what would the signor do?"

"He may lose his temper. It may be in a way that won't show, but it's possible that he'll hit you with the flat of his sword or call the watch."

"He won't use the point of his sword, will he?"

"He'll do nothing that would make him stand trial, let alone go to prison. Just be sure that you don't put yourself where you'll be charged with theft."

"You're well acquainted with Antonello's story," Gregorini remarked.

"Why, yes."

"Lucia was your mother, this man is your father, whom you hate. Why yes, I'll do it, for anything you want to pay me, or no payment at all. It will be a small stroke of revenge for a member of my guild. Also—if I'm attacked without cause, the people will rally around me. I'll show them they haven't given their plaudits to a craven!"

With this last his voice rang, his shoulders squared, his nose rode high, and quite a noble expression graced his commonplace face. *We are all showmen of a sort,* I thought—*only some of us are more transparent than others.* I had no doubt that Gregorini would do his part well.

As the hour drew near I dressed in my very best, hired a gondola, and made for the rear of the Casa Polo by a little-used canal. There was no reason to believe that the postern door would be bolted while the servants were up and about, and the narrow quay on this side was largely screened by a bridge. A short distance up the canal I heard shouting, singing, and the shrill notes of a treble flute. The jongleurs were pausing only briefly at the smaller houses, doing a trick or two and picking up thrown coppers, but it would be in character for them to make a good showing before a mansion as extensive as the Casa Polo. Apparently they would arrive before the front entrance precisely on time.

So all had gone well thus far. The fact remained that I heartily regretted engaging the troop at all, since a band of serenaders would have served my purpose at much less risk. Especially I cursed my extravagant folly in having them bandy Antonello's name. Already their caller was shouting it at the top of his voice. They would overdo the business. Gregorini would appoint himself a tragedian and end by giving me away. Nicolo would not lose his head and rush out to pummel him; instead he would become thoughtful, immensely capable, and steel-cold.

As I waited in the shadow of a bridge, my coldness was of a different sort. It caused a clammy dew over all my skin and chilled the cockles of my heart and frostbit my spirit. I thought at first it was the foreboding of failure, a clearheaded gloom brought on by a fatal rashness. But presently I exposed the lie. It was nothing in the world but terror.

There was nothing the matter with my scheme. I was simply frightened almost out of my wits of Nicolo Polo.

The discovery had a startling and quite mysterious effect upon me. An angry shame sent a hot flash through me on the heels of the dismal cold, and that boiling-up made me crave exertion as might a roweled horse. Happily, the jongleurs were almost at the portico. I heard casements opening in the front of the house and then a wench's squeal of laughter.

"Ah, princess!" the caller shouted at her. "I fear a small brown knave will invade your bower——"

The monkey would be climbing the wall by now. Nicolo's sons would be rushing to the windows of the supper parlor; the servants could hardly mind their duties; Nicolo himself would grow dark in the face and Maffeo would await his brother's cue. . . . I made for the postern door. It opened to my hand. After a brief pause in the shadows, I gained the staircase on swift and stealthy feet. At its top the close sound of voices reached my burning ears. I barely rounded a corner when two abigails, the young, pretty one carrying satin pillows and the old, ugly one a chamberpot, ran through the hall. I sped into my mother's room. It had become Nicolo's room—my eyes swept in the evidence in passing without recording what it was. If now I found what I was looking for, stored in reach of his hand and under his nose, my victory would be sweeter on that account.

But my spirit flagged as I reached out the open casement to the tile water pipe. My arm being visible from the promenade if anyone looked this way mattered not at all in the dismal face of failure. The upraised pipe easily admitted my hand—I felt around the bend. And then the interior no longer felt smooth and hard. . . .

For a matter of a foot, and except for a gap of about two inches, some coarse-grained substance lined the pipe. . . . It was not leather but something like it. . . . Instead of being water-soaked and rotten, it was somewhat stiff. . . . My clawing fingers tried to cramp it into smaller space. I felt it tear, but it did not fit as tightly as before. . . . With a frantic heart and boiling blood but with my hand still moving with my will, I tried to work it down and out of the pipe. . . . I would be captured rather than retreat without full trial.

Again the substance tore, and part of it came free. I brought it out without looking at it, and my next clawing dislodged the rest. Clutching both pieces, I whirled to fly.

A measurable period of time must have passed between that start and the sudden stop I made on the threshold of the postern door, but I was not aware of it, nor would I ever remember any intervening event. I stopped as might a fleeing fox as he beholds with his narrow, cold-fire eyes an unexpected block to his intended course. But that does not cause him to concede defeat. Such a notion could not enter his intent brain. Although his heart had been beating full blast before, it does not burst apart. He stops and picks another path that, with good luck and good running, may gain him his goal.

A footman of some sort whom I had seen in Nicolo's train was standing within easy view of the narrow quay, and with him was a pretty wench, probably from a near-by domicile, for whom he might like to display his prowess at catching thieves. In any case he would raise an alarm at sight of me. I must choose between ducking back into the house and hiding there until the coast might clear or making boldly toward the fondamento, with the hope of gaining a cluster of people hanging close to the performers. The latter would be my only screen from watchers at the windows of the supper parlor; still, the choice was an easy one. At least I would not be entering a cul-de-sac, and I could still breathe.

I walked briskly and gained the crowd of gapers without anyone's raising a cry. But my intent to conceal myself among them was thwarted by new developments, and it came to me that I would not get off scot-free.

Out of the door came Nicolo, his face cold and gray. His eyes swept the performers in brutal contempt, and they were superb eyes, missing almost nothing that concerned him; likely, my own sharp vision was rooted in them. I watched them wheel toward me and then light. I thought the expression on his face changed very slightly, but it gave me no clue to his next act. I knew that if my face were white, he took note of it, and that he observed what looked like two pieces of dirty parchment in my hands.

His voice rose in an imperious command.

"Stop the show!"

The laughter and noise of the crowd had been diminishing since the instant of his appearance, causing the performers to sound louder, more strident, somehow more showy and crude. Now the abrupt, complete cessation of their antics had a shocking effect on all the simple people gathered here. Silence fell with a sense of crushing weight. The caller's patter stopped in mid-air. A red ball, a white ball, and a red-and-white bottle spun flashing when all else had stilled; then Gregorini's incredible hands caught the first, second, and finally, with the merest suggestion of a flourish, the third. A dancing bear went down on all fours and hung his head. A monkey in a gay red coat and breeches and a little cap ran along the edge of the balcony till his rope tightened. Then he perched there, watching with a worried face.

Nicolo approached me in the lithe strides of a man in his first prime. *What are you doing here?* I could hear him saying it, the exact sound, while his handsome lips were still closed. However he worded it, my answer was ready.

Instead he said something completely different and in an utterly unexpected tone.

"Marco, is this your troop?"

"Signor?" He had flushed the word out of me as a hunter does a rabbit, and my expression had been as vapid as a rabbit's.

"If it is, I'll let them finish their show and throw them some money. Otherwise I don't want them disturbing me at supper."

"Why should you think it was my troop?"

"Their name—I heard it cried all down the canal—and the fact of your presence. You must be aware that some of these troops are owned by gentlemen, and I dare say their owners sometimes mingle with the crowds to get some idea of the collections. I was quite ready to congratulate you on a beau geste. But your patent surprise at my question seems to mean that I guessed wrong."

"Yes, signor, you did."

"Then your arrival together is nothing but a remarkable coincidence?"

"Perhaps not as remarkable as you think. I too heard their uproar and was struck by the name of the company, so I left my hired gondola and intercepted them. I wanted to ask if Antonello the Younger was the son or some other close kin of the jongleur you spoke of. I thought it possible he could give me some information useful in court, in case a suit is ever made against me."

This was in effect what I had intended to say in case of an encounter of this kind. It came forth cold and stale, and a lame parry to his adroit, deep, barbed thrust.

He looked me up and down and I thought his gaze lingered a perceptible instant on the torn sheet in my hand. I was quite sure that his curiosity was aroused and perhaps the Devil whispered in his ear that this was the very object of his search, the loss of which was the greatest loss he had ever suffered; but his common sense denied the inkling.

"In that case I'll ask you to do your business with him elsewhere," Nicolo said curtly. Then to the crushed clown, "Take yourself and the other trash out of my sight and hearing, as fast as you can."

Doubtless Antonello noted that Nicolo Polo made no threats and had need of none. Without waiting for his master's nod, the bear-leader began tugging the pitiful brute across the quay to a big brightly painted gondola. The monkey man drew in the tether so swiftly that his squeaking pet was in peril of falling. Nicolo's cold eyes were not on them now—he had turned back to his door —but they did not stop even to wipe away their sweat. The clusters of spectators appeared to dissolve and avoided one another's eyes.

"I wish to talk to you, Antonello, so I'll board your gondola," I said as grandly as possible.

Except to pay him his fee, he wished that I would stay away

from him. All his noble feelings had dissipated. Antonello the
Great was rotten and forgotten, and I was his luckless bastard.
Probably it was to raise myself in his estimation rather than to
console him for a rebuff that I gave him a gold piece instead of
the three lire I had intended. This I handed him on the approach
to the first bridge.

He accepted it with no sign of gratitude. "So the gentleman
thought you owned my company, did he?" he remarked, with a
sneer on his painted face. "I would have told him I owned every
stick and stitch myself if I hadn't been afraid I'd spoil your game."

"You were a great man yesterday, Gregorini. Don't turn into
what the signor called you."

I hailed a gondola and turned away from the Casa Polo. In
case Nicolo had found out or surmised something to take action on,
I chose obscure canals instead of the great thoroughfares for my
homeward route. Then I approached Mustapha's house only after
careful reconnaissance. Meanwhile I had concealed the two pieces
of dirty fabric under my shirt.

For ten minutes or more, Mustapha and I conversed. I sat down,
apparently at ease; I had almost the feeling of it; certainly I made
him no short answers and listened to him not impatiently, or even
patiently but with an interest that was real even if somewhat
forced. All this was some sort of propitiation of the Devil. All the
time I heard soft sounds behind the wall where Miranda moved
about, opened and shut drawers, and sang. I considered going to
speak to her as a kind of preparation for a coming ordeal—perhaps
to take bearings to determine my position—but I rejected the idea
by instinct.

Alone in my room, I looked in a glass, mocked myself, cursed
myself for a spiritual bastard. Then, sitting on a chest, I got out
the two pieces. Instantly I was sure that they were no sort of
parchment that I had ever seen, and under their dirt and stain
there was writing.

The coarse-grained, slightly spongy material was of inter-
woven fibers. I passed a damp cloth over it, greatly afraid that
wiping off dirt might wipe away the writing. This did not prove
to be the case, so I grew bolder. As the stuff cleaned, the writing
became plainer. The script was bold, and by fitting the two pieces
together, I was soon able to read it.

My eyes slowly widened, for here was the answer to one of the
greatest enigmas in Christendom—the legend of the Salamander.

The Parchment

My dear niece Lucia:

When I came to the Court of Mangu, Khan of Tatary, I was made to walk between two fires ere I was admitted to his presence. I escaped with painful burns, but if the fires had been set closer together, I might have perished.

Their wizards walk through fire unharmed. I discovered that their secret was a long cloak, boots, and a hood that looks somewhat like leather. Some legend of the stuff has reached the West. It is called salamander skin, and many alchemists and philosophers have experimented with the hides of these reptiles, believed to be impervious to fire, in an attempt to produce it.[9] These attempts are doomed to failure. Actually the garments are made of a mineral fiber found in the High Altai on the western border of Cathay. The wizards guard the secret not only from the people, who make rich offerings, but also from the Khan, who believes in their seeming supernatural powers. Yet the latter would pay richly for the protection the stuff could afford his documents, his most rare treasures, and even his royal person.

In the city of Fuchow, whence a caravan road makes into Eastern Dzungaria, I was able to obtain a small piece from a magician. On it I have inscribed this letter, with India ink. I think it is the same incombustible substance that was used for wicks in the lamps of the Vestal Virgins. It is all I have to leave you: care for it as though it were a precious locket, adorned with pearls. Perhaps husband or son will find it a key to fame and fortune.

I write this in my cloister in the archiepiscopal palace in Dalmatia, as I approach my death on earth and, I most humbly pray, my eternal life in Heaven.

Your loving uncle
Johnannes de Carpini
Archbishop of Antivari

Then, below, was what seemed written in fire itself. As I read it, in my mother's handwriting, my hair rose up as in the presence of the walking dead.

Nicolo knows something of this. My son Marco, do not let him have it, or I cannot rest in my grave.

Mama

CHAPTER 8

DEPARTURE

IT WAS MENTIONED ON THE RIALTO THAT PAULOS ANGELOS, THE
most considerable slave dealer operating from Venice, had returned from a journey to a near-by market. Perhaps he had
laid in enough of his special kind of wares for his next journey
eastward, and had lost his lively interest in Miranda. When several
days had passed without any reply to my letter, I put myself under
the disadvantage of approaching him again.

He received me in an office so plain that it would do for the
cell of a monk. I had seen him several times before; only the
present business opened my eyes to his peculiarities and distinc-
tions. He was soberly dressed, small, swarthy, with well-carved
features, curly black hair, magnetic eyes, and hands that an artist
would love to paint. His manner was quiet and quite winning.
I thought that he was better born and educated than most slave
traders.

"Miranda is a lovely child," he remarked, after the amenities
had been seen to. "I was very eager to get her for a Thessalian
duke of special tastes—I think she would have suited him to perfection. As it happened, he was in great haste for a new concubine—to console him, I believe, for the loss of a favorite—and when
I was unable to deal with her keepers, I bought a beautiful blonde
Asturian in her stead."

"I'm sure you haven't delivered her yet. Perhaps it's not too
late——"

"For this dealing, it is. You see, signor, I've promised Celesta
the place—a very favorable one—and of course I can't disappoint
her. There will be many more dealings. I would be pleased and
proud to present Miranda to my clients, but I'm not in the business
—as the old saying goes—for my salubrity. If you'll quote me a
price on which I have a reasonable expectation of fair profit, I'll
buy her here and now."

"My price is three thousand lire." Then, as he seemed to hesitate,
I added from a cramped chest, "With an understanding between
us as to her disposal."

Paulos Angelos gave me a slight bow. "Your considerateness of
her does you credit. I don't think we would have trouble on that

score. And I'll not deny she's worth more than that, in the eyes of a connoisseur. But the question is, what can I get for her? I was prepared to pay seven hundred bezants to make a quick sale to the duke at nine hundred. To please him, although against my better judgment, I might have paid eight hundred bezants. But it's unthinkable that I would pay such a sum with nowhere to place her. I assure you, signor, that six hundred would be a very fair price indeed."

"I've been offered six, and rejected it."

"I see very little chance of my offering more than that. However, if you wish, I'll look at the girl again. It may be I'll see her as suiting some good customer."

It was in my throat to tell him he must decide now—one thousand gold bezants and not a dinero less. At least she would be saved another inspection. What would I be saved? Was that what I was getting at? I must not work in the dark or shrink from the light. Did I fear that he would reject her or that he would accept her? I did not know. I was not only deeply torn but inordinately perplexed.

He was speaking again. . . .

"I can see her the day after tomorrow, if you're at leisure then."

"If you please, I'd rather you saw her today."

He looked at me curiously, then with a winning half-smile, "I've been through it myself, young man," he told me, with grave charm. "She's the first you've owned, and truly beautiful. If you can afford to keep her for your own, I'd envy you."

"I thank you for your expression."

"Since I know you wouldn't offer her to me if she weren't a virgin, I'll present myself at your abode at the second hour past noon."

When I went home, I found Miranda seated in the sunlit window, mending with thimble and thread some of the household clothes. Her eyes rose slowly to meet mine.

"Miranda, the slave dealer Paulos Angelos will be here at two o'clock," I told her, standing still in the middle of the floor.

"Am I to dress to be shown or to be taken away?"

"He's coming to look at you with a view to buying you."

"Don't tell Mustapha Sheik until after his meal."

Paulos Angelos came in what I thought was his richest dress. When he had paid due honors to the house, I escorted him to what Mustapha called our durbar—merely our best room overlooking the lagoon. Then I opened a door and summoned Miranda.

She came in, light-footed, and took her stand by a window. Her eyes were darkly glimmering and her face was calm. Angelos looked at her a long time.

"Maiden, will you turn a little to the right?" he asked. . . . "Now a little to the left. . . . Signor, she's more beautiful to my sight than the first time I saw her—but also, more nearly unique."

"I take it that will affect the business in hand," I answered.

"To some degree. I would prize her more, but find her harder to place. Signor, any price I offer for her is with the understanding that she is virginal and has no unsightly mark of canker."

"I guarantee her virginity. She has a red scar from a severe burn on the sole of her right foot."

"A brand?" Angelos asked, palpably startled.

"It might be called that. It's in the shape of a crescent."

"How did she come by it, signor?"

"She told me in confidence. I may say that it does her credit. You may look at it if you like, or make any examination you wish."

"None is necessary. I'm prepared to make an offer for her."

He paused, plainly waiting for me to dismiss Miranda from the room.

"If you have no objection, Messer Angelos, I'll have her remain while we conclude our business," I said on sudden impulse.

"I've no objection," he replied, almost but not quite concealing his surprise. "It's not customary, as you know, but if it won't rowel her feelings——"

"I don't think it will, and I'd like to have her hear what you tell me about your plans for her, in case you buy her, and the various clients to whom you would offer her. I'll invite her to express her own hopes and wishes in these matters, to which I'll pay heed."

"They would influence me also, I've no doubt." And Angelos gave her a slight bow.

"Would you like to stay, Miranda?" I asked.

"Yes, master."

"Then seat yourself on the divan. Messer Angelos, will you now make your offer?"

"It's seven hundred gold bezants. I have in mind to offer her for nine hundred to a Parisian perfumer living in Constantinople. He is a cultivated gentleman and quite rich. His art carries him on long journeys throughout the Farther Levant, buying musk, spikenard, attar of roses, and suchlike ingredients of fine perfumes. He sent me word that he wants a lovely young girl as his companion on these journeys. I can't guarantee it, of course, but

I have every reason to believe that Miranda would suit him admirably."

"Miranda, would such a buyer suit you?" I asked.

"If I must be sold for concubinage, instead of for farm labor, he would suit me better than any buyer I've heard of so far."

"Are there any questions you want to ask about him?"

"Only one, and I fear that Signor Angelos can't answer it."

"I'll try," Angelos said, his eyes oddly lighted.

"I'd like to know if he's reputed to be kind."

"I can tell you, with utmost confidence in my words, that he is. The faces of his slaves bear witness to it."

"In that case, it would be a happier outcome than I had expected."

The room fell silent. There was no movement either except for the almost unobservable ones of our bodies and the slow wheelings of dust motes in a broad shaft of sunlight coming through the window. It happened that I occupied the great chair—a ceremonial chair, I thought, that Mustapha had brought from some quiet schoolroom beyond the desert. Paulos appeared lost in reverie. It was hard to believe that he was thinking of so many lire profit, or of pleasing customers either. I wondered if he were wondering at fate.

Miranda's presence gave the scene a profoundly moving quality. Her bare feet were together, her hands in her lap, her two long braids glistened like pale-colored gold, her eyes appeared dark and quiet under the arched brows. I had drunk to intoxication on her lips. My lips knew as eyes alone could never know the beauty of her breast; my hands were learned as to the loveliness of her whole flesh; my mind rejoiced in hers; my spirit bowed before hers, knowing it was greater than mine in all eyes that see. So why was I considering letting her go? I could keep her for my own! The incredible promise was true! I could have her waking and sleeping, eating and working, moon shining and moon hidden, in rain, sunlight, gray fog, mist of morning, black of midnight, in pain and in joy. She would cleave to me. I would grow in strength with her hand in mine. I would uncover great mysteries. I would plumb deep secrets.

Beautiful Miranda with the blood-red brand. You sit there, not trusting me to save you. Why then do you love me?

"Then it's understood that if you buy her, you'll do your best to sell her to this perfumer of whom you spoke." So I heard myself speaking to the slave trader Paulos Angelos.

"Yes, signor."

"Will you give him the first refusal of her, regardless of what offers you receive before then?"

"If we both live to meet again, I'll do so. And if he won't buy her, I'll strive to satisfy her as to a purchaser."

"Still, I can't let her go for seven hundred gold pieces. My price is a thousand."

"I'll offer you eight hundred. If the Parisian will pay me nine hundred, I'll barely come out moneywise, and have to take my profit in good will."

"I wish I could favor you, Signor Angelos. I'm bound to that price."

"Consider that she's sixteen. Consider that she's branded on the foot. Consider that most buyers don't want beauty of her sort. But I'll go one step further—to cut in half the distance between your price and my offer. That will mean nine hundred pieces of gold. There's no dealer in Venice that wouldn't dub me a fool."

"I can't accept less than one thousand."

Angelos smiled faintly, sighed, rose to his feet. I would have believed this was a trick of his trade if I had not seen him rubbing his hands together as though he were washing them.

"Thank you for letting me see her, Signor Polo," he said. "Good-by, Miranda, and may you have your heart's desire."

"That last is denied me, Paulos, but you may have a good profit from me, if you'll be bold."

Paulos gave her a great wondering glance. It seemed almost a moment before he could speak.

"First, why do you address me as Paulos? Is that fitting in a slave?"

"Signor Polo has caused me to forget, for a while, that I'm a slave. I pray your pardon."

"You must be accustomed to calling wealthy merchants by their given names."

"Whatever I was accustomed to is gone. I won't do it again, signor."

"How did wealthy merchants address you, if you'll tell me?"

"It will do no harm to tell you, and it may do good. They called me 'my lady.'"

"By Saint Theodore, I should have known it! But what did you mean by saying that I'd make a good profit from you?"

"Buy me at Signor Polo's price, a thousand pieces of gold. Venice is only one dot on the face of the earth—don't weigh me by its scales. If you'll offer me only to buyers of my liking, I'll bring you two thousand."

"By Heaven, I believe you will!"

I started to speak but the hand of Fate clutched my throat. I saw Paulos turn slowly, his eyes glimmering.

"Signor Polo, I'll meet your price of three thousand lire, payable in gold bezants within thirty-six hours. In earnest thereof, I pay into your hands the usual three per cent, which comes to thirty pieces of gold."

He counted them out from a leathern bag and put them in my cupped hands. I gazed at them in soul-sick dread of a miracle sent from on high whereby they would change to thirty pieces of gilded silver. But they remained the good gold coin of Byzantium, of fair and lawful fineness. My weakness passed away.

2

On All Saints Day, four days distant, my cousin Leo would celebrate his twenty-first birthday. I remembered the date well for having repeatedly measured his exact seniority to me. The occasion would justify a feast at the home of my uncle Zane, and it was almost as sure that Nicolo and Maffeo Polo would be invited as that I would be left out. However, as brazenly as might one of the blackbirds in the Polo coat of arms, I intended to intrude. At that feast table would sit witnesses to my bargain with Nicolo, and long-eared servants with long memories would wait on them. It would be a good time and place, I thought, to seal the deal.

To anticipate the scene did not chill me as much as it would have before I received my mother's legacy. It was as though my temperature was somewhat higher.

Meanwhile I had other business of moment. It caused me to waken at cockcrow on the morning following Miranda's sale. The merest milky mist on the eastern waters betokened the waning of the night, but I was glad to get up and shed my troubled dreams. A dream witch had tried to persuade my spirit that the maiden was still mine, but a stubborn, dark-browed fellow with his hard head on the pillow spoiled all the sport.

Paulos Angelos would no doubt take possession of her sometime today. I thought to open her door softly and gaze upon her at the last hour of her last sleep in our house, but I mastered the impulse, or else the fear of needless pain mastered me.

Making for the gardeners' market that Rosa frequented, I wore my best raiment instead of the plain clothes I had worn before. In my purse were five gold pieces of the earnest money for a gift to her, such a sum as she might have dreamed of possessing when she was young and hopeful, but in these late years as remote as the moon. I thought that her face would light up at the sight of me, and she would be pleased by the people watching when I greeted her, and a little later, when I slipped the lordly gift into her hand, she would not believe her eyes. Such a worn old hand to hold so much red gold!

How gladly and proudly then would she perform her last service to Lucia's son—only to signal to me, from an upstairs window, as Nicolo sat at meat with his kinsmen.

But at the market I looked for her in vain. I waited long past her wonted time, then went to inquire for her at a certain stall where the lentils were extra-fine.

"I'm looking for old Rosa, whom I think you know," I said to the gardener.

"Aye, I know her well, and I saved some leeks for her that she'd ordered, but she hasn't come."

A tall, thin woman, older than Rosa unless I missed my guess, sniffed at some garlic and laid it down.

"Are you speaking of the beldame who always wore a tire-woman's habit, and spoke oft of her dead mistress Lucia?"

"That's the one," the gardener answered.

"She won't come for the leeks."

"I'd like to know why not."

"Leastwise, if she does come, you wouldn't see her, or if you did see her, you'd faint."

"What news do you have of her?" I asked in a firm voice.

"According to Amelia, a charwench who's friend to my grand-daughter, she died in her sleep three nights past."

The conversation between the two went on. I heard it, thin and strange, like voices in a dream.

"Why, I'm sorry to hear it," the gardener announced.

"In the midst of life we are in death, the Good Book says."

"Only three mornings past she was standing where you are now, looking at white turnips."

"She'll look at them no more, unless they're planted in the churchyard, and she gazes up at 'em."

"I could count on her Tuesdays and Fridays, as sure as the bell peal of San Marco. She'd only a few coppers to spend, but 'twas worth counting at year's end. Signor, she'd be pleased to be asked for by a gentleman of your kidney. 'Tis a pity she won't know of it, and that the business you had with her—to her benefit, I don't doubt—has come to naught."

I found my voice at last.

"Is she buried yet?" I asked the lean old woman.

"Why, gentleman, this is the third day! What would they be keeping her out for, an old bag of bones like her and me? The wench told my daughter she was buried the very day they found her. They can't get us into the ground fast enough, us who's outlived our use."

I gave Rosa's survivor some silver and walked away. When my head had cleared a little, I made for the Church of the Last Supper, where she had worshiped ever since she had first come to Venice in my mother's service. Moneywise, this church was poor, its congregation mainly folk of humble station, but, to my joy, it had an ample cemetery, where the dead need not lie crowded, and their bones could stay undisturbed till they molded away. A young priest spoke so warmly of the crone that it brought tears to my eyes; then he showed me her tomb.

"I should like to have Mass said every fortnight for a year, and on the anniversary of her death every year for ten years, for the forgiveness of her sins."

"I didn't know she had any," was his surprising answer.

"You'd never guess it, it was true. You'd think she'd been shrived of every one by Father Time himself. But she did have. She died hating one who had done evil to one she'd loved."

"She needs no praying for that. It's a sin of the flesh, and when the flesh is off her bones, she'll be rid of it."

"Worse than that, she died praying that the son of the one she loved would take vengeance on the one she hated."

"Vengeance is a great sin, especially when it's in the marrow of one's bones, but when her bones are dry, it will trouble her soul no more."

"In order that the son of the one she loved might find his lost heritage, she sent him to the Witch of Endor."

"Have naught to do with witches. But the sin will be on the son's soul, not on hers. Did she keep faith with those who loved her?"

"Yes."

"And with those she loved?"

"Do you mean she wouldn't sell them into slavery?"

"That would be a sin far beyond her reach. I meant would she

speak harshly to them without need, or deprive them of their due
for her own pleasure, and suchlike great sins that poor folk may
commit?"

"She's guilty of none of those things."

"Then the money that you would spend for the saying of prayers
for the peace of her soul, give to the poor for the peace of your
own soul."

"I'll do so, holy Father, but my soul will find no peace."

3

All the rest of the day I roamed about the city as though I were
looking for something I had lost. I visited the scenes I had most
loved, or admired, or marveled over in my childhood, and looked
upon those wondrous things that were the sea's gifts to his bride.
It did not seem possible that these things were wrought by human
hands—the countless marble sculptures that awe the heart, the
acres of mosaic pictures that exalt the spirit, and the lavish works
in gold, jewels, enamel, alabaster, glass, and multicolored stones
that dazzle the eyes. Atop of one of the giant pillars crowning the
Piazzetta stands a bronze lion to keep watch and guard over the
queen of cities.

But the noblest token of all of her temporal power and glory
was the four gigantic horses on the frontal gallery of San Marco's
Church, tossing their manes and tails. They had been brought to
Venice in my grandsire's time. But no one knew what dreamer
had conceived them centuries before, or what master builders had
cast them in indestructible bronze, or for what great pagan
triumph they had been raised. Yet by means of a plasterer's ladder
left on the narthex, a boy of twelve, alone and in the dead of
night, had mounted every one. Only God knew to what unearthly
realms his soul had ridden.

Roaming from bridge to bridge, I stayed too long. The sun
would set, closing the business day, before I could reach home.
If by then Paulos Angelos had come and gone with the purchase
money, he might repent his bargain and sacrifice the earnest.
Thirty pieces of gold would make a beggar rich, but its loss or
gain would be small figs to a merchant of his ilk. He was not one
to throw good money after bad. His common sense had objected
to the price, and only the strange words of the slave herself, floating on empty air, had caused him to disobey his better judgment. . . .

This was my train of thought as I started home, and my mind kept on it, in tireless repetition, until I saw the afterglow on our casement glass. Dasa, Mustapha's servant, opened the door to me. I spoke to him in Arabic.

"Did Angelos Effendi come today?"

"No, young master."

Then he would not come until tomorrow. Perhaps he would never come.

I went through the curtained arch of our durbar to find Miranda and Mustapha playing an Arabic game known originally as *shatranj*, but which we called *shah mat*, meaning "The king is dead," and which the English called chess.[10] Mustapha could beat me in a few minutes all around the board, boresome to both of us, but by his bating her several manikins, he and Miranda had close and pleasant contests. As I drew the curtain I heard them laughing in merry concert. Mirth was still on their faces as I entered. I feared that black jealousy was on mine.

None of us had spoken a word when Dasa followed me into the room.

"He comes now, effendi."

"Who?" But I knew too well.

"The slave trader who bought the *lilla keiberra*." The latter meant "great lady." Trust the eyes of a trained servant not to be deceived!

"Admit him to my gulphor." Then to the others, "Paulos Angelos is arriving. Miranda, I assume he's come for you."

I put a mask on my face as I spoke. I could read nothing in hers as she replied:

"I assume it also."

But Mustapha's face became as pale, the skin as tightly drawn over its bones, as in an attack of his sickness.

"Have him admitted here, Marco my son, if you will," Mustapha said.

Presently Angelos was present in the room, a small man, not as tall as Miranda, yet its dominant figure. His eyes were brighter than their wont, I thought; his manner, although punctilious, did not quite conceal a nervous eagerness. With hardly a word he handed me a certificate of deposit made out in my name by the moneylender Phineas of San Martino, for nine hundred and seventy pieces of gold. In return I gave him a letter of title to "the Infidel slave girl known as Miranda." I had written it ahead of time, away from his and Miranda's eyes, so if my hand shook I could still it without shame.

"Now I entreat a favor," said Paulos Angelos, when he had pocketed the document.

I could hardly keep from giving way to some fairy-tale hope. . . .

"Signor?"

"I can't sail for Constantinople short of a month. Meanwhile, I have no suitable quarters for Miranda in either my home or my pens. Will you ask Mustapha Sheik if he'll keep her here, under his protection, until I can claim her? I'll gladly pay a lira a day for her keep."

When I looked at Mustapha, he spoke.

"I will gladly assume the charge, Signor Angelos, and the pleasure of her company will more than compensate me for her provision."

I could not bear to look at his face, it was so childishly bright. Tears stood in Miranda's eyes and those eyes avoided mine. At my request, Angelos agreed to keep the transaction secret until I had made certain arrangements; then, with impeccable manners, he took his departure.

Three days passed without tangible event. My fate seemed as quiescent as a sleeping dog; I dreaded waking it by any move of mine. Most of the daylight hours I spent ordering stores and equipment for a trading journey eastward of Acre. Since the dealers were accustomed to merchants' stealing marches upon one another, they too promised secrecy in these matters until time for me to set forth. At dinner with Miranda and my aged mentor, we seemed to make as merry as before. As though by some strange kind of flight out of myself, at night I slept as though I had been drugged.

In the early afternoon of Leo's birthday, I dressed in my best to appear at the feast. There would be no cup of wine for me to quaff, but my uncle would not refuse me a glass of rain-water from his reservoir, to judge by the lowering clouds; and I would be lucky not to be drenched aforetime. The shower held off while I made to a wine booth within arrow cast of his house in San Felice.

A fine gondola that Nicolo had bought or leased had not yet docked there. I was a little uneasy lest the threat of rain had kept at home the travelers to China, which perversity in human kind would make a donkey laugh. As usual, I misjudged the

signor and his walking shadow. Well before I had finished a goblet
of good red wine of Provence, let alone before my old friend the
tapster had completed his first long-winded tale, the golden
dragon painted on the hull's burnished black came swimming
down the canal. A servant disembarked first, to lend his master
a hand, then Nicolo, then Maffeo, then Nicolo's two sons, then
two footmen bearing gifts. Nicolo wore a suit of dark-red velvet
and a silver cloak; the others' regalia did not take the eye. Uncle
Zane came to the quay to greet them.

Without haste I finished my wine. The tapster wound up his
tale, which was merry enough. A moment later my uncle's porter,
my oldest friend in the house now that Rosa had gone, had me by
the hand.

"I'd not like to blow my horn for you, as though you were a
stranger," he told me, after we had talked a moment of old times.

"You'd better, for your skin's sake, but it's not your fault if I
dash in without waiting to be ushered."

"That it's not. Must you stand on ceremony when you come to
give birthday greetings to your cousin, who was never the lad
that you were, nor is the man now? I'd rather you gave him the
toe of your shoe where he needs a donkey's tail."

How dared the old man speak so frankly of the heir of the
house? Plainly he held me worthy of his trust! I knew better, but
my heart warmed to him just the same.

"Blow your horn, old friend, as loud and fine as when Nicolo
returned."

"Nicolo? So that's what you call him! I've heard talk—but I'll
name you in my prayers." With that he blew a fine blast.

I entered the unbolted door and quickly passed through the
anteroom into the dining hall. Because the window light was dim
except for occasional flickers of lightning, my uncle Zane had
lighted a great spread of candles, and the short, sharp view that
I caught of the assembled diners before any of them glanced up
was clear enough to paint a picture by. The seven people there
sipped from cups or forked meat or worked their jaws, while the
servants gave them assiduous attention. For one instant of treachery I wished I were one of them. I stood in the dusk beyond the
candle shine, and a cold wind of loneliness bit me to the
bone. . . .

Nicolo had the sharpest ears, the most watchful eyes. He
glanced up and looked at me, but he did not start or seem more
than mildly surprised. At once he turned to Zane and spoke so

soon that his level voice eclipsed the sound of caught breaths all around the table.

"Why Zane, you didn't tell us that you were expecting Marco."

"I told you just the contrary, but I guess you didn't hear me," Zane replied. "Marco, you've gone your own way of late, which is not our way, and that's why I didn't invite you to join your kinsmen at this feast. I mean, of course, your kinsmen by marriage, you being Lucia's son."

I was instantly cool, confident, and strangely happy. Entirely competent to speak now, I waited for a better opening.

"Now he's here, my lord, let's make him welcome," my aunt Flora entreated in an anxious voice.

"Why, I'll not gainsay him, if he's come in honor of my son's natal day. What say you, Nicolo?"

Nicolo's faint smile warned me that I had waited too long.

"I don't believe it's what he's come for," he remarked in a pleasant voice. "I think he's come to tell me he's found the money that he needs to go with Maffeo and me to Cathay."

All eyes had been drawn to Nicolo as he spoke—now they turned on me. There was no other movement in the room, and no sound until Leo gave a harsh burst of laughter.

"What amuses you, nephew?" Nicolo asked in the same pleasant voice.

"You're joking! Where could Marco get a thousand pieces of gold?"

"Now that's a question, but there's none, I believe, about him having it. He came in here without waiting to be ushered in. He didn't fail to see my boat at the quay, and I think he expected it here today and waited for its arrival before he made his dramatic appearance. None of that smacks of a peace offering or even of paying birthday honors to Leo. Isn't it far more likely that he wishes to tell me something in front of witnesses?"

"I swear to you that the old Arab couldn't have raised that much——" The loudness of Zane's voice did not hide its tremor.

"Of course he didn't. Marco, did I guess right?"

"Yes, signor."

I came toward him and held out the certificate of title in a shaking hand. He took it with a steady hand, looked at it not too briefly or too long, and handed it with a faint smile to Maffeo. The only sign of deeper feelings was a dangerous one—a contraction of his pupils to bright points, causing the eyes themselves to look more large and bright.

"I'd 've never believed it, by the bones of God!" cried Uncle Zane.

"Marco, we'll sail on the calends of May, or thereabouts, on the bireme *Our Lady of Salvation*. I advise you to bespeak the captain for cabin and storage space, and to lay in goods to the amount of two or three hundred bezants for sale in Lesser or Greater Armenia. As for your share of the expenses, I'll draw on you as we go along. All this depending on whether, after all, you decide to attempt the journey."

"I've already decided, signor."

"You may have a few minutes in which to change your mind. Meanwhile I'll make another guess—this time as to the source of your wealth. I think you obtained it in the Casa Polo on the night you hired a troop of jongleurs to perform on our fondamento. I don't know its form, but I'm sure it's a product of alchemy for resisting fire that your mother's uncle brought from Tatary. I suggest that you learned of its hiding place, entered our house to get it, and sold the secret to Phineas or some company of Jews."

"In that case, Nicolo, doesn't it belong to you?" Uncle Zane asked, barely able to control his excitement.

"Everything that Lucia owned to the day of her death was mine, and this is not the first theft. When I saw that torn parchment in your hand, I had a strange inkling of what it was, but I didn't believe it and let it pass. Only just now, when you showed me the certificate, did my mind leap to the truth. You're not the first of your blood to resort to housebreaking to get what you want. But the other came to a quick and a cruel death."

Nicolo put no stress on the last phrase, but his smile had died and his face was a little lifted and its expression was like that of a god in marble lately found in Crete and brought to Venice. His sister Flora grew wide-eyed.

"Marco, don't go with him!" she burst out.

"Stay out of it please, Flora," Nicolo said. "Marco, the theft would be difficult to prove. I've neither the time nor the inclination. But I advise you to stop there. You're young and rash and not as cunning as you like to believe. In plain words—although I rebuked her, your aunt gave you good advice."

"I'm sorry I can't heed it."

"Marco, I don't want you to go with Maffeo and me to the Court of Kublai Khan. First, you're a living witness to my wife's whoring, and I want you out of my sight. Second, your character is such, inherited from a rogue, that you could bring our caravan

into disrepute or to disaster. I made the bargain with you fully
persuaded you could never raise the sum—anyway, at that first
meeting with you, when you weren't full-grown, I hadn't realized
how perfectly you reflect the adulterous union between my highborn wife and a wandering jongleur. If in spite of this you choose
to hold me to my bargain, you won't find me off guard again.
Sooner or later the base blood will tell; then I'll show you no
mercy. Choose, Marco, now."

"I choose to hold you to your bargain, and I'll return the enmity
you give me with all my heart."

"Marco, will you work with us the best you can?" Maffeo broke
in.

I could hardly believe my ears. "Yes, if you'll let me."

"Then, Nicolo, make the best of it. You're a born leader and I'm
not, but you're making too much of a cuckoldry nigh twenty years
cold. You made a deal with Marco, and you must give him his
chance to work it out and profit by it. That's the first law of a
merchant."

"And if you two kill each other," Aunt Flora cried, suddenly
emboldened, "you'll be chained together in Hell."

Nicolo and I looked at each other, and lightning through the
windows must have lighted my face as it did his. It was as though
we were already chained there. It was as though both of us were
gazing into a slightly distorted glass.

4

There had come the day appointed for my departure. Today
I had a rendezvous with sorrow, with loneliness, with a ship and
the sea. Since sunrise Miranda, Mustapha, and I had kept company with one another, mainly sitting on a divan with her between
the old man and the young one, talking at times, sometimes laughing over jokes and incidents that seemed of a bygone age. We
pledged one another in wine. Although the drink was forbidden to
good Mussulmans, Mustapha smiled and told us that what he
drank now, he would take off his allotment in Paradise.

At our neighbor's fondamento hung the gondola in which I had
borne Miranda on a silver sea. On her little deck was a piece or
two of hand baggage, and impatiently waiting to take me to the
ship was Arturo, her regular gondolier, lent to me for the occasion.
The window told me that the weather was favorable for sailing
—somewhat bleak for this time of year, a gray sky lighted here and

there by shrieking sea gulls, and a sharp wind out of the Carnic Alps, but that wind drove down the Adriatic in the way we wished to go; and with a little tacking we could clear the shoals of the Foci del Po before another sun.

"Many winds have made whitecaps on our sea since you brought me my medicine that day," Mustapha said.

"It was a lucky day for me."

"I wonder if it was. In my case, there can be no doubt. The potion I bade you bring was for my aching head, but you brought another for my old and lonely heart. I could not pay you for it, even with lore. And lore is a strange mistress. Once we start to enjoy her, we can't get enough of her. When we cohabit with her, she insists on bearing children that are inclined to be unruly, and cause us trouble. If she hides away from us, we will search the world——"

"Master, it's by no motive as noble as the seeking of knowledge that I'll set sail," I broke in with painful truth.

"That I know. But except for the knowledge I helped you gain, you would not set sail. And now the time has come to make you a parting gift. Look in the chest."

I did so, and brought forth an astrolabe of a model and a perfection of workmanship I had never seen. Showing off a little for my master, I explained to Miranda the essentials of its use. Figuring the arch of the sky as one hundred and eighty degrees, I could measure with this instrument the altitude of the North Star. This rose or fell as we traveled north or south: thus we could determine our degree of longitude, and by measuring other stars we could get a rough idea of our degree of latitude.

"With this, you can never be quite lost," Mustapha told me. "Although you may suspect that you've passed the outmost rim of the world, by making your calculations you will know that the distance between you and home is measurable in miles. With more nearly perfect instruments, which time will bring, you could discover the exact number. Perhaps that number known in some distant age will not be quite as terrifying as the rough estimate you will make before the year is out—provided you live and do not turn back. I have a strange feeling that the world is as large as Eratosthenes calculated.[11] And it's a sphere hung and probably revolving in the midst of the heavens—make that the basis of all your orientation, or you will sink in a bog of error. But Marco my son, in all its unbelievable expanse, it is yet one world. The same sun causes sap to flow in Italy as in Cathay; the same moon sails the sky, the same stars burn in ineffable and eternal mystery. It cannot be but that the great seas interflow. The waves that rock your ship off the Spice Isles are made of water drops that have been blown in spray on the beach of Rimini. The rain that falls in your face might have come—and in the passing of the ages I believe it did come—from your own Lake Trasimeno."

"It will be cold rain and lonely to hear," Miranda said quietly after a long pause.

"I'm more afraid of the blown sand of the desert," I said.

"Remember, it is all part of our world, the birthplace and dwelling place of man. What a strange habitation! Consider the brooks that meet and form streams, and the streams that join to make rivers, and the rivers winding in divine grace to their mother the sea. We know of the Danube, the Dnieper, the Don, the giant Volga, but is it true that beyond these is one that dwarfs them all? If so, there will be men like you venturing forth in boats or casting nets. They may vary from you slightly in form and face and color of skin, but they are men as sure as God exists, and I am sure of God because He made them. Take the far-flung steppes of Tatary, the wandering sands of the Kara Kum, and the wasteland of the Gobi that may be wider than Spain. Yet you will find them there, bravely battling the hell of heat or the deadly cold, watching their herds, building their tabernacles, hunting, fishing, daring, living. Is it true that north of India there are mountains snow-cloaked halfway down their sides under the burning sun? If so, you will find man's tracks along with those of wild sheep, the wolf, and the bear. How can man live on the slopes of these colossi, beside craters belching fire, and in the track of avalanches, harried by winds that scream like lost souls in Hell and blow the snow in blinding, freezing clouds? Yet he does. He has found a way. He has acquired knowledge and cunning and craft whereby he can parry the cruel blows of nature."

Mustapha paused to collect his thoughts. The beauty of his face was incomparable except with that of solemn seas or skies of stars. When he spoke again, his voice had the beauty of a great singing of all the people on some memorial day.

"Marco, it is well that we join hands with them. We have much to teach, so much more to learn. By common talk, by trade of good things, and by the fellowship of humanity itself, all the more thrilling because of our slight diversions from one another, men's lives will be better, wars will cease, hate will die, scorn will be drowned in the sea, and God's purpose—as far as I can see it with

my weak eyes—will be fulfilled. And the first task is the opening
of the roads. Not by men who go with noble aim, but by adventurers seeking gold or fame or just the burning, brimming cup of
utmost life. It comes to me you are one of them. I had an inkling
of it long ago and I dreamed of it in great joy. It is for that that
I can bear to see you go."

His throat worked, then he leaned back, spent. I rose and went
to a cubby and brought forth a parting gift for Miranda. It was
a lute, one as fine as she had played in the house of Simon ben
Reuben. She gave me one great proud glance, then, without our
asking, tuned the strings and began to play.

The room became brimful of lovely sound as with light from a
magic lamp.

> Beggarman O beggarman, out on the lea,
> Did you pass a bold knight of high chivalry?
> I gave him a kiss, I gave him a flower.
> For he's my true lover, Young Rob o' the Tower.

I sat beside her, feeling as though the music came partly from
me. Her hands were mine by some mysterious projection, their
movements in harmony with the strange stirrings of my soul; her
lips were mine by an old bond and they shaped the song as they
had shaped a kiss she gave me. I was looking at her for the last
time. That glance would hold a few minutes more, then, unless
by some strange stroke of fate, I would never see her with waking
eyes again. The word "desire" means "from a star," and she had
come to me as strangely as one star to another in the deeps of the
sky. Her face and small, proud form were cast in beauty.

Of late, that beauty had increased. The change did not wholly
derive from my own clearer sight; there had occurred a delicate
transfiguration. Was its cause such a common thing as love?

*I love you, Marian Redvers, daughter of a great house, who
should be mistress of Castlebrook. I love you, blue-eyed waif.*

> I fear he'll not wed you, fair maiden of Devon,
> He died in the battle and rode on to Heaven;
> And gifts that you gave him in sweet unbless'd hour
> Will fetch you to Fire, not to Rob o' the Tower.

The song, the melody, that particular shape of beauty, died
away. And at that moment there rose Mustapha from his seat, tall,
brown, his black eyes tear-wet, the skin drawn tight over his facial
bones in augury of death.

"I'm going now to my gulphor, Marco my son, and I'll bid you farewell."

He put his hands on my shoulders and kissed me between the eyes. Then a door closed behind him.

"Then, Miranda, it's time I said good-by."

"Full time," she answered.

"Why did you tell Paulos Angelos that he could sell you for twice the price I asked for you? Otherwise he wouldn't have bought you."

"You've no right to ask me, but I'll answer. I wanted him to buy me."

"Why?"

"I wanted to be chosen."

"I don't understand that."

"Why should you?"

"For him to choose you as a slave to sell, or some buyer to choose you to keep?"

"Both of them."

"Did you tell him the truth?"

"That's not your lookout, but I'll answer that, too. I told him the truth. Someone will pay that for me, and I'll be worth it. He shall have my body and the joys of it and they will be greater joys than you can yet imagine. If I can give it to him, he shall have my love."

"You knew I loved you."

"Yes, but you didn't choose me."

"Do you know that I'll love you greatly and forever?"

"You told me so, and I believe you, and my heart tells me so."

"I want you to be happy."

"Since I've fallen so low, it will take very little to make me happy. Anyway, I'll strive for happiness."

"Will I be happy? I bid you prophesy."

"No. If you'd chosen me, you would be happy, but at what price?"

"Won't even being a king in Cathay make me happy?"

Miranda laughed softly. "You can never find happiness now. You sold it for what you thought was a just price. It comes to me that every human being has one fair chance to buy it, one fair chance to sell it, and neither will ever come again. But Marco, you are doomed to wander over the face of the earth in this life and perhaps in the life to come."

"Will you love me all that time?"

"You've no right to ask, but I'll answer just the same. Yes, I'll love you always. Now I'm done with prophesying, and my heart aches."

"Tell me one more thing. Will I ever see you again?"

"We'll see each other in dreams."

At that instant Dasa, Mustapha's servant, clapped his hands once, then drew aside the curtain.

"Young master, there is a marriage in the city, the bridegroom being a cousin of Arturo the gondolier, and he has left his post."

"No matter. I'll row the gondola myself, and leave it at the quay where hung *Our Lady of Salvation*."

Dasa bowed and withdrew.

"You sang so beautifully," I said to Miranda. "Will I ever hear your voice?"

"I'll sing to you in your dreams."

I looked at her, and this was the rendezvous I had with sorrow and loneliness. In its crying to her, my heart forgot to be proud.

"Have I lost the right to kiss you good-by?"

"Yes, but I'll kiss you good-by."

She came and put her arms around my neck and her lovely mouth against mine. I felt her whispering:

"When you lie cold and lonely, call me, and I'll come."

Doors closed behind me. I unfastened a rope from an iron ring. I mounted to the platform in the stern and dipped the long oar.

I could have headed straight into the lagoon but instead I rowed past our little quay. Then out on the balcony came my beloved, her eyes glimmering with tears, her lute in her white hands. The sunlight glistened on her flaxen hair.

She sang to me of a little maid of Devon and her lost lover. I stroked in time with the music, long, strong strokes, and the boat bore me swiftly on my way. When I was too far for notes to carry, I still saw her, her hand raised in identification and salute. And the music seemed to linger in the little cabin, as though I were taking it with me across the world, to be my companion always.

BOOK TWO

CHAPTER 1

TOWARD THE RISING SUN

NICOLO POLO, MAFFEO POLO, AND I, MARCO POLO, TRAVELED
eastward.

We rode a well-armed merchantman down the Adriatic
Sea, across the Ionian Sea, out along the Mediterranean Sea past
Crete, past Cypress, at last to Acre, the great Christian strong-
hold that Richard the Lion-Hearted had conquered from the Infidel on the Lebanon coast. Other merchants took passage on the
same ship, some servants followed Nicolo until he should replace
them and send them back, yet the stars looking down knew we
were alone. Our navigator estimated the distance at two thousand
miles, which might be thrice the wild-goose flight from Venice to
London.

From in and about Acre to the great port of Aegae two hundred and fifty miles up the Syrian coast, we three had company.
The new Pope had not been able or else had not seen fit to appoint
one hundred wise churchmen to carry Christian beatitudes to the
Cathayan multitudes, but he had sent two, Nicolo and Guglielmo,
worthy friars both. But at Aegae, at the mouth of the caravan
road whose gut led to India, there came word of Tatar raids
athwart our path. His Holiness had chosen the two friars on account of their wisdom. This wisdom caused them to turn back.
Nicolo, Maffeo, and I went on alone.

To my sorrow, we did not pass the great Capital of Trebizond,
on the southeastern shore of the Black Sea. Its royal family were
esteemed the most beautiful human beings in the world. All the
kings of Christendom and the Sultans of Islam vied for their tall,
fair-haired, black-eyed daughters. But the fly in the ointment was
—or so we were assured—that the sons were born with short tails
that their robes of sable and ermine could hardly conceal.
Mustapha Sheik would have doubted the tale of tails, although
he would not have denied it without proof. I needed no proof to
know that if it were true, the regal tailbearers made no real effort
to hide their odd distinction, and indeed took pride in it as Satan
does in his cloven hoofs. Only common men fear departure from
commonality. The uncommon spend their whole lives, by and
large, proving their condition.

The caravan road eastward fetched us to the south of Trebizond, through Sivas and Erzinjan. The great lords of these noble cities paid tribute into the hands of short, swart, button-nosed collectors, and some of it at long last poured into the coffers of Kublai Khan, halfway across the world. Our caravan moved on, a little southward now, losing track of the marches we had made since our friars turned back—thirty or suchlike—and did not trouble to dream of the count ahead. We passed some thousands of loaded camels every day, their backs piled high with silks, satins, brocades, rugs, musk and spikenard and spices, swords and armor for everlasting wars, ebony and ivory, gold and silver, amethysts and amber and jade. Wild-eyed captives of all colors and tongues walked in chains, while slave girls rode in curtained litters. These last were mainly veiled, but sometimes the veils were lifted by quick sly hands or perhaps wind played the wanton, revealing the arresting beauty of fair-haired Circassians or the beautifully molded brunette faces of the daughters of Persia, or sometimes ivory-skinned, slant-eyed maidens whose nation I could not name.

Swinging a little southward, we crossed a mighty range of mountains, cold as the moon on a winter night, absolute cold, it seemed, where the last warmth in the last tree heart had died away, and the green waters of the rock-bound lakes looked frozen to their depths.[1] Here the snow drifted before the moaning wind, or was blown in eerie clouds, and except for that moaning and the hiss of the frozen snowflakes there was no sound. But we could bless the bitter weather, for only we and silent, lean gray wolves dared venture forth, while the wild Kurds, whose very name was Wolf in the Tatar tongue, almost as hairy and more cruel, must hang by their hidden fires instead of raiding our caravan. And out of those white passes we came down onto a wide brown plain, where the wind was bleak and biting but the winter sun gave forth a perceptible glow, and where grapes grew in summertime, and sweat ran off men's faces as it did in the vineyards of Lucania.

Days passed, nights sped, and we came to the Kingdom of Mosul. This was the homeland of the great merchants who we called Musolini, sellers of the cloth called muslin (*musolino*). Here dwelt many Nestorian Christians, living at peace with the Saracens who worshiped Allah, but both paid taxes to the king of the Tatars, who bowed only to a distant emperor and a rag doll over his bed. And just across the river lay some ruins strangely differing from most we had seen along the route, in not being the handiwork of the Tatars, who had passed here less than twenty years ago. The new desolation had looked almost as old as this, but men said it was as the age of a kitten compared to that of a sea turtle. Men said that the rubble of the immense double walls marked the battlements in Nineveh, the capital of Assyria two thousand years ago, and that the great pile atop the hill was once the palace of Sennacherib, and a blackened spot amid the waste was the temple of the goddess Ishtar, on which God poured His wrath.

Now we followed the River Tigris as it wound through a wide, rich plain shut in by impenetrable mountains and pathless deserts. The land widened and warmed with the slow weeks; great reaches of it were garden-green, crowded with towns and villages; the spires of the Nestorian churches stood as thick as the minarets of the Infidel; and except for an occasional scar on the face of the land, or suddenly met stretches of desert in the midst of plenty, you would never know that the Tatar had passed this way.

He had come in the person of Hulaqu the Mongol, brother and viceroy of the Emperor Mangu Khan, who preceded Kublai Khan. He had brought a host of mounted archers and spearmen, and his destination was Baghdad. We too came to Baghdad, in due course, and at first glance you would wonder at his charity and restraint. He had not lost his temper once, so the whole vast wondrous city, the capital of Harun al-Rashid, was not razed and laid utter waste. True, he had shut the Calif in his own treasure tower with only gold to eat, but the Calif was known to love gold above all things, and he handled full much of it, piling it about, before he died of belly hunger and thirst. Hulaqu had marched only a hundred thousand of the people, on the pretense of counting them, to a nearby plain, but their bones lay out of sight beyond the city walls and half-a-hundred thousand children and babes nearly filled the gap. The huge caravanserai were a good half-full. The merchants offered great stores of silk stuffs and gold brocades, some of this so lavish with figures of birds and animals that the material for one robe cost two hundred bezants, or the same number of Persian dinars. And a Tatar governor still held court in the great palace of the Emir, made of sandalwood, ebony, ivory, jasper, lapis-lazuli, and black-and-white jade, and whose meanest stone was alabaster white as snow.

Yet it was whispered that a little way back from the caravan roads where his envoys rode amid pleasant sights, the mark of the Tatar was plain. There, half the water reservoirs and their aqueducts and wheels had been destroyed as if by playful giants, whereby whole countrysides were turned to desert, and this ever marched against the fertile farms; and in time all Mesopotamia, once the Garden of the World, the pride of kings, would become the sun-baked abode of a few shepherds, the lair of the lion, the pasture of the wild ass, and the haunt of the desert asp.

What did I care? Five years ago I had scarcely heard of Mesopotamia.

2

When we had reached the city of Hormuz, atop the straits of the same name, midway between the Persian Gulf and the Gulf of Oman, and so far from Venice that I could hardly believe in the same sun, it mattered greatly to me whether we continued our journey by land or by sea.

Nicolo wanted to go by sea. The voyage would be star-far, all around India and God knew what other vast lands outthrusting into the Indian Ocean, and then northward up the illimitable shores of China—but he reckoned it as shorter in the count of days, weeks, months, and years than the journey overland through the body of Asia. True, it would be a longer sail than any European had made since the world began. But men with dark or yellow skins sailed between port and port, goods were carried and traded, king's horses were transported, and every pilot's knowledge of reef and shoal overlapped his neighbor's. The danger should be no greater, Nicolo said, and the hardships somewhat less.

Maffeo believed what Nicolo said and did what he told him, but he was badly frightened of the Persian dhows on which we must seek passage—wooden craft innocent of an iron nail, their planks held together by ropes of coconut fiber.

Nicolo was a little less afraid only because he had other matters —mainly, to reach our destination as quickly as possible—on his mind. I was the like for a different reason. A good half of the people in and about the docks were either Arabs or spoke Arabic as well as Persian. Knowing a nation's language is a shibboleth whereby its queerest customs and strangest ways begin to show merit. These rope-stitched boats, anointed with whale oil, rode the choppy coastal water as limply as a Tatar did his rough-gaited pony. However, the great billows hurled by the tempest in the high ocean might tear one of them into scraps and tatters in one swoop.

Had the ships been as sturdy as a Venetian bireme, I would still have striven to go by land. In the first place, I was in no great haste to reach the Court of Kublai Khan—the longer in journey, in reason, the better schooled and muscled I would be for the tasks ahead. In the second place, riding the road across Asia was a harder and hence a far better school for a man of my abilities and ambitions than being batted about a hired cabin over the albatross path; before its end I would come closer to Nicolo in the lore of travel and the science of success.

In the third and fourth places, it was somewhat less expensive, and far more exciting. In the fifth place, if we went by sea, I could not get my hands on a helmet and a cloak and boots fashioned in a city called Fuchow, so far from us that you would think that ministering angels would lose their way.

"We'll go by sea," declared Nicolo to his brother Maffeo in the hearing of his unacknowledged son.

"If you say so," answered Maffeo, "but I shall leave moneys with the Nestorian priests to say Mass for my soul."

Still Nicolo would have held to it if a Tatar-speaking Persian had not come along selling opium pellets to ward off seasickness, and engaged him and Maffeo in a conversation of which I could not translate one word. However, this proved to be its general drift.

"Effendi, is the ship you are to take a new one or an old one?" the Persian asked, when they had made friends over the fact of knowing the same tongue.

"The latest from the yards, of course," Nicolo answered. "I don't trust those fiber fastenings not to weaken with use."

"Malik, if I tell you a secret known to the shipbuilders, but closely guarded from the merchants, will you give me back-sheesh?"

"If I count it of profit to know."

"It's true that the fiber ropes binding the planks grow weaker with age and use. The sailors care not for that, for if the ship falls apart in a gale they will speed straight to Paradise, to drink nectar and break maidenheads throughout eternity, but sober men think twice before entrusting their goods to these bottoms, let alone their lives. But if your Kismet ordains that you go to sea, in Allah's name—and there is no God but Allah—go forth in vessels five or more years old, and eschew the new."

"What's the sense of that?"

"The sixth year past was the Year of the Locust. They came in black swarms and stripped and killed the palm trees of Oman, whence came the strong fiber most prized by shipbuilders. In its place they bought fiber of Yemen, greatly inferior to the other. If you do not believe me, count the score of lost ships in these waters since that dread year."

"Could it be that you are in the pay of the owner of a fleet of old ships falling apart at the seams?"

"It must be that you've found me out, for now I'd accept no backsheesh even if you'd give it, and I beg that my saying go in one of effendi's ears and out the other."

"We must be on guard against tricksters, but it comes to me that you are honest, and I'll give you a silver dinar."

"I can't go back on my word, effendi, but I'll implore you Allah's blessing, and if it comes to you in the form of good offices from humble men like me, and thereby you live to pass this way again, you may give me a feast."

The opium seller salaamed deeply and went his way. When Nicolo investigated the report, he discovered that a new variety of fiber had been used in shipbuilding for about five years, although the builders maintained that it was fully as strong as the old. The more they thumped their palms with their fists, the greater the doubt raised in Nicolo's mind. Also the single-sailed craft, undecked except for hides, were small, foul, and crawling with rats and roaches.

So it came to pass that on Maffeo's next protest at the sea journey, Nicolo yielded, with fine handsomeness, to his wishes.[2]

As we set forth up the caravan road to Shamil and Nevergun Pass I pondered with my usual anxiety the words and deeds of Nicolo. His guess that the Tatar-speaking opium seller had been employed by owners of antiquated ships was on the right street but the wrong corner. The real truth was, the man also spoke Arabic, and had been employed by me.

The trick was of the caliber of the first I had played in my life-long war with Nicolo—falsifying his letter for the eyes of my uncle Zane. The cunning was of the same low sort and the immediate success of its operation as notable. Both had been hazardous, and in the first instance I had ultimately paid the piper. The piper's fee would be a great deal higher for the present dancing, and I could only pray to my saints and trust to my luck for deliverance therefrom.

But the saints are not supposed to support artifice and deceit, and Luck is a famous whore.

3

It is hard to believe that Hell itself is hotter than Hormuz. Sometimes a wind blows across the plain that must be the breath of Hell, for men breathe it and fall dead and their bodies give the appearance of being baked in a long, slow fire. During our stay there, it smote an army of nearly seven thousand marching to collect the king's tax from a recalcitrant prince, and since there was no water in which they could lie till the pall passed, not one life was spared.

Throughout the hot season no eyes in the city can shut with sleep, the rich seeking the coolness of their well-watered country villas and the lowest beggars fleeing the walls to lie beside the roads. With this, and the death wind striking without warning, you would think that folk would abandon the country to beasts, birds, snakes, and evil spirits. Instead it throngs with dark-skinned Mohammedans who appear to enjoy life almost as well as Venetians. They eat vast quantities of dates and fish. They drink a date wine, marvelously spiced, and a cordial more fragrant than musk and spikenard, known as Mohammed's Bouquet. They keep orchards of peaches, apricots, pomegranates, and oranges. They are born and die, hope, despair, fear, challenge, love. You would think them children of God, the same as ourselves.

Only two days north of Hormuz, we came on rough, rocky, gullied ground climbing steeply for a distance of twenty miles. Here we overtook some merchants waiting with their caravans for reinforcements ere they ventured on, and we were glad of their company in the journey forward. This wilderness, and that which lay beyond the great rich plains, were the abode of beasts more savage and terrible than the black-maned lions of the desert. They were some breed of Mongols, calling themselves Karaunas, and their business was raiding caravans. Our band being strong, we saw no hair or hide of the murderous rogues clean on to the Plain of Rúdbár.

This too had been fertile land until its towns and cities were laid waste. Still my eyes found much to brighten and delight them. On the sun-baked pastures ranged the fat-tailed sheep, almost as big as the little donkeys of Hormuz. The carts and plows were often drawn by immense oxen, snow-white, with a great hump on their shoulders—some of them kneeling like camels to receive their riders, and all of them beautiful in the noble way of beasts. Turtledoves winged from thorn grove to palm clump in multitudinous darting flocks, their pace ever seeming to quicken until it suddenly stopped short at the place of lighting. And among them ranged and slew the swiftest falcons I had ever seen—some sort of peregrines, I thought—their business in life declared by their blood-red breasts.

We ate of citronlike fruits with what appeared to be tooth marks in their skins, known as the apples of Paradise. It was said that they had grown from seed in the core that Adam dropped when he and his mate had shared a forbidden feast. And in the thickets dwelt a large black-and-white grouse, like to a francolin except for his flame-bright beak and feet; our Arab cameleers told us they had brought corn to Mohammed starving in the desert. Truly their evening cry sounded like Arabic words, saying,

"Sweet are the corn ears! Praised be Allah!"

The great plain was slightly tilted toward the distant mountains. Every day was cooler than the last, the landscape more wild and desolate. On an afternoon that we saw a lion asleep on a rock and met a gray wolf trotting down the road as though going to market, we were glad to find a mud-walled village in which we could seek shelter from the Karaunas. And since the settlement seemed indistinguishable from a hundred others scattered over the plain—a stretch of white road, a cluster of houses of sun-baked brick under date palms, a well, sheep and dogs and donkeys, and some score dark-skinned Infidels—how could we expect such a heart-warming scene as this we came upon at the village gate?

Two people were standing there, as though waiting for us, both of them a sight for homesick eyes. Not I, but most of our number, had some venerable kinsmen beyond the deserts whom one of the two recalled—this an aged man with snowy beard and hair whose proud bearing set at naught his shabby dress. That we could see his hair, instead of its being hidden under a turban, lifted the heart of every Christian in our company. It was almost certain proof that he was a Nestorian, cut off from all his kind except for one companion.

That companion was a damsel of not more than eighteen, unveiled, modestly but poorly dressed, and with a bright piece of embroidered cloth in her hand. One glance told me that she was among the few most beautiful, perhaps the very most, of all the damsels I had seen since leaving Venice long ago when I was young. Nor had the sum been small or its quality scurvy. My eyes had brushed a thousand agreeable faces since that departure to find out if even one could be as lovely as the one I had lost. A good many had been virgin slaves being transported to distant bazaars—and merchants who must count centesimi did not waste costly transport on homely faces. The girls I had seen in windows and on roof tops had wanted to be seen; since God made Eve, the plainest women have behaved the most properly. Moreover, God had scattered female beauty or its semblance from Ethiopia to Ultima Thule. It had been as rife in Baghdad as in Bologna.

Since leaving Venice, I had been true to the one I had lost. That was neither good sense nor sound philosophy—how can truth be kept with the nonexistent? Better say I had been continent out of respect to a memory. Even this was not the truth—continence does not count on Saint Peter's book unless it tugs against temptation. Suddenly it came to me, with a rush of joy, that I was cured of the distemper. Time is a gentleman, say the Chinese. He is a good physician, too, and while he had not healed my strange raw wound, I thought that he had reconciled me to inevitable loss. But perhaps I would be sorry that this particular damsel had been the one to waken these yearnings from their long, cold sleep. The captain of our company had seen her too.

There was no doubt of that captaincy. We were three caravans, traveling together for mutual protection, embracing about a dozen merchants rich enough to ride horses instead of Bactrian camels, but by the end of our first day together, Nicolo had become its acknowledged chief. Nor could I doubt the discernment of his eyes as he gazed upon the darkly glowing face and small, voluptuous form.

He drew up beside the gaffer and swept off his hat.

"I salute your years and honors, and hope that I may serve you and your charge," he said handsomely in his rich voice. This was duly translated into Persian by our Armenian interpreter.

"May Saint Thomas and Saint Theodore behold your charity to the aged and the weak and bring you benisons from the throne of God!" the old man answered in a firm and somehow thrilling voice.

"I rejoice to find a Christian in this unregenerate wilderness." Nicolo's large gray eyes glistened with emotion.

"Verily my granddaughter and I are of the True Faith, although poorly instructed in it. We're followers of Nestorius like our fathers before us, but I fear we are touched by heresy and tainted with heathenism. Think you the Holy Father would have mercy on us for the sake of our striving?"

"I've no doubt of it." And Nicolo too would forgive the taint, I thought. The heathen customs of some Central Asian folk often prove most convenient to Christian travelers.

There was something strange and no doubt heathenish in the maid's appearance and manner, but as I rode up with the other merchants to view her at close range, I found that bewitching. Perhaps she *was* a witch. Her mouth was redder by nature than any I had ever seen, and her oddly set black eyes more bright. They shone out of the dense forest of black lashes. She looked more like a picture of Pharaoh's daughter that I had seen in Alexandria than anyone I could recall. Her skin was a rich olive and her hair was dense, long and raven-black. She was wide between the temples, as are the Tatars, and perhaps there was a trace of Tatar in her sparkling blood. In spite of our gazing at her, she did not pretend to be shy, looking us over with a like lively interest. Her little unconscious movements appeared so graceful that I thought them lovely.

Above and beyond all this, there was something about her to excite the passions of every man, from youth to dotage, who looked at her. What that something was, all seven wise men of Ancient Greece could not have told.

"May we help you in some way?" Nicolo asked.

"Effendi, we're in great need of help. Know that my granddaughter, Araxie, has lately lost her husband. Hearing of it, I went from my village in the north to fetch her home. What gold and silver he owned was seized by his mother, and the little I have saved we spent on the road, but Araxie has left one piece of silk of her own needlework. If you will give us a place in your caravan, to ride upon the poorest of your beasts or to walk behind you in the dust until you gain Kerman, we will beg to give you the unworthy gift as a token of gratitude."

"Why, this is as fine embroidery as I've ever seen. It's fit to cover a pillow to rest a prince's head. So I take it you fear greatly the two-legged wolves, or you'd not pay such fare."

"I myself, effendi, have nothing to fear. I have no red money, let alone white or yellow, and I am too old to be worth my ironing as a slave. But when I travel with my grandchild, it's as though I go heavy with treasure. Forgive me, lord, my boastful words."

"They were not boastful, father, only a statement of fact I myself invited. Truly you may come with us, and without fee. But the sun is low and we'll not press on till tomorrow if the sheik will give us shelter behind his wall."

That worthy stood forth from the small crowd of turbanned onlookers. In the salaaming and other ceremonies going on between him and Nicolo, attention was drawn from the vivid dark face among the bearded ones. As far as I could tell, no eyes but mine were on it. She must have felt them, for her eyes wheeled to meet mine.

A slight lift of my brows asked a question. She raised her chin a little—perhaps it was a half-nod—and her lips curled a little on one side in a witchy smile.

CHAPTER 2

THE ARGHUN WOMAN

AS HAS BEEN SAID SINCE TIME OUT OF MIND, ONE LARK DOESN'T make a summer—and one half-smile is not a pledge of a maiden's favor. Yet I felt an inkling of happy fortune.

The next good augury came to pass well after the evening meal. A long-winded sheik and other worthy villagers had occupied Nicolo's time for a good hour; then he retired to the pavilion he shared with Maffeo with every sign of seeking a good night's sleep. He could be disguising his purpose, but I doubted if he would take the trouble. More likely he was not in the mood for adventure and chose to wait a more favorable time and place.

Throughout the journey I had made a point of greasing our interpreters' palms. Although they were a lying lot by nature—by pure human nature they could not resist taking advantage of their in-between position and all words passing through their mouths must pay a kind of toll—they were glad to lie in my favor if to their best gain. The Armenian Rusas, whom we had hired at Hormuz, was more my creature than Nicolo's. I had kept him reasonably honest by what seemed an uncanny penetration of some of his schemes—the simple matter of knowing Arabic—and besides, I paid him well.

"Rusas, has Signor Nicolo made any arrangements for obtaining the maiden's favor?" I asked when the camp had grown still.

"He bade me carry certain compliments to her. She thanked him kindly in her own name and the name of her husband in Heaven. Perhaps she was only whetting his appetite, but more likely she was a little afraid of one of his years and station, ambassador to the Great Khan."

"Perhaps her grief is still too great——"

"What could comfort it like a lover's arms? Of those she's been bereft for half a year—so her sire confided—and she's young and beautiful and, I would hazard, fiery. The gelding Patience was a good horse according to the tale, but the great stallion Impetuosity won the race. Although the signor is far from old, he's no longer a boy, and he wants all things in order, delivered to him at his own convenience, and not to miss a good night's sleep. And remember, young master—youth calls to youth."

Pleased with his show of sapience, Rusas took himself off. I lay down around the corner from the flood of moonlight and as still as though sound asleep, but my eyes were as open as an owl's and soon almost as sharp. A merchant setting down figures in a book closed it and blew out his candle. The last stirrings of the camp died fitfully away. The cameleers lay like casualities of battle, each under his white aba, unmoving as white rocks. Each flock of sheep reclined in its place, its members close to one another in some sort of love that awed my heart tonight, and the huge white oxen dozed on their feet, sometimes lowing softly. A whole great history of man was written here, I thought. I waited and watched for the sight of a beautiful maiden. . . .

After an hour's vigil I was all but certain that Araxie would not keep rendezvous. I had given her more than enough time, and it stood to reason that she had missed the signal I sent her, or was unable or unwilling to comply. Then I decided to give her another hour. Giving it to her was the right term, but in the way of a compliment or a tribute instead of a gift of value—I did not want it or have any use for it except to sleep through, and that was a dull employment. And while most maidens would come to meet a lover in the first hour, perhaps Araxie would not yield to his longings until the second.

What was sleep to me but a dark bridge between one adventure and another, and what were my dreams but the rippling waters that flowed beneath? The vigil was quiet and lonely and uneventful, but what I heard and saw and smelled was far more sharp than dreams. And this living of that hour instead of merely living through it—making something out of it instead of begrudging it—appeared to please the gods.

I saw what might be a peculiarly nimble young ghost floating among the shadows of the houses. It did not pass close to my lying place—if I were to see it at all, I must be wide-awake and on the lookout. As it started to move along the wall, I rose and took a course that would intercept it not far from the gate. I too avoided the spaces of bright moonlight. I did not want to catch some evil eye, or the attention of anyone who lay awake. Soon the byres hid me from any doorway or pavilion.

When I had drawn within a hundred paces of my tryster, she was no longer ghostlike, but as hard to see as a sprite in the web of light and shadow. If she had seen me, she had not acknowledged me. As she came close to the gate she stopped and looked back, but not as though in expectation of my coming. When she did see me, she gave the impression of being startled. She stood motionless a few seconds, then drew back into the shadow. I waved my hand.

When I came up to her she was standing midway between light and shade, her hands clasped, her raven hair flowing, her eyes long and lifted a little at the corners, and a dreamy beauty upon her face.

With this expression and her whole posture, her costume was in poetic keeping. A silken robe tucked in under her arms laid bare the swell of her breast and confided her small voluptuous form; over her naked shoulders hung the piece of embroidered silk her grandfather had offered Nicolo today; her black hair flowed, and her feet were bare of sandals. She let the shadows partly conceal her beauties in a show of shyness that was no doubt some old propriety among her people. Indeed I got the impression of time-honored formality not only in her bearing but in her dress. I was almost sure that a concubine of the sultan presented herself in this fashion when he summoned her to his couch on a moonlit court.

"*Koba* (Evening Star)!"

Her eyes that had avoided mine wheeled in surprise.

"Do you speak Arabic?" she asked in that tongue. But her pronunciation made it sound like some other language.

"It's almost my native tongue."

"Why, you speak it as it's spoken in very Oman!"

"I delight that you speak it also, moon of beauty."

"But the great malik—I think he's your father—spoke Tatar to my grandsire."

"I doubt if the Tatar language lends itself well to talk of love."

"It is good for discussing horses, hunting, and war. Arabic was my mother's tongue, and it has been pleasant to my ears, so the effendi will forgive me for lingering this long."

"I wouldn't forgive you if you left me."

"Lord, it's not fitting that we should meet so in the dark, both of us unattended, and I in immodest raiment. I was hot and could not sleep and the moon beguiled me——"

No doubt this was what a Sultan's concubine was supposed to say to her master, part of a time-honored ritual, when she had gone walking in her master's garden after a eunuch had whispered something in her ear.

"We needn't waste time or breath on the proprieties, bringer of delight," I broke in. "None are necessary after our eyes had met today, and you had given me a smile."

She stood quite still for several long-drawn seconds and an expression stole into her face that I could not read. If I were to guess it, she was half frightened, half wonder-struck. She gave me a furtive glance, then moved enough to bring her face and breast full into the moonlight.

"You called me Cobah," she remarked in a thoughtful tone.

"I think it fits you well."

"Perhaps you've mistaken me for a virgin. Instead I'm a widow of half a year, and I'm soon to become the wife of my husband's brother. That is the custom among my people."

"Then for the moment you are free."

"Effendi, is it your desire——?"

"My great desire."

Then my scalp tightened with the effect of creeping, for I remembered another meeting under the moon. It was far off in time and space. The stars were grouped the same, although some I had known had dropped behind the western horizon, and some I did not know had risen in the east. Our island there had been surrounded by silver waters instead of silver desert.

The beauty that I sought then was of another birth and order than that I was seeking now. Still, as the shock of remembrance passed I felt only gray regret. I had bartered away my pearl never to be reclaimed and I must make the most of my returns. I must no longer let the dead past cast shadows backward over the glimmering present.

2

I bent my head and kissed Araxie's rose-red mouth. And that rose was not of delicate and subdued hue, but the scarlet rose of Persia, red as the breast of the desert falcon. Her eyes began to shine with intense excitement.

"It's too dangerous here," she whispered.

"Where can we go?"

"Outside the gate. There's an old Mohammedan tomb close by——"

"Let's not have anything to do with death."

"Why, those bones have been dust a thousand years!"

"Still, we can't go out the gate, because there's no one to lock it behind us."

"There's no danger from the Karaunas tonight. There might be a greater danger inside the wall."

"I don't know what you mean."

"It doesn't matter. Follow me, my lord."

She stood poised—reminding me of a beautiful black-and-white bird with gay-colored wings about to take flight—until I nodded. Then she could hardly resist running in the light way of village girls, and when I would move cautiously from shadow to shadow, she became impatient. She clutched my hand and tugged it and hers was damp with sweat, but it was a smoother hand and more voluptuous than I would have expected from a field-working village girl.

"Take care, lest your grandsire see us," I whispered when she started to cross half an acre of smooth-spread moonlight.

"He's half-blind and sleeps like a babe," she answered in great impatience. "I'm more afraid of the sharp eyes of your sire."

"Why should you be? Has he——" But I did not know what to ask.

"He desires me himself, and I take him for one as proud and unyielding as a king."

"Would you rather have him? Decide quickly."

"No, I've chosen you."

"If you leave me to go to him, I'll kill you."

"By Gog and Magog, I never will."

Instead of angering or frightening my companion, the savage threat fanned her passion. With rough ardor, she clutched my neck and pressed the full length of her body and thighs against mine. Her belly thrust slowly forward until she stood in the shape of a drawn bow, my shoulders drawn atop hers and pressed down with great strength.

"Fall with me, man of the West!" she cried. "Am I not cushion enough for your tender bones?"

"Not into the dust." But I was half ashamed of my squeamishness, so out of place on an adventure of this kind, and troubled by some distaste of mind about the escapade itself. Whatever its cause, it did not curb the sudden, avid hunger of the flesh. I felt no tenderness toward the desert girl but knew she wanted none. She was beautiful in her wild way and I, and I thought she, had kept a long fast.

"Have the women of Frankistan taught you nothing, or are they eggshell frail?" she asked. "This is the way we Arghun women prove our lovers."

Arghun was a Tatar word I had heard Nicolo use. I thought it meant of mixed blood.

"I'm no Arghun man, but a Venetian."

"Then in Allah's name make haste."

Again she took my hand, and as fast as I would follow, led me by way of the shadows to a picket fence. It enclosed not more than half an acre, protecting from the livestock a stack of new-cut unthreshed millet. I felt a brief chill in following Araxie though the gate and closing it behind us. I had heard of capturing wild stallions on the steppes by tying a mare in heat in a pen with a drop barrier. The ground was bone-bare except for the dull glimmer of the high moon.

But we were a good way from the houses and largely screened by the cattle byres. Our only watchers that I knew of were huge white cattle, some of which lurched to their feet as though in good manners, and Bactrian baggage camels of low caste and malodor. Araxie uttered a low cry and flung off her beautifully embroidered silk scarf. It fell in the dust and her white robe fluttered down beside it in dishevelment. My own hands were busied now, but not fast enough to satisfy the itch in hers. Yet this frantic passion and my own response to it, more brutal in many respects than was ever aroused in me before, did not quite overcome what seemed self-disdain, but which might be only deeply submerged fear.

In some Asiatic tribes, the young women are frankly and overtly the wooers. That did not explain the culmination's seeming more a predatory binding in the dimness of the jungle than an embrace of human lust. But if she were a strange woman, she was also strangely beautiful. I knew ecstasy and felt exquisite pain.

At her peak of rapture, Araxie gave a high-pitched, convulsive cry. She had failed or had not tried to muffle the sound, and it would carry far through the stillness and disturb the villagers' sleep. I had no care for that, but was surprised by my own grim thought, like an eerie phantasy, that they would mistake it for the shriek of a desert fox. The spell slowly dissolved. Araxie lay still, her eyes uprolled and revealing silverlike crescents under the half-closed lids. I rose and saw that her pale-brown breast was smeared the same color as her lips, and these were even redder than before.

I looked at my chest and shoulders. But on touching the wounds, I found them trifling. I must wait till their flow ceased and wipe it away; then my shirt would hide the short twin rows of little cuts. I felt no need of haste—all fear of our tryst being discovered had passed from me. It might happen but I did not believe it. It seemed to me that the adventure would have some other end.

Araxie stirred, uttered a long sigh, and slowly opened her eyes. When she saw me she gave me a sleepy smile. But it checked quickly when she saw my chest.

"Did I do that?" she gasped.

"Unless a succubus took your place."

"Oh, do you know what it means?"

"No."

"You won't believe me, effendi, but it's true. You've put me with child." Her eyes glimmered incredibly in the pale light.

I shook my head in instinctive rejection of the thought. She wiped her mouth on the back of her hand, licked it clean, then spoke eagerly.

"Isn't it your blood? That's a sign that it will flow with mine in a new life. Already that life is kindled. It happened so with me only once before on the first full moon of my bridehood—and the sign did not fail."

Against my will, I swayed to the conviction in her voice.

"If that should be true, what would be the consequences?" I asked.

"None to trouble either you or me. I told you my husband's brother would make me one of his wives in a few days. He'll never know that the baby isn't his."

"Was your other baby—the first time you were given the sign —a boy or a girl?" But I did not know the bent of my own mind.

"A boy!"

"Was he a phoenix, born of fire?" I was flattering her because of some unknown fear.

"He was beautiful and bold, and if he had lived, he would have been a chief!"

"Did he die like so many babes of summer fever?"

"Not he. He was sick not one day in the month that he lived. He tugged at my teat like a pig, and grew fat and lusty."

"Then how did he come to die?"

"My husband, the babe's father, lately lost to me, became jealous of him and killed him."

I had heard the words clearly but I must have mistaken her proud tone.

"Why didn't you kill him in revenge?"

"He was my husband who had stolen me from my father's house when I was a virgin, and I loved him. Oh, I tell you we Arghun women know how to love."

Then a sign was given to me. It was only the shriek of a desert fox far away on the moonlit plain—a belated answer, I thought, to a cry he had heard several minutes ago and had thought upon in vain. I did not know the meaning of the sign.

3

The desert sun, threatening imminent heat, brought a great stirring. The cameleers yelled; their beasts twisted back their necks and tried to bite them, and the horses looked down their noses at such goings-on. The baggage wallahs heaved bales and boxes and fastened ropes; we merchants exchanged pleasantries until Nicolo bade us take our places. He had greeted me affably and asked if I had rested well. I could read nothing in his quiet smile and brilliant eyes.

Araxie and her grandsire were given seats atop a lightly loaded baggage camel. All hands were glad to have them with us on the road, the old man so venerable, and the damsel so beautiful; no one could look at them without pleasure. Otherwise the traveling was about the same as yesterday. Rather it was a gradual development of yesterday's trends. The plain's tilt became more pronounced; hills were more frequent and steep; brooks flowed swifter and straighter; there was less sand and more rock; the air was clearer and the copses larger and greener.

We came on a beggar clothed in vile rags, grimy hand outstretched. The merchants looked at him impassively and rode by; I turned in my saddle to watch the cameleers and the baggage wallahs look aside to avert the evil eye. But Araxie's grandsire gazed upon him with sorrow and pity, grieving that he had no money to give him, and of all our company, only Araxie herself leaned down and put something in his hand. The movement was wonderfully graceful. Her face was alight with happiness. I wondered if this were an act of gratitude to her gods.

"If there be honor among thieves, as the adage tells, a beggar maid can give to a beggar man," came a harsh voice beside me.

I felt a touch of anger. The speaker was Daniel, a swarthy Jew of Tabriz. If he had spoken slightingly of a Christian girl on the Rialto, he would have been spat upon. But remembering Simon ben Reuben and his parting gift to Miranda, I held my tongue.

"He gave her something in return," Daniel went on. "I suppose it was a charm of some sort. These foolish people buy written charms from so-called holy men, wash off the ink in a little water, and drink it. They think it brings them all sorts of benefits."

Such as the healthy growth and safe delivery of an unborn babe?

"She showed more charity than any of us," I remarked.

"Anyway she's a very beautiful girl. I would think her an Arghun—that's a Tatar word for a person of mixed blood. She has a dash of Tatar from a quarter other than the old man's. There's some fine Arab blood in the cross, and most likely Persian of Khurasan, famous for its beautiful women. But don't fall into the error of thinking of her as a Christian. In many of these regions the Nestorian Church has been contaminated with rank paganism."

"The old man told us that——"

"In effect he did. I'm still puzzling over it. The hooded duster that Maffeo Polo wore last evening looked something like a friar's gown—it may have been for his benefit. Anyway, young man, don't get involved with either of them. No doubt the girl would afford good sport and that's all right——"

I turned curtly away.

The heat mounted as the road roughened, and I would be glad when we stopped for our Mohammedan cameleers to say midday prayers. The beasts slipped and stumbled on the rocks, their drivers cursed; of all our company I saw only two who appeared unwearied and unruffled. One of them was Nicolo. He had made some sort of truce with the hardships of the way, yielding gracefully when he must, keeping intact his reserve strength, lithe in the saddle. The other was Araxie. Not merely serene, she took a positive joy in the long, grueling ride, and it was almost as irrepressible as her beauty. Trouble came into her face only when she glanced at her grandsire and this she tried to hide, I thought, lest we share her worries about him and begin to regard him as a burden on the caravan. While retaining his dignity of manner, he looked pale and under deep strain.

About half an hour short of noon according to my sand glass, we came to a ford on a tributary of the Halil Rud. Apparently it had offered a fairly easy crossing until lately: now the banks had slid, leaving them impassably steep. Detour would be difficult because of gullied ground and thorn thickets. As the drivers scratched their heads, Araxie called to her grandsire in a pleasantly excited tone and in a language I did not recognize. He answered gravely, then spoke to Nicolo through an interpreter.

"My granddaughter has reminded me of another crossing not two arrow casts from here. It is used by the villagers at Konsalmi, and is reached by a bridle path we crossed a stone's throw back."

"God's grace upon you both, and you've earned your passage," Nicolo replied.

We retreated the short distance and took up the path. Rough and little-used, it led into a natural amphitheater, its brush-grown rims about two hundred paces broad, and fronting on the stream. The ford looked easy but we were not to essay it yet.

With a low groan, Araxie's grandsire clutched his throat and began to topple from his seat.

Three stout drivers checked his fall and eased him to the ground. At the same instant Araxie leaped down and ran to him, crying. Drawing his gray head into her lap, she began to stroke his brow, meanwhile murmuring a prayer.

The whole caravan had stopped in disorder. The marchers left their ranks to crowd about the fallen patriarch, and we horsemen in the van turned back to his help. Most of our number dismounted. I kept my seat with the thought of riding ahead to a village about half a mile beyond the ford, whose sun-baked white walls glimmered through the thorn scrub and whose oasis of date palms raised cool green plumes against the burning-glass sky.

Then I noticed that the Jew Daniel had not dismounted or made any other move to help the gaffer and was looking down at him with cold, alert eyes.

Daniel felt my angry glance and flushed. "I'm sorry I can't join in the commiseration," he told me in low tones.

"What do you mean?"

"This is a show of some kind. He knew those cameleers would catch him. I think the young beauty's going to need twenty dinars for some rare drugs. I suspected her when the old man told that lie about the scarf."

"What lie?"

"That she'd embroidered it herself. I saw it a good month ago in the stock of Kamul, the silk merchant, as he was loading his caravan at Shiraz."

"Didn't you know that caravan was ambushed by the Karaunas and wiped out?"

"*What?*"

I did not answer. Instead I wiped sweat from my brow, meanwhile peering through my fingers with every strength and effort of my eyes. I looked to the heavy thorn scrub that grew halfway down the walls of the amphitheater. A silver twinkle, instantly disappearing, was sunlight on a polished spearhead or harness metal. Then there was a stir off and on along the edge of the thickets, as if a giant serpent lying there were shifting his coils. It was inaudible and it would have been invisible except for the desperate probing of my eyes, and I would not have guessed its meaning if my mind had not already leaped to a dreadful truth.

The stir was caused by a line of a hundred or more horsemen slowly raising their bows.

Their mounts stood statue-still, silent at the scent of ours blown to them on the breeze, and this was not all their training. After the first flight of arrows they would leap down the steeps like stags, needing no guiding but a little shift of weight by their in-human riders. Our horses and camels that did not fall or stampede at the first volley could not carry us far in the winged hail to follow. And for that little way, only our best steeds could keep pace with the Tatar ponies.

All this came to me as a vista revealed by lightning. I saw the arrows being nocked with slow, steady movements and the bows stealthily drawn. My mare was headed away from the ford. She bounded forward as I roweled her cruelly, but wheeled to my drawn bit. The quick turn fetched her on the course I must take and my howl had already drowned out every other sound and rang against the rocks.

"*Karaunas! Karaunas! Follow me!*"

Leaping from my spur, the mare did not quite clear an obstruction. I felt her front hoof sink into what seemed soft wet ground. No doubt the patriarch opened his eyes and saw the sky once more before darkness filled them, and his death scream had just started its sky climb as I dropped my reins over the pummel and bent low in the saddle. With one hand I clutched a big rope-like hank of Araxie's hair. With the other I caught in her armpit as with a hook. Her upper garments ripped away and she screamed with pain, but my grip held, and by a great wrench of muscle and bone I heaved her in front of me, half in my lap in the chairlike saddle, and half jammed against the peak. She had little room to struggle and at once became helpless to do so under the press of my arm.

I made one dash straight away from the ambushed horde. For the instant I did not think they had eyes for anyone but my captive and me.

I began to wheel toward the ford. Our other horsemen bounded into their saddles and followed Nicolo on a cut that would intercept my course. With a half-turn I got between them and the bowmen. I was quite sure they would not let fly in my direction.

But with a howl like the hungry chorus of a hundred wolves, they broke from their ambush and came bounding down the slope. At least twoscore in the vanguard set off in our pursuit; the rest cut off the flight of the cameleers and surrounded the rest of the caravan. Yelling like devils, they shot arrows into the backs of all who tried to fly and drove lances into the breasts of the few who chose to fight rather than be sold for galley slaves.

I watched these killings over my shoulder and was very glad of Araxie's close company on this ride.

We splashed through the ford—Nicolo leading now, Maffeo and seven other merchants in a band, I on the rear flank between them and our pursuers. As the Karaunas took a short cut to bring them on our flank, I dashed forward with joy in my heart that I wore such magic armor, protecting me and nine of my fellow travelers. Araxie might be the daughter of a Karauna chief, I thought; more likely she was his mistress.

Our horses ran with their necks stretched, tails arched a little, picking up their hoofs cleanly, for they were mostly excellent Badakhshans, costing up to two hundred dinars. But Darchill, a stingy Georgian Christian, had bought him a lowborn nag, priding himself upon his thrift; and now the jingle of the gold he had saved was a poor buckler against the nearing howls of the Tatars. Their ponies were shorter and shaggier, not quite as swift as ours on good ground, but wondrous coverers of rough going, impervious as their masters to heat or cold, and tireless as wild asses. Happily we were running on a cattle track between ford and village, and at the very longest, the race would be short.

"Let me go!" my captive wailed.

"In due course," I answered, stopping her wriggling with my arm.

"It wasn't my fault. I've been true to you, I swear before Jesu and all the saints! How could I know that the black horde lay in wait——"

"The beggar brought you word where to lead us. But you missed the chance for a clean sweep last night when I wouldn't go with you outside the gate."

"May I fall dead if I lie——"

I did not hear the rest. I was watching Darchill on his cheap scrub. He had dropped five yards behind our body, farther than the wildest Tatar arrow would miss its mark. At least ten came arching from the wild riders' bows. The range was a hundred paces, aim was impossible from the bounding backs of the rough-gaited ponies, yet all but one of the ten passed within twelve feet of the horror-stricken rider. The tenth arrow took him at the base of the neck. He screamed, flung wide his arms, and tumbled to the dust.

"Last night you seemed surprised to see me," I told my light-o'-love. "I thought you were pretending for propriety's sake, but you really were surprised. You hadn't given me a sign—I imagined it. You didn't want to be seen when you crept out in the dark. You were making for the gate, and you intended to open it to your companions waiting outside."

"Yes, but that was before I lay in your arms. Truly I'm a woman of the Karaunas, but I only obeyed the orders of our Khan. And after we had become lovers, I sent word by the beggar that you were to be spared."

"You intended to stay with me?"

"I would follow you to the world's end!"

"You are very beautiful, Araxie. Your back shines in the sun, and I wish we could stop and make love. But I must go into the village and close the gate behind me."

"Those villagers know me and will kill me. So check your speed a little just before you dash through and let me slide off."

I did not answer. I was watching the race and anticipating its finish. Our shouts had aroused the villagers, who had come in from their fields for noonday rest and repast, and at present were gathering about the gate of the earthen wall. They paid taxes and obeisance to a district governor. He might himself be a Tatar—at least he was remotely subject to Kublai Khan, a Mongolian Tatar —but the prosperity of the land stemmed from its commerce, and he would raze any village that took sides with the bandits. We had gained a little on our pursuers and they were nearly out of arrow cast. Except for some unforeseen disaster we could dash through the gate in time for the waiting villagers to swing it shut behind us and drop the bar.

There would probably be time enough for me to check my speed a little and let Araxie slide off. She would be flayed and bruised and perhaps break a bone, but she would live to remember our love-making.

"Let me go!" she cried.

"Not yet."

"Remember our embrace under the moon!"

"I'll never forget as long as I live."

"Let me go! Their arrows can't fly this far."

"Why, I think you're right, but we'll wait a moment more."

In the moment that we waited, one of the horses of our fleet band stepped in a gopher hole. I heard the sharp crack of his leg bone breaking, then saw him shatter down. I caught only a glimpse of his fallen rider, then lost sight of him in the dust. He was Daniel the Jew.

"You're waiting too long," my companion wailed. "The villagers will kill me."

"No, you'll be safe from them."

"You'll gain the gate in a moment more. Check your horse as you let me off, or I may break my neck."

"The fall won't hurt you, I promise."

"But you're riding as hard as before! Let me off now—quick —before too late. Remember what's between us! I'm your woman and your seed is in my womb!"

"That I know, and it pains me to part with you. Still, I'll let you off."

But before I did so, I drove my dagger blade deep between her beauteous breasts.[3]

CHAPTER 3

LORD OF THE RUINS

I T IS A LONG, DESOLATE, AND WEARY ROAD FROM KERMAN NORTH-
ward, and its only mercy on us was of a perverse sort. Because
we had met the Karaunas, we traveled light.

Of the five merchants other than Polos who escaped alive, only
two were going our way to Meshed. They, like us, were as naked
of stuffs as a new-hatched jackdaw of feathers, having saved only
their gold and jewels carried in saddle pouches. One of the pair
gladly fell in with our notion not to lay in any more until we had
crossed the desert, whereby we would need transport only for
food and water for ourselves and the beasts and a few belongings.
The other merchant yearned for the riches of Kerman—saddles,
bridles, and harness fit for kings, embroidered pillows and quilts
for favorites' beds, and casts of falcons—but Nicolo told him that
the most he could take would be a quart or two of turquoises;
otherwise we would leave him to eat his goods on the road.

It would be a dreadful road to be left on. For three days' march
it was only a dusty track through desolation. We were used to
gazing far and wide without seeing a human habitation; now we
often looked in vain for a living leaf. It was a land accursed. The
only water was green and poisonous. Riding through it on a half-
crazed horse, I feared God as I never had in snow or storm, and
beheld the Devil just behind my shoulder.

My heart leaped at only the sight of the moon, old and sick
though she was above the waste, for she told me that this was
still part and parcel of our dear world, and my tears nigh flowed
from being made to think of Miranda, Mustapha, and all the rest
I had lost. Perhaps God's purpose in fashioning this desert was
to remind us how little worlds were worth without people and
their fellow living things.

On the first night, the sun-baked ground turned quickly cold,
its heat sucked out by the moistureless air as the warmth of a
man's body is by the kiss of death. But on the second night, a hot
wind blew across the sands as though to stop our mouths with
dust and shrivel us to mummies. And in the gray and gruesome
midnight, the merchant whom we knew as Lazarus, some sort of
Syrian, the one who had yearned for the fleshpots of Kerman, rose

from his bed with a dreadful cry and ran off from the camp and vanished in the murk.

We followed his footprints as demons followed ours. After we had gone a quarter of a mile, walking instead of wildly running like our quarry, we doubted whether we would find him alive. Presently we heard a noise that must be of his making, although dreadful to believe it the issue from a human throat. With harrowed souls we pushed on to behold him lying crumpled at the foot of a cliff with his head twisted about on his neck. No doubt he had stared behind him as he ran—at God only knew what pursuer—and such was his posture as he fell. He lay on his belly and side, but his face was turned to ours as we came down to him, and his pale eyes stared into ours.

We searched his belongings for some clue to his kith and kin, but we could find none, nor discover his place of habitation, nor even what God he worshiped. Then we remembered that this stretch of sunburned hell lay within the kingdom of Kerman. Its king paid tribute to a distant emperor but ruled with a haughty hand. One of his laws read that if any foreign merchant died in his domain, all of his goods above the cost of a winding sheet must go to the royal coffers.

So, sitting in the dark, Nicolo, Maffeo, our last companion, and I reckoned the worth of Lazarus's horse, saddle, and camels, added thereto the price of his turquoises and the count of his gold, and divided the total into four shares. He was far richer than we had thought, and the windfall more than recouped the loss of our goods to the bandits. Then we wrapped his body in the cloths of his pavilion and buried it in a deep grave in the sand. There we left him, so lonely that I wean he wished for a desert wolf to updig his bones and gnaw them.

There were no wolves here, not even vultures in the way of birds, no lizards on the stone. Late in the afternoon of the third day we saw a black-and-white bird that seemed of unearthly beauty, and at sundown a long narrow strip of sparse, sear vegetation marking the course of an underground canal. It stretched farther than we could see and had holes dug here and there for travelers' use. It had been built by slaves in the days of Nebuchadrezzar.

Here we rested and refreshed ourselves and our beasts for two days.

The desert was a little less absolute in the next four marches, we seeing some creeping things and most marvelously running things, the last being wild asses. Then we came to the good city of Ku-banan, whose name means "The Hill of the Wild Pistachios." Here we laid in medicines and iron and steel works of surpassing quality, including mirrors that would reflect a face as perfectly as a deep, moss-grown well. It was pleasant to see people doing something besides traveling, and we were sorry to leave them when, after a fortnight's trading, again we pressed on.

In eight days, that in my nightmares seemed eight years, we crossed another wasteland to the province of Tunocain, well peopled, and famous for the beauty of its women. Here we were shown a Holy Tree, the breaking of one twig therefrom being punished with death. Some said it supplied Adam his staff and Moses his rod, while the devil-ridden Nestorian Christians, not to be outdone, declared that the Cross had been cut from its mighty limbs. But these tales were probably mythical, while the story of the Old Man of the Mountains, who had lived and reigned in my own time, was based on truth.

He was the hereditary head of a sect of Ismaelians, themselves heretics outside of the Mohammedan fold, and according to their hocus-pocus, an incarnation of Divinity itself. By walling in the entrance to a beautiful valley between mountains, he laid out a magnificent garden, with palaces, fountains, and orchards, and even mechanical runnels from which milk or honey flowed when a tap was opened. When his mullahs spied a likely youth fit to be a member of the murderous band that served him, he was given a sleeping potion, brought within the garden, dressed in jeweled raiment, and wakened by sweet music. All-but-naked maidens of singular beauty brought him fragrant fruits, delicious viands, and exquisite wines; they danced or sang at his pleasure, and when a more rampant hunger came upon him, he could have one or all of the beauteous bevy at his nod.

After some days of this he was again drugged and restored to his former place. Pining for the Paradise he had lost, he was told by the mullahs that he had made a trial trip there, and could return if he took the Old Man of the Mountains for his god and ruler. Thus was recruited a troop of robbers whose raids enriched their master, and who slew all who stood in the way of his supreme power. Since they smoked or ate bhang, Indian hemp, which in Persia was called hashish, they called themselves the Hashishins. On Western lips, the name became Assassins, and as such was known in Venice.

The Old Man of the Mountains became the actual lord of a

vast territory, only to be besieged and slain by an army sent by
Hulagu Khan, brother of the Emperor Mangu Khan, eighteen
years before. Of his band of Assassins, most were slain, but a few
found eyries in mountain fastnesses, from which they still harry
the land and rob the caravans.[4]

A venerable silk merchant, wearing the badge of a hadji, was
pointed out to me as a former member of the murderous horde,
but having made a pilgrimage to Mecca and his peace with Allah,
he had the favor of the Calif and hopes of a real Paradise behind
the sunset.

"Is the story true?" I asked him, after he had given me a long-
stored sherbet of figs.

"The garden, with its bright pavilions and gilded palaces, was
as real as yon doorpost. So were the fruits, wines, and beautiful
maidens. But only the dullest lumpkin ever dreamed he was in
Paradise. He pretended to do so only to enjoy its blessings."

"What disillusioned you?"

"A melon that was served me was overripe—that alone was a
flaw I did not think Allah would countenance—and it fluxed me."

So be it with every garden and every gardener that presumes to
be divine!

2

We crossed the great land of Dasht-i-Lut. The old and yellow
moon that had shown us the dead face of Lazarus on the desert
of death rose silver-white and full, its second or third waxing,
over the great caravanserai of Meshed. The city lay near the
eastern borders of Persia, below the endless sands of the Kara
Kum; and ten thousand caravans passed through the gates in its
ninety-foot earthen wall from year to year. Within were pleasant
running streams, rich hostelries, bazaars without end, and the
Brides of the Oasis.

So were called the thousand beautiful young girls whom the
Imam allowed to marry travelers for as long or as short a time
as they remained in Meshed. Since there was always a rush of
recruits, virgins were not difficult to find, many of them belonging
to well-off families; however, they expected a larger bridal gift
than the many-times-widowed. We merchants and many of our
followers had been looking forward to the treat for long, dusty
days, and we could hardly wait for our goods to be stowed ere
we went wife-hunting.[5]

I was shown the prettiest in the bevy. So a dragoman had assured me, his eyes rolled to heaven and both hands on his heart and his voice atremble with emotion, and if he had lied, by witness of my own eyes, I could cut his throat. She was a virgin in her fourteenth year. The reason that I might have her was that she had agreed to become a Bride of the Oasis only if her initiator was a presentable youth, under twenty, and of good station. And since this had straitly limited the number of candidates, her bridal gift need not be more than fifty dinars for my fortnight's stay.

Her name was Esther and she came into her father's rose garden to look at me through her veil. Evidently she was satisfied to take me for her mate in her bridal adventure, because the silk became caught in a rose thorn and disclosed her face. To think that I could have her for those days thrilled my flesh and, unless the Devil gulled me, exalted my soul.

She was lovely as any Venetian girl of fourteen and the slave trader Paulos Angelos would gladly have bought her for nine hundred pieces of gold.

This meeting occurred in the morning after my first night in Meshed. Abdul the dragoman promised to deliver her to my quarters in the caravanserai at sundown. All day I walked on air, but when the sun winked out of sight behind the western rocks, and the light began to dim, and the breeze off the desert blew fresh in my face, and the sand kept running through my glass, I fell hard to the ground.

Posting a boy at my door in case somebody came, I went out into the crowded square to look for Abdul. I did not find him, but before the moon was over the roof tops, I spoke with a *chokoda*, a kind of gate keeper, just outside the wall of Esther's garden.

"Abdul is an underling to the serai master," the fellow told me. "You should have dealt with the effendi himself. A great sheik looked at her, and to her great joy, she found favor in his sight. So he sent for her in a handsome hired palanquin at the fourth hour past noon."

"But she promised to come to me."

"I am sorry, effendi. You know the fickleness of youth."

"You say he was a great sheik. Such are not commonly found in men under twenty."

"She changed her mind about that condition when she saw him. But truly he is not a day over thirty."

"Will you give me his name? I will send him a peacock plume in tribute."

"Why, it's no secret. He's an ambassador to the Great Khan from Frankistan—and his name is the same as the game played on horseback by the lords of Kabul."

"No matter. There are many fine fish in the sea."

But I did not drop a golden hook to catch one. I would not so dance attendance on Defeat.

From Meshed, it was no great feat to get to Balkh. The distance might not be more than five hundred miles by crow flight, provided a crow could find his forage in the mountains and desert, and not stay to gorge on the melons of Shibargh. But we went on camelback and horseback and shank's mare. We wheeled four days to pass a single well of brackish water. Then, making our way up the valley of the Upper Oxus, amid watered fields and orchards or blackened earth, we came unto Balkh, above the Hindu Kush and almost at the western gate of the mighty Pamir. This was known as the Mother of Cities. It had boasted mosques as beautiful as Samarkand's, which were upstarts compared to the Buddhist temples and reliquaries, which were innovations compared to the shrine of Zoroaster, who had died within these walls. But only fifty years ago, the city had come into the disfavor of Genghis Khan. After promising them immunity, he caused all those who could keep pace to march onto the plain—men, women, and children to the number of fifty thousand—and slaughtered every one. The halls of the college and the towers and palaces were razed to the ground.

A few sick got well. Old men and women doddered about cleaning out the wells and gathering a little corn. Babes in the cradle grew up, and with the strangers drifting in, they catered to the caravans from Tehran or Khotan, Samarkand or Kabul. So once more there were caravanserais within the walls, along with bazaars and beast marts and wine booths and bagnios, and even people's abodes if you looked for them. But all the attar of rose, spikenard, musk, myrrh, and frankincense borne back and forth from the sands to the snow could not sweeten its smell of death.

We spent nearly a month there, prospering well, then set forth again. About three miles beyond the city walls toward Talekan, our caravan was delayed by a sudden panic among the beasts, caused, we thought, by the smell of a leprous beggar on the road. While the baggage wallahs were reloading and roping, I rode my mare Fatima across a rubble-strewn field to the ruins of a con-

siderable court. I was thinking of the kings that had gloried there,
very Tiglath-pilesers according to their courtiers, and in their own
conceits except for a small, chill doubt that sometimes smote them
in the belly more than the brain. My thoughts were arrested by a
stirring in the reeds around a broken water tank. Thinking it might
be caused by a wild pig, as such animals frequent the long-for-
saken abodes of man, good meat to us Christians and unabhorred
by many good Mohammedans who gag at the thought of tame
pig, I strung my bow.

The movement ceased. Since I had foolishly approached from
upwind, it seemed likely the beast had smelled my mare and me
and crept away. I could go no further on horseback because of
the broken rock, and was at the brink of turning back when I saw
Nicolo making toward me on his beautiful dappled Arab stallion
Godfrey. His strung bow was handy on his back and his hand
grasped a borrowed lance, a favorite arm for swine-hunting in
this part of the world.

The fever took me to beat him to the kill. Quickly tieing Fatima
to a shrub, I crept behind the ruins of a magnificent marble terrace, my arrow cocked and ready to draw. I hoped to surprise
the quarry in what I now perceived was the remains of an aque-
duct, rank with growth.

At that moment I discovered that not all the kings had gone.

3

One king remained. In many qualities honored in kings, he was
the greatest of all.[6] He was a black-maned lion, weighing a quarter of a ton, so bold that he made his lair within three hundred
paces of a caravan road. At night he roamed far and wide, preying
on deer, wild boars, and cattle and horses in their arid pastures,
and slaughtering helpless sheep with what his fellow monarchs
call the divine right of kings. Where most he showed illustrious
was in hunting the wild ass, most swift and one of the most beautiful of all created things. He would stalk them, a dun shadow
in the scanty grass, until he drew within a stone's throw; then
swift as a stone cast by a sling he rushed upon them. They could
outrun him at full tilt, but often he overtook them before they
could get their hoofs under them to fly.

Sometimes he stalked and sprang upon a man, only to be perplexed, almost frightened, a sense of something strange and evil
clouding his brute brain, that so tall and seemingly such glorious

quarry should die before he had half bared his fangs. Ere he had bloodied half the crooked spikes set in his great mauls, the great trophy he had sought had turned into a limp, loose bag of broken bones. Its head that had loomed so high burst apart like an ostrich egg at a glancing lash of his paw. He had no use for the awful fury and blazing power set off within him, and his veins almost burst from the thwarted surging of his blood; and to worry the dead thing made him feel silly in the sight of God.

He had not killed last night, otherwise he would have gorged, lolled back to his lair at dawn, and slept like a swine. All his stratagems had failed, and now his shame and anger as much as his hunger pangs kept him awake. He sprang from the ditch, cleared the terrace in two unbelievable bounds, and rushed upon my mare. She saw him and whirled to fly. Her stout rein broke like thread at her first leap, but death was upon her before she could stretch her legs. It was a death she had seen when a foal on the deserts of Oman, and her most evil dream.

He did not mount her and I did not see the deathblow that he gave her. One instant, they were both in extreme exertion, she to live, he to kill. There was nothing else than that, at this instant; and the ruined palace on the brown desert was its perfect setting. My eyes had never beheld such violence, and started from their sockets. The next instant, she had been hurled down with a broken neck, her killer crouching over her with his great head turning and his blazing eyes seeking some new outlet for his rapturous rage.

As his gaze met mine, I launched my arrow.

The bow and arrow is a weak weapon for such game as this. A Tatar lance or even a Toledo spear would stand me in far better stead should the beast attack me; by crouching under it and holding it firmly, his own furious rush could drive it through him as if it were thrown by a giant. An arrow may kill from a good distance if it strikes the quarry in a vital spot; but the more strong-lived beasts usually lived until inward bleeding overwhelmed their hearts, and in that interim they craved to avenge their death wound. In this case the range was short. The lion was already in his rage like a Northman gone berserk in battle, so his life force was many times magnified and he could fight on and kill after his heart had stopped and his soul had passed. If he retaliated with all his might to the sting of my arrow, I would have no time to launch another. Thus my shooting at him at all had been a most rash act; and my thoughts, flying arrow-swift, told me that this moment, among these ruins, could be my final moment.

Even so, excited strength of my arm and shoulder, pivoted against my loins, had gone into the draw, and the long English bow became a deep inverted D standing for Death. I loosed cleanly and the string thrummed. I saw the shaft in its swift dart and its plunge of half its length in the beast's side.

He gave forth a short roar and with a sideways lunge of his head he sank his teeth in the shoulder of his dead prey. This action, eloquent of the brute brain, gave me time to snatch another arrow from my sheaf. Then it was as though I had snatched at time and missed. I counted time's dreadful lack in an instantaneous calculation such as may be the last mental process of thousands of men meeting sudden death. The lion had recognized me as his enemy and directly moved to attack. I saw the movement start and fate had decreed I should live long enough to contemplate it as it was etched on my memory. No wild beast's action could be more splendid, more beautiful in its perfect functioning, and more declaratory of the glory of God.

During his first bound toward me, he marshaled himself for his charge. You could think of it as girding up his loins, but he could not bear one instant's delay in joining battle, and the efficiency of the act was a terrible testament to its ferocity. He landed with his head down, his feet under him and already driving at great speed, his tail rammed out. Speed was his extreme compulsion until he could reach me and kill me. He raced against the fury in his heart—as though it would explode unless he could straightway sink his claws and fangs in enemy flesh.[7]

In that little interval not yet ended, I too functioned at the extreme height of my powers. My battle was not with my attacker, but with myself. I had almost no sense of a continuity of events; all seemed one explosion. Only by reaching beyond myself could I perceive the drag of time—that it had not yet gone and I must still strive on. Terror lashed at me to run. Thereby I would not see the fangs and claws as they closed in, and by my living a second or two longer, I might better the chance of an extraneous force, now bearing down upon the scene, moving in my favor. Nor could I abrogate Death by looking him in the face: I could only defy him. I was nocking my arrow now, but except for a stroke of fate I would not have time to draw.

I continued the effort in some strange and tragic defiance of known and unknown foes. My soul gave the command as though it were a haughty thing instead of the poor thing it often showed itself to be, and I obeyed.

If Fate struck, it would be by the hand of Nicolo. He had been riding fast when I first saw him; when he saw the lion he had spurred the tall dappled Arab into its utmost run. The course he had taken was intended to intercept the lion's course at almost his last stride. Long and lean though the chance was, there was no other.

I did not believe it. Instead I actively disbelieved it without any recognizable process of thought. Nicolo might pretend to try to save me, more for my eyes than for those of onlookers, and at the last instant let me fall. This was my preconceived conviction. He had not unslung his bow—no doubt he knew as well as I did that he was not equal to the shot—and his apparent purpose was to catch the beast on his lance point. Beliefs stored in my brain denied that he could force the Arab that near his ancestral enemy.

In this last supposition, I was wrong. The stallion never faltered from the course his master had set and ran as fiercely as a trooper's steed in the full charge. It had slipped my mind that many of the finest horses in Central Asia were trained to intercept running game. His neck was stretched, his ears laid back, his snowy mane rose and fell, while Nicolo rode like a dervish. The dun killer's big black mane set off his pearl-bright fangs and he gave forth a deep-toned coughing roar. Their nearing courses gave the effect of the two lords of the desert being drawn together by some elemental force.

For any of us four who survived, the scene among the multi-colored stones, under the steel-blue sky in the white sunlight of midmorning, would be one to remember always. It might return and return to the dreams of the drowsing beasts, or suddenly cast Nicolo or me into deepest reverie.

Nicolo leaned forward and half out of the saddle, thrusting the long lance. The point missed the tawny side and only gashed the beast's shoulder with a glancing blow, but it arrested his terrible charge. As he turned to fight, the rumbling thunder in his throat changed to a short growl of surpassing violence. Then the gods must have looked down in wonder and admiration, for the stallion reared up on his hind legs, tall and taller till he loomed giantlike in form as well as in valor, and tried to strike with his forefeet.

These great events had dwarfed my own struggle to survive, but I was no bystander. Drawing my bow with my full strength, I drove an arrow as with a sledge hammer into the lion's flank. As he whipped his maned head to bite at the shaft, Nicolo's spear leaped forward again. Its lightning played against the tawny hide while its steel plunged deep. The beast's great start as it pierced his vitals wrenched the weapon from Nicolo's hand, and his throes broke the shaft.

Once more he reared up to attack, in an awful silence now, but his strength was waning fast, and a terrific blow from the screaming stallion knocked him on his back. He rolled over—tried to get up—fell back with a groan. For a moment more he lay sobbing in the dust, then he stretched his legs and his neck and tail, shuddered, and died.

"You came at a very lucky time for me," I told Nicolo as the dust began to settle. I could not keep my voice from trembling.

"It wasn't altogether luck," he answered gravely and with deep calm. "I suspected that the caravan beasts smelled something more frightening than a leper. And there was talk at the caravanserai of lions hereabouts."

My head swam and my knees almost buckled under me. To cover this, I walked over to look at Fatima, vultures' meat now.

"You'll need another horse," Nicolo remarked thoughtfully.

"I wouldn't've if you hadn't arrived when you did."

"Probably you'll have to make out with a scrub until we get to the great horse market in Badakhshan."

"Both the mare and I would be in the same boat," I persisted.

"It's said that the breed of Bucephalus was obtainable there until very recently, but the widow of the breeder killed all the pure stock in some act of revenge." Nicolo swung down for a better view of the lion.

"I'm under great obligation to you, signor, for coming to my help," I said, the cords of my neck taut.

"Not at all."

"Will you accept my thanks?"

"Certainly not, when you don't owe them."

"Will you enlighten me as to why I don't owe them?"

"I owed you a debt. Your quick work saved Maffeo and me as well as several others from the Karaunas. I don't like owing debts to anyone, much less to an upstart bastard out of my wife. Now the score is paid."

He rubbed his hands as though washing them, sprang lightly on his horse, and cantered away.

CHAPTER 4

KING OF THE SNOWS

IN TWELVE DAYS' MARCH FROM BALKH, WE CAME TO THE FORTI-fied town of Talikun, in a fertile land close by a mountain of solid salt. Here the Mohammedan population is almost as wayward from the tenets of the Prophet as Nestorians from the teachings of the true Church. But they are great hunters as well as heavy topers of their thick, sweet wine; thievish but hospitable; half-civilized but good to look upon, with tall, well-molded bodies, ruddy skins, yellow to brown hair, and hazel eyes. I enjoyed meeting them on the roads and the close company of one of their prettiest daughters at the caravanserai at Qishm. Near the town stands the Mount of the Zend-Avestam, sacred to the Parsis, where burned the holiest fire in all the world, brought there by the hero Jamshid. Myself and Roxana—to my delight, the maid was named after very Alexander's bride—lighted a fire of our own. It was not holy that I knew of, but most certainly beautiful, and it would glow in my memory for many a moon.

Beyond Qishm lay desolation as complete as it seemed without end, but we crossed it in three days. Then we came upon wonderful highlands, part of the great kingdom of Badakhshan under the Hindu Kush, and here I bought a marvelous red-bay mare with a white star on her forehead. It was the mark of Bucephalus, the seller told me, but I cared naught for that, when I had taken her down a rocky defile at full tilt. She was as sure-footed as a goat, swift as a mountain sheep, and I believed brave as a lion. I named her Roxana in remembrance of my good companion.

We moved among high mountains now, in the coolest and most bracing of air. We ate wild-sheep meat, the best in the world for flavor and strength-giving according to the people, wheat bread, and brook trout fried in walnut oil; we drank the cold, crystal-clear water in place of barley beer; and generally we thanked God for the life within our bosoms. Still we were not quite content with the common blessings of the days. On this cold, magnificent plateau, with manifold green parks that God laid out, there were mines of silver, mines of azure, and the richest mine in the world, for all we knew, producing the balas rubies of which very Venice had heard, red as pigeon blood, fiery as a hill girl's heart, and almost as unobtainable as a roc's egg.

If we could get hold of some of them, we could trade them for the favor of kings or the favors of their daughters. But the Emir owned the mines, amassing almost the whole output in his treasury, and selling only a few at extravagant prices. Only a very few went down the rathole, as the saying was. The Emir's guards searched the mineworkers to their bungs; a guard caught with one was chained in the mine until he died, a poetic punishment that the Emir learned from the Tatar. If a slave girl was seen to wear one at the Court, the courtiers began bowing and kowtowing as though she would soon be queen.

You could wonder that no Tatar army had ridden hence, to loot the treasury and work the mine. The answer lay in the high, narrow passes, colder than Iceland, which alone gave entrance to the kingdom, and where a company of lean, wine-bibbling catapultists could hold off a button-nosed horde. Indeed the Emir remained one of the few independent monarchs in all Asia.

Yet Chance, in the person of the young and amorous wife of a road guard, put me on the track of a fair balas ruby. It had been presented by the present Emir's father to a master goldsmith, with the right to sell it in his need; now the recipient's hands had lamed and his eyes dimmed, and his grandsons had no money to buy wives, and he would sell the precious trophy at a bargain. The upshot of it was, after a night of backing and filling, the old man wept, kissed his pride and joy farewell, and laid it in my palm. Into his scrawny hand went a goatskin bag containing two hundred dinars in gold.

Considering the extreme rarity of balas rubies elsewhere in the world, and the unthinkable ranges, deserts, rivers, and kingdoms still stretching between here and the capital of Cathay, surely the flawless, fire-hearted jewel of five carats' weight could be a modest and not unseemly gift to Kublai Khan.

When the custom officer at the border asked me if I had rubies, I could not resist bringing forth the stone in Maffeo's sight. The official admired it, and after examining its carefully inscribed pedigree, assigned to me, he congratulated me on its possession. Maffeo's smile seemed frozen on his face by a blizzard out of the Pamirs, and presently he entered the pavilion he shared with Nicolo.

In a moment he emerged and beckoned to me. I had been

summoned there a good many times before—usually to receive instructions as to giving false information and withholding true, sometimes to plan mutually profitable buying and selling—and I resolved to be very casual about my acquisition. That it would be a subject of discussion I could not doubt.

"Maffeo tells me you have acquired a very beautiful balas ruby," Nicolo began as soon as I was seated. The bluntness surprised me.

"A fair one, I think."

"May I see it? The matter concerns the safety of the caravan."

I showed him the stone. He examined it carefully with vividly lighted eyes.

"It's very fine. Maffeo and I did no little jewel-buying on our previous expedition, and I flatter myself we both learned something about jewels. You could fairly ask five hundred bezants at the great Alexandrian bazaar."

"I paid two hundred for it," I said, wondering whether Nicolo would at last stoop to use me or trick me.

"An excellent bargain. It would be quite an attraction to the bandits that infest the mountains eastward. So I'd like to put two more with it, for a use I have in mind."

He spoke pleasantly, as was his wont, but I could hardly bear to look at what he held in his palm. To my great relief, neither stone was the equal of mine.

"If I appraise your ruby at five hundred bezants, I should think these two together would be worth another five hundred," Nicolo went on.

"Certainly."

"If you agree, we'll book them at that figure, and use them for bandit bait. If we can't keep clear of the mountain wolves, and the stones are lost, you're to be paid on that basis out of the great sum we have saved by the trick. But first, you'll want to know its necessity."

"I would, signor, truly."

"Unlike the renegade Karaunas, who have their own gods and king, the bandits we're likely to meet are devout Mohammedans and nominally subject to the Emir. So they'll think twice about killing envoys and merchants in lawful passage. They probably wouldn't strip us of our heavy goods, since they couldn't readily dispose of them. Nor would they lay hand on our golden tablet, and would likely kowtow to it. But they'd certainly make off with all the money and jewels they could find. And if they suspect we've hidden some, they have ways, not at all pleasant, of un-covering them."

"You said to use these jewels as bait——"

"Precisely. The bandits won't expect us to have balas rubies, but they'll not overlook the possibility. So we'll have them hidden with what seems a great deal of cunning. One of us will give the secret away through a faked blunder or slip. Then when the rascals find them, they'll never doubt but these are all we have and won't look any further."

I was able to hold my tongue but not the rush of color from my face.

"Well, do you agree?" Nicolo asked.

"Yes, if the amount to be saved justifies such a severe loss."

"Show him, please, Maffeo." And as Maffeo bent over a saddle-bag, Nicolo continued to address me in a tone of pleasant casualness.

"Technically they're not mine, although I have carte blanche as to the use of all but one. As the Khan's envoy, I sought an audience with the Emir, and it happened that he had heard of me from the Khan's viceroy at Samarkand. When I asked if I could convey his compliments to my master, he straightway decided to send him a gift. The main item was an especially fine ruby, but he furnished me with several more, to give the Khan and his family or trade along the way for equally noble gifts." Nicolo paused, took a leather pouch that Maffeo handed him, and drew forth a double handful of cotton wool. It appeared about to burst into flame from seven balls of cold, blood-red fire glowing within the fleece. All were balas rubies to make up the lucky number of nine. The largest was the size of a crimson cherry of the *Halil Rud;* none of the others was less than twice as large as mine.

I had been slow in getting through my head the might, the majesty, even the meaning, of the word "king." And that was only one of my fallings-short.

2

The road from Badakhshan to Kashgar and Yarkand is a long road, taking thirty days of fast travel. By avoiding narrow defiles where cataracts roared, glassy steeps where avalanches swept with their awful thundering brooms, we took nearer fifty. And it is the highest road, I reckon, in all the world.

It crosses Little Pamir and Great Pamir. It comes by a lake of crescent shape, which a genie cut with Mohammed's sword, and which is the birthplace of the great, strange Oxus River. There was hardly a moment that we could not hear the distant deep-toned rumble of a snow slide. Everywhere and forever blew the snow clouds. In the lower valleys there were oases watered by melting glaciers, and here fruit ripened and birds sang and yellow grainfields rippled in the breeze; here were temples and schools and marts and crowds. But atop the vast plateau dwelt only wild men, in huts of stone and turf, and beasts and gods. The people called it Bam-i-Dunya, which means "Roof of the World."

In these hanging gardens of God, even the cooking fires went against nature. The flames under the pot danced and dispersed; the water bubbled fiercely but was slow to scald your finger, and hard corn would not soften in an all-day boiling. Looking down from these heights, we saw the Oxus winding to the rim of the sky, the wild white streams that fed it bounding out from under bridges of snow, and the mighty ranges running without count or end. Amid them hung valleys so deep and savage that even the devilish wolves dared not venture down, and on a thousand peaks no man's footprints had ever marked the snow.

In the mountains of Badakhshan we had seen and fed upon wild sheep. Fine, fat, and stoutly horned, they could not hold rushlights to the wild sheep of the Pamir, known as argalis.[8] At first I saw them as gray dots on the high grass slopes, and knew them only through their immense twisted horns left about at hunter's camps, or which were set in the snow to mark a trail. Often a horn was nearly five feet along its spiral, and a big pair measured an equal distance between the points. That a mere sheep could carry such a load upon its head I could hardly believe.

It was not a load, but a crown. This I perceived at my first close glimpse of a big ram. He was standing atop a crag, his head lifted, his feet together, his back arched, his whole bearing noble beyond description. I began to perceive that God had created him expressly to befit and reveal the Great Pamir. No lesser creature could concord with its sublime concept—one vast garth halfway to heaven, tall as the sea is deep, walled in a white wall whose towers and battlements pierced the sky.

His horns were of little use to him in defense against his natural enemies, the wolves that hunted in small, bold, villainous bands or the lone, long-furred, heavy-tailed gray-and-black snow leop-

ards, among the most beautiful of beasts, that lay in wait for
him on banks and ledges, sprang, transfixed the bounding neck
artery with their fangs, and slew. He butted his rivals for the swift,
smaller-horned ewes—their collisions could be heard afar through
the still air in the great tournaments of the rut—but only to van-
quish, not to kill. The horns were a God-given decoration not to
the good servant but to the high born. Their wearers must bear
them up steeps that would break the heart of an unburdened
horse, bound with them from rock to rock, run with them along
ledges and across the deadly crevices. Yet they would rather die
than lay them down; their very weight, like that of a king's crown
of massive gold, made demands upon their strength which they
gloried to meet.

I longed to test my courage, cunning, endurance, and other
human gifts against his splendid strength—eyes eagle-sharp, nose
and ears as keen as a fallow deer's, the swiftness and sureness of
his feet, his prowess to ascend where I could not follow. I wished
to pursue him into his snowy fastnesses, slay him if I could, and
bring back his horns to adorn my lodge, a memento of our conflict,
and to eat of his flesh with no mere belly hunger but in the ancient
ceremony of obtaining a share of his powers. Thereby, as all wise
men knew, I would become more sure-footed, swift, stronghearted,
and long-winded, and perhaps more lustful. Countless rams had
been foreordained to win or to lose magnificent contests with hunters; that went with their appointment and birthright. And this
contest would be more equal than most and hence more thrilling,
because the villagers usually went forth in bands, picking no particular quarry but killing any of the flock whose escape they could
cut off, while I would hunt alone for a lone mountain king.

Our caravan could not stop to let a junior merchant spend a day
on the lofty sheep range. But an avalanche in a defile stopped it
until such time as some fair-haired, blue-eyed falcon trappers,
calling themselves Kaffirs and bivouacked near by, could shovel
out a passage. That would take about five hours, I thought. It
would be folly to essay the lofty grass slopes in that short time.
. . . But the skin on my neck prickled when I came on a pair of
ram's horns laid out on the sod roof of the chief's house. They
were the largest I had yet seen.

When I admired them, the Kaffir answered me in high spirits.
I caught only one word of his language—Iskander, the Central
Asian rendition of Alexander, almost synonymous with "king" in
this part of the world. What Alexander the Great or his many

namesakes had to do with sheep hunting I could not guess. But the fellow's gestures—an expansive stretching of his arms and vigorous pointings to a mountaintop—arrested my deepest attention and stirred my imagination. Presently a cameleer of the Sarikol addressed him in some lingua franca of the snows, who in turn spoke to me in the base Turki-Persian dialect larded with Arabic words, which I had picked up long since.

"The chief says that these horns are small compared to the horns of the ram that his people have named Iskander."

"Why have they named him that?"

"Because he is greatest of all the rams they have ever seen."

"Where are his pasture and his fold?"

"Straight up this mountain."

"Then why don't they pursue and kill him?"

"Because he and his ewes, being sharp-eyed as saker falcons, discover their approach, and take off from the grass slopes over a ledge that leads to inaccessible rimrock. It is out of arrow cast and they dare not follow those sure feet across a void deeper than Gehenna."

Suddenly I was struck by a thought resounding within my skull like a thunderstorm in a mountain chasm. I had remembered Nicolo's speaking of Kublai Khan's interest in distant lands, and the delight he took in wonders of all sorts. It was somewhat doubtful if any of his viceroys had sent him horns of these magnificent wild sheep, and highly unlikely that he had seen a head so great that illiterate tribesmen would name its bearer after their hero-god, Alexander. And if the Khan was as illustrious as I liked to picture him, perhaps he would consider such a head, presented to him by its winner, almost as fine a gift as a priceless ruby.

It happened that my red-bay mare Roxana was daily proving herself as beyond praise. I tightened her cinch till she grunted, then mounted her with no load other than my gold and jewels, bow and quiver, a piece of dried goat flesh, and my woolen barracan to wear when I met the wolf-fanged wind on the open mountainsides. The Kaffirs gave me careful directions. Roxana began her long, grueling climb.

I rode her up the broad shoulder of the mountain, across treacherous slide rock, and around the rim of a gully. Already the wide green parklands looked like garden plots, the lakes were as sapphires set in the stone; eagles skimmed screaming over the hollow gorges half a mile below us. If I sat horizontal to my horse's back both of us would topple to our deaths, so I lay along the saddle, clutching her mane. Not until her eyes were bloodshot and her nostrils red and she sobbed for breath did I get down and fasten her to a pillar-like abutment of a weathered crag to wait for me. She had saved me a little time and perhaps a crucial amount of wind, strength, and sweat.

Now I made my way on foot, by such routes as I could find, toward a lofty grass slope running up to a sheer cliff under the crest. Scattered over it were fifty or more small forms, revealed by the clear air as heavy-headed beasts, some lying down, most of them in the broken movements of grazing. All but one varied in color from snow-white to dark gray. With that one exception, they resembled other flocks that I had seen, made up of lambs, ewes, half-grown rams, and full-grown rams. But the darkest of the lot—showing almost black in this light—was by all means the largest.

I felt a great surge of suspense and feverish desire.

I climbed steadily and steeply for half an hour, and the scope of the adventure widened and deepened every minute. It was partly the effect of my human solitude in all this vastness of mountain and sky. It was like the coming-true of a forgotten dream, which must be the way that Heaven breaks upon the newly dead—a place unimaginable by the living brain and yet instantly recognizable by the soul through some previous instruction. No Heaven would be so empty, cold, silent, and forlornly beautiful, I thought; but some last Hell might be. Beyond the seventh Hell that doers of great evil have dared fear, there may be another in which every soul wanders alone in an ineffable vastness of mountain and sky. There is no pain except a little in his legs and chest, but he must contemplate himself forever in a last, utter, irredeemable divorcement from God.

I stopped, rested a moment, and steadied my swimming head. It came to me that the sheep had already seen me, that even the spring lambs knew of my approach, but being the great argalis, lords of the realm, they took no notice of me. It might be for sport or some symbol untranslatable to the human mind. Those lying down rose one at a time, and I thought that the flock grazed closer to one another and looked up more often. I drew within six hundred yards. Now there was a movement going on, so slow and calm that it was hardly apparent. The ewes with lambs were feeding closest to the rocky flank of the grass slope, the barren ewes were next, then the young rams, and then the heavy-horned and lordly elders. But the king had not partaken in this action. From a dead stop, light as a bouncing ball, he bounded to the top of a six-foot boulder. There he stood in motionless majesty, gazing not in my direction, it seemed, but over my head.

I gained the same slope and almost the same elevation, although still four hundred paces distant. A ewe and her lamb strolled around the curve of the hill and disappeared. Others of her kind followed with gradually quickening pace. The barren ewes left in a group—they were ashamed, I thought, of their dry teats, and hung together for company—and then the half-grown rams in a dignified file, not deigning to look back. As I drew within what we call arrow cast, but too far for any hit but a lucky one from a falling shaft, only mature rams remained on the slope. Five of these had withdrawn to its end, near the top of a ridge. The sixth, who was Iskander the King, remained on his dais, obviously poised, immobile and magnificent. He had turned enough to show me his profile sharp against a snowbank further up the slope. I could hardly believe his magnitude and beauty.

All the lesser rams had made off along a ledge so narrow it looked like a seam in the rock, dipping to what mountain men called a saddle and leading to a shelf projecting from the face of a cliff. Leisurely the five elders made the crossing. Iskander remained as still as the stone itself.

I worked my way over dangerous slide rock to the slippery grass. Now I crouched within two hundred paces of my quarry, at which range a broadhead arrow may kill clean. The shot would be an extremely difficult one, worthy of Coeur-de-Lion in the mountain breeze, yet I was amazed at the beast's boldness. Suddenly I conceived of the explanation. The savage huntsmen of his acquaintance had weak bows that could not cast that far. Indeed I had never seen them attempt a shot at more than half the distance. Perhaps Iskander would scorn to fly from a tall form with an evil smell twenty bounds distant. He would wait until the humming hornets fell only a little short. That was his pride before his liegemen and his ewes. . . .

I decided to close within a hundred and fifty paces, then try the shot. The breeze was more cold than strong; with a full draw and a hard aim and a clean loose I had a fair chance to win. But when I had got that far, and the moment came to play the chance for all it was worth, I could not bear not to pass it by.

Whatever its first cause—perhaps superstitious fear of the gods— it was one of the most worthy actions of my life. Gaining these heights had been an inspiring experience and its glow was on me still. I was seeing Iskander not only as king of the rams, but as more than as a protagonist of the Pamir, even as a proof of the magnificence and mystery of life itself, and hence its hope. I did not want to win the great prize by taking advantage of his ignorance of the strength of my weapon. I would keep to my original intention—to follow him where other hunters had never ventured, or to give up the quest.

The issue was as clean-cut as though by Fate's contrivance. The retreat of Iskander's flock, where presently he would withdraw out of my arrow range, was a cul-de-sac. There was no possibility of his climbing up the sheer cliffs rimming the shelf; as before when men drove him from his pasture, he would wait there until they went away. And I could engage him by one operation only—following him along the ledge and across the saddle to his citadel.

I advanced a few more steps. Iskander sprang down, shook his rump, and trotted after his flock. At the very end of the grass slope he stopped, nibbled a moment, glanced back at me, and leaped nimbly onto the ledge. But now he began to progress with portentous care.

Following slowly, I felt a great deal of inner tumult. While hating the thought of turning back, I did not know how great a risk I was willing to run. The flock was in plain sight on the shelf beyond the saddle. Their king joined them, and all gazed in my direction. It was a strange thing that they would seek a retreat from which there was no outlet; I could account for it only by its serving them before. It might indicate that even wolves and leopards eschewed the passage, or that the rams could hold it against them.

I gained the ridge and my gaze made the journey that my feet must soon make, if I were to win. My eyes bulged at the narrow way along the face of the precipice, overhanging the profound gulf. Then I felt them thrill to a magnificent discovery.

The Kaffir tribesmen had said that the gulf was as deep as Gehenna's. As I gazed down, the expression struck me as only too apt—the cliff fell away fathom after dizzy fathom until my head reeled, then leaped down in a series of steeps to a dimly descried glen where maybe demons dwelt. To fall off the ledge would mean to drop sheer, perhaps turning over slowly in the air for several seconds, each as long as a term in Purgatory; then striking the steeps, to bounce, leap, and careen into the glen three cables' lengths below. But it was the depth of the void, rather than the narrowness of the bridge, that had blanched the faces of the mountaineers and had made them turn back.

I firmly believed that if this same ledge had overhung an ordinary ravine, they would have essayed to cross it without crippling terror. Yet a sixty-foot fall on rock will kill almost as surely as one of sixteen hundred.

So my adversary was still myself. My feet would be equal to the passage if my soul kept faith with its high birth by valor and resolve, both proofs of implacable pride.

I considered depositing here every ounce of impedimenta—all my arrows except three, my pouch containing keys and a little sand glass and a few other belongings useful or beloved, even my dagger. Why not all my clothes except my sandals? But thinking of the figure I would cut in the eyes of my quarry made me grin, and I decided to go as I was. Up and down and across mountains, Iskander went as he was. I was not a naked anchorite looking for visions in the wilderness, but a Venetian gentleman on a superb adventure.

For the first hundred feet, I kept my eyes stoutly on the footing. But this was a false stoutness. As the ledge narrowed ahead of me, deeper and deeper in my mind's eye yawned the chasm. It was at my side and a little behind where the Devil walks. Its unseen presence made my eyes ache and my thoughts muddle and my belly sicken. Already I yearned to grope with my hands at the treacherous shale. I was going to fall. . . .

Then I stopped, looked up at the sky, thought upon the marvel of my being here, alone for the moment in the Great Pamir, then without hanging on, slowly swept my gaze downward into the void.

I saw the multicolored rocks of the opposite side of the chasm, not nearly as steep and high, but to look down the precipice to the series of cliffs below, ending at last in the dark glen, required that I lean my shoulders a little outward and bend my head. With my sweat cold upon me, but my eyes narrow and hard and perhaps a turning-down of my lip corners in almost a sneer, I did so. I gazed into the Pit. It differed only in externals from those set in the path of millions of my fellow men. The evil spells cast by its demons are greatly weakened by the power of the human eye.

At that moment, I won the victory.

It did not matter as much as before whether I laid Iskander low and took his horns. But King Fate had decreed—or his pet monkey Chance had prayed—that the adventure would end fittingly, in a beautiful sweep of event. I had passed the most perilous span of the ledge and was approaching the saddle. Still more than a hundred paces distant, Iskander had become restless. He moved back and forth in front of his flock and tossed his crowned head. Presently he stopped, gave me a long, unflinching look, and then uttered a deep-toned bleat that carried far in the airy silence. Resolutely he started back.

I could not doubt that he had perceived my almost completed crossing of the moat guarding his citadel, and had come out to do battle.

I flipped an arrow over my shoulder onto my bow. Iskander walked briskly, then broke into an easy run. I stood with my right leg braced behind me, my left bent in front, and put my shoulder into the draw. I could not wait until he crossed the saddle into point-blank range. That would bring him onto the face of the precipice, from where he would plummet to ruin on the rocks below. My movements were timed to loose the shaft when he was about sixty paces distant, coming into the rise of the saddle. To strike the base of the burly neck would not be a difficult shot on the good wide ground. But whatever the adversities of the time and place, I dared not miss.

My bow rounded. Iskander gained speed. A slight action of my fingers freed the string and the long arrow with its broad head of whetted steel sped smoothly on its way. I was not fixed to shoot again, lest the sudden movements make me lose my balance, so I held my stand, trusting all to the well-loosed shaft. As it struck and plunged deep, the great ram rose on his hind legs, his horns in a magnificent last flourish against the sky.

Giantlike he toppled, but with a final wrench of his body, he fell with his head toward me. Kingly still, he raised his head to look at me. Slowly it lowered, not as though cast down by the hand of Death, but from the weight of a crown he could no longer bear.

CHAPTER 5

VOICES ON THE DESERT

DROPPING DOWN AND DOWN FROM THE PAMIR, WE WATCHED the snow fields and naked rock and windy grass slopes give way to parklands and forests and mountain meadows, while the weather slowly warmed.

It would cool eftsoon. The fourth summer since our spring departure from Venice was waning as inconspicuously as a common moon. But in spite of necessary rests and much unavoidable waiting, these more than three years had gained us about two-thirds the distance to Peking. Nicolo and Maffeo Polo had journeyed by another route and so had traveled no part of this road, this long road from the Levant outward, and they knew no better than I what to expect, and rarely better how to cope with it. I had become so great a strength to the company that Nicolo might save my life in some deadly pass from sheer practicality, and I was almost sure that he would not try to take it until we had crossed the last river.

A curious change had come over my mind, although so gradually I could not remember when it began. From the first I had refrained from looking back to Venice, refusing to dwell on people and events I had known there, and of late this disregard had changed to a kind of forgetfulness. At first they had come to visit my dreams, but I paid them little heed, never went back to visit them, and in time they had ceased to trouble me. It had been my desire, and it represented a victory of my will, although sometimes I felt it might prove a costly one. Lately I had found myself no longer looking forward to the Court of Kublai Khan; indeed I did not worry with matters beyond the immediate reach of road. I had no occupation, no identity, but that of a traveler. I was in no haste, neither did I want to tarry. I cared not for the next year or the next moon, but lived for the day, the hour, sometimes it seemed for no longer than the present moment.

Far and away from the far-flung Arabic civilization and its remote outposts, I heard and spoke no more its rich and beautiful tongue except as it larded Turki-Persian, the lingua franca of Central Asia, now merging into Turki-Tatar. Thus I had less cause to remember Mustapha Sheik. And if I had lost beautiful Venice, the Bride, the very Saki of the Sea, behind a lost horizon, why should I try to keep one small, yellow-haired maiden I had met there? So it was neither in her memory nor to obtain forgetfulness that at Kashgar, whose name Venice had never heard, I took a Bride of the Oasis; it was merely the custom of the road. I kept her for ten days in the caravanserai, ten more among my baggage eastward, then sent her back, weeping, with a westbound caravan.

Also in Kashgar I traded for half a gallon of jade, black, white, yellow, vermilion, and a piece or two of dark green with golden veins. It had been fished by jade divers from the Kysyk So, and it

would pour through my hands and shine before my eyes long after
I had forgotten my bride's name.

At summer's end we went to Yarkand, where almost every person has a great swelling on the side of his throat and very large,
bright eyes. In the early fall, we gained the great and wonderful
oasis of Khotan. The best of the fruit was already harvested; what
remained was grateful to my eyes—so strangely clinging to the
boughs, or heaped in baskets, red or purple or golden, as though
we were back in Italy instead of down from the Pamirs—and sweet
to my lips. The yellow stalks of ripe grain bent down from the
weight of their bearded heads.

Beyond the oasis lies the approach to the terrible Takla Makan
that sweeps east and north to join with the Gobi in what the people call the Kingdom of Evil. I thought at first this was a figure of
speech, but was soon to learn it was a literal expression of their
belief. They thought that in some old conflict between God and
the Devil, the Prince of Darkness had seized upon this vast domain, a year's journey long from Khotan northeast to the Manchu
rivers and generally half as broad, perhaps greater than all Europe
west of Constantinople.

The Devil had turned back the rain-bearing clouds, so except
for some mountaintops reaching close to heaven, and still disputed
ground, there was no rain, no snow, no dew for a thousand leagues.
The land was turned into one vast melancholy waste with a few
seepage-fed wells along its fringes, a suitable place for his legions
of demons, imps, monsters, and all sorts of evil spirits.

It was said that only his worshipers could pass freely and safely,
after performing flagitious rites. All other human beings, and
Christians especially, entered the kingdom at great hazard to their
lives and souls.

From Khotan to far Cherchen, the caravan road crosses a high
plateau at the feet of the Kunlun Mountains. To the southward
we caught glimpses of peaks rearing up and piercing the ethereal
cirrus clouds, and one, called Muztagh Ata, the name meaning
White Mountain, was sublimely beautiful. A few cattle drivers
have cots along the road, and secret water holes away on the desert
to which they fly when the Devil-worshipers come riding. Now
the autumn winds shrilled across its sands and hard-baked clay.

This was an outer borderland of the dread Takla Makan. At
Cherchen we loaded food and water for a three-day forced march,
and God knew you would think that desolate stretch lay out of

the world. Instead it was a corridor between the two realms, a kind of Land of Nod. At its end lay the thriving city of Lob, where there were wells and even baths, shops and caravanserais, and temples to Buddha, Allah, and the Christian God. Luxuries of most sorts could be had at exorbitant prices; only the favors of the beautiful fair-haired Turkman damsels were dirt-cheap.

Yet we knew well, by means of inklings beyond our common sense, that Lob was no common city, part of man's world. No one dwelt here; the people came, hung for a while on the brink of Gehenna, went away, went mad, or died. Many became mystics and dreamers; others fashioned new gods and strange cults; a great number practiced sorcery and divination. A good part of the folk within the walls belonged to caravans resting here after the terrible crossing, but they had seen and heard what is not good for the souls of men, and it was a common thing for them to linger on through weeks and months and years, wasting their substance, and never return to their homes. An equal number, eastward bound, reveled in the fleshpots ere they set forth; but it came to pass that some never found the strength and the will power, each day finding a good reason to wait another day, till their bales too were empty; then they borrowed or stole for a season, and disappeared. Perhaps the Devil met them in the dead of night and persuaded them to join his legions. There were strange things. . . .

"Heed me well," spake a Nestorian priest to Nicolo, Maffeo, and me on the eve of our setting-forth. "Not tomorrow night, or the next, or perhaps for seven nights, will you hear from the demons dwelling in the Kingdom of Evil; but they will be about you ever, and no later than the tenth night they will move against you. You will hear what seems a great company of people out in the dark. The jingle of harness, the creak of ropes, the shouts of the cameleers, even the shuffle of sand—all this will come clearly to your ears. But leave not the road or the rest ground to search for them. They will lead you to your death. And on no account shall any man straggle from the company. If his body is ever found, it will be beheaded or dismembered or deboweled by a clawlike hand."

Nicolo looked grave, Maffeo frightened, I tried to wear a mask. But Maffeo gave the Nestorian priest two pieces of gold—to be laid on the altar—and somehow this caused the warning to ring less true.

We rose and loaded our beasts and took our places soon after midnight, so we could make our march when the winds were low and the air more clear of sand. We need not fetch water save for a two-day journey—the road lay close to the snow-capped ranges, and wells of scanty store were found at almost all caravan rests for the thirty-day march—but food for man and beast must be transported by camelback. I had known wastes of rock and snow to be bitter cold, but not the desolate sands. So the cold stars and the icy air of late fall seemed to add to the strangeness and the wickedness of the scene. And we had followed a made road less than a league when it ran out and disappeared.

Every footprint of beast or man was buried in wind-blown sand. Yet there were signs in plenty to guide our steps, strange-looking in the moonlight—an endless train of white bones. Some were of cattle and horses and camels, but frequently I saw a rib case, half filled with sand, that caused my skin to prickle, and now and then a skull too round to fit the neck of a beast.[9]

Where seepage from mountain snows fed underground veins, tamarisk bushes found root. These would bind fast a pile of sand, more would be blown onto it by the wind, so that green-topped mounds, twice man's height, dotted the plain. Sometimes there were stretches of loose clay on which no beast, bird, reptile, or insect cast its shadow. Mostly the Takla Makan was a waste of sand dunes, the larger running east and west, crisscrossed with smaller ones, so that the effect was that of a sea of sand arrested by enchantment in an instant of wildest tumult.

We should have waited at Lob for the intense cold of winter. If we had, we could have loaded our camels with ice, perhaps to save us from death from thirst in some awful pass, or, held to our faces in a dust storm, to help us to survive the worst pass of all. No, there was greater calamity than this to be met on the desert, although it smote with great rarity at this time of the year. It was called a dry fog, and was a lowering of dust-laden air that sometimes hung for days, from which there was no flight. If the fog was light, the traveler suffered torments past description. If heavy, he quickly smothered and died.

On and on into this earthly hell we forced our way. From dark to dawn the sand was cold as snow, the wind bit to the bone despite our woolen barracans; it was as though we wandered on the opposite side of the moon, divorced from the sun. The sun's rising brought a gentle warmth, but on many a day it turned to parching heat, with the sand burning our feet and the dust hot in our eyes, nostrils, and mouth. The worst was our solitude among the dunes and the white bones under the dust-darkened sky. Our realization of the world of God and man dimmed every day; ever more credible became our sense of having passed its bourns into a realm of dreadful dreams, more awful than any we had ever dreamed, which had come true.

Various people in the caravan began to see visions and hear voices. Some were illusionary, I thought—not one of us, unless it be Nicolo, was in his perfect mind—but many were strange twistings by our fancies of real sights and sounds. What appeared as lakes, surrounded by lush meadows and verdant trees, was a common phantom; many-towered castles and walled cities hung in the empty air; one day our whole party saw what seemed an armed host on the march. Banners fluttered in the wind; horses pranced and armor gleamed; captains rode up and down the lines. I had trouble staying clear of believing this deceit and could not have done so save that ten thousand hoofs raised no dust and the army moved in an eerie silence. Perhaps such a force had passed here in some forgotten war and had been blasted by the sirocco, and this was an army of ghosts.

Demoniac faces and forms thrust out from tamarisk mounds, sworn to by every heathen in our company—and perhaps we Christians would have testified the same if we would believe our eyes. Creatures that looked half human, half beast, appeared to dodge behind the sand dunes. If we could believe our ears, zither players surrounded our camps in the deep of night, playing not in harmony, not in melody that the mind could catch, but in weird discord, harrowing our souls with the sense of unfathomable evil.

One lurid afternoon I made out some small, moving objects in the dust haze two arrow casts distant. Had they kept to the caravan road, I would have thought them survivors from some waylaid caravan, retracing the steps of their fellows by scent to some picket ground they knew. Although of camel shape, I thought, they moved too swiftly to be real, and suddenly they vanished. My head became dizzy and aching from the seeming realness of the illusion. . . .

Revulsion from this weakness came upon me quickly. Perhaps it was a deep-lodged terror of going mad. I had seen the figures, whether substance or empty air, betwcen the road and a two-humped sand dune clearly distinguishable from any other nearby, and this lay directly toward the setting sun. I resolved to ride to the ground, see what I could see, follow my mare's own footprints back to the road, and overtake the caravan.

Ten seconds after I had left the road my companions disappeared in a defile. I rode in the cold shadow of dunes and remembered that since this was the seventh day since we had left Lob, the Devil had only three days left of his allowance of ten to deal someone in our caravan a deadly blow. The wind seemed to be rising, lifting more dust and causing the sands to creep a little, as if with the wicked mind to cover my tracks. When I caught sight of the sun over the dunes it seemed to hang in a different place in the sky.

I rode on, my gaze fixed on the two-humped dune. Almost at its base, when I had thought a dozen times of turning back, I found the fresh track of camels, unmistakably real. Although our caravaneers had told us they were nonexistent in all this part of the Takla Makan, beyond a doubt I had seen a small herd of wild camels on some swift and portentous errand.

I regained the road and soon caught sight of the caravan. Of the many who had seen me turn out, not one looked back in concern for my befalling; the all of every man was straining ahead to the next rest, and God, by whatever name, forbid that the well be dry! I decided not to tell my fellows about the camels. I would let them think I had dropped behind to answer a call of nature, which was the truth in a deeper sense than they would know. I must be true to my own nature, such as it was; and if the Devil struck before the end of the tenth day, I could fight him a better fight if I fought alone.

2

On the following march, the course was long, rough, and dangerous to flesh and spirit. Coming to the mouth of a road out of the far Tien Shan, by an ancient well supplying brackish water, we hoped to find and fall in with other east-bound caravans, but all was silent and forsaken, and the tracks of the last comers were so nearly erased by blown sand that we could not judge their age. And in that same hour I was weighed in a balance with Nicolo and found wanting.

I was riding in the van with the head dragoman, employing my long-range eyes in finding the far-strewn markers hard to descry under the dust clouds that hid the sun. Presently they became abundant, the bones in little piles or clusters. Such neat assortments, each the bracing of a beast's body or a man's only a few weeks before, should have put me on my guard; instead I followed the course they set, the caravan behind me, for a good half-mile. Then Nicolo rode up beside me.

"I fear, Marco, that you're off the road," he said quietly.

"I think not, signor." My brain seemed clogged with dust.

"I believe that a caravan, crazed and dying from thirst, left the road to follow a mirage. It was their last effort, and the beasts and men began to drop out like locusts flying over burning grass. I believe the road swung to the right instead of to the left, southeast instead of northeast. I saw what I thought were markers to the southeast."

"Truly we should go southeast, and I believe we are. If we could see the sun, I think it would be over there." I pointed to a faintly luminous patch in the sky.

"I think that's a thinning of the dust cloud and the sun's behind us. Since I've appointed you the watch, I would like to have you turn back from your own conviction. Let's see if we can get a shadow."

He put the point of his small dagger on his thumbnail. It cast a discernible shadow on the pink sheen, a trick I had not seen before. The sun was where he had indicated and we were heading down a devil's road toward Death. With self-hatred in my heart, I ordered the retreat. Nicolo rode nonchalantly to his place.

Midafternoon before the midnight that would complete nine days out of Lob, we rested by a meager well below a dune-ringed plateau of sand stretching northward as far as we could see. There was only a half-measure of water for every man, none for the beasts; and many whirlwinds raising brown towers that suddenly collapsed in falling palls might foretell the dread sirocco. The most flamboyant sunset I could remember ushered in the most chill, desolate twilight. By the time the leprous moon, gourd-yellow, cleared the eastern dunes, the cameleers lay wrapped in their barracans, each beside his picketed mount, trying to dream away their hunger, thirst, and dismay before the midnight call. Between times of hanging their heads in despair, the horses neighed and stamped. Occasionally a camel raised a horrid bubbling cry that stretched every nerve in hearing to the breaking-point before it as suddenly and unaccountably subsided.

Once I thought I heard an echo of the yell up and away on the plateau.

I thought so without any great conviction. But soon after this, there was no doubt of my hearing what we called zither music all about our encampment. My gaze wheeled to Nicolo, posting accounts by the light of a sputtering tamarisk torch. He did not raise his head and some little tension in his body told me that he too heard the devilish sound.

It died away soon, and the eerie whist disclosed another sound that I had thought was only a trick of my pulse and breath. It appeared to be carried on the breeze from far out on the plateau and was imaginable as the harsh utterance of a cicadalike insect at the last dim edge of hearing. On that frontier, it rose and fell a little, never any louder than the hum of a mosquito when one is half-awake, and whatever its origin, I believed it to be a genuine sensory experience, not an auricular illusion.

I lost it for a moment, but groping in the silence, found it again. It became discernibly plainer with the passing moments, and I began to search my memory for its likeness. I had heard many natural sounds that it faintly resembled, but the one that it fitted best was the one that caused the most unpleasant tightening of my scalp. That was the sound made by a moving caravan at a good distance.

Truly I had expected to hear a sound of this general sort long before tonight. Not only the Nestorian priest had promised it; the old cameleers who had passed this way before had given me detailed accounts of its manifestation, usually associated with disaster. Trying to put myself in Mustapha's shoes, I had thought of it as some natural sound of the desert, transmuted by human imagination into a thing of terror. But as it came clearer, I was awe-stricken by its uncanny familiarity. Drivers appeared to be shouting and cursing at their beasts the same as on any rough road, horses neighed, goaded camels uttered their inimitable complaints. I could not resist the impression that a marching caravan was much nearer than the volume of the sound would indicate, as though it was muted by some barrier other than distance—as though it broke through from some other world. But that might be an effect of its source's being well over our heads on the sandy plateau, whereby only a kind of echo floated down to us.

The camp was waking. A few of the drivers covered their heads so they could not hear; others sat up, fingering their amulets. I rose and walked into Nicolo's torchlight. He saw me and laid down his pen.

"Excuse me, signor, for interrupting your work," I said.

"It was already pretty well interrupted by the sounds out yonder," he answered in a pleasant tone. "I would almost think they're real."

"I do think they're real."

"Of course they are, in that we really hear them, not imagine them. So is the zither playing. I meant I can almost believe that there's a caravan of living men and beasts out there in the dark."

"I think there is."

"Men go in search of such caravans—and never come back. You might think of them as a mirage of the ear instead of the eye. Perhaps the sound is mysteriously borne from some caravan road scores of miles distant. Listen! I fancy it's growing a little fainter——"

I thought the same.

"I believe it's a lost caravan within a mile of us," I insisted, "and you should order fires built and pots clattered."

"What will we use for fuel? There's no dried dung—not enough tamarisk to make a torch. Would you have us set fire to our stores? Anyway, could they see it behind these dunes? As for a clatter of pans and pots, it wouldn't carry far against the wind, and the drivers would think we were summoning the Devil and kill all three of us. But suppose it was a lost caravan, and we found it and brought it here. They're out of water or they wouldn't be traveling at this hour, and mad or dying. What could we do for them. What might they do to us?"

"I'm considering riding up on the plateau."

Nicolo's eyes glistened in the moonlight. "If you believe it's a real caravan in distress, of course I'll do nothing to stop you."

I turned away and my thoughts turned inward. The sounds of men's shouts and beasts' cries were as plain as the shape of the camels I had seen two days before. Perhaps there was a natural sound heard often in this region that resembled the noise of a caravan on the march, but my unusually sharp ears had tonight discovered evidences, missed by other listeners, of the thing itself. I remembered the faint prints at the junction of the northern road with ours—one hard local wind might have made day-old tracks appear several weeks old. Then another memory stopped my heart.

What of the false road I had followed half a mile? If a day or two earlier another caravan had been similarly led astray and had followed the course to the last white bone, the captains might even now be seeking their lost way. Tonight they might have wandered within hearing of our encampment, and just now had yielded to despair and turned away.

But the Devil that had sent a legion of demons to call me to my destruction could put logic in my brain to make me follow on.

3

In the light of day, my mare Roxana was a lively red-bay. The night had turned her black, and it seemed I hardly knew her as I got her between my thighs, as though a hell nag had been picketed in her place to bear me to my doom. It seemed that I hardly knew myself as I made up the dunes, as though my identity had been washed out in the thin flood of moonlight, and I was some sort of puppet being led on a string by the Powers of Darkness. I felt the enmity of the sands, the wind, the strange shadows, even the moon, whom aforetime I had loved. All were ineffably menacing to the little torch of life within my breast.

Instead of one long sand dune climbing up the plateau, there was a series of dunes of increasing height and steepness, with black valleys between. I could hear nothing but my mare's grunting and the shuffle of sand all up that strange ascent, but as we gained the plateau, the sounds I had followed became suddenly much louder and more sharply accented. These were not natural phenomena. Either a caravan of living men and animals moved to the windward, or else a legion of demons was deliberately and perfectly imitating its characteristic clamor.

The ground appeared to be weathered clay, perfectly level, covered with a finger-deep layer of wind-dropped dust. It would rise in a cloud under my mare's hoofs, and blowing back, would fill her tracks as fast as she made them. The vision of my being lost on this awful empty tableland under the dying moon chilled my soul, there was no pity in my heart for the wanderers in torment, and I hated myself—this little shell of me that the dogs of the wind bit—for leaving the encampment. Yet savagely spurring the good beast, I rode wildly toward the sound.

If this were a feat of will, it was the last one of the episode. None was needed to ride on long after my bestormed brain told me I should have reached my goal; the reins seemed no longer in my hands. When the clamor suddenly ceased and the silence held and held as in an evil dream, I tried to think that despair had run down the line of men and beasts as I had seen it more than once on our own journeys, throttling the heart and throat of every one. Then it broke with the howling of a curse in the Turki-Persian tongue. It rose just beyond the dim rim of my sight.

I hallooed with all my might. In the next few seconds vague blotches of darkness on the pallid plain began to take shape as loaded camels frozen into immobility by my shout. Men stood beside them. Horsemen wheeled toward me. A captain came riding fast.

"Who are you?" he cried, his voice shaking with hope.

"I'm Marco Polo, a Venetian, from a caravan resting not a mile from here."

"Are you on the road?"

"Yes."

"Is there water?"

"There'll be a mouthful apiece for the people. If need be, I'll kill one of my camels for its water sack."

"You'll not lose by it, I'll promise that. But give me one assurance, before God—remembering I'm half-crazed by terror and privation, and dare not believe my own eyes and ears. If you are a Venetian, you are a Christian. I am Baram, a Mussulman of Bukhara. We have rich lading—what use to try to hide it?—and we will pay well for any help you give us, and sell you what you desire without a dinar's profit, and give good gifts besides. But swear before your God you'll not use our weakness to rob and murder us!"

All this came forth in one shaking high-pitched burst.

"We travel under the safe-conduct of the Great Khan."

"Allah! Allah! Allah!"

With hardly a word more, Baram turned and shouted to his followers. He fell in beside me as I turned back toward the encampment, with the whole caravan noisy in our wake. The trail of footprints was soon erased by dust, and for half the distance I had only the moon, sicker than her wont in the dust pall, to set my course on, and the beasts could not smell the water because it was down the wind. Then we caught a glimmer from an invisible moving torch. Soon the flame itself gleamed just below the rim. We rode on in silence until I made out the figure of a horseman crossing a tall sand dune. His course was a short cut from the resting ground to the place I had found the caravan.

"It's Nicolo Polo, master of our caravan," I told my companion.

"I thought you were the master."

"No, I'm Marco Polo, a merchant of the company."

"He's looking for us too. But you are sure that he'll treat us——"

"You need have no fear."

Baram spurred his horse and rode ahead. The moonlight showed him clapping his hand to his forehead and his heart, a Mohammedan greeting to Nicolo that in his distress he had forgotten to give me.

"God be with you, friend," Nicolo answered in his rich voice.

Bright pride in my victory, strangely mixed with the dark pride of concealing every shadow cast upon it, would not let me tarry to hear the talk between the two captains. As Nicolo fixed his eyes on me, I barely drew my rein.

"I promised this man that there would be a little water for him and all his people," I said. "If it's necessary to kill one of my camels——"

"It won't be necessary. I have a skin bag full in my stores, and we're only one march from one of the best wells on the road."

I half expected him to offer some explanation for not thinking of this before, but I might have known he would not.

"By the way, Marco, your ear was better than mine in tracing the sound."

"You might explain it by the ear for music of Antonello the Jongleur."

"I do so, to my great regret."

Nicolo turned to speak to Baram. I rode on to my pavilion. There, standing in the shadow, I watched the laden camels file stolidly down to our camp ground. Their drivers unloaded and picketed them; pavilions were raised; our sleepers were up and scurrying; shouts rang out. Nicolo said that there was not enough tamarisk in the camp to make a torch, but several flared in the pallid moonlight with a rigadoon of shadows. Presently it showed Ali, Nicolo's servant, passing a dipper among the gaunt, bearded, dust-blackened newcomers, every one of whom blessed Allah ere he wet his lips. I would lie down, I thought, and go to sleep, and dream.

My will to do so failed until it was suddenly too late. A Persian lamp with the soft shine of burning palm oil came into view from behind the pavilion. It disclosed Nicolo's steady hand and young, princely face.

"I hoped I'd find you awake," he said. "Baram the caravan master has sent you a gift of great price. It's a token of his gratitude for your deed tonight."

Nicolo held out his palm bathed in amber light from the lamp's shining on a saffron-colored jewel nearly as big as a walnut, with a score or more facets. I recognized it as a yellow sapphire, not as valuable carat for carat as slate-blue or sea-blue sapphires or those with shining stars, and of course not to be measured with diamonds, rubies, and emeralds, but because of its great size worth, I believed, about a thousand gold dinars.

"It's a noble gift," I said, "and I accept it with many thanks."

"Perhaps you don't know that yellow jewels are in great esteem in Cathay—it's a sacred color."

"I didn't know it, signor."

"Baram gave me a jewel of the same color, which I'll show you presently. They were the two most valuable single objects that he possesses, he said, although he thought mine had deteriorated during the march. For the moment it's not much to look at—one could hardly imagine its being worth so much ready money. But in the first place, I don't look for long teeth in a gift horse, and in the second, I think he disprizes it unduly. In the end it may be worth more than the sapphire, which doesn't seem quite fair."

"You're the master of the caravan," I said with stiff lips.

"I agree it might have been in the way of cumsha instead of gratitude—he wants us to buy all his China-bound goods, so he can make a quick return to Bukhara. He thinks his narrow escape was warning from very Allah. Actually, of course, he's lost his nerve. But he needn't have had the least concern as to selling his stuffs. He's an epicure and I don't doubt he expected to sell directly or indirectly to the Khan. His whole lading will be offered us."

I nodded and waited.

"I think you're entitled to first choice. That will more than recompense you if my gift proves more valuable than yours. Maffeo can have second choice, and I'll be content with what remains. How much money have you available in gold and silver, jewels apart from this one, jade, and precious stuffs of small weight?"

"About three thousand dinars."

"I'd suggest you venture a third or a half. He's not eager to sell his jewels—he has only a few of the sort he gave me, and not as fine." Nicolo gave me a pleasant smile. "But he offers us gold and silver brocade, embroideries, Samarkand of the finest, ermine and sables, bejeweled scimitars and daggers of Kerman steel, and Arabian medicines. Also a lot of ten Badakhshan horses, skin and bone but still sound."

"I would like to see the wares," I said.

"You may within the hour. We should be on our way soon after midnight—Baram will wait for morning to get what water seeps into the well during the night and then make a forced march to our last night's rest. I've given him hashish to stimulate him for the effort, and enough to keep his men going eight or ten hours. Traveling light, they should make it without trouble. Now come with me."

Nicolo walked beside me, talking spiritedly, to Baram's pavilion. "This young man is very pleased with the sapphire," Nicolo told him. "Now I'm taking him to see the gift that you gave to me."

"It will look better when it's polished, and it will improve in a warmer climate."

Nicolo led me to a pavilion that I thought must be occupied by some merchant in his company. When he called for admittance in the Turki-Persian dialect, the door curtain was drawn aside by a dark, pink-palmed hand. The light showed first a young, shapely Nubian girl in the dress of an ayah. A small charcoal blazer took the chill from the felt-lined and carpeted chamber; plainly, Nicolo and Baram had had dealings here. But there was another girl lying on a heap of raspberry-colored rugs, wearing a padded coat over a shift of transparent Samarkand silk. Either the soft, yellow radiance seemed slow in falling upon her or else my eyes were briefly and strangely darkened.

As the maiden sat up, her hair fell about her shoulders. It was of much paler color than my sapphire, still the excuse for Nicolo's jest. But at first blush it seemed strange that he would regard her of greater worth, she being so inordinately pale and gaunt from famine.

She was older, too, than the prime offerings in the slave markets. She was a young woman, not a child in her first flower—perhaps eighteen. Her eyes were pale brown and oddly set. I could hardly see her lips, they were so pallid. Her throat was slender and her breasts were small. Surely, surely I was lucky to be given a yellow emerald worth a thousand gold dinars instead of this wasted desert waif with yellow hair.

The maiden bowed her head and touched her hands to her brow in obeisance to her new master, then drew her coat closer in modesty before a visitor. When again she raised her eyes, she gazed straight forward without a trace of expression on her face. And now I could see the delicate carving of its bones.

The light fell full upon it and my eyes opened wide. Then I too was blinded by a sudden hope—almost a belief—bound round with terror. It had moved upon me under burning tears that Nicolo must not discern.

CHAPTER 6

THE STRANGERS

*L*ittle slave girl met midway on the ocean sea of sands, are you Miranda of England? Unless you give me a sign, I cannot know.

Not that my common sense rebels. It hammers within my head that although she and I have been parted for four summers, and that parting came to pass halfway across the world, all that time and all that way she too could have been bound for the Court of Kublai Khan. Does he not collect the rarest and most beautiful things on earth?

Thousands of his agents comb all Asia for the most beautiful virgins, slave or free. Could I wonder that Paulos Angelos or that some later buyer, discovering he had obtained a pearl perhaps beyond price, aspired to set her among her peers to his great gain? She and I started for the Levant within a few days of each other. Would it be a miracle that on the only eastward highway between the Tien Shan and the Kunlun Shan, we twain should meet again?

If this slave girl is Miranda, I went searching for her in the moonlit waste when she thought that her rendezvous was with Death. But was this strange encounter out of keeping with the pattern of my life and fate? Still, I cannot believe unless I am given a sign. For I kissed her good-by forever, put her out of my life, buried her among my lost memories and effaced her grave.

"Why man, your eyes are full of tears!"

This was Nicolo's voice, breaking into my reverie, its tone mainly curious but holding the merest trace of suspicion.

"They're full of dust from my ride and the lamplight burns it in." I wiped them on my kerchief.

"Now take a good look at my new jewel, and tell me who got the best of it, you or me?"

Nicolo's eyes were bright with happiness. I believed he had an inkling that his triumph was even greater than he knew. They were also extremely alert, but I did not fear self-betrayal as I made my search. I was used to guarding my countenance in his sight.

But Miranda was not so practiced. If this was she, she had known me at first glance; she had been expecting all these months and years to meet me again; if she had been in hearing of my voice when I came up to her caravan, she had recognized me then. The fact that she sat so still, with only a slight rise of color easily caused by the visit of strangers, argued that she was not Miranda. My dry eyes caught differences more marked than I had at first thought. Miranda could look like this after such a journey in space, time, and event, but so could many other maidens of her coloring, features, and form of equal beauty. Miranda was nearly twenty now, while this girl looked about eighteen. I had long ago put Miranda away because she had become the concubine of some prince, nobleman, or goldsealed merchant; I had divorced her phantom from my bed and her wraith from my board. Yet Nicolo had spoken of his new prize as a maiden. . . .

My heart cried that this was Miranda, but it had lied to me before. I asked a bold question in the Venetian tongue.

"What is her nationality, Signor Nicolo?"

"I haven't inquired into that, as yet. She's not a blonde Hun, as they are called—Kaffirs and the like from the Hindu Kush—and I doubt greatly if she's any sort of Circassian. My best guess would be she's a White Russian or even an Eastern German. But I've got the strangest sort of feeling, which my common sense denies, that she's English."

"What language does she speak?"

"She knows a few words in Turki-Persian. She didn't respond to any other that I tried."

"And you say Baram bought her to sell to Kublai Khan?"

"You seem greatly astonished by it, Marco. I don't believe I've ever seen you so taken aback."

"She's rather old to be a virgin, is she not?"

"She told Baram that she was, and he believed her. He's no fool, and I believe him."

"What is her name, signor?" And my heart stood still.

"He calls her Linda."

Miranda . . . Linda. One might have derived from the other, but actually they were no more closely related by sound or letter than Maffeo and Marco.

"Signor, I don't deny that the girl has beauty of an odd, wistful sort," I said, my heart drumming my side. "No doubt it will be more marked when she puts on weight——"

"And when she has bathed," Nicolo broke in, sniffing as he smiled. "So far she's had only a little oil to remove the dust from her face and breast. They were covered with it when Baram showed me her—yet I was overjoyed by the gift. I believe I would have given my second-best balas ruby for her as she stood."

"The ruby would bring about two thousand dinars, I believe."

"Perhaps I'm bewitched, yet I'd lay you a hundred bezants that my eyes are as open and my business judgment as sound as ever in my life."

"I would have chosen her myself, had I been given the choice of gifts. I see in her a pearl of first water, worth more as she stands than the sapphire. What do you see in her?"

"One of the most beautiful girls on earth."

Little slave girl that I found on the mountain, must I deny you still? Yes, if only in self-protection. For if you are Miranda, what then? I have found you only to lose you again. And this time I have lost you not to some unknown whose face I cannot see; this face resembling mine, except it is aglow with triumph over your possession, is one I know full well. And it must be that I loved you more than I knew, for it is not true—my heart denies the evil prompting—that I would rather see you dead.

If you are Miranda, will you acknowledge me? Why should you, when I have only got my deservings? When I sold my sweetheart slave, it may be the deal was fair, but I drove away the little ghost who tried to come to me, and shut your love and beauty out of my heart. Except for that blindness and crassness, I would have guessed your destination and looked for you along the road. I would have asked a lavishness from the gods, so when I answered a cry in the night, I would have expected to find you. I have been a measly trader instead of a nobleman, or I would have put more faith in fate.

"Are you considering her as a gift for the Khan?" I asked, my voice holding well.

"If she's as beautiful as I believe, she'd be a fitting gift."

"She would have to be flawless as well. No doubt you know that even a small mark—an unsightly mole or scar anywhere on the body—bars a maiden from consideration for the Khan's harem." And my heart flung into my throat with reborn hope.

"Everyone knows that."

"Why not look well? If there's only a slight disfigurement, I'll take her off your hands and you can buy something from Baram's stock as a gift for the Khan. I'll hold the lamp for you."

"I don't think it would give you much pleasure until she's bathed and fattened. Anyway, she's rather frail to expose to a room no warmer than this. Still, I can tell fairly well." Nicolo turned to the Nubian girl and spoke in Turki-Persian. "Help the Lady Linda off with her coat and tell her to stand."

Actually the room was quite warm. It was to my eyes that Nicolo was not willing to have the girl exposed. I wondered if he were surprised by or was even conscious of deeply submerged jealousy, seemingly so needless. It was proof to me that almost all intelligent men have a sixth sense, but often it does not explain its impartings.

"To hear is to obey!" the Nubian girl replied.

Then she addressed her mistress in a base Arabic, larded with Ethiopian words, which most Nubian slaves employed. By cutting corners and jumping over the jargon, I understood her well enough, and so did the white slave. This could come about in a few weeks in each other's company. Miranda had known a few Arabic words when I first met her.

"Is he trying to sell me to the young loon, do you think?" Linda asked.

"Be careful. They may speak our tongue."

"They are both Franks, to judge from the sound of their talk. But the older is richer and stronger and I hope he'll keep me."

Meanwhile she was slipping out of her padded coat.

"Did you catch what she said, Marco? It was a corrupt Arabic."

"I got part of it, and I'll tell you later."

Clad in a shift of diaphanous silk, the white slave rose gracefully to her feet. Only her face that had been veiled from the sun and wind and lately cleaned and her throat, shoulders, and breast were of a luminous whiteness I thought I had seen before; the rest of her body was gray with dust. I thought she might attempt some sort of apology for this, but she did not—nor would Marian Redvers of England. The wasting of her flesh was more severe than I had at first perceived. Her ribs stood out, her hip bones were plainly outlined under the taut skin, and her gaunt legs looked unseemly long. I felt my throat tighten and almost fill.

"Why are you so frail?" Nicolo demanded in Turki-Persian. "You couldn't have lost that much flesh in these few days."

"I think it's the wasting sickness," she answered quite distinctly, "and I will soon die."

"If she dies, I'll wish he'd given me a Badakhshan mare instead," Nicolo told me in Venetian.

"I'd take a chance on her recovery," I replied. "What would you sell her for?"

"Why? Do you want to buy her?"

"I have a yellow jewel, but your jest of having one too doesn't hold water. This girl's white as a pearl except for her hair. Pearls are lucky for me, but Mustapha Sheik cast my horoscope and told me I must never wear a topaz or any yellow jewel. I can't see any mark on her, but you are deceiving yourself if you think she's worth giving to the Khan, and if you'd given the second-best balas ruby for her, you'd repent it. But I'll make you an offer here and now, and if her back is striped or she has any other disfigurement disqualifying her for the Khan, I'll stand by it."

"What is your offer?"

"The yellow sapphire and two hundred dinars to boot."

"That's handsome enough. But since she's a free gift and I have nothing to lose——"

"You'd better not refuse until you look at her back."

"It's true she might be striped. Many owners wouldn't like her aloof ways." Then in Turki-Persian: "Turn around, Linda."

The slave girl turned impassively.

"No whip has been laid on her," I said. "Of course if a Saracen wanted to teach her a lesson, he'd give her the kurbash on the soles of her feet—but I'll risk that too."

"You might be sorry if——" Nicolo turned again to his chattel. "Linda, lift each pretty little foot in turn and let me look at it."

The girl did so, first the left, and as my heart stood still, the right. . . . *In an instant more I would hear him speak and she would be mine.* . . .

Then my head rocked with pain and my belly sickened and cold sweat bathed me from head to foot. On the sole of the girl's foot black with dust there was no red crescent burned in with a branding iron.

"She's without mark and her aloof ways are only a sign of high birth," Nicolo was saying.

Although rallying now, I did not dare speak.

"I'll set no price on her," he went on, "and if I don't present her to the Khan, I'll keep her for my own."

I nodded, and aware of his searching gaze, I turned as calmly as I could look at the Nubian girl.

"You puzzle me greatly, Marco," Nicolo remarked.

"In what way, signor?" I asked, steadying my voice.

"You're not your usual self, or else some very strong feelings have taken hold of you."

"If you'll pardon me, both are true. Chasing ghosts on the desert is an unnerving experience. Also I was taken enough with the white pearl to make an offer for her—and now you've refused it. I find myself tempted——"

"To a black one?"

"How did you know?"

"I saw your gaze wander."

"She has delicate features and a beautiful form. Do you own her too?"

"No, although I intended to buy her to serve Linda. And I agree with you, she's fine to look at. Baram said her Nubian name is unpronounceable, but he calls her Sheba. As a good Mohammedan, he's as well acquainted with the story of Solomon as we Christians and I relished the pleasantry. I'd venture her rich brown skin is very like the famous queen's."

"You promised me first choice of his goods, and if I buy her, she could remain in attendance on Linda except at such times as I summon her to my pavilion."

"That would be entirely satisfactory. If you'll authorize me to offer one hundred and fifty dinars, I'm fairly certain Baram will accept."

"You can go as high as two hundred. I could certainly get that for her in Cathay." Then I fixed my gaze on a leather case in a corner of the tent. "If she can play a Persian lute—and many Nubian girls play well—I can get more."

"The instrument belongs to Linda, I believe. Baram mentioned her as a good singer and musician."

"I'd like to hear her if only to get the zither playing out of my ears."

Nicolo opened the case. My eyes began to start, sure that they would see the Grecian lute I had given Miranda on the day of our parting; then they darkened in fear of Fate and the gods. The instrument was indeed a Persian lute, and I knew my lute was rift.

"Will you play it for me, Linda?" came Nicolo's quiet voice, speaking in Turki-Persian.

"Yes, my lord."

Nicolo put it into her hands. Her attendant had not cleaned

them in the fragmentary toilet making and their dirt touched me almost as much of their gauntness and seeming frailness. But with movements bold and strong she plucked the strings.

I heard the opening chords of an almost forgotten melody. Then the maiden Linda began to sing in a language I could neither speak nor understand, although I knew it was her native tongue. It was a ballad of her own country that Miranda had translated into my native tongue and sung to me long ago. Her voice was low and glimmering with beauty and the words came soaring out of the past, across the mountains and deserts, back into my heart.

> Pikeman O pikeman, red from the fray,
> Did you pass a bold knight in battle to-day?
> He promised to wed, I gave him a flower,
> O fetch him to me, my Young Rob o' the Tower.
>
> I fear he'll not wed you, fair maiden of Devon,
> He died in the battle and rode on to Heaven;
> And gifts that you gave him in sweet unbless'd hour
> Will fetch you to Fire, not to Rob o' the Tower.

2

In the business that followed, Nicolo represented both Maffeo and me while we stayed in the background. He had met several of Baram's kinsmen during a stay in Bukhara on the earlier passage; over cups of long-stored sherbet, he got us better bargains than we had hoped. In addition to the Nubian girl, Nicolo bought for me silk stuffs, mainly gold and silver brocades, to the amount of a thousand dinars. The quantity was as much or more than I could have got in Bukhara for the same sum; in effect it had been transported free across fifteen hundred miles of mountain and desert. If I did not make a thousand dinars' profit, I would miss my guess.

Nicolo and Maffeo bought all the remainder of Baram's offerings for five thousand dinars.

With some bought camels and hired tenders transporting our new goods, we set forth in the biting cold of midnight. I did not seem to look twice at the curtained litter, heaped with felts, atop an old, shaggy, perfectly trained riding camel belonging to Nicolo. I was deep in wonder, which is a deeper thing than amazement or astonishment.

We had traveled about two hours when the shape of a horseman showed on the moonlit road behind us. To behold such a figure, silent and solitary in this empty waste, flung our hearts into our mouths; he was very Death coming to summon us, for all we knew. But before long he had turned into a common-looking fellow named Zurficar we had seen at the rest ground. Some fashion of Tatar calling himself a Turk, and bound for Inner Mongolia, he had taken a puny captain's position in Baram's caravan. It developed that he had been torn between his desire to continue his journey and his desire to turn back with his chief. The former urge prevailed upon him shortly after our departure, whereupon he set out to overtake us. So however ordinary he might look, he was of extraordinary courage, or he would not have journeyed that road of bones alone in the dead of night.

Nicolo's face lay in shadow as he spoke to him, and from his voice alone I got the impression that he took no pleasure in the addition to our company, and even lacked a little of his usual self-mastery. However, when Zurficar explained that he had served the Great Khan in Mongolia and knew the country fairly well, the cold shoulder warmed.

The night waned, the cold dawn cracked, the pale sun rose, the genial warmth turned to heat. Just before noon we came to a good well, one of the best on the road, the waters cool from underground seepage from distant mountains, and abundant not only to slake the thirst of man and beast, but to wash hands and faces and a few clothes, and even the bodies of us three merchants and the slave girls. The camp stilled in the early afternoon and remained hushed until early night. When I had wakened and eaten, I sent word by Nicolo's servant for Sheba to come to my tent.

I had had it pitched well away from any other, which had caused the cameleers to exchange nods and winks. To reply to their jests I got out my ram's horns and posted them beside the entrance, and since these were the largest they had ever seen, the men roared with mirth; perhaps it was a good healthful human sound that I thought God liked to hear, and perhaps the desert demons stopped their evil occupations to listen and snarl with hate and perchance tremble with fear.

I lighted a small palm-oil lamp. The flap of my doorway jerked, and I drew it aside. Sheba, wearing a barracan of gaily striped cloth, threw back her facecloth and raised her hands to her bowed head.

"You may take your ease," I told her in the Arabic of Oman. She understood me and squatted on the felt floorcloth. I paid her no more attention for a matter of ten minutes, partly so she could familiarize herself with my appearance and the surroundings, partly to provide the silence that any lecherous cameleer, eavesdropping in the dusty dark, might well expect. Then I blew out the lamp and coming close to her, spoke in hushed tones.

"Sheba, do you know why I bought you?" I asked.

"Effendi?"

I reworded the question, employing the simplest forms and words. She tossed her chin in a sign of understanding and pleasure.

"I do not know, but I guess."

This meaning I derived from the girl's bewildering mixture of base Arabic with some Nubian language. Still I did not switch to Turki-Persian, in which she had appeared fluent: I wanted her to make a habit of mind of addressing me in this dialect, so if ever she spoke unwisely in others' hearing no harm would be done. By patience on both our parts and Sheba's quick ear and tongue, we were soon getting along without much trouble.

"What was your guess?" I managed to ask.

"You want me to carry secrets between you and the Lady Linda."

"Did she tell you so?"

"When I asked her, she said it might be so, but it would bring no good to anyone, and likely harm."

"What made you suspect it?"

"She told me of a lover she had had in—in some city in Frankistan—and that we might meet him on our journey. When I saw your face, I believed you were the one. When I could look into Lady Linda's face, I was almost sure."

"What did she say when I sent for you tonight?"

"I beg not to answer."

"You must answer. You are bound to me, now."

"I remain bound to her as well. Lord, she told me if you desire me for your concubine, to give and take every pleasure that I could, for the road was long and lonely, and we might soon all be dead, and she was sorry that I had been made to attend her all the way from Samarkand."

"Do you think she spoke from her heart?"

"How could I doubt it, effendi? She told me that she had begged you to take her virginity, and instead you took a thousand pieces of gold; but since I was not a virgin, and you had no sum to lose, you might be more yielding."

"Did she speak in bitter jest?"

"No, effendi. She spoke quietly, with her small, beautiful smile."

"Do you love her, Sheba?"

"She's the beat of my heart."

"Do you think she has the wasting sickness?"

"Has the slender-legged gazelle of the Libian Desert? She has made herself thin by much walking and little eating, so she can better endure thirst and hunger and great heat."

"It is cold now, and she should fatten. Why did she tell the signor she had the wasting sickness?"

"I don't know."

"It was not that the signor might sell her to me?"

"I think not, effendi."

"Why not? Has her love for me turned to hate? Speak truly, or I'll lay on the kurbash."

"She told me only that you did not call her, effendi, as you promised, and so I think her love for you died on the desert."

"How could I call her——?"

Then my throat cords twisted, and I stopped. Miranda's own words in farewell rang out of the past: "When you lie cold and lonely, call me, and I'll come."

I opened the tent flap and looked up at the dust-dimmed moon. It seemed that I said something to her without words—made some sort of promise without thought. Then I tied the strings and returned to my place.

"Did Miranda—the Lady Linda—tell you any of her history after the Greek Angelos bought her and before you knew her?"

"She spoke of it to pass the time. Angelos tried to sell her to a perfume buyer of Byzantium, but without success. Then he sold her to a Syrian slave dealer named Abu Kyr."

"Did she tell you the price?"

"When I asked, she told me. Fifteen hundred bezants."

"Angelos could have done better, if he had faith. What happened to her then?"

"Abu Kyr brought her to Isfahan, intending to sell her to the great Emir there. Instead he sought Baram of Bukhara, buying treasures to sell to the Great Khan and his couriers, and Baram bought her."

"At what price?"

"When I asked, she told me. Two thousand bezants."

"Then her boast was true."

"Effendi?"

"At what price did Baram hold her?"

"I heard him say he would get three thousand bezants—or dinars

—from a buyer for the Great Khan. This was before she got so thin."

"Three thousand! One who owned her sold her for a thousand and thought he'd done well."

"He was a blind fool, effendi."

"Sheba, your mistress—but she's not so any more except by my sufferance—bade you take pleasure in me and give me pleasure. If it is my desire, it is your duty as a slave. But if I do not command it, and leave it to your preference, will you do so or not?"

"I cannot, lord."

"Why not?"

"Even though you have bought me, the *Lilla Keiberia* is still my mistress."

"You said her love for me died on the desert."

"But the dead walk sometimes. I have seen and heard them."

"Without your meaning to, you've given me hope. No, I seized upon it and made it my captive, but you've fed it when it wouldn't eat from my hands."

"Is it like a lion cub, or a fledgling sand dove from a nest?" Sheba broke into a shout of laughter.

"The listeners about our tent will think I've done well. What will your mistress think?"

"Do you think she would deign to listen, effendi? Your hope is dove-frail if you know her no better than that."

"You speak too boldly, but I'll not reprove you, only give you an order. Arrange for her to meet me alone, as safely as possible, at tomorrow's rest."

"She won't do it, effendi. She made a promise to her gods to be a dutiful slave."

"In that case, arrange for my coming to her, taking her by surprise. Leave the tent flap untied and do all else for my ease and safety. Take pains, and let me know when all is ready. If you do your part well, I'll give you Persian sweetmeats. If you fail, you may have only a half-measure of water on the next day's march. If she cries an alarm, I will shield you if I can. Now you have my leave to go."

Sheba rose and touched her forehead with both hands.

"Effendi, if I were not bound to her, I would ask for sweetmeats of another sort."

With a deep-throated bubbling laugh, she vanished in the darkness.

3

The office I had given Sheba was no sinecure. We camped on a clay flat, shadowless except for heaps and crude windbreaks of sun-baked bricks, probably the rubble of some long-ago military post. Happily the well was deep, clean, and abundant, but its only help was to give her an excuse to stay up late, washing her own, her mistress's, and her master's clothes. It was by no means certain that Nicolo would stay in bed through any term of hours. To transport our new inlay of goods, we had bought some of Baram's camels and hired their tenders; the newcomers had not yet settled down and required frequent surveillance. Also, Baram kept spies among the drovers.

Nicolo ordered his new slave's tent erected within thirty paces of his own. But because both were near the well, the seeming blow to my hopes might prove a boon. Sheba would go to her clothes-washing soon after nightfall. Nicolo should be sound asleep by then; and if he rose in the next hour, she was sure to see him in the light of her dung fire, in which case she was going to run to him with a loud cry of *Shair Allah* (The Justice of God)! By pleading for holy water to protect her and her mistress from night demons—we were never without a ewer blessed by Nestorian priests—she hoped to arrest him while I beat a quick, furtive retreat.

I had enjoyed the hatching of the crude but sound plan—actually, any working or mere plotting against Nicolo was joy to me—and I did not dwell on its quite possible if not probable uselessness. For instance, Sheba had told Miranda not to fasten the door ropes, since she would be close by and going back and forth. But if Miranda did fasten them, from nervousness, I could not expect to get in. If I succeeded in entering, I could not even guess how soon I must come forth.

The last dusk died in the seventh hour; the decaying, jaundiced moon would not rise until the tenth. When the coast appeared clear, I moved too swiftly to be oppressed by my thudding heart. The strings of the close-drawn curtain had not been fastened, but the thick dark I had counted on within held a pale, bluish-yellow globe around the jewellike flame of a taper. Miranda lay in its umbrage. I made out her shape and guessed at her white face and a ghost of highlight on her hair.

"Who's there?" she asked in Turki-Persian. Her voice was low, not it seemed from stealth but by nature.

"Marco Polo."

"If you are looking for Sheba, she's at the well."

"I know it—keeping watch."

"What do you want?"

I started to say humbly, "Only to talk to you." But that was a mere fraction of my wants and maybe the time was short, and maybe Fate would give me no more or less than that, so I spoke the one Venetian word that came upon my lips, springing there from my heart.

"You."

She did not seem arrested or amazed.

"You can't have me now, Marco," she answered in the Venetian tongue. "It's too late."

"It's not too late as long as we both live."

She gave a muted laugh. I knew her by it as well as by her song.

"That might not be very long, if you're caught here," she said.

"If it comes to killing, Nicolo will die, not me."

"You were always a great boaster."

I knew her by her truthtelling, too.

"I have to be to win." It was true, but I did not know why.

"It may come to that. You hate each other far more than I ever realized. I smelled it on both of you when he brought you into my tent to show me to you. That was an act of hatred on his part. This may be one on your part."

"What may be?"

"Your coming here. You don't want me any more. You wanted me only when you were young and innocent, and even then you wanted something more. You said you did, just now; but what you meant was, you want Nicolo's slave girl. I don't care about that, but is it fairly safe for you to come here? Don't lie to yourself or to me."

"Fairly safe, yes."

"Are you taking into consideration that he's even more cunning than you are—at least he's far more experienced in cunning—and may have seen through our pretending the other night and may be sneaking up on us this instant?"

"If he had suspected we had been lovers, he would have tried to keep me from buying Sheba."

Miranda laughed again, then her eyes grew big. "You still have a grain of innocence," she told me in a different voice, utterly lovely in my ears. Then she paused, fought and won a little battle of some kind, and went on in the almost sprightly tone of a moment ago. "It's just what he would do, Marco, to encourage you. And you know, if he wanted an excuse to kill you, catching you with me would afford him the best he could ever find."

Deep inside my brain I felt a slight shock, as from the impact of an idea.

"Why, it would be a wonderful opportunity," Miranda went on. "All the caravan men would applaud. They're fanatical Mohammedans, and the killing of a purdah-breaker would exalt them to the skies. In their eyes it would earn Nicolo, an uncircumcised Christian, the right to go to Paradise. Your being his son would thrill them all the more. He tells everyone you're not—only a relation of his wife's—but of course they know different. The dimmest-eyed of the lot can see the resemblance."

"How do you know all this?"

"Sheba sees everything, and I'm not exactly blind."

"He wouldn't like to kill me until we cross the Hwang Ho."

"Then he won't try to catch you before then. He'll only make sure you do no damage to a slave worth three thousand dinars."

I drew in all my thoughts and set them at one task. Presently they performed it to their best ability.

"Miranda, I don't believe he suspects we know each other. I've seen no sign of it and many signs that he doesn't. He'll expect me to covet you and try to get you when I'm tired of Sheba, but he'll not look for any stroke this soon."

"In that case, you may sit."

"A slave girl giving leave to a Venetian merchant?"

"I'm the mistress of this pavilion."

I bowed to her and sat down.

"You've grown from a child to a woman—from the great ladyship you were born to almost to a queenliness that perhaps you aspired to—in three and a half years," I said.

"That's one reason Signor Nicolo and I are going to join forces in the matter I mentioned."

"What matter?"

"Making sure that you'll do no damage to a slave worth three thousand bezants."

I stopped and looked at her. My eyes had grown accustomed to the candlelight: it was no longer a pale blue-yellow globe hanging in pitch-dark but a diffused glimmer dimming away to vagueness. Miranda's eyes were big and shining. In better weather, as Baram had expressed it, her gaunt face would regain all its former beauty, added to a new beauty I was discovering there, which had come upon her on the long road. I did not know its source or exactly where it lay. Like almost all real beauty, it was unanalyzable. On the night that I swam beside her to Sea Pig's Wallow, I saw her amazing aliveness, expressed in physical grace, behind her quietude. Now I saw the same thing behind serenity, which is born of power.

I could believe now that she had rid herself of her ornamental flesh in order to travel light and better withstand hunger, thirst, and heat. When she needed it, she would put it back. And what remained was still beautiful and ineffably desirable. I could hardly breathe. . . .

"You've come to a new attitude toward your slavehood," I remarked.

"I wondered if you'd noticed it."

"How could I help it? It's a far cry from your wanting me to keep you a while, then sell you as a farm wench."

"That was before you cast me out."

"Do you mean—before I sold you?" But I knew she did not mean that.

"No, I still forgot myself in love of you. But when you forgot me—and I knew it in my dreams—I knew I must quit you and look out for my own interests. Instead of a farm wench, working in the sun, I decided to be a queen ruling a palace."

"When did that happen?"

"About two years ago. I belonged to a Syrian trader named Abu Kyr. He paid fifteen hundred bezants and hoped to sell me to the Emir of Isfaham for two thousand. The Emir would not pay it, and in the meantime I had heard of Baram of Bukhara, buying treasures to sell to the great Khan. I persuaded Abu to take me there along with some other things Baram might buy. Besides selling me for five hundred bezants' gain, the journey profited him well."

"Do you mean you had the ambition to be one of Kublai's concubines?"

"No. I meant to be one of his queens."

I could not keep my eyes from widening and some scales from falling from them.

"When you decided to go to his Court, the brand on your foot must have mysteriously healed."

"That would have taken a miracle. Miracles aren't given to slave girls wanting to be queens—they've got to run risks, as Esther did. When Abu Kyr had brought me to Bukhara, Baram wanted to buy me for his main offering to the Khan—until he saw the brand. Then he said he couldn't consider me for his venture, although Abu Kyr could make a fair profit on me in the market there. I asked Baram if he would take me provided I got the brand cut out without disfigurement. He said he'd gladly do so. I had already heard that the greatest physicians in the Mohammedan world, including amputators and trepanners, practiced their arts at the University of Bukhara."

She spoke calmly, without haste. My wonder at her poise changed to alarm at her complaisance.

"Wait just a minute, Miranda."

I stole out of the tent, afraid that the time had flown even faster than it seemed. The hush of sleeping men and beasts—not quite silence, yet without distinguishable sound—hung over the camp; its only breach was a splashing of water near the well in time with low, wailing song. Dust murk hid the stars and Sheba's dung fire glimmered fitfully. I looked at my sand glass. Not half an hour had passed since I had entered Miranda's door.

I approached Sheba from the direction of my tent. "*Sall' ala Mohammed* (Bless the Prophet)," I told her in good Arabic.

"*Al*," she answered without looking up—the accepted abbreviation of "*Allah umma salli alayh!* (O Allah bless him!)."

"Half an hour more?"

"If those zither players out on the desert don't come for me. If they do, I'll need holy water sure."

I left her, went to my pavilion, and made my way through pitch-dark to Miranda's.

"I was sorry to have you go," she said, "but I hoped you wouldn't come back."

"Why?"

"You'll make me so much trouble. But after a minute or two I wanted you back."

"Why, again?"

"To triumph over you, partly. My story is one of triumph—you can't help seeing that. Instead of disappearing in the house of some rich burgher or a palace of a prince, I'm almost to the Gobi Desert on the way to the Court of Kublai Khan. Your rejecting me made a woman out of me. Much more of one than if I'd become your concubine, or even your wife."

"What's the other part?"

"I think I've fallen in love with danger."

"Why not? He's been your companion for many a moon."

"Not too great danger, you understand, only enough to be exciting. Tonight there's just the right amount. The chance of murder or a duel to the death for you, but only a scolding, at worst a slapping, for me. I'd tell him you came to ask about Sheba—that she wouldn't surrender to you—and tried to make love to me. I'll say I couldn't get rid of you without alarming the camp and bringing disgrace upon him——"

Her eyes gleamed in the candlelight. I had cast a pearl beyond price before swine. No, I had dropped it where the connoisseur, Nicolo, could pick it up.

"My time's short. What about your foot?"

"Oh yes. I got Baram to take me to one of the greatest physicians, a disciple of Avicenna. He said I couldn't cut out the brand without possibly laming me or certainly leaving a scar, but because it was on the sole of my foot, where the skin is thick and has great power to rebuild, in six months he could wear it off with drugs. Of course Baram couldn't wait half a year, so I asked if I could take the medicine with me. That was possible, he answered, but its application would be a long, uncomfortable process, most awkward on the road.

"When he explained it a little more, I saw what to do. The drug was extracted from the root of a scrub with pointed evergreen leaves—it was similar to what we call barberry in England. It ate flesh away and was used for removing warts and wens. Then why couldn't I put a little in my sandal and walk on it every day? He said if I mixed it with olive oil, it would destroy layer after layer of skin while new layers grew from inside. Baram could hardly believe it, but agreed to pay down sixteen hundred bezants for me, and to sell me at the great market at Samarkand if the medicine had no effect. If it worked, he would in due time send Abu four hundred bezants more. I walked all the way from Bukhara to Samarkand and most of the road to Hokand. That's the real reason I'm so lean. With the burning and the walking, I wore the brand away."[10]

I saw her tramping that endless road under the sun and the moon. But a brand had been put on me that I could neither walk, work, nor pray away. I did not know what it was, and I could get rid of it only by conquering Nicolo, winning Miranda of England.

"I must go in one more minute. When can I come back?"

"Never."

I laughed at her. She laughed too and wiped her eyes.

"Still, it's no use, Marco," she murmured earnestly. "I'm not going back in love with you, and I'm going to do nothing to interfere with my being a queen in the Court of Kublai Khan. And in that I have support so great that you'll know I'll stick to it."

"The support of Nicolo?"

"Your mind runs on him. No, my saints."

"Did your saints object to what we did before?"

"No, because I was your slave. But I'm not your slave now—I belong to Nicolo. You think we can still make love as we did before until you can get me back or make some other deal, but we can't. Even if I wanted to, I'm still safe—I can still abstain. And that's because of a contract I made with my saints."

"What contract?"

"I told you once. When I tell you again, go. On that night, I wasn't at all sure I could go into slavery. I had been burned and thought it would happen again and again until I told my secret, and so would be ransomed. So I promised that if I won, I would be a dutiful slave—a loyal slave."

Miranda was speaking very quietly and her face was still, but I felt a force within her that I knew by no name but steadfastness. What else could I expect of one who had gone, not been led, three-fourths of the way from Venice to the Court of Kublai Khan?

"Do you realize what you're saying?" I asked.

"Partly."

"I've got to take you from Nicolo before he takes you himself or presents you to the Khan. And he won't sell you."

"I don't think you can, when he has so much more power. But you have another course—to let me alone."

"If he should die, I could make full claim as his heir. There'd be a will disinheriting me, but Maffeo would be glad to divide with me out here on the desert."

"You told me once that if you kill him, you will fail in your venture and go to Hell."

"I think he may meet his death trying to kill me. If I pick the time and place and provocation, it would be almost sure." And that was the idea that had struck and lightly stunned my brain early in the visit.

"Your minute's up and I want you to go."

"I must go, but I'll come back."

"I don't want you to and you have no right to."

"What are your wishes to me? What is right out here on the desert? Ask the lion and the falcon and the snake."

CHAPTER 7

THE TEMPLE OF SWASTI

I WAS A GREAT BRAGGART, MIRANDA HAD TOLD ME, BUT UNTIL NOW I had made good a fair share of my words. Now there came a time when I seemed to go slack as a ship's sail in dead calm. Not only did my schemes boggle in a morass of indecision and self-doubt. I committed few bold acts. So far Miranda would not consent to secret meetings—Sheba's office in the matter availed nothing, nor did my own mutterings whenever she was within earshot. To invade her tent again would be dangerous and, unless all signs failed, profitless. I daydreamed of seducing her, and in the gray, almost silent secret world of sleep the passage became so rapturous that my flesh was satisfied and I could imagine her knowing and sharing the experience in her own dreams. Through all our long parting, she had never been my partner in these flights; at least she had not identified herself as such. My only reading of that mystery was that I refused her the place, my soul unwilling to enjoy the mirage of a reality I had put away. This was a feat of will, an exercise of abstract justice, but inhuman and therefore wicked. The fact that lately I went seeking her on these gray paths, found her, and loved her physically was a momentous fact, although I did not penetrate its meaning.

These passing days brought us through the ordeal of the Takla Makan to the town of Shakow, where the religion and language of Tibet prevailed among a mixed populace of Turks, Tatars, Tibetans, and Tukuhuns. Countless images of Buddha stood or crouched or lay in the rocky caves about, and on the mountainside reared a vast abbey, where a thousand yellow-robed monks performed heathen ceremonies, including devil dances and blowing on a horn as long as an Indian python. As the oasis unfolded before us, two hundred square miles of well-watered, crop-bearing land, we stood smiling like little children and touched one another's hands. But the place had a special and secret meaning for me. I had better lay my plans and gird my loins for the greatest venture of my journey. Shakow indeed was the last inhabited spot on the road to Suchow, ten leafless days' march over the Gobi Desert.

And at Suchow dwelt the magicians who walked unharmed through fire.

The enterprise of obtaining salamander skins had taken new shape in my mind since my tyro days. Unlike my mother's uncle, Friar Johannes Carpini, we travelers would not be forced to pass between the fires at the Tatar viceregal courts; the Khan's golden tablet protected us from all such trials. On the other hand, the tales of the Tibetan magicians' supernatural powers almost always began with their immunity to flame, and the most knowing and learned travelers whom we encountered had offered no explanation. The wizards derived a rich revenue not only from the duped tribesmen; it was said that the Khan himself also granted them favors and fiefs. In this report, I perceived a thrilling promise. If such a great and sapient king knew the secret, surely he would make practical use of it. The gift of fireproof garments, along with the pertinent facts of their fabrication, might be counted greater than any jewel animate or inanimate.

It seemed that in contemplating the coup de main, I found relief from the aching problem of regaining Miranda.

A circumstance that raised my hopes lay in my growing companionship with the newcomer, Zurficar. He was once gatekeeper of a market in Kamul famous for its beautiful female slaves, and when I nicknamed him Pietro, on the ground that he had held the keys to Heaven, he was greatly taken with the lame and impious joke. Far from a nobody, indeed a man of some parts, he was shrewd, affable, bold, unscrupulous, and intensely ambitious to get ahead. I used him first in perfecting my speech. The Turki-Persian dialect employed by the people west of the Pamir had gradually changed to Turki-Tatar, still rich in Arabic words, but a more unified argot; and we Polos had picked it up as we went along. But Pietro knew Jagatai, which was the literary form, named for a son of Genghis Khan, and the tongue of the courts. Turki-Tatar and its blood brother Jagatai were mutually understandable, so merchants very rarely bothered with the latter. I did so, and in fact never missed a chance to practice it, with the hope of shining in the greatest of all courts.[11]

"Do you believe that the magicians of Suchow really have magical powers?" I asked him as we rode side by side out of Shakow.

The question caught his interest. "If it's trickery, it's of an impressive sort," he answered.

"Have you ever seen it with your own eyes—walking through fire, and so on?"

"They don't call that magic. It's in the way of proof of big magic made before. Let me explain that the magicians' chief job is killing dragons by secret rites. The people believe that dragons cause sickness and murrain and loss of crops, and although they propitiate live dragons, they'll pay the most to be rid of them. The magicians explain that to lay eyes on a dead dragon would turn a common man to stone, and to prove their killings they exhibit what they say are the horns, claws, and scales of a dragon, and the skin from the dragon's belly, which has no scales. How do the people know it isn't some common leather? Because if the wizards make garments out of it, they can walk through fire. Since everybody knows that dragons live in great halls of fire, that settles it. I've seen them do it several times. It's usually done at night as a climax to various other feats, and it's extremely impressive."

"Have you ever seen the garments at close range?"

"Not very close. The magicians won't let any layman examine them or touch them, saying they're deadly poison. One piece is a kind of hood, with eyeholes of some sort of crystal. This is loose-fitting and tucks into the collar of a robe. It's put on the last thing. The sleeves of the robe are tucked into big mittens, and the divided skirts into big boots. The leather is almost snow-white."

"Couldn't it be ordinary leather fireproofed in some way?"

"In what way? I've seen one of the walkers stand a good half-minute in raging fire."

"If it's trickery, it's strange that the Khan permits it."

"He permits it, and rewards it too, in every city where it's practiced. But Suchow seems to be the center of the dragon-killing cult."

Suchow was also on the caravan road from the High Altai, where Carpini believed the fiber mine to be located. Indeed it was the only notable oasis on this crossing of the Gobi.

Not daring to press the matter in my present excitement, I waited until some easy riding suggested casual talking.

"I've been thinking over what you told me about the dragon skin," I began.

"So?"

"I think it's the same as certain alchemists in Frankistan call salamander skin. Anyway, I'd give a great deal to get a suit of it."

"That would be extremely difficult and dangerous, if not impossible."

"Why?"

"In the first place, it may be poison, as the priests say. But certainly if they caught you trying to penetrate their secret, they'd kill you."

"Still, it might be done. Do you know any of the magicians?"

"I know one of the priests—if he's still alive and in Suchow. He's a graybeard, and the last I saw of him, he was trying to save enough money to return to his birthplace in the High Altai."

Coming from there, he might know the location of the mine and the process by which the fiber is woven into cloth. If he were old, he had probably grown tired of the frumpery, sick of his fellow fakirs, and long since enured to all sorts of compromise; and if he needed money, he would likely sell out to get it.

"When we come to Suchow, find him and bring him to me in stealth. If I obtain the garments, I'll reward you with a hundred dinars. If I prosper from them as I hope, I'll make you my bailiff and bring you to good fortune. But if you break faith, you'll be killed by a sword blessed by an archbishop, whereby you will be dispatched to the Christian Hell, where no salamander skin can save you from the flame."

Ere we came to Suchow and the fate awaiting me there, I noticed a change in Nicolo.

The first sign was a definite rise of his spirits. I had never seen them violable—under hardship or danger, he became grim but undiscouraged, and in victory he held them in tight rein—but I could not mistake the ring in his voice, the swing of his stride, and the look of a king in his face. When I sought for the reason, at first I found only his increased confidence in the road ahead and a greater ease in conquering its difficulties. It was an unwritten rule that I must keep out of earshot of his and Maffeo's talk, but careful observation gave an easy answer to the puzzle thus far.

Obviously the two brothers had regained familiar ground. Their earlier journey had taken them through Bukhara, Samarkand, and north of the Tien Shan, but from Kamul they had turned sharply southward to strike our present road at Shakow. I had no doubt that they knew every major landmark between here and Peking.

Although we were still in the Oceans of Sands, about a thousand miles from our destination, Nicolo took his own and Maffeo's safe arrival as a near-foregone conclusion. The sobering fact remained that in this happy augury, I was left out. He did not tell me the one or the other, I surmised it from his manner. My youthful strength and abilities had been useful to him in the long, long road behind us, but he could dispense with them now. If any account with me called for settlements, he need not let the exigencies of time and place stand in his way.

He stopped summoning me to his tent for conferences with him and Maffeo. If he spoke to me at all, it was as to a servant. I was no longer posted to the van nor was I given the least authority. Of course the cameleers and baggage wallahs noticed the change fully as soon as I, whereupon I lost face with sickening rapidity. So when I gave an order even to one of my own crew, he must answer sullenly or obey insolently, lest he too lose face before his fellows.

Perhaps it was in some weak attempt at retaliation that on a bitter night under an icy moon three marches past Shakow, I again invaded Miranda's tent. I came on the excuse of ordering Sheba to repair a ripped surcoat beside her mistress's charcoal brazier; she, coached in advance, pretended to go to my tent in search of other needed mending. But except for a darkling pleasure of defying my wiser self, I was sorry I had come.

Miranda was wrapped in a woolen barracan, causing me to remember a warmer clime and lovelier nights. Her hair glimmered wanly in the green glowings of the burning charcoal and her face was more beautiful than I had ever seen it. Partly this was a final clearing of my own eyes, for I had defied and scattered their last cloud. Mostly it was a flowering after long growth. She was more beautiful than I had ever dreamed—strange dreams of long ago, which I had not believed; and for not believing them, for doubting them with crass and vulgar doubt, I could not have her now they were proven true.

"You're no longer so skinny, Linda," I said in the Venetian tongue.

"No, I'm not. My master bade me put on flesh, now that the hardships of the journey are almost over, so that the Khan would be more pleased with me, in case I'm given to him."

"And if you're not?"

"So my master will be more pleased with me when he takes me to his couch."

"Which would you choose?"

"As befalls at last all dutiful slaves, my choice is my master's will."

"Then you must choose that I go at once."

"I don't know his will in the matter. Perhaps he'd like to have you stay awhile, to look upon my face and to imagine what's beneath my robe. He knows I'll do nothing that would displease him. Also, he might take satisfaction in your trespassing as that much more rope to hang yourself with."

"You know him well. I would almost believe that he knows you already."

"Why not believe it? If I say differently, it might be because he's ordered me to lie. In twenty nights on the Takla Makan, nearly thirty more at Shakow, and now the third on the road to Suchow—do you mislead yourself that he's a laggard or a reed? If he's neglected me, it's because he may wish to give me to the King of Kings."

"He'll expect favors in return, so is giving you away greatly different than selling you?"

"Giving me to Kublai Khan? Selling me on the street? It's the difference between a prince and a peddler."

"Your tongue is sharper than it used to be."

"So are my wits."

"You say it may be Nicolo's wish to have me stay awhile. Except for his will being yours, what is your wish? I leave myself open to your retort."

"I want you to go at once."

"You take no satisfaction in my fall?"

"In the little way you have fallen, I do take satisfaction. But I fear you're fated for a great fall."

"Then you've noticed something——"

"I've noticed that we're in Mongolia, only a few months from Peking. My master would not mind my warning you—he's warned you himself, by various means, several times." Her tone became deeply earnest, indescribably beautiful. "As once my owner—as once my halfway lover—you put a bond on me, the shadow of which remains. I don't want my fears to come true."

"Perhaps you had better fear for your master."

"You are always the braggart."

"At least put by your forebodings for a fortnight or so, and see if my fortunes fall or mend."

"I'll remind you of a foreboding that came to me on the day of our parting. It was that you'd lost your chance of happiness and must wander over the world in search of it as long as you live. Now I have an amendment to it."

"What is it?"

"You may not live very long, perhaps not even the fortnight or so that you bade me put by my fears."

"Is there any special reason——?"

"Only what I feel in my bones. What price is death out here? Ask the lion, the falcon, and the snake."

But now that I was glad that I had come—loving her face in the dim light and her voice that breathed remembrance of all we had shared—I must suddenly go. The tent flap jerked; without stood Sheba, the whites of her eyes glimmering in the wintry light.

"He's awake, and is lighting a lamp," Sheba whispered.

I walked silently and swiftly away.

It seemed likely that Nicolo had been wakened by a spy. The unpleasant conjecture wove through my dreams that night and begloomed my thoughts throughout the morning's march, and as the midday sun began to dissolve it, suddenly it had the solid shape of fact. Nicolo left his place at the head of the caravan, hung by the roadside, then fell in beside me.

"I've something to show you, Marco, in a few minutes," he said.

"I'll look at it with interest."

"I think you will. Whether you take any good from it, I have no knowledge or concern. However, I felt it my duty to call it to your attention."

I inclined my head in acknowledgment.

"Actually it is only a signpost pointing to a new world. That is, brand-new to you, and barely glimpsed before by Maffeo and me. It's a world that no Venetian could believe until he sees it. It is at once glorious beyond imagination and perilous past description."

"You mean, of course, the Court of Kublai Khan."

"The Court is only a symbol of his kingdom, citadel of his empire, an iota of which you've seen. Until now his hand seemed far away, his power and glory as remote, almost as legendary, as Prester John's. It will be different soon."

"May I ask, signor, why you condescend to warn me?"

"Because you've done your best for the caravan throughout many trials, and you served my brother and me well when you found Baram's caravan on the desert. While your wealth has increased threefold, and you have received a rich jewel besides, my obligation remains. But I'll discharge it in a few minutes. Thereafter you'll set your own course."

The big man rode free in the saddle, and his hands rarely tightened the rein or raised a whip. Yet the great gray stallion, high-mettled as a Kurd, paced along under perfect mastery.

"For instance," he went on after a brief silence, "I won't speak to you again about entering the pavilion of my slave girl Linda."

"It is also the pavilion of my slave girl Sheba."

"When you want Sheba, call her outside the tent. Of course I'm aware that you did no more than talk to Linda, or my present recourse would not be to words. A word, indeed, to the wise, as Solomon put it."

"I've heard it, signor."

"When you realize a little more what's ahead of us, you'll understand better a thing far behind us now—my telling you I didn't want you in our company. I gave you my reasons—both personal and practical. On the rough road, you've proved an asset rather than the liability that I expected, but soon the scene will change. Then if you want my protection, you may have it at a certain price. If you won't pay that price, you can pay the Devil."

"What is the price?"

"To resign as a partner in the enterprise, and accept subordinacy under me."

I was watching dust clouds swirl through the upper sky behind an errant wind. Down here the cold air scarcely stirred. I waited till the breath clouds disappeared from about Nicolo's lips.

"In plain words, you would not present me at Court."

"Perhaps not. But you would retain your gains and have an opportunity to increase them by trade."

"I bid you remember that in the beginning I offered to come in a subordinate position. You answered I must become one of the company, furnishing my own capital, or stay at home."

"I made a mistake. But you needn't make one now."

"Signor, I'll not resign my position in the company."

"What will you resign, I wonder? But before you speak further, see what we have here."

A monument had been erected beside the road, consisting of a block of alabaster at least six feet square on a pedestal of brick. Characters carved in the snowy stone indicated a writing of solemn import. I recognized the language as Jagatai, the literary form of Turki-Tatar, which I could speak tolerably well and was learning to write. Nicolo beckoned to Pietro. To my amazement, the hardbitten fellow fell prone and touched his head four times to the dusty ground.

Then he rose with a solemn face and read, his voice trembling with emotion:

BY THIS SPOT
PASSED THE FUNERAL CORTEGE OF
MANGU KHAN

GRANDSON OF GENGHIS KHAN

On its way to his burial ground in the High Altai.
And with him passed one hundred snow-white steeds,
To be slain without bloodshed and buried with him,
To ride in the Hereafter.
And with him passed three hundred maidens of perfect
        beauty,
To be wrapped in carpets and thrown back and forth
        until they die,
Whereof their flesh will remain unmarred,
For Mangu Khan to enjoy in the Hereafter.
And with him passed twenty thousand men and women
        of varied sort,
Chosen from the cities and villages along the road,
To be strangled and buried with him and become his
        servants in the Hereafter.
For he was Lord of All Earth
King of All Kings.
And this stone was raised by his brother

KUBLAI KHAN

FOR WHOM THE WORLD WAS MADE

2

"Does this reveal the matter I broached to you in a different
light?" Nicolo asked.

"No, signor."

Nicolo rode ahead. I waited a moment, listening to the soft
sound of camel pads in the sand, then resumed my place. In the
following days I had cause to meditate Nicolo's words, because
this reach of our journey was truly the beginning of its end. We
remained in the fastnesses of the Gobi. There was no permanent
dwelling house from the beginning of the march to its end, but
the Tatars—and now their name had changed to Mongols, but their
nature remained unchanged—passed here at certain seasons with
their flocks and herds in search of upland pasture. Caravans became more frequent and many of the rest grounds boasted huts

for the Khan's messengers and envoys. Where great folk had died, their companions had more often stopped to bury them and to raise cairns.

To gain Suchow, we passed through the Gate of Jade in what is the single largest handiwork of man since the world began. This was the Wall, made of brick or stone facings packed with earth to the height of twenty feet, with strong, square towers erected every hundred or so paces of its fourteen-hundred-mile length. It ran along hills, valleys, mountains, gorges, deserts, and oases, and had been raised by the great Emperor Shih Huang Ti two hundred years before Jesus Christ. Since "great" means something more than large, I wondered if the same adjective could be applied to the immense barricade. Certainly it had helped to fend off the wild Mongols for more than ten centuries; but if one-tenth of its cost had been spent in taming and civilizing the horde, perhaps it would have never broken out of its grazing grounds to rape all Asia. Shih Huang Ti, when your spirit beholds a Mongol Khan on the throne of Cathay, do you turn over in your grave? But only the gods can look down the road you might have taken, only they can count and measure your mistakes.

Suchow was the capital of a rich oasis, and its thronged caravanserai made us remember Baghdad, Mosul, Kerman, and Meshed on the other side of the world. On the third night there, Pietro reported that he had found his old friend, the priest of the Swasti, still in need of money to retire to the mountains of his native Dzungaria. I was to know his name no more than he knew mine—I could call him Jadugar and he was to address me by the common Mohammedan title malik. Pietro arranged for us to meet beside an abandoned well in a little-used courtyard of the caravanserai. He would serve as interpreter as far as needed; neither of us was to see the other's face.

In her second quarter, the moon hung almost straight overhead as Pietro and I made our way to the rendezvous. We paused by the well; in a few seconds I made out a dim figure with long hair and what I soon surmised was a red gown. That he was a Swastika, meaning a worshiper of the mystic cross Swasti each limb of which turned at an angle from right to left, I had no doubt.[12] The cult was an ancient one, mainly devil and nature-goddess worship euphemized with Buddhist terms and forms. Five hundred or more of the order dwelt in a huge castlelike abbey overlooking the city; of this number, at least fifty openly practiced magic. Certainly I need have not the slightest scruple about bribing him to betray his fellows and what Christians might call his faith. The most respectable lamas I had seen spent their time begging, toying with rosaries, and sillily turning prayer wheels while they intoned a million times "The Jewel is in the Lotus." At best they professed a debased Buddhism, while the Swastika were the most ragged and dirty, lousy and low, of the whole Tibetan priesthood. I regretted only that I must pay the scoundrel good gold or silver for the stuff required, instead of kicks and cuffs.

Pietro had warned me that I must even be polite to the foul-smelling shaman.

. "For how many pieces of gold will you deliver to me here a full suit of the fire-fighting dragon skin—hood, cloak, boots, and mittens?" I asked.

"Not for all the gold of the caravans, malik, would I do so," Jadugar answered in self-righteous tones. "Until you've gone through certain ceremonies to protect you from its deadly poison, the merest touch——"

Jadugar intended the preliminaries to occupy a good hour. He would present as many difficulties as I would pay to have removed; by then he would know how much he dared charge for the garments themselves. I spat on the ground in contempt, then Pietro handed him a piece of the fabric I had brought from Venice.

"*Shakya Thubba!*" he burst out. The term meant the mighty Shakya, and referred to Shakya Buddha. But I would have felt more secure if I could have shaken out of him the name of one of his own depraved gods or goddesses of the Swasti, such as Dreuma. Ordinarily these shamans invoked Buddha only for effect.

"You may see how weakened and wasted I am from the deadly poison," I said.

"Malik, you've been to the High Altai."

"No, but one of my kinsmen has been there." Friar Carpini had touched Karakorum, which is near enough.

"If you obtain the garments, will you tell all who see them that they are from the white bellies of fire dragons, slain by the magicians of the Swastika?"

"What else could I tell?"

"You might say something that would cost my order a good part of its revenue. Then if my brothers of the abbey found me out, they would boil me alive, cook the meat off my bones, and devour it. Malik, you've been to the High Altai."

"I've been nigh there, and I can keep a secret."

"Still I can't bring you dragon skins. I'm not one of the devil dancers and have no access to the Room of Wonders where the skins are kept. The most I'll do is to tell you how to find your way there, and for this you must pay me one hundred gold pieces in hand."

"I'll pay you only when I've got the garments and brought them to my lodgings with no alarm raised. Pietro will witness both our pledges."

"Then heed me well. You've seen the reliquary on the lowest terrace of the abbey grounds?"

"Yes." This was a tower in the shape of a big-bellied bottle.

"Just opposite is the Bride's Gate, whereby bringers of delight may visit my brethren's cells. But very few of them pass through in the first three hours after sundown, for these are the hours we Swastika sit in order in our pagoda and humble ourselves before our gods. Even so, take every precaution against being seen. At the head of the second flight of stairs, there's a long hall, completely deserted at this time. Its right-hand corridor leads to a balcony, and on this you'll find a door fastened with a wooden lock. A small, sharp saw of steel, such as are sold in Hind, could sever the lock in a few minutes with little sound; if this is unobtainable, use a sharp knife with a heavy blade. It's the door to the magic Room of Wonders—where the magicians keep certain gear. The suits of dragon skins hang on the wall."

"Why do your brethren trust to a wooden lock?" I asked.

"They have never needed even that. The folk hereabouts, and even the bringers of delight, would not open that door for a full chest of gold."

"What shall I do for light?"

"There are dim lamps along the corridor and on the balcony. You must make your own light in the Room of Wonders."

"What will happen when the theft is discovered?"

"Unless you've blundered badly, it will be blamed on our enemies, the Bonpo, stealing upon us from their abbey across the valley."

"If the Bonpo came raiding, would they wear their black robes with blue borders?"

"It would be a great sin, as well as evil fortune, to put them off."

"Don't you and the Bonpo worship the same gods?"

"Both sects bow down to Dreuma, the snake goddess, and to the great magician Tamba-Shi-Rob, and the Giant Dwarf Tampami-ber, god of fire with his crown of skulls. But their god Kye-p'ang is made of wood instead of plastered earth, and the four arms of their Swasti bend from left to right instead of from right to left as Tamba decreed."

"Such heretics should be burned alive!" I remarked.

"Malik has spoken truth."

"I'll speak now," Pietro broke in. "Jadugar, do you know what vengeance will be visited on you if you've lied to us, or if you cause an ambush to be laid for us?"

"Fear not——"

"You'd better tremble with fear. Your liver will be torn out and fed to the pariah dogs before your eyes."

"Why should I betray the son of my old friend and a great merchant from the setting sun? With the hundred gold pieces added to my hoard I can return to my own homeland, there to buy cattle and mares and three young wives to milk them, and do such magic as is pleasant and profitable, with no long-nosed abbot to complain!"

Warmed by this common humanity half-hidden under his foul rags and matted hair, I felt new confidence in the enterprise. Thinking over what he had told me, I saw no serious obstacle to its success. The risk was considerable, but the fact that cautious, hardheaded Pietro, native to the land, would cheerfully run it beside me showed it was not large. Truly Fate had been generous in setting the conditions. Had they been much harsher, still I might have attempted to meet them. It lay as near to inevitability as any act of my life.

In my cold cell in the caravanserai, I dreamed wildly, warmly at times, dismally for a space, but at last triumphantly. My mother was near me in several of the scenes, although I could not see her face. Rosa stood mute with tears in her eyes. The Black Woman of Martyrs' Walk had me look at a candle flame, then held me in her arms. The jongleur whom I had renamed Antonello to plague Nicolo became merged with Jadugar of the Swastika, and deep in my dream I realized for the first time, with that strange lack of surprise that marks the dreamer, that "jongleur" and "jadugar" were the same word. When it seemed I had climbed countless stairways and stolen through endless passages only to lose my way in defeat and despair, I reached into a disused water pipe and brought forth not the two torn fabrics, but a pearl-studded crown. I wakened, got up, and read by candlelight the almost faded writing on the fabric.

Sleep was hardly out of my eyes in the cold morning before those eyes were welcoming the sun. Every man looks for certain

signs of good or evil fortune, and all of mine were fair. I was a
Venetian, while my adversaries were louse-bitten, devil-ridden
barbarians. Beyond that, it was my great stroke against Nicolo
in the war that began before I was born. No doubt Kublai Khan
would be pleased with the gift of a blonde slave girl of surpassing
beauty, but would he count the gift as great as a suit of fireproof
fabric, no mere curiosity, but a natural wonder that he could put
to practical use for his whole empire's gain?

*Miranda, go from my visions till I find the answer! Do not
let me see your hair combed smoothly back and braided into
hempen ropes on each side of your slender neck and hanging in
front of your steep, snow-white shoulders, or I cannot judge fairly.
I must not behold your mouth, which in my heart means lovely
smiles, and kisses, and song. Your eyes make me perceive the
limitation of the brilliance and beauty of jewels.*

*You do not go because I won't let you go. Is that to tell me
that no matter how I triumph over Nicolo in the Khan's Court,
I must still have you for my greatest and final prize?*

3

With Pietro's help, I took many a stitch in time. Long before
dark, he had obtained two red robes for us to wear during the
actual thieving, and two blue ones with black borders for use on
our flight. We chose suitable ground for posting our horses in the
care of my slave girl Sheba; she was to have the sheet in which
she carried washing and be able to make her way on foot in darkness from our place of rendezvous to the woman's ghat. Most
likely I would need no weapon for killing at a distance—this was
my only consolation for its enforced lack—but my dagger hung
handy in my left armpit. In my heart was a growing exultation.

As soon as the dark thickened, Pietro and I met in the courtyard
and made our quiet way to the posting ground. Here we were
glad to put on our disguises, for the month was bitter February,
the thin dry hair of these highlands would hold no heat, and the
fangs of the frost bit through our numbed flesh to our aching
bones. Next to our own garments we donned the black robes with
blue borders. If we were seen during our flight, we would presumably be taken for raiders from the Bonpo, and if this did not cause
the smoldering feud between the two sects to blaze into bloody
war, my pleasant fancies gulled me. Over this Bonpo raiment we
wore the red robes of the Swastika. If we were met in the dim

halls by a bringer of delight, arriving early to warm the bed of some favorite wizard, we could avert our dirt-smeared faces and peacefully go our way. We intended to shuck the red robes at the Bride's Gate. Our black ones could be stuffed with the bulky garments of the fire-walkers into Sheba's sheet, having every appearance of innocent laundry on its way to the woman's ghat. Thence she should be able to transfer them safely to my saddlebags.

She was waiting at the rendezvous, knowing her part well. Although she did not mean to let me know it, I discovered her deep-biting fear in her wide eyes and shaking voice, and this I did my best to hide from Pietro, lest his spirit quail. Before we parted she wished me the favor of Ahriman, the Zoroastrian devil of whom we had been hearing ever since we penetrated Persia, and who was of great potency throughout many sects of Central Asia.

"Why not seek me a blessing from Ormuzd instead?" Ormuzd, or Ahura Mazda, representing Good, shared with Ahriman, Evil, the rule of the universe.

"Because the work you do tonight is evil work."

"To steal from a temple of devil dancers?"

"In what cause? Do you serve good or evil? It is great evil to hate your sire, no matter the ill he has done you. He was God's instrument in causing you to be born." She was speaking in bastard Arabic that Pietro could not follow.

"Your theology is too deep for me, Sheba. But here is a thing that stands to my common sense. The devil dancers themselves worship Ahriman in some form or other. Won't he then withhold from me the favor you've asked, and give me his curse?"

"No, because he's not true to his own. By whatever name you call him, he's still the great traitor. That is why I sorrow to see you, my master, join his caravan."

"I?"

"You've done so, I believe, to get at Nicolo. I fear that you crave my Linda more for his pain at her loss than for your joy in her gaining. It might be better for her if you die tonight. Then only your shadow could visit her in dreams."

"Yet you asked a blessing that I might live!"

"What else? I am only a black woman of Nubia, alive for the hour."

Regardless of which caravan Sheba or I had joined, the magicians of the Swasti belonged to the Devil.

All men know that certain of God's elite can perform miracles.

The power is given them to use for others and for the Kingdom, never for their selfish gain. In repayment for the services of his own priests, the Devil gives some of them a power resembling this, actually its hollow mockery, the power of magic. By its exercise, the magicians can break the laws of nature, presumably the Law of God, but only temporarily and in trivial ways. They can hang suspended in the empty air. They can cause a mango tree to grow before your eyes, or at least cause you to believe this; or to dismember a man and make him whole again; or to throw a rope end up into the sky, climb the rope, and disappear; or to cause sudden rains or gales or thunderstorms. From these feats they derive a stingy revenue, but their treacherous master has no intention of letting them become vastly rich or powerful. His viceroys on earth are emperors, kings, barons, and the like, who can hire magicians by the drove. When all is said and done, they are his mangy coxcombs.

We came to the great abbey crowning the hill. What looked like angry eyes here and there about its walls were luridly lighted windows; others showed a flickering glimmer; most were dark holes. There seemed only silence until we listened with pricked-up ears, then we could detect a ghostly echo deep within the pile, not any sound of nature, it seemed, nor yet of man. Guided by gleamings of the moon, we made our way between stone outbuildings to the foot of the reliquary. On our previous survey, from two cable lengths' distance, it had showed as a white jug, tall as a house. Now it loomed above us like a monstrous bottle of polished alabaster, big enough to hold the whole body of the fisherman's genie, and wiping out half the lights of heaven. But in the cold dark we found the Bride's Gate, opened it, and found our way to a steep flight of stone steps.

The whisper in our ears became a rising and falling murmur. It could be caused by hundreds of priests chanting orisons to their gods behind thick stone walls; but sometimes it was broken by what might be the faraway clang of gongs and horn-blowing and bursts of laughter and shrill cries. "They're saying Mass to the Giant Dwarf," my stout Tatar whispered in a tone of contemptuous mirth. Then I saw him shiver in the gloom.

We gained the top of a second flight of stairs and started down a crooked corridor, dark everywhere except for pallid islands where stone lamps had been set in niches in the wall. It was supposed to come out on a balcony, in due course, but it ran on and on like a gray road in a nightmare. Around black bends or in the murk where the dying beams of the far-spaced lamps could not meet, I must run my fingers along the walls in order to find my way. Suddenly I cursed myself for venturing into what might prove a cul-de-sac.

I would not have gone so readily, perhaps not at all, except for Pietro's willingness to go with me. But in my passion for the prize I had not scrutinized this; I had taken it for proof that my plan was sound and the danger slight. Partly to busy my mind against the horror of imagination, I marveled over it now, only to find that I had been self-betrayed. Any plan I had proposed would have suited Pietro. He had let me decide how great a risk to run, as I might have known had I remembered that he was a Tatar. Slaves of his tribe had brought the highest price of any male slaves in Venice, simply because of their wholehearted service and their unshakable loyalty. They did what their masters told them with the thoughtless directness of a dog.

Still I did not turn back. I could not, my will to go on being thoughtless and direct. For all I knew we were a dog leading a dog to a dog's death.

Where the last lamp dimmed out we found the exit to the balcony and then the door of the Room of Wonders. From an Indian merchant in the caravanserai I had obtained a small saw of extreme hardness that ivory workers used, and after hundreds of thrusts and withdrawals, it scratched through the ancient wooden padlock. With a quick stroke of a plunger in an ivory cylinder I ignited tinder and brought it to a lamp with only one bright face no bigger than my hand.

Its beam moved slowly about the room. First it revealed the ugly faces of an idol with ten hands and three superimposed heads, perhaps a great god of yore now discredited and shamed and stuffed away, but more likely a deity of awful potence, revealed in the temples only at foretold and eerie hours. In spite of my aching haste, I could not stop the round ray from exposing every one of a long row of devil masks fastened to the wall, and looking at them, I could not hold it steady. These were fashioned of wood, leather, hair, and the like; their teeth might be stones and their glaring eyes no more than light-reflecting glass. Yet it seemed that I knew every one. Each was a flawless image of a face beheld in nightmares or delirium or in madness and perhaps in intimations of Hell—sights that in our sunlit hours we deny that we have seen, but which our souls remember all too well.

In a corner leaned a thin, long chalkwhite trumpet that my

gaze would not skip. Its slightly crooked shaft was of human thighbones hollowed out and set end to end; its mouth was a cleverly carved human skull. Gongs for calling friendly spirits and driving away inimical ones hung from the rafters; baskets and boxes used in human decapitation and dismemberment tricks stood about, and their dusty, shabby genuineness appalled my spirit. There were wooden and copper idols representing the male and female principles in nature; drums hooped with human rib bones for rainmaking and thundermaking; a girdle of infant skulls; and dried human hands and feet that were caused to move and walk by diabolical arts.

Then the lamp jumped in my hand, for among multicolored robes and frumpery of various sorts hung some suits of salamander skin, snow-white from being newly washed in fire.

When we had rolled one of them into as compact a space as possible, there began the long agony of our retreat. Perhaps I walked in the Devil's care tonight, as Sheba had entreated, because I led my companion safely off the balcony, passed the wan lamps of the stone corridor, and down the upper stairs. I found myself half believing in the auspice, my scalp tingling and my cold skin thrilling—then it seemed that the Devil had played with me only to let me fall.

From the dim flight below rose a sudden murmur of voices. They were obviously male, and an instant later the lamp in the wall niche revealed the shapes of two of the red-robed Swastika priests climbing the steps. Their heads were bent to find good foothold but they had only to look up to discover us. And we could not retreat to certain exposure in the lamp-studded hall.

The plan of defense taking instantaneous shape in my mind was violent attack from above. I visioned both of us pouncing down atop the bent-headed pair and stabbing them to death before they could resist or even cry an alarm. Swifter than thought, my terrors were being transmuted into that animal fury which alone, storming the brain, can empower such a violent act, when quick-witted, keen-eyed Pietro snatched me by the arm. He had seen a dark recess in the wall beside the landing. In an instant we were both pressed against the wall. Unless the two lamas looked fully and sharply to one side they would surely pass by us. But Pietro saw me draw my dagger and with what I thought was a beaming smile on the dim blur of his face, he bared his own. If at any instant we should be discovered, I had no doubt of our concerted attack in the very next.

Then there came an instant in which Pietro's good tactics came close to failure from a strange cause. As the foremost lama was about to finish crossing the open space and his fellow was just emerging into our sight, the impulse to kill now gripped me with great force. It seemed composed of an unreasoning terror that had usually spared me in the climax of great trials—certainly I saw no sign or likely prospect of our being discovered. Still, I resisted it with a sense of darkening hope. Perhaps I could not have done so except for Pietro's shoulders having edged in front of mine as he took a warlike stand. The trifling obstacle weighed on the side of my inertia. I accepted it as a provision of Fate.

The two monks passed out of sight. The shuffle of their bare feet on the stone quickly died away. Pietro and I resumed our flight; and now Good Fortune kept company with us, and I could be glad I had not risked battle, and Fear became a little cold snake in his den deep in my brain. We found Sheba at the meeting place and I laughed at her popping eyes. She stuffed our loot in her washing sheet and took off by a picked route to the woman's ghat. Pietro and I rode furtively until we passed a famous bagnio, then went to the caravanserai by separate paths. I stood watching a caravan unloading in the courtyard when Sheba came into the firelight with a white bundle on her head. When I saw its wet glimmer and a trickle of water down her face, I blessed the head that was as long as her heart was loyal.

We appeared not to notice each other as she made for my quarters, but I caught the sharp glance she threw. That it was deeply troubled I could not doubt. After a few seconds' wait, I followed her and found her shivering in the dark passage. She led me through the door and closed it softly.

"Two men followed me to the gate," she whispered.

"When did you first notice them?"

"On the way back from the ghat. But I think they may have been behind me all the way."

"Perhaps they wanted only——"

"No, they took too much care not to show themselves. I think they were following you when you came to the meeting place. Are you sure no one saw you?"

I remembered the two monks who walked by the alcove looking straight ahead.

"No, I can't be sure."

"Is there an empty room with an unlocked door where I can hide this?" she asked quickly.

"It would take a long search. You'd better put it on your head again and go out the main gate of the caravanserai. I'll see if the coast is clear."

I walked quickly ahead of her as far as the courtyard, then what I saw caused me to turn back.

"Put it in my room and lock the door and bring me the key," I told her.

She went about obeying the order as swiftly as she dared. Yet by the time she had finished the shape of coming events became far more clear. Of the fifty long-haired, foul-faced priests of the Swasti whom I saw entering the gate, all but one had squatted in two long rows before the dung fire. One, who wore a larger rosary and carried a longer staff, stood in front of the rest, beating his breast and yelling in a high-pitched gobble.

"Sacrilege! Sacrilege! Revenge! Revenge!"

CHAPTER 8

THE MAGICIANS

THE MONKS HAD MARCHED IN SILENCE TO TAKE ME BY SURPRISE, and so had collected no long tail of riffraff. Since the caravanserai lay at the outskirts of the town, I could hope that the guards would close and lock the gates before devil-ridden crowds could gather. There was one other factor that I could count as favorable. Suchow was the only oasis of any size or importance in many days' march, and the Khan's law was executed with respect to frontier conditions. Here, as in many remote cities, the merchants were granted autonomy within the caravanserais as long as their verdicts were not appealed to the Governor. I would surely stand my first trial before them under the rulings of the serai master.

Such underlings as cameleers, hostlers, baggage wallahs, water boys, and sweepers gathered swiftly into a compact crowd, silent but greatly excited. Singly or in pairs, the merchants came out of their quarters as the news reached them, and before long the serai master, wearing an iron key and other badges of authority, made a dignified appearance with his bailiff and clerk. The gates swung shut. The dung fires mounted and cast a lurid light on the two rows of ragamuffins and their now silent chief. I caught a glimpse of Pietro standing among the middle fellows but averted my gaze from him. As Nicolo and Maffeo Polo made a lordly entrance—for the whole city knew that they were ambassadors to the great Khan —it may be that my cheekbones flushed, but my lips curled in a sneer.

Attendants brought an iron chair for the serai master. A bench was placed for the abbot of the magicians, and some horse tenders with slanted eyes and button noses gasped to see him seat himself Buddha-wise, with his legs tucked under him. A long silence fell. A big rat that was neither black nor brown but snow-white crept out from the rows of squatting magicians full into the firelight. When one of them uttered a squealing sound, the beast ran back.

"What is your charge, O Abbot, and by what evidence and against whom is it made?" the serai master asked in Turki-Tatar.

The Abbot replied with great vehemence in a high-pitched frantic voice.

"While worshiping the Giant Dwarf in our temple, two of our brethren of the Swasti beheld the selfsame vision. It was of two violators of our temple, making their way to the Room of Wonders. Driven by that vision, they left the temple, and lo, as they passed the landing on the stairs they beheld the two miscreants, hidden in an alcove. It being against their faith to lay hands forcibly upon even the vilest thief, they feigned to avert their eyes. Passing by, they brought word to me of the violation, but the blasphemers had fled with their loot, being a suit of the dragon skins that defy fire."

When he paused to catch his breath with a sucking sound, the serai master spoke in a calm, judicious tone as might the Doge of Venice.

"The fire-walkers have told that these garments are the most deadly poison to all except themselves. Why did not the thieves fall down dead?"

"Only by casting horoscopes and certain ceremonies of divination can we know the full truth. But my brethren thought they recognized one of the desecrators, whose face was less hidden, as a monk of Bonpo, the abominable heresy practiced across the valley. If so, he could have learned the secret antidote of the poison and rendered the garments harmless."

"What then?"

"We wished for the eyes of a desert owl that would penetrate the darkness and reveal the evildoers. The God of the Night had not given us such eyes, but he sent her whom he had so endowed, and she flew to our help."

Suddenly the whole assembly caught its breath. Perched on the Abbot's shoulder was a little brown owl such as dwells in the same burrow with marmots and desert asps. I had been watching all his gestures and expressions that the firelight disclosed, yet I had not seen the visitor's arrival.

"You were able to trace the thieves?"

"We found where they had tied their horses, and soon we caught sight of a slave girl carrying a bundle as though it were clothes for washing. We followed her to the woman's ghat, and then to this very courtyard. Also, one of our number saw two horsemen whom our gods whispered to him were the evil twain. One was without doubt a priest of the Bonpo—presently he parted with his fellow and rode away. Our brother followed the other, and was about to lose sight of him, knowing not his countenance, when a pale light, such as might be cast by a giant firefly in summer forest, played upon him. Behold, he was a tall man on a red horse, and his countenance was like that of the Khan's ambassador from Frankistan."

"Do you dare accuse Nicolo the Frank——"

"I looked upon the great Emir as he took his place. My brethren told me of his resemblance to the rider in face and form, as though they were brothers, but the rider was somewhat younger."

"None of your followers have spoken to you since Nicolo Emir took his place."

"Ah, but one has—with the tongue of the spirit."

"Nicolo Emir rides a dapple-gray horse, but a younger kinsman of his wife's rides a red horse."

"Aye, and we behold him among the merchants."

"It's a grave charge, O Lama."

"I do not make it, lord. I ask if he owns a female slave of Nubia, and whether she came hence tonight with a white bundle, and what might be the contents of that bundle."

"Is there anyone here who can answer those questions?" the serai master asked, turning to the listening throng.

"I can answer two of them, master," a cameleer replied.

"You may do so."

"The merchant Marco Polo owns such a slave girl, and I saw her bring a white bundle through the gate and carry it to his lodge."

At that, all the squatted priests raised their arms, palms up, over their heads. Lifting their faces, they gave forth a cry such as might rise from a pack of desert foxes about a lion's kill.

"Silence!" the master demanded. Then, turning to the cameleer, "Does that complete your testimony?"

"Yes, master. I don't know what was in the sheet, although it was dripping wet."

"Deceit! Deceit!" shrieked the priests in one voice.

"We shall see. The evidence surely justifies a search of Marco Polo's quarters. But before that he shall have a chance to speak." He turned to me with great dignity. "Marco Polo, have you anything to say in rebuttal of the evidence brought forth against you?"

"No, malik."

"Then you confess that you have the stolen garments?"

"I have them, malik, but they weren't stolen."

"How, then, did they come into your possession? I warn you that the telling of any lie will go hard with you."

But which lie I told did not matter very much, provided it brought out one fact—my possession of a weapon that in my terror and despair I had almost forgotten.

"It's true that my companion of tonight was a brother of the Bonpo. He had come from the High Altai, and there he had known my mother's uncle, Friar Johannes Carpini, who visited the Court of Kuyuk Khan at Karakorum a quarter of a century ago. There may be some graybeard in this company who remembers the event."

The serai master turned to an old Tatar gatekeeper with a hawk face. "Toto, you are a Karakorumian. Did you hear of the coming of this Frankistani priest?"

"The very wolves on the steppes heard of it," the old man answered.

"My uncle knew this holy man as Surab," I went on. "To him he gave moneys to obtain for him a suit of what the Swastika call dragon skins, but this skin was obtained from a den deep in the ground, and that dragon was not killed by magic worked by priests, but by picks and shovels in the hands of common men in the High Altai."

Over the gathering hung a breathlessness more strained and still than I thought my words could cause. I did not know the reason until I felt a stab of pain, devilish sharp, in the calf of my leg. I whirled in time to glimpse a brown, furry animal, of a larger frame than a housecat's, but much leaner, run off with a monkey gait and instantly disappear in the shadows. But my pain and fright passed quickly, while my dismay at the throng's behavior lingered on. Although almost every watcher had seen the beast's advance upon me, no voice had been raised in warning.

"Abbot, the Frank hasn't been convicted of any crime, and he or no one else is to be molested while giving testimony," the serai master said sternly.

"I have not done so, malik."

"That animal—some kind of monkey—belongs to one of your band."

"Malik, we've never seen him before. I think he was once a man who'd done great evil, and has been reborn in that form. In trying to atone for the evil, he rebuked with his teeth one with a lying mouth. But the avatar won't molest him further if from henceforth he speaks truth, and he'll fare much better at our hands."

I no longer doubted that the Abbot had caught my hint and its implied threat, but its effect upon him was far less marked than I hoped. There came a chill of ill omen upon my spirit.

"He's not put in your hands yet," the serai master replied. "Marco of Polo, you may proceed."

"The holy man Surab promised to deliver the garments when my mother's uncle Johannes or any emissary called for them, whether in one year, or ten, or three times ten. If he had gone to his gods, his heirs would discharge the debt. The years passed, and I, Johannes' heir, had word from Surab that he had joined the order of the Bonpo at their monastery at Suchow. To him I sent word that I would surely come here to get my legacy, but when at last I arrived with Nicolo and sought him out, and met him in secret, he told me that the garments had been stolen by the magicians of the Swasti."

Again the dirty hands shot up, palms and faces raised, and a howl of "Lies! Lies!" shook the icy air.

"Marco of Polo, can you produce the monk whom you call Surab?" the serai master asked.

"I can't, because I vowed that if he would help me recover my lost legacy, I would consider the debt discharged and protect him from all ill consequences. This vow I made before my saints, never to be broken."

"How could you be sure that the suit you took was the one your uncle had bought?"

"I couldn't. I took the first my lamp shone on."

"What proof can you offer this court that the story is not an invention intended to save you punishment of a high crime?"

"Malik, here are two keys. The large one of iron unlocks the door of my lodging. The small bronze key opens a cabinet in my right-hand saddlebag of Tabriz leather, in which are torn pieces of white fabric. Bid a trusted messenger bring them here, as well as the fire-walker's suit wrapped in white sheeting."

"You may go in Toto's charge and get them yourself. He won't be required to touch the suit or to get within arm's reach of it, and I wouldn't in his place."

"I'll not, master, and on that you can bet a horse." So spoke a good Tatar.

I had long since caught sight of Sheba at the gate of the harem-lik. I signaled to her and she came on light feet and followed me ahead of Toto. In a moment she reappeared, carrying the bundle on her head, her hands swinging free at her side. As she calmly set it down before the serai master, the spectators freed their deep-drawn breaths and most of the merchants and hard-bitten cameleers looked faintly sheepish. But the eyes of the magicians half-hidden in unkempt hair were hot and angry.

I put into the master's hands the two pieces of fabric.

"They were torn in an accident," I explained, "but your Honor can see that they fit together. On them was written the letter from my mother's uncle, Friar Johannes Carpini. And you will see too that the material is the same as the suit of the fire-walkers."

At this last, the master came nigh to dropping the pieces, and clung to them only to save face before the watchers.

"They do seem the same," he said, when I showed him the helmet. "But the writing here is in a tongue I don't know."

"Will you have me read it aloud?"

"That would prove nothing. Ask one of your company to read it and give us its burden."

"Then I'll ask Nicolo Emir, ambassador to the Khan."

I had never in all my days done a bolder thing. The thin ice was instantly apparent to all members of our caravan, and their acute suspense spread fire-fast through the throng. Yet the chance I had played was my best chance, for unless my instincts lied to me, Nicolo would not dare disavow me altogether. The other merchants knew me for his kinsman, countryman, and fellow Christian and never really doubted that I was his son. And while they would take care not to make enemies of the lamas and knew I must be punished for my grave offense, they wanted no precedent set for tossing aliens of position and substance to these louse-bitten dogs. Indeed as Nicolo took the torn pieces I could see that he was nonplused.

Then slowly he raised his head and looked at Maffeo. He began to speak in the Venetian tongue, not loudly, but full-voiced, so that I could hear.

"Do you remember, at our last feast with Zane and Flora, I expressed the fear that Marco would bring our caravan into disrepute?"

"I remember it well," Maffeo answered.

"I remarked on how he had committed theft to get what he wanted, as his lowborn father had done before him. But you told me I was making too much over a cuckoldry twenty years old."

"I did say that, yes."

"Maffeo, you were wrong. Do you confess it and resign this matter to me?" His bearing, like his memory, was like that of a king.

"Nicolo, I've long ago resigned all matters to you."

2

Nicolo nodded gravely. Fitting together the two pieces of fabric, he read in silence. All eyes were fixed on him; everyone knew that the verdict of the court would hang largely on how far he backed my story. The magicians sensed the crisis and the leering insolence of a moment ago passed from their dirty faces. And perhaps because they feared that Maffeo and the other merchants were putting silent pressure upon him, they cast another spell.

I noticed that one pair of eyes after another withdrew from Nicolo and slowly widened. I followed their gaze to behold the most remarkable piece of legerdemain of the night. The faces of the wizards appeared as blank and flaccid as the faces of the dead, but their loosely opened mouths were filled with light. There was not one that did not show an unmistakable pale glimmer and many were luridly bright. I was quite sure that the effect was achieved by small mirrors held by the teeth and tongue as every magician gazed steadfastly into the fire.

Nicolo looked up from his reading. He could not help seeing the weird show but he paid it not one whit of attention.

"Master of the serai!" he called in a strong voice.

The big-eyed man in the chair rallied with a visible effort.

"Aye, Nicolo Polo, ambassador to the Great Khan."

"The material bearing this writing and the garments of the fire-walkers are undoubtedly the same stuff."

"That's of interest to this court. Please continue."

"The writing bears out Marco's story that his great-uncle meant him to have a set of garments that he had ordered in Dzungaria. But it mentions no one named Surab, nor does it bear out the account of them being stolen."

"Part of what I told was recounted to me after Johannes' death and part by Surab himself," I broke in.

"Does that complete your testimony?" the master asked Nicolo.

"Yes, your Honor, and I give it in great pain."

His voice had hardly stilled when the weird lights in the magicians' mouths went out. Animation slowly returned to the cadaver faces. The serai master spoke with renewed energy.

"Then the offense of Marco Polo becomes more understandable, considering his impetuous youth, but no less criminal," he declared. Then, turning to the head magician, "What do you ask in the way of punishment?"

"That he be delivered to us to take to our abbey. I promise that no drop of his blood will be shed."

"We all know what that means. And you know that the merchants here will not consent to such a decree."

"Our abbey has been desecrated. Woe will be upon them if they forbid us our revenge."

"And you know too that Marco of Polo will appeal the sentence to the Governor. If so, every detail of the case will be investigated by agents of the Khan."

I had started to speak, but my tongue was almost stuck by terror, and a Persian Jew, dispatched by the Khan to India on some mission, spoke for me.

"Especially, my lord, the Khan's agents will investigate the dragon killed by picks and shovels in the High Altai."

"What do we care for that?" the chief magician shrieked. Still I thought the shot had told.

"I have it," cried a jade-buyer of the Koko Nor. "The law of the Mongols is that if a thief can repay nine times the value of the article stolen, he may go free. In that case, the article too may be returned to its owner."

"So be it!" another merchant cried.

"But how may we set the value of the garments of the fire-walkers?" the master asked.

"At the very least, five hundred gold dinars," the Master of Wizards cried.

Terror was upon me more deep than I dared show the crowd or myself. Otherwise my cold heart would not have surged at this pronouncement. Nine times five hundred dinars was forty-five hundred: I could pay it and save myself, at worst, death by torture, and at best, a cruel lashing that would cripple me for weeks and disgrace me forever. The magician's miserliness coming upon him in long years of taxing frightened peasants had overridden his piety; if he had not craved my gold more than atonement to his gods, he would have cried a thousand dinars. Even so, he had cut it almost too fine. It was as though he had appraised every bolt of cloth and pod of musk in my bales.

"Five hundred shall it be!" the serai master cried with great energy. "And nine times that figure shall be the penalty, paid out of hand by Marco of Polo to the magicians of the Swasti. If he can't pay it within the hour, I order him nine times nine lashes on his naked back."

My head was reeling from the delayed shock of the blow, yet it worked well. It sent ghostly hands and eyes to search my bales and boxes and count my baggage camels; on an invisible score sheet I added up the findings. The thousand gold bezants I had got for Miranda were equivalent to a thousand dinars; good trading in nearly four years had gained me twice as much more in money and goods; Lazarus' death on the desert had enriched me by a thousand, and the prize I had won for finding Nicolo a beautiful slave girl should round out my total wealth at five thousand dinars. About five hundred of these had gone into my personal equipment—my excellent horse and saddle and my wardrobe, pavilion, and two extra camels for their transport. If the appraisers accepted my valuation, I could satisfy the judgment without loss of my gear.

Like most Venetian merchants I could calculate quickly in my head. In my half-madness the power became strangely increased, and I knew the cost in dinars of every stripe that my naked back was saved. It was fifty-five point five carried to infinity, a weird number somehow, such as often turns up in calculations of multiples of nine. . . . If the judge would let me and I could be spared the shame, I would take nine of the eighty-one lashes to save five hundred dinars.

The serai master had waited for his pronouncement to be written down. Now he was speaking again.

"If any gentleman in this company objects to this verdict, let him speak now."

The thought came to me, as through the dark, that Nicolo might object. I did not dare expect it but my soul was too sick to feel shame at wishing it. A great many of the audience were looking at him. Especially the Mohammedans, blood feudists to a man and intensely loyal to their clans, could hardly believe his silence. Truly the amenities of life, all but unknown to the wild Tatars but more strictly observed by civilized Orientals than by Europeans, required him to make at least a nominal protest if he were only my fellow countryman. Even that would save me no little face.

He did not speak nor did he glance in my direction. There was an expression on his face that I could read only as thwarted fury, and since its cause could not be the heaviness of my punishment, it must be its lightness. Had he wanted me publicly whipped, or given a bloodless death at the clever hands of the magicians? My brain wavered from the thought and my heart grew faint: in spite of everything I had not believed he could hate that hard, simply because, until now, I could not. Perhaps his fury was at himself for not disavowing my story entirely. Perhaps it was aimed at the master of the magicians for letting me slip whole-skinned through his greedy fingers.

The silence had held long. One after another of the listeners turned his gaze back to the serai master.

"Marco of Polo," came his voice, "do you wish to appeal this judgment to the Governor?"

I was beaten to my knees and sick at heart.

"No, your Honor."

"Then deliver your moneybags and keys to me. I shall appoint three merchants to seize upon your possessions to the amount of the judgment."

The three appeared well posted on market values and did their duty well. Quickly they appraised my treasures—gold and silver brocade bought from Baram, embroideries, precious carpets, jade, turquoises, ointments and medicines—and these made a pretty show in the bright, fresh-fed fires. But they would not accept my appraisal of three hundred dinars for my balas ruby, and put it in at the paid price of two hundred, a strange end to my expectations of a handsome profit now so sorely needed. When I disclosed the yellow sapphire, it passed from palm to palm and caused a brief, weighty discussion. I found myself watching the sober faces in intense anxiety: I took note of every headshake and hand-waving. It was my first lesson in the meaning of poverty—how things once counted little now loom large, and what would have been a trifling loss could now bow down the heart.

"What did you pay for this jewel, Marco of Polo?" one of the merchants asked.

"It was given to me."

"At what do you appraise it?"

"A thousand dinars."

The discussion was resumed, then quickly ended.

"Two of us are not willing to allow that much," the same merchant told me. "We've set it at eight hundred. That means we are still short by nearly five hundred dinars of the amount of the judgment. How many of your camels can you spare, now that your goods are reduced and you are not likely to buy more in the near future?"

"I need only two for my pavilion and personal baggage. I have four others that I used for baggage, and eight spares that carried food and water on the desert."

"We will allow you ten dinars per head. That appears to exhaust your patent assets, with the exception of a Nubian female slave and your personal belongings."

"I can dispense with my pavilion, now that the main of the desert is behind us, which means I can spare another camel. And I can get along with a greatly reduced wardrobe."

The pavilion, almost new, was appraised at fifty dinars. When my chest was opened, some of the less rich merchants as well as middle fellows attached to the caravans and the serai crowded about. My richest garments, showing no wear, sold readily at half-cost, as was customary at bankrupt sales; these and the rest that I could spare brought a clean hundred. Mustapha's parting gift, a fine Arabian astrolabe, went begging for a while—less handsome but no less accurate types were common in China—then the Jew who had spoken for me at the trial, a doctor more learned than rich, offered ten dinars with a shamed face. I took it gladly, certain that it would be put to good use. My wonderful English bow, that could shoot a lion but not a star, was set and immediately sold at forty dinars.

I needed a hundred and fifty more. The merchants told me they would allow that much on my Nubian slave girl, one of whom would put her in his harem.

"What price would you set on my red mare?"

There fell a sharp silence and at least one of the appraisers, a horse-trading Marwari from the Indian city of Bikaner, looked embarrassed. That question seemed to bring home to several listeners how low I had fallen.

"Why, I'd pay the same sum out of hand," the horse dealer said. "But Christian, a man who calls himself a merchant can't walk in the dust!"

"I think he can, if he must. Before, when I sold a slave girl to buy transport, I came on ill fortune."

"By Saint Thomas and Saint Theodore," a Nestorian jeweler broke in, "it may be you needn't part with either."

"I don't read your riddle," I answered.

"Those horns there. Unless I'm mistaken they're off the great wild ram of the Pamir, and the largest I've ever seen. I'm a collector of curios of varied sort and sometimes I indulge myself in the way of cost. Suppose I offered you a hundred dinars. Couldn't you scratch up the extra fifty you need from some of your other gear?"

"No, sir, I don't think I can." In truth I had fifty dinars left in my purse, but these must be hoarded against my turning beggar on the road.

"Mark you, there's no ready market for trophies of the chase. That pair of horns could gather dust in my *kiffir* for twenty years without an offer of twenty dinars to take them off my hands. But I've taken a fancy to them—you've had your full share of trouble— and by God, I'll give you the hundred and fifty you need to get you clear."

He looked at his other listeners, not at me, giving the effect of waiting their comments on a deal already closed. Actually his ear was pricked up for my reply.

Instead of making any, I looked back and far and high to a scene of the great Pamir. I stood on a narrow ledge on the naked rock with what must be a pearly heaven, so pure as it was, gleaming above me, and Gehenna yawning below. The great ram had fled from me to his retreat, but now he returned to do battle. He wore his great horns as proudly as Kublai Khan wore the crown of Tatary. As the clean-loosed arrow plunged deep in his breast, he rose to his full height and brandished them in the air. Then he fell and looked at me awhile with lifted head, which at last sank down.

His name was Iskander, the Persian form of Alexander, whose power and glory rivaled that of Kublai Khan.

"I thank you kindly," I heard myself saying, "but I'll sell the nag."

The jeweler spat on the ground and walked away. The horse trader went to look at his new mare and the crowd lost interest in me. I thought that the last stripe had been laid on.

Only a moment later a stir passed through the two rows of squatting magicians. Suddenly their master stood up and held his staff aloft.

"Hear ye all!" he yelled. "Tonight we've seen an alien in our land deal fairly before our gods even though his own kinsman might take harm therefrom. He's known as Nicolo Emir, and an ambassador to our Khan. Since he did not protest the judgment, already too light, we present him the suit of dragon skins that our gods have returned to us, so that he too may walk safely through fire."

I felt in the middle of an evil dream. This was an unbelievable thing, yet I found myself accepting it without surprise, almost without anger at the gods, and with only a further withering of my spirit in the bleak cold that is the climate of such dreams. Surely the magicians would not risk their fire-walking secret by giving the mineral garments to an alien—yet I saw their master humbly lay them at Nicolo's feet. . . . A servant carried them to his quarters. He handed another servant two pieces of torn fabric that had once counted so much; and he and Maffeo exchanged smiles as the man brought them to me.

Don't let him have it, Marco my son, or I can't rest in my grave.

There came a remembered pain across my brows, but it soon passed. The seized camels were being laden with the confiscated goods; presently some yellow-robed youths whom I had not noticed before, probably neophytes in the monastery, led them out the gate. As the magicians rose to leave, they looked like a band of ragamuffins instead of great necromancers, mystic priests of the Swasti. They were behaving with circumspection, the watching merchants thought. . . .

Then our attention was drawn to the smoky murk overhanging the fires. Countless small black forms had come out of the dark and darted back and forth uttering mouselike squeaks. Thousands flew in frantic circles narrowly missing our heads, or skimmed low over the fires, or cut elaborate figures as in a dance of fiends. Their squeaking became an ear-piercing agony and their rank smell turned our stomachs and their numbers sickened our minds.

It was only a vast swarm of bats. Since they did not weigh ten to a pound, hundreds of them could cling under one loose robe. But perhaps some strange accident caused them to be abroad in this unseasonable weather. Presently they vanished and their horrid outcry grew dim and died away.

When again we lowered our sick gaze, the magicians had gone.

CHAPTER 9

THE FALLEN GOD

THE CARAVAN OF MY ONCE BELONGING LINGERED AT THE SCENE of my overthrow for fourteen infinite days.

When it finally formed for the march southeast to Kanchow, I had abandoned any notion of false boldness, and had set my will against flight, whether of body, mind, or spirit. So I took a place behind the merchants, in front of the baggage camels where the head dragoman was wont to ride his pony. The rest of my arrangements were as simple and cheap as I could make them. Sheba and I together had loaded our single camel and she would take charge of him on the road, an easy task for a desert girl like her. I expected to buy our food at the road stalls and eat with the cameleers. Thus I hoped to escape all the drover, baggage wallah, and servant hire—provided, of course, Nicolo permitted the arrangement.

As to this outcome, I was in grave doubt. The terms of my membership in the company specified that I travel in good style for face's sake, a condition that had gone by the boards. He had once refused to let me accompany the caravan in a lowly capacity and his memory, like mine, was long. While waiting in aching hope to hear the trumpet, I was bleakly ready to have him send word for me to take my camel, my female slave, and myself out of the line.

He did not. Slowly we went our way out of the gate of the caravanserai, down narrow crooked streets, through the great portal in the Wall. By now my joyful wonder was being slaked by hindsighted acumen; I could tell why I had been spared as convincingly as a Paduan lawyer. Nicolo did not want to be seen kicking a man when he was down—especially a fellow Venetian and an acknowledged kinsman. But it would not be like Nicolo to go further than this—and the fact fetched up short the vaunting that so often follows a lucky event. He would not treat me better because some knaves and fools whispered that I was his son; instead it would cause him to treat me worse. Nicolo would play the

gentleman in his fellow merchants' sight only at his own convenience and whim. Too well he knew the gains from his fame
for ruthlessness.

No doubt he wanted Sheba to continue in Miranda's attendance.
The road stayed lonely and the land harsh; and his prize would be
happier, eating and sleeping better, and hence in better fettle
when he brought her to the Court of Kublai Khan. This factor
would remain in my favor all the way to Peking, but it carried no
great weight. And to curry not his favor but his neglect, I had
taken one step that instinct told me was on the right track. I had
begun it the day following my fall, a fortnight before this departure.

The less I looked like Nicolo, the better he could stand the
sight of me. He wore a fine mustache, with shaven jaws and chin.
I too had grown a mustache, perhaps to irritate him, and on account of some dim perception of distant events, I did not want to
shave it off; but I had started to grow a small, shapely beard. By
now it had altered the aspect of my countenance and made me
look older. I stopped dressing my hair in the Venetian fashion
favored by Nicolo, and my wearing plainer clothes differentiated
us still more.

Walking in the dust and begrimed by it, I was generally less
conspicuous than before. Eating the cheap, rough food of the
cameleers and sleeping by their dung fires, I managed to stay
almost altogether out of Nicolo's sight. I did not believe that this
truce with him, if I could call it that, could last long; actually he
was granting me quarter for a little while for his own uses. Yet for
four days he gave every impression of ignoring my existence.

In those four days much happened inside me. I did not know
exactly what it was or what good or ill it would bring me. Walking the road was in itself mildly pleasurable, my body being equal
to much harder work, my lungs liking the thin, cool air, my brain
calm after its late storm, and my heart warmed by the companionship of my clean-striding, quick-handed slave girl. It came to pass
that I found a certain fellowship with the cameleers. I had lost so
much face that the remnants were not worth spitting at—they
themselves would not gain face by insolence to me—and since I
was no longer a poor master but had proved their match as a man
I even gained a little face of a kind they prized. As for getting
caught in thievery, why, I had paid the fiddler.

In the afternoon of the fourth day we came to Kanchow, the
ancient walled capital of Kansu, a city heaped with great abbeys

and thronged with immense idols. The word flew over our rest ground that Nicolo and Maffeo had been invited to feast with the Khan's Governor, and presently I saw them, bejeweled and bedizened, mounting their horses to ride in state to his palace. Perhaps I was inadequately hidden among the cameleers and other pedestrians of plain dress, for Nicolo fixed his large eyes on my face. Perhaps he had merely waited our arrival at a new scene to settle matters, for he spoke in an undertone to Maffeo, then came riding toward me.

Looking down from his high seat, he addressed me in an impersonal tone.

"Our invitation from the Royal Governor is an official one to bearers of the golden tablet of the Khan," he said. "Now that we are approaching the frontier of Cathay, it carries far more weight than in the hinterlands ruled by subject kings beyond his immediate control."

I had noticed this. Until now the tablet had been largely a token of honor and Nicolo had rarely employed its latent powers. Now it was turning into an Aladdin's lamp.

"While the authority and the safe-conduct it betokens are vested only in Maffeo and me, in practice they pertain to our property and trains and even to fellow travelers whose interests march with ours and whose missions benefit the Khan," Nicolo went on. "Obviously it must not be employed for an offender against the Khan's law. The murmuring of the people would surely reach the ears of the Governor and thus probably the Imperial Council. But your manner lately indicates you're aware of this."

"Yes, signor, I am."

"Of course you know too that since the terms of our agreement are not being kept, you can no longer claim membership in the company."

"I resigned it, sir, when I lost my goods and my horse."

"I take it you still wish to go to Peking."

"Yes, and to find employment there to help to mend my fortunes. I think I could be useful to a merchant wishing to import Occidental goods, and perhaps could obtain a fellowship at one of the universities in astronomy and geography. In due course, I could find my way back to Europe."

"I think that's a sensible course. As ambassador to the Khan, I might prevail upon some official to find you a post. Also, I'm not averse to your traveling with the caravan in your present capacity, provided Sheba can continue to serve my slave girl Linda. At Peking I'll decide whether to present Linda to the Khan or to keep her for my own delight; then you can sell Sheba or make other use of her. Meanwhile I'll do more than quarter her; for her services you may quarter with my bailiff. However, there must be one clear understanding."

I inclined my head and waited.

"Make no further call upon me of any kind, and do not ask me to present you to the Khan."

"I agree to that, and considering the trouble I was in, I think it would be very dangerous for me to come near him."

I spoke unvarnished truth, and Nicolo knew it. His great eyes shone and his big hand loosed the rein. As the gray stallion bore him off, large and effulgent in the sunlight, I became lost in reverie. It came to me that Nicolo was better satisfied with his victory than at first. It was more nearly complete than he had realized or, which amounted to the same thing, I was more easily broken than he had believed. Now he was wondering whether he need expose himself to danger, no matter how slight, to deal me some sort of coup de grace. It seemed to me that he was willing to wait for that, even to let Fate finish me off, meanwhile throwing me enough crusts to keep me from any act dangerous to him. Too harsh treatment might drive me to a deed of revenge. Certainly it would cause unwelcome comment among other merchants.

Was there only so small a hole in his coat, or had he Achilles' heel?

2

Tonight Nicolo would ride five miles from the caravanserai to the Governor's palace. My thoughts made a little turn that I often forbade them and lighted on Miranda. It would be a victory for me just to lay eyes on her—for I was rid of the folly and frailty that would make it out a defeat—and I needed a victory sorely. I thought it lay in something more than brooking his will. I had not seen too clearly lately, and I thought she would do my eyes good.

I had calculated the risk of entering her quarters and found it outweighing my hope of gain when Sheba, crossing the courtyard, tossed her chin at me. I followed her into my cell.

"My Lady Linda has gone to the Nestorian temple for her soul's sake," she told me. "There's no one there now but some old priests chanting before the altar, and she said she had something to tell you if you'll come and hear it. And she said that there was no sin in using the temple as a house of assignation, because the Nestorians were heretics, and anyway she forswore Christianity when she became a slave."

"Tell her that if she can so beat the Devil around the bush, so can I. I'll come as soon as you're out of sight."

I did so, but at first barely glanced at the two female slaves, both veiled, at a kneeling bench in the rear of the small nave. I was surveying the whole scene, which I had not done with sufficient care in the case of a heathen abbey at Suchow, or perhaps I would have been in a different fix. Indeed Mustapha Sheik had tried to teach me that lesson long years ago.

Above the altar was a large silver cross, its center and four ends adorned with jewels. The altar was bedecked with a cloth of gold in which pearls had been worked to make holy pictures, and lighted by an elaborate lantern with eight wicks. Three priests wearing haircloth tunics and black wool-lined jackets crouched before it, performing ceremonies in the warmth of a charcoal brazier. Presently I discovered that besides this and their warm robes, they had another way to fight the devil-sent cold. At first I could hardly believe my eyes, these being some sort of Christian clergy, but their singing and chanting out of tune, and their falling against one another and their difficulty in getting up and down, left no room for doubt. Presently one of them reached for a ewer behind the altar, quaffed deeply, and passed it to his mates.

The lantern light almost died away before it reached the two girls, then gave the illusion of reviving. They too were warmly clad, and anyway they were used to cold weather by now. I was startled to remember that this was March, and the fourth year of my journey was almost done.

Almost four years ago I had laid eyes on Miranda for the first time. When I looked toward her now, she raised her veil so I could see her face as plainly as the dim light allowed. "This is what you've lost," the act told me, a strange, proud act which like so many proud things, was deeply sad. *It's what I'll win back,* my heart's surge answered. But I was always the braggart. . . .

I came and sat beside her, wonder-stricken. She waited while I gazed upon every aspect of beauty now revealed, and yearning wracked my heart and lust stormed my brain. Then she spoke quietly in the Venetian tongue.

"As I feared and warned you, you've been brought low."

"That's true."

"I sent for you to give you another warning."

"I'll thank you for it, and it may be I'll heed it better than the other."

"You don't matter to my master any more, and as long as that's true, he'll not harm you. So be careful what you do that might make you count with him again."

"Are you speaking for my profit, your own, or your master's?"

"I'm duty-bound to speak for my master's profit when it conflicts with yours or mine; but I don't think it does in this case. If he'd kill you, he'd commit a most awful sin and have to make terrible atonement. I know him better now, and there's not the slightest doubt that you're his son."

"Perhaps he knows you, at last, and the water of giving you to the Khan is already over the dam."

"Well, it isn't."

The twisting went out of my throat and the roughness from my voice.

"Do you want him to give you to the Khan? When I asked you that before, you said you were so deeply enslaved that his will was yours."

"I've thought it over since then and have decided I want him to give me to the Khan for his good and mine too. He doesn't need me like you needed me. He's already a giant in strength—his great ambitions are sure to be fulfilled. But that fulfillment will come quicker if he becomes the Khan's favorite. For what is a suit of fire-walkers' garments—even a fireproof mineral woven into cloth—compared to me?"

"There must be a hundred great beauties hoping to be queens of the Khan who feel the same."

"I didn't send for you to quarrel with. I saw that you are desperate and in danger of making some fatal mistake. Remember, he can kill you now with impunity—except for punishments from beyond the earth—for any story he tells, the judges will believe, you being a confessed thief. He could have had you killed in Suchow, but he's always torn between getting rid of you entirely and bringing you to heel. One's easy and the other's hard, and he likes hardship. Also, he was never able to bring your mother to heel, and that would make it a double satisfaction."

"Truly, you know him better than you did, and you talk plainer."

"I'm no longer an English child who fell in love with a Venetian bravo. But your gods made you save me from the desert—to punish you, I think, for casting your pearl away—and so I'm telling you the truth."

I did not boast again. I looked her in the eyes and said, "I know it."

"I'd like to tell you something else, and have asked permission of my saints, but whether they've granted it I don't know."

"What have they to do with it?"

"I promised them I would be a dutiful slave. To tell you this, perhaps I must break my vow. But I would be doing good, I think, while to remain silent would be doing harm."

"It's a hard choice that you'll have to make yourself."

"I thought of asking those three priests to help me decide, but look at them!" Just now they were singing *Vexilla Regis Prodeunt* at the top of their voices.

"Miranda, we're a long way from home."

"If I tell you, will you go?"

"Yes."

"At once, not asking any questions?"

"Yes."

"Baram was very kind to me and is a good, just man. I don't want you to brood over his ingratitude to you and perhaps, if you get a chance, strike back at him. He didn't know the truth about your going out to look for us that night—I didn't know it at the time—but I've found it out since from an old camp tender who erects our pavilion. Baram believed that you went out on Nicolo's orders and he was looking for us at the same time. If he had known that you went of your own will and at your own risk, against Nicolo's advice and wishes, and that we all would have died except for you, he would have given you his most precious possession as a reward."

"Instead he gave it to Nicolo?"

"Yes."

"So Fate—I don't want to say God—gave me a second chance to have you, but the chance went wrong?"

"It was partly your own fault, Marco. You should have looked for me in the caravan instead of going to your tent. You should have found me and claimed me. You might have known you'd be given another chance if you wanted it enough."

"How could I know it?"

"At least you could have kept trying instead of giving up."

"Maybe it's written that after I'm punished enough, I can still have you."

"I think if you did, you would only sell me again."

"Miranda, how did Baram come to make that mistake?"

"Nicolo saw me and wanted me and lied. By keeping you away from Baram, he ran no great risk of his finding out the truth; anyway, he's a bold man who takes risks. This one won."

"Yes, it did. It won more greatly than I once could dream." Made in this half-heathen church on this wintry day, here was my profession of faith.

"If you believe that at last, it's too late."

"You said I ought to keep on trying——"

"I take it back. But you'll try something, and whatever it is, I don't want you to be brought down to defeat and possibly death by treachery."

That last word stopped my breath. I wondered if she were using the wrong word—that she meant something much less, such as trickery. Perhaps because of the drunken priests' caterwauling, I had misunderstood her.

"Did you say. . .treachery?"

"Yes, and that's the main reason I had you come here. You promised me you wouldn't ask me any questions, but I don't think you need to. I'm doing right when I say this. There's no longer any doubt in my mind—I was confused before between letter and spirit."

"When you say. . .what?"

"Don't trust any more of your secrets to Zurficar the Turki-Tatar, whom you call Pietro."

3

Mustapha Dey had once told me for the love of Allah not to hang upon his words as though they were a life line thrown to me on a sinking ship. It seemed that my ship was sinking now in a calm, cold, wine-dark sea of doom, and there was no life line thrown to me, no words in its stead, no Mustapha to fill the breach, no Allah to turn to at last. My spirit was as withered as all my laurels, I was bankrupt of hope as of pride, and every wind blew cold.

Instinct warned I must not act, speak, or make any irrevocable decision until again, if I ever could, I gained firm ground. I must peer out and keep guard like a rat in its hole, but must not myself be seen. And I dared not dull my mind with potions or enflame it with passions lest these injunctions fail.

This was not life, only its shadow. At least the man walking in the dust, keeping these rules like a slave, did not seem me, Marco Polo, bold, crafty, licentious, vindictive, willful, a man of deeds, a son of Venice. I had a bleak feeling of being depersonalized. It was as though I had dropped out of my identity when I had lost my way. I felt little, and perhaps my strongest feeling was in the form of an intimation of early, peaceful death. All my faiths had already died, it seemed—faith in Miranda's innocence and even in her beauty, faith in the greatness of Mustapha, for had he not believed in me? And even faith in my mother's trust to me, as sworn by her delegate on earth. So I could no longer be certain that I was Nicolo's son. I no longer believed in it as I had believed in the uniqueness and the immortality of my soul. My resemblance to him might be extreme prenatal influence. Or was it a trick of the Devil to lay me by the heels?

Throughout the caravan's fortnight stay in Kanchow and down the long road to Yungchang, I made no real effort to realize myself and shake off the waking dream. It seemed I was too stunned to know what had hit me. But perhaps my inertia was some sort of natural protection. Vulnerable in the extreme, perhaps I was trying, not intelligently but instinctively, to stay out of trouble.

At Yungchang the merchants bought musk and yak wool from the Koko Nor. The mountain breeze with its smells of spring was like a tonic to me, and I found myself tempted to give a gold bezant for the favor of a damsel of the town, white-skinned with rosy cheeks and raven-black hair, who dropped me a flower from a roof top. Miserliness made me refrain, but I had been pleasantly surprised to find myself once more a man in at least one respect, and instinctively I began to seek other signs. Still guarding every action and word, I set my thoughts free. When they had larked it awhile they were refreshed enough to undertake a hard problem.

Ever since the trial I had avoided Pietro, at first to save him loss of face and possibly from the contagion of misfortune, lately because I could not play the necessary part. During our stay at Yungchang, I dared to drink rice wine with him, and on our taking the road I sometimes walked beside him. I noticed that he took not the slightest interest in my general conversation—the hare was no longer worth the skinning—but if I said anything worth telling Nicolo, he became all ears, plus cold, glittering eyes. No doubt he loved the man as might a captured wolf.

We came to the summer capital of the subject king of Kansu at the foot of the Ala Shan. This was an immense castle on a splendid terrace, the main palace surrounded by armories and pleasure domes. Paying tribute to Kublai Khan, the king was permitted much of his former magnificence and the trappings, although not the scepter, of power; he dwelt in a luxury undreamed by Western potentates, with lackeys and eunuchs without end, a harem of five hundred chosen beauties from all over Asia, game parks, hawks and hounds, and, for his parades, a thousand snow-white camels from the famous stud of Ningshia. Before his surrender he had boasted too of five thousand pitch-black yaks, larger than the common kind and very fierce, but since they were ridden by crossbowmen in guarding the passes into his realm, giving Kublai no little trouble before he could break through, they had been taken away from him. In their place he had been given an equal number of white fallow deer.

The greater part of these pets had escaped or died, and the walled park where he had kept them had fallen into neglect. Few passed through the tumble-down gates, and one barren hilltop stayed completely forsaken for an odd reason. Here lay a colossus of perhaps greater dimension than any other in the world. It was called the Dead Buddha and had once stood here as the titulary deity of the land, towering over the king's palace and visible—so legend had it—for a hundred miles. No swan, raven, elephant, or serpent was old enough to remember its raising; it was already ancient when Shih Huang Ti built the Great Wall ere Caesar conquered England. But within the memory of living man the ground under one side had sunk and the enormous idol leaned slowly over until it fell.

Its peculiar interest to me was that the vast form, probably built up slowly of clay, shimmered in the sunlight as though covered with gold leaf. So when the full moon covered the whole countryside with silver leaf, the hours that the malign influence of death was most high and the scene most forsaken, I had Sheba follow me there with a pair of scrapers. I thought likely we could scrape off enough gold before moonset to fatten my purse a little; in any case I hoped to practice some necromancy, which means to foresee the future through communion with the dead. Mustapha told me how he had visited the Great Sphinx under the midnight moon in the solitude of the Egyptian desert. He had asked her about the meaning of life and the mystery of the human soul, and some enlightenment had been given him. I did not seek answers to such vasty riddles, but I would like to know if some thinking I had done was straight, and if the path I had taken lately was the right path. There was nothing to stop Sheba, whose heart was Eve's and whose wisdom was as the serpent's, from acting as the oracle of the dead god.

My first study was of how the mighty had fallen. But as though the hand of the Devil had half-caught him in the Devil's way, the god did not smash, and the only damage was a rift across the back of the head, strangely comparable to a fractured skull. His hand that had been lifted and open in some solemn admonition now thrust skyward as in a last spasm fixed by rigor mortis. His toes turned up. Between his feet was an animal of some kind, apparently a cat, tail down and legs in the air.

We paced the length of his corpse—fifty of my long strides. The other hand that pressed against the ground was fifteen feet long, and the foot a good twenty. When we climbed to his forehead to look into his face, we could not stand high enough to see it well; and the curl of the lips that had doubtless represented a blissful smile suggested the awful grin often seen on the faces of cadavers. The eyes were half closed, and their rims, never covered with gold leaf, had bleached white. I could lie along the slope of the nose, and if I had won Miranda instead of lost her, she and I could have made love on the broad of his chin. It was just what we would have done, if she were here with me instead of her bondwoman. It would have been the perfect act of defiance of the ravages of Time, the answer to Death.

I was wondering how many ingots of gold had been beaten eggshell thin to illumine the vast form. The chest was forty feet broad and thirty thick, the swollen belly a third again as gross, and the wall of the well-molded, deep-sunken navel had taken at least six square feet of gold leaf. But the god-makers of long ago had saved much yellow stuff, and labor as well, by substituting drapery for manly loins. If their motive was modesty instead of economy, I doubted if the god would like it any better.

I had once seen the complete skin, carefully flayed, of a tall man, and had judged its area in square feet to be his height multiplied by half his height. By this figuring, some ten thousand square feet of gold leaf had been used to adorn the god. But now he needed it no more than Mangu Khan the three hundred maidens of perfect beauty who had been buried with him.

But when I applied a scraper to the region of his belly, I found the leaf not eggshell thin but almost as intangible as sunlight. When I had scraped clean a square-foot patch, I had collected a teaspoonful of yellow dust as light as fool's gold. It seemed likely that the leaf had been removed by other desecrators, and a gilt paint applied in its stead.

But my heart was light and my head strangely clear and my companion's eyes intensely alive. It was as though I had been lost in the desert, but had come upon an ancient landmark, and with her help I could find my way back to the road that led to the Court of Kublai Khan.

"Sheba, when I told Zurficar, whom I call Pietro, of my desire to obtain a suit of the fire-walkers' garments, I thought he was loyal to me," I said. "But it may be he was loyal to Nicolo."

"Is the moon shining upon us, or may it be the sun?"

"How can you be so sure?"

"My Lady Linda became sure on the night of the trial, but she didn't tell me so, lest I tell you, and you strike in revenge while your wits were out and be whipped to death. She had surmised he was a spy on the fourth day out of Shakow, when Nicolo learned of your visiting her. The old *gibbaleen* who erects her pavilion told her that Nicolo and the Turki-Tatar had many meetings. But she didn't know you'd put your trust in him."

"When did she think Pietro became Nicolo's creature?" I was dreading the path my mind was taking, but it could not turn back.

"On reflection, she thought it was the night of his joining the caravan. You remember he caught up with us on the road. Linda thinks he had discovered the lie Nicolo told Baram to cheat you out of the prize—for Tatars have ears like asses—and decided to follow him."

"I remember Nicolo wasn't pleased by his coming. And at the first hint of extortion——"

"Pietro threw no such hint. It was furthest from his mind. Remember, he's a Tatar—he admires cunning and craft almost as much as cruelty. He saw in Nicolo both of these, and great strength besides. Linda believes he wanted him for his master as might a dog—to be faithful to him as a dog, and to fatten from his leavings as his reward. That too is like the Tatar. Why do Tatars bring higher prices than any other male slaves on the market?"

That had been true even in Venice. Once a Tatar knows his master, he is faithful until he is sold or death breaks the bond.

"I think he threw himself at Nicolo's feet and was taken into his service," Sheba went on.

"In that case, when Pietro made up to me it was on Nicolo's orders." Although the spring night was chill, I wiped sweat from my face.

"Yes, master."

"At Shakow I asked Pietro about the fire-walkers."

"He'd been waiting for you to ask him, master. Nicolo knew that you would as you came close to Suchow. You told Linda, long ago, that he'd guessed half the truth——"

"I heard it from his mouth. Did I think he'd forgotten, blind fool that I was? But I'd have thought my mother would have risen from her grave to warn me."

"It's not easy to rise from one's grave, master. I think it can be done only by clutching the Devil's hand."

"A few days later I asked Pietro if he knew one of the fire-walkers. No, he did not—Nicolo was afraid I'd be suspicious of such good luck as that—but he knew an old priest who needed money to go home to the High Altai. It was a good story—Nicolo had coached him in it. And when we got to Suchow, behold the old priest was still there, but he couldn't bring me the garments—I must go after them."

"Have mercy on yourself, master, and let it go."

"No, I want it to sting so bad I'll never forget. Since Miranda—Linda—warned me against Pietro, I thought he'd merely told Nicolo of my plan—for a price—and Nicolo had warned the priests. But it wasn't my plan—it was Nicolo's. Pietro provided the fellow I met in the dark, and was Nicolo's emissary to the abbey. The magicians were perfectly willing to set the trap for the price he offered. But I wonder if they kept their bargain to the last."

"Do you think they took more than he promised them?"

"I think he may have promised them a thousand dinars or some such sum if they would agree to demand a greater fine than I could pay, then give him the stolen garments. I could have appealed to the Governor but certainly I would have been whipped in Tatar style. But they saved me from the lash to get more gold."

"That last may not be true. It's bad enough as it is."

"Good enough, you mean." I laughed loudly, as might a new-risen phoenix.

"You've gone mad. It's this place—you and me, a white Venetian and his black slave girl, perched like sparrows on a dead giant——"

"No. I've just seen the truth."

"You want to hate him, so you can kill him?"

"Not particularly. I want him to hate me—as hard as he can. I didn't know until now that that's his Achilles' heel."

I had no doubt of Sheba's understanding the allusion. The tidal wave of Greek culture, long since receded, had washed all North Africa.

Sheba's long black hands lay flat on her cheeks and as she gazed at me the moonlight picked up the porcelain-white of her eyes.

"Why?" she whispered.

"Because it's an unreasoning, blind, and lying hate. It isn't worth my hating in return. But I mean it to give me the victory."

Sheba laughed wildly, sobered quickly, and wiped her eyes. "We're both mad!" she cried. "How will you win it? You have no gold, no power, no friend, only one camel and one slave and the horns of a wild sheep."

"Answer one question. You have heard of the power and glory of Kublai Khan all your days, and you have a way of sifting people's talk to find its gist. What kind of a man is he?"

"He's not a man. He's the King of Kings."

"What do you mean by that? There's a man underneath."

"No. If there ever was, he's ceased to exist. He's not even a Tatar any more—he's the Tatar's god. He thinks, feels, breathes, lives what you read on the stone beside the road—Kublai Khan, for whom the world was made."

"But he hasn't conquered all of it, yet. There are kings in India who don't send him tribute—kings in Europe who doubt his omnipotence."

"He means that they shall, before he's done."

"How does he choose his viceroys and councilors and governors? By birth and blood, by favoritism, or by fitness for the office?"

"If his own son shows himself a fool, he builds him a palace to play in, but doesn't let him command one troop of horse."

"Then walk beside me in the dust for six hundred miles more. Invoke your witches and help me all you can. Then if I can still hear Mustapha's voice—if I dare to mount again the four bronze horses of San Marco—if once more I can follow Iskander across the chasm——"

"If you can see the face of Miranda of England," Sheba broke in, chanting in a glimmering voice.

"If I can do all these things—why, Sheba, I'll play a game of chess with Nicolo."

CHAPTER 10
ROAD TO XANADU

THE SCOPE OF MY STUDIES WIDENED APACE AS WE DREW INTO the shadow of the long and mighty arm of Kublai Khan. So far we had seen the least paring of his little fingernail, for we followed the northwest frontier of Cathay at the edge of the desert, yet this minuscule was enough to cause a queer, cold quiver up my backbone. In the desolate stretches, the rest houses of the Khan's couriers stood forty miles apart. In the more peopled areas they were spaced at something over half that distance. Each was a great hostelry with scores of richly furnished rooms, hundreds of attendants, and from two hundred to four hundred fleet horses, half of which stayed groomed and ready to run. Thus if an important message must go to or from the Khan, belled riders would ride in relays day or night from post to post; if, at his pleasure palace in Xanadu, he desired a dainty fruit from Peking, ten days' journey by caravan, it could be started on its way in the morning and arrive at his table the following evening. And woe betide any rider who was tardy, or any lord, no matter how exalted, who delayed him on the road.

Between these posts, at intervals of about three miles, stood the posts of the foot runners, each the size of a small village. The couriers carried messages and very light freight from local officials to their chiefs, who dispatched it on by horseback if they saw fit. And there was no danger, now, of their losing their way. Instead of a long strewing of white bones, the roads were graded and graveled, lined with trees wherever trees would grow, otherwise marked by stone pedestals and signposts.

Nicolo and Maffeo carried a golden tablet that declared them ambassadors to and from the Khan, so they need not turn out for any caravan on private business. I had never had it in my hands, but the Persian Jew who had taken my side at the trial had shown me what appeared to be its duplicate. It weighed nearly two pounds, and bore an inscription in Jagatai that, at last, I was able to read:

By the power of the great God, may the name of the Khan be holy! All who pay him not reverence must be put to death.

Yet we must wait more than an hour beside the road while

drovers brought past a thousand snow-white horses, for these had been bred for the Khan, and were being driven to Peking, where they would be consecrated to his use at a great religious service in early May. They would become part of his private herd of ten thousand, each without a blemish, used not for war but for ceremonies and parades, and the mares supplying milk forbidden to all except his family and blood kin and some followers of a certain tribe whom his grandsire, Genghis Khan, had seen fit to honor in this way. And while we did not give ground for a five-mile row of carts that came out of a road from Yulin, my eyes came close to popping from my head. The carts were loaded with broken black stone from mines beyond the Wall and were used in the thickly settled country south of us for fuel. In truth it was almost pure carbon, hardened by nature, and it burned longer and with more heat than the best oakwood.

Nicolo and Maffeo had known of this marvel ever since their previous journey to Cathay, but counted it so little compared with much else they had seen that they had never mentioned it in my hearing. Nor had they spoken of the paper money we began to see in the towns and posthouses—paper very like the Arabian sort, made from flax, cut into strips and bearing a writing designating a certain sum in silver as set by the Khan. Peasants in the fields accepted it as readily as silver, never questioning whether it might be counterfeit; thus a man could carry a fair-sized fortune in his bootleg, and a one-horse load would buy a thousand horses.

The season advanced, the road ran on, and by the end of April we were in northern Shansi along the great bend of the Hwang Ho. For many moons and a thousand miles I had heard mention of Kuku-khoto, the Blue City, the great mart of Middle Tatary above the Wall, and the abode of the Living Buddha. I had thought it would be so strange to come to it at last. But now we came to it and the merchants traded there and we saw the wondrous temples with their countless idols and after a while it dropped behind the horizon. We had come now to a populous plain, strewn with cities and towns, and paying immense tribute to the Khan in gold, silver, and paper money and in the stuffs of their manufacture, especially gold and silver cloth gorgeous beyond description. And far and wide, down every road and across every water, the name of Kublai Khan was a name to make men catch their breath and women turn white with awe and little children grow round-eyed. And as we moved eastward, it was around and about us like the bowl of the sky.

No name of mortal man that was ever breathed, I thought, held so many in such awe. In Christendom not even the name of God sounded and resounded with the same thunder, perhaps because His face and hand were hidden from mortal sight, and He dwelt in Heaven instead of in a man-built palace across a river, a mountain, or a plain. Indeed Kublai Khan was more than a name; it had become a watchword, an appellation at once terrible and sublime; millions upon millions of human beings pronounced it in their prayers.

His couriers rode furiously on every turnpike. From every lane came droves of horses, camels, cattle, and sheep for his use, and caravans and trains of carts loaded with the produce of the farms and factories bound for his treasure houses. There was no law but the Khan's, no right or wrong except what increased or reduced his power and glory; every body and soul and stick and stone was his personal possession to do with what he pleased. The sun must shine or the rain must fall by his imperial leave, for if they balked, his horde of wild-eyed magicians from Kashmir and Tibet conjured them to his sway. This last was told us by the most learned men we met. After many tellings, I did not believe or disbelieve, only put it out of my mind. If I were to survive on some desperate day not far off, it must be not as a king-worshiping Oriental, but as a Venetian.

We journeyed to Siuen-hwa-fu, a considerable city devoted to making harness and leather and fur garments for the Khan's troops, not far below the Wall in the far northeastern corner of Shansi. Three days beyond lay a country of far-flooded rivers and lakes, black with water fowl on the spring flight, and at a place called Chagan Nor, meaning White Pool, the Khan was having erected a hunting lodge, for his ease in hunting the birds with his thousands of falcons, and in hawking the pheasants, partridges, and cranes that swarmed the plains. The edifice would be of marble, and with its additions and outbuildings it would house ten thousand souls, the least number that accompanied him on pleasure trips, not counting the Imperial Guard, which would quarter mainly in the town.

From thence a great turnpike made for Peking, and in hardly a week's easy march we could have laid eyes on the greatest palace in all the world. But we would not see the Sun of the World shining in glory there, for the sun in the sky told us this was May, and he and his train were making for Xanadu, his summer palace and pleasure dome ten days to the north in the province of Jehol.

He would arrive toward the last day of May. A few days later he would hold a Fete of welcome, receiving emissaries and gift-bringers from all this corner of his empire. And since Nicolo and Maffeo were his accredited ambassadors whose duty it was to bring him tidings from Christendom, they too turned north. And since my slave girl was a prized attendant upon Nicolo's slave girl, I followed them, walking in the dust.

On that ten-day march, it was as though we were drawing nearer some kind of heaven, where an infinite number of angels strummed harps and sang, and no shadow could exist in the manifold rainbow light, and every moment held more thrilling pleasure than a lifetime on earth. We heard no music, saw no radiance, but the converging caravans, loaded with gifts and tribute, and the travelers pouring from every lane and footpath, had the same effect in heightening our excitement. Hence came subject princes with their gorgeous trains, governors of provinces who swayed more power than many a king in Europe, barons bejeweled and bedizened, mighty captains of hosts with guards of honor, ambassadors riding fast with sealed documents and royal greetings, wealthy merchants from all lands, artists hoping for sudden fame, wandering players, jongleurs, and musicians, peddlers of all sorts, and, in ever increasing numbers, humble pleasure-seekers and sightseers. These last were spending in one fling their little stores of hard-earned coins and ill-afforded leisure. The greater part of every day they spent on the roadside, making way for dignitaries and their trains. Yet I saw no resentment in their faces; they gaped at every wonder and thrilled at the displays and aspired to no happiness better than merging with the laughing bright-eyed crowds, and dreamed no dream of glory greater than beholding, with their own eyes, the very Khan.

Some of the families had bullock carts in which the women and children rode, along with food for the journey, cooking pots, holiday clothes, and even a rude pavilion. Others had loaded their gear on a single animal, the parents and the older children walking, and usually carrying babes on backs, in arms, or in wombs. If they had no baggage except bundles, as was true of thousands of poor pilgrims, their cares seemed proportionately light. Why not? When their money was spent and their bellies were empty, the Khan would fling out largess. There was no danger of rain or any disagreeable weather, because the Khan would forbid it. And the little fields to which they must return would yield better crops next year because they had basked in the effulgence of the Khan.

The unexplainable rise and the swift flight of one rumor after another added to the general joy, and no one mourned the sudden death of its predecessor. The Khan would give away one hundred elephant-loads of silver alms. . . . The Khan would feed a hundred traitors to his hunting tigers. . . . The Khan would name which of his twenty-five legitimate sons would succeed him, and three would be thrown to death in carpets for gazing through a window into his harem. The Khan had a new drinking mug, to hold a gallon of mare's milk, carved from a single diamond. . . . To my amazement, our caravan was the subject of one swift-winged tale—that Nico-lo-po, a great baron of Frankistan, was bringing testaments of surrender and subjection, along with vast tribute, from the Emperor of the West to be laid at the Khan's feet. Only the Emperor's name was in dispute. Some thought it was Richard the Lion-Hearted—the far-flung fame of that long-dead doughty Englishman had stirred me before now. Others maintained it was the Pope, and no few held it to be Prester John.

The air favorable to the flight of rumors lay close to the ground, heavy with human scent, so Nicolo and Maffeo, riding high at the head of the caravan, were not likely to hear many. I did nothing to bring the story about him to Nicolo's attention, let alone scotch it. Since the report of his world-spanning journey had caught the imagination of the pilgrims, there was a fair chance of its living on, gathering plausible detail as it spread far and wide, until it became current in Xanadu, where it might, through palace chit-chat, reach the ears of the Khan. I took pleasure in fancying a devastating anticlimax to these sensations. . . . But I could not afford such empty dreams, and soon put them by.

2

The golden tablet and the fact of their long-belated returning to the Khan's Court lent Nicolo and Maffeo large and genuine importance in official eyes. Three days out of Xanadu, a district chief appointed them a kind of beadle, to clear their way through the crowds and to determine precedence between them and other official parties. Thereafter the journey sped as in a dream.

These last days we traveled the road that the Khan took on his return from Xanadu in September; hence there were rest palaces for his use from ten to fifteen miles apart. The courier posts had been imposing enough, these were fit for the year-long residences of the second order of kings. Such noble edifices were preparing me, I thought, for the summer palace known as Xanadu Keibung. While it was neither as great nor as costly as the great palace of Peking, the drivers told me it was a pleasure dome not unworthy of the Great Khan.

Our last day on the road was the next to the last day of May according to Christian counting. By traveling late, our caravan could have entered the main south gate of Xanadu city, and Maffeo and Nicolo have gained admittance to a guesthouse on the palace grounds. Instead we stopped at sundown at a cara-vanserai three miles from the city wall, and before dawn flushed up, we took a leafy lane that led us in the general direction of the west gate. This was by the beadle's arrangements. He was aware that the two had never seen Xanadu Keibung and had planned a pleasant surprise for them, he too being a gentleman of refined tastes. We followers were not forbidden a share in the treat pro-vided we had the wit to appreciate it.

As we gained the crest of a high hill west of the wall, the sun heaved up in the east. Then I thought that our camels must gaze with a thrill in their dull hearts, and I would not wonder at them, only weep, if the dumb beasts knelt down.

When a jewel is mounted among lesser jewels by a cunning lapidary, they set each other off. Yet the central stone remains the subject of the invention and takes the eye first. So it was with the main edifice of Xanadu Keibung.[13] At this distance it gave the effect of a superably set gem infinitely magnified. It had the shim-mer of a pearl and, as the sun mounted, the changing hues of an opal.

The eye looked close to discover the most obvious source of the illusion—the three wide-eaved roofs crowning the three retracting stories were of polished tiles of gold, silver, pearl, scarlet, azure, emerald, and every variant tint known to the rainbow; the pillars supporting these aglitter or agleam with precious inlay and lac-quer; and the multicolored marble of the half-glimpsed walls. Its square dark-red terrace was about twenty acres in extent and set in what appeared to be a ring of turquoise three or four times larger, perfectly imaging the palace in all its manifold lights, and the forest at its rims. But this last was not magic. The Jewel is in the Lotus, so chant the Tibetan monks to infinitude. This jewel was in a lake.

Four marble causeways, green, blue, black, and white, led to the four entrances of the palace with the effect of an enameled cross. On one shore of the lake stood numerous double- and single-roofed mansions of noble state and dimension. These were the lodgings of some of the Khan's kinsmen and guesthouses for visiting princes and other exalted folk. All of these, with their gardens, arbors, courts, and colonnades, and the lake itself with its solitaire and landscaped shores, were enclosed in a gleaming white wall, almost as high as the trees, fully a mile square. From this distance the fountains looked like white or rainbow-hued lilies, the rills like silver threads, and the seasonal flower beds, multicolored bridges, and canopied barges suggested fine inlay in a richly jeweled medallion. The effect of the whole extravaganza at close view we could only imagine.

Far out over hill and dale ran outer walls, enclosing, it seemed, the whole countryside. The inner enclosure was a mere fraction of this expanse, estimated by the beadle at sixteen square miles. They constituted the most beautiful park I had ever seen.

It lay generally between a high ridge, plumed with tall, dark pines, and a long loop of the sluggish, low-lying, slow-flowing Lan Ho, sometimes called the Alph, nearly half a mile wide at this reach. The upper landscape was wild and rugged in the extreme, with black forest and gray heath, cliffs, crags, and glimpses of a white cataract that appeared to burst full-grown well under the rimrock. It leaped down a deep-cut chasm at the bottom of a wooded glen, its roaring distinctly audible at this distance of at least two miles. Every interopening ravine had its singing brook to swell the violent stream, so when it debouched from the chasm, it was a young river, flowing boldly and with majesty. Where its banks began to level off, hardly a mile from its source, a towered bridge, pale gold in hue, spanned the shining waters. These lulled quickly and turned dark blue below the bridge, and took a winding course on to the Lan Ho.

A road from the town crossed the bridge, and to this and some adjacent ground, the people were given free access. Here they could enjoy entertainments the Khan provided, picnic, and watch the training of several hundred of his best gerfalcons kept in the park in mew.

Actually the main purpose of this park was to afford the Khan hunting and coursing on a small scale. The large buildings and pens that we glimpsed through the trees housed the birds, as well as the hounds and the hunting leopards belonging to his entourage. However, we were not to think that this walled enclosure of sixteen square miles, thronging with game, furnished even a considerable fraction of the Khan's sport. To his great hunting camp on the Hwang Ho, he brought ten thousand giant mastiffs, as well as hounds, leopards, and hunting tigers. These and his hawks supplied the Court with one thousand head of game, whether beast or bird, every day of the winter months. The hawkers, doghandlers, watchers, and kennel and mews men numbered thirty-five thousand. At least ten thousand of his barons and courtiers, with their slaves and trains, could lodge in luxury at this vast encampment, and follow the hawks and the hounds in their master's wake.

An ample supply of game to furnish their fill of sport was provided by two short ordinances of the Khan. No other person in the vast province, not even the Royal Governor, was allowed to keep mews and kennels. If any person in all Cathay killed any wild animal or bird during the winter months, he was whipped to death.

The lower half of the park contained many beautiful woods, emerald-green meadows, fishpools, and meandering streams. Dreamy pavilions stood beside flower-banked ponds. But its prime feature was a smaller palace, crowning a hill, that seemed built of solid gold. This was a favorite retreat of the Khan's during his stay in Xanadu, especially on hot and sultry nights; and although it could house a thousand souls, it was built entirely of giant canes covered with gilt. An equal wonder was that it occupied ground which only a fortnight ago had been empty. The entire structure could be taken down, loaded with its furnishings on several thousand camels, transported at the Khan's whim, and re-erected—all in a matter of days. If one of his favorite concubines grew tired of the view from her window, he needed no Aladdin's lamp to work a wondrous change.

"Are the people allowed anywhere in the park except in those precincts?" Nicolo asked in his clear, far-carrying voice.

"No, and the region of the chasm is forbidden to his foresters and keepers. It's said he wishes to keep that part as Nature made it." More than that was said, to judge from the beadle's face; but he quickly veered from the subject. "When the Khan holds durbar, the people may come into the inner grounds through the lower gate and hang around the doors and balconies of the great hall. Indeed, they'd be allowed to enter if they could find room. The Khan holds by the ancient law of the Mongol that his meanest subject may have access to his imperial person, along with the right of petition."

"I can't remember any of the common sort attending the great durbar in Peking."

"They aren't forbidden to do so, after the great folk and their attendants have taken their places. Moreover, if they have petitions, they can raise their hands. But sometimes the Khan is busied with other matters, in which case he doesn't point his scepter at the petitioner. It is a risk that few of his meaner subjects care to run."

"What happens in that case?"

"He is taken out and strangled."

Nicolo did not answer but turned with a charmed expression to sniff at a gentle breeze coming up with the sun. It had blown across the park and had gathered up the incense of flowering trees. I could not recall a more exquisite perfume. As Nicolo savored it, seated atop his great gray stallion, a passer-by would have thought him a very king.

CHAPTER 11

THE CHASM

WHEN WILD-RIDING COURIERS AND EXHAUSTED RUNNERS brought news that the Khan's train had been sighted over the hill, I gathered with a large number of the common sort on the precincts reserved for us in the park. After awhile there came a glimmer as from a rising sun in a little niche in a wooded crest where the road ran. An involuntary utterance, one of the strangest I had ever heard, rose from our crowd. I could best describe it as a prolonged grunt of happy wonder.

Knowing what to look for, as did the others, my sharp eyes were among the first to focus on the Khan's equipage. He journeyed in a howdah at least twenty feet square and borne by not one elephant but four, all of them tuskers exactly ten feet tall, perfectly trained, and marching two by two. As it caught the sunlight it began to show reddish in hue, since the outside was covered with tiger skins. The interior was known to be lined with beaten gold, and the roof could be thrown open at the Khan's wish.

Although we did not see them, three thousand of his personal bodyguard of nine thousand were riding out and ahead of the equipage on both sides of the road, but not setting foot in the road itself lest they raise dust. Behind the Khan marched a file of about twenty elephants, all richly caparisoned and bearing how-dahs bright with inlay and lacquer and shining in the sun. In these rode one or more of the Khan's four queens, and members of his family, with favorite attendants and outriders. Next in order were not his barons and courtiers, but fully a thousand horses white as speckless snow, semidivine beasts to the Tatar mind, bred for the Khan alone, and their like forbidden to any of his subjects. Occasionally he rode one of the stallions; the mares supplied milk and *karvas,* the Tatars' mainstay and their ceremonial drink, to his kinsmen, wives, and concubines.

Behind these beautiful beasts came a mile-long file of carts bearing favorite hounds and hawks with their keepers, at least a hundred fierce eagles used in killing deer, and, which I had heard but could hardly believe, a score of hunting tigers, each in the company of a small dog to smell out game for it when the game took cover.[14] These gorgeous beasts were not caged, merely kept in leash, and either rode in the carts or paced beside them in charge of their trainers. Other carts contained wolves for coursing wild cattle and heavy stags, and fully a hundred hunting leopards rode on horses, each in charge of a groom.

By the time all these had emerged into plain sight, the Khan's equipage was not far from the eastern gate of the park, a great portal magnificently adorned and used only by him and his immediate family. As his equipage turned into its approach, we saw two gerfalcons rise from the opening in the roof of the car; obviously, they had been cast to hawk at a passing flock of cranes. This pair were the finest in all the royal mews of many thousand or they would not be riding with the Khan; quite possibly they were the best on earth. Perhaps that was why I took no joy in watching them tower and stoop. Their quarry had been doomed when the Khan's eye first fell on them. That fall had been as crushing as a giant tree falling on their nests.

The Khan's car passed through the sacred gate of the park and into the palace grounds. The file of elephants followed, while his immediate bodyguard of three thousand fell into close ranks and entered an adjacent gate. Led now by the drove of white horses, each with its groom, his train made their way through the south gate, then each section went its own way like the divisions of a well-trained army coming into camp. Behind the hawk and tiger carts, and the leashed wolves and the mounted leopards, marched another file of elephants, not as tall or as richly caparisoned as the first, but fully ten times as many. The men and women in the open howdahs were obviously great folk of the Court; I suspected that the curtained ones bore favorite concubines. And from these to the niche in the hills, as far as eye could see, rode company after company of horsemen. Some were richly dressed and evidently minor officials of the Court. Whole companies wore the same apparel, representing various services to the Khan—falconers, cooks, costumers, physicians, jongleurs and acrobats, vintners, tailors, jewelers, goldsmiths and silversmiths, and, in regiments of nine hundred riding ten abreast, his bodyguardsmen not today on duty.

These streamed from the ridge top to the various gates of the park and the city for more than two hours. So we spectators almost laughed at a mere hundred dog-handlers, each dressed in blue and holding two giant mastiffs on leash. We had better not laugh. We had better remember that Xanadu was not one of the Khan's great hunting seats, where hawks and hounds, falcons and beaters and watchers, were numbered in thousands. In Xanadu the Khan kept cool, hunting only an hour or two each day. In other respects, his Court here was only a skeleton Court. For instance, in Peking the ménages of his four queens, each occupying a separate palace, numbered forty thousand in eunuchs, handmaidens, and slaves.

Behind the dogs, there walked barefoot in the dust a hundred men in rags. Indeed they were as tattered and dirty as the troops of beggars that many a Christian king hires on feast days to receive his alms and prove his charity. But no great baron, who sometimes played chess with the Khan, smirked with such pride as these matted-haired beasts. They called themselves the Khan's astrologers. Actually they constituted the most powerful body of necromancers, sorcerers, and seers in all the world. They were the pick of all Asia and every one was a master of some diabolic art.

They brought up the rear of the imperial procession. The host of men and beasts coming into view in the dust clouds was made up of drovers, baggage wallahs, herds of cattle and sheep, and loaded camels without end. Only a few of us gapers stayed to watch them pass; the greater number of us sought good lookouts for a sight less magnificent but more heart-lifting and lucky. In the cool of the evening on the day of his arrival it was the custom of the Khan to ride out into the park, to see how the game had flourished in his absence, and to take a few head to start the season well. On the croup of his steed would ride a hunting leopard or perhaps a huge eagle, whom he would loose at a fallow deer. The open glades might give a glimpse of him as he raced behind the spotted cat or under the nine-barbed harpy. It might come to pass they would watch the very kill.

But I had business elsewhere.

Three days from today the Khan would hold durbar in the great hall of the palace. My own plans for that day were hardly worthy of the name: they amounted to one simple stroke, the results of which would depend on how well it was delivered, on circumstance, and on how close was my guess at the characters of Nicolo and Kublai Khan. I might be prevented from dealing it at all. That was in the lap of unknown gods and hence no immediate burden on my mind. My poverty would impair my preparations, but making the best of it brought me to the town's old-clothes market, busy enough, but where no one ever smiled.

I was looking for a robe of a certain color and kind. I did not care how thin it had worn, provided it would hold together for one wearing—after that, I could get along without it, will I, nill I. Finding nothing barely suitable among these sorry relics of better days, I was cursing my own low spirits when I felt them take a sudden lift. I had caught sight of my former copemate and fellow night-hawk, Pietro the Tatar. He was treating himself to lichi nuts from a street vendor and had not seen me yet. Instead of avoiding him, I raised my voice enough to attract his attention. Although the gains would be small at best, I thought to give him good news to take to his master.

At once he came strolling toward me, his eyes glistening. I affected chagrin at being seen in the ill-smelling resort of misfits, human and cloth.

"I take it you're about to sell your old turnout, to fit yourself anew," he said.

"I have a few winter garments that I can spare, now that summer's come," I answered. "But the prices paid at this raghouse are too low."

"I doubt if you can do any better in the town."

"I suppose I'll have to let them go. I need a little money to dress Sheba for the slave market. With the hundred and fifty dinars that she'll bring, I can lay in camel wool to sell in Shengking. There are several eastbound caravans that I can join."

"Aren't you going to offer her to your—to Nicolo Emir?"

"I thought he wouldn't want her, if he gives the white slave girl to the Khan."

"Why, he might take her anyway. He couldn't lose very much on her."

"I'm not going to ask him for any favors."

"Why don't you wait to see if he keeps the Frank Linda for himself? I heard him tell Maffeo malik that he hasn't decided yet. If he does, he'll probably pay you two hundred for Sheba. Anyway, you ought to see the durbar. I've asked our beadle to find me a stand in the outer gallery, and he can do the same for you."

"Someone might recognize me and cry me for a thief. You were lucky that night—but I wasn't."

"My Tatar face didn't stand out like yours did. And although you had nothing to gain by implicating me, some men would have done it anyway. If there's any little favor I can do you——"

"I won't want the place in the gallery, but I thank you anyway."

"Is there anything else? You've had a lot of misfortune—I've prospered moderately—and if a dinar or two would help you dress Sheba——"

"Five dinars would help me a great deal, and I'll repay them after I sell her."

"Why, I'll lend them to you gladly." He handed me the five gold coins. "And I'm sorry you'll not see the great sight."

"I suppose Nicolo will cut a fine figure." This was merely to make an assurance doubly sure.

By nature cruel, and sharing all his master's triumphs, he relished my bitter tone.

"I suppose he will. He's bought a new robe of ceremony. His servant took it into the sunlight to look for moths, and several of us saw it."

I had been enjoying the game and had considered it merely that—to raise my spirits rather than make gains, although the five dinars was a windfall and if Nicolo had a last lingering doubt of my abjectness, Pietro's gleeful report would set it at rest. Suddenly, though, it had proved of immense importance, and I had to guard my countenance from his sharp eyes.

"Why, I thought he'd wear his blue brocade with the golden pheasants."

"This is dark-red brocade, of ankle length, with heavy golden eagles and silver deer, very large and splendid. It cost four hundred dinars."

"Four hundred? If he'd given them to me, he'd have never missed them, and I could have kept my horse and my longbow and now Sheba."

But I need not dissemble a deeply anxious face. The fear that had never lifted from me, awake or asleep, these last few days—

never intense but ever dismal as a dull toothache—was of the failure of one straight, bold stroke aimed at Nicolo. Now I must face the likelihood of not being able to deliver it at all.

I had cause to remember some folk wisdom Miranda had learned from an old hostler in England:

> For a nail rusted through the mare lost her shoe;
> So she slid on a crack and fell and broke her back;
> So her rider walked late where robbers lay in wait;
> So dying unshriven he went not to Heaven.
> O the wailing he did on the Devil's hot grid
> For iron worth a penny when thrift he hadn't any.

2

If my mare lost the race it would not be by my lack of thrift. I spent the following morning searching for an accouterment I lacked, combing all the ground that offered the least hope. But the merchants would not rent to me any rig that would suit me well—they were suspicious of poorly dressed aliens with thin purses, especially when the town thronged with fly-by-nights—and what I could buy for my last handful of gold fell sorely short of my need.

I wished I could find a shrill-laughing, hand-waving Jew of the kind that owned pawnshops in Venice. Not that his heart might be softer than these quiet Chinese, but he would be more of a cosmopolitan and have more imagination. For some strange reason, no Jews had ever found their way to Xanadu.

The least sorry substitute for my requirement that I had money to buy turned up in the stock of a Bengali tailor. It was of ankle length, not badly worn, and made of brocade, although of inferior sort, but the wrong color, dull-looking, and without decoration. Still I paid a piece of gold to have the dealer hold it until tomorrow noon; unless Fortune turned her wheel to bring me something better, I was resolved to take it, make the best of it, and play the game. I was an adventurer and this was my great adventure. When my lips turned down at the corners in an evil sneer, I knew that I would risk everything to win.

At my cheap, mean, but private room at the caravanserai I found Sheba completing the task I had set her and her shining eyes signaling exciting news. After guarding against eavesdroppers, she spoke to me in a husky whisper thrilling to hear.

"If it's your wish, Miranda will meet you tonight."

"When and where?"

"At the third hour after midnight, three hundred of your long steps above the bridge in the Khan's park."

A cold thrill ran over my skin, the same as on the haunted desert, and I had to guard both my countenance and my voice.

"You misunderstood her. She meant three hundred paces on one side or other of the bridge along the road—her saying 'above the bridge' probably means toward the town——"

"No, master. She meant up the chasm of the stream."

"But that's forbidden to all except the Khan and his barons. I heard the people say it's the most sacred——" I stopped to wonder at that word.

"His barons don't go there. They wait for him on the rim. Not even his queens can go with him there. The people say he goes to meet the ghost of Genghis Khan and take counsel from him. So it's the safest place you can find."

"If we're seen going in or coming out, we'll be straightway whipped to death. Not only I—both of us. No doubt he has spies everywhere——"

"I spoke of that, but she doesn't believe it. She says it couldn't cross his mind that anyone would dare come near such a terrible spot. Anyway, the moon has almost waned away and there won't be much light to spy by."

"One of his soothsayers could find out——"

"She doesn't think their magic will work against what's good."

The chill stayed in my flesh and blood and the marrow of my bones, but I drove my brain to pay heed to a memory seeking entrance like a shaft of sunlight probing its way through clouds. In a moment I had captured it and saw its bearing on the present pass. The hardy men of the Great Pamir dared not take Iskander's path across the face of the cliff as tall as a mountain. If the same ledge overhung a ravine of ordinary depth, they would have essayed it bravely. But the fall from either one was down to death. Perceiving this, I had won a splendid prize.

"Tell Miranda that I'll come with pleasure."

3

The truth was, I went in great terror. I had gained the river edge where it flowed through the public precincts, then walked up its grassy bank in the light of the withered moon. Before long I came to a little fence, two feet high and made of frail bamboo, marking the forbidden ground. I stopped, my body drenched with sweat, and must shut my jaw to keep my teeth from knocking. But I could remember stopping at Iskander's bridge, gazing down into the pit, and walking on. I stepped over the fence in one stride and again walked on. The wide stream hunched up and rushed past me with increasing speed and gathering sound. But my terror had passed from me as though by the breaking of an evil spell, and only an eerie sense of things not of this earth made my skin creep.

No doubt Miranda had chosen this meeting place because it was one of the most lonely in the world. She had chosen this hour in the late ebb of night because it was the least employed except by dreamers, spirits good and evil, and night birds and beasts. But I felt there were other causes in the first case, and I now discovered one, strangely warming my heart, in the second case. Tonight's moon rose late. She had returned to the shape she bore when she was young and beautiful and promising great things—a deep-drawn bow with long pointed ends—but now she faced her western burial ground instead of her glorious birthplace, and almost all her promises had failed, and she had turned into a witch with a weird lamp. Yet because I needed her pale beams to guide my steps, Miranda had arranged for me to have them. Our appointment was the hour that she hung high. Pouring straight down, some of the beams fell into the deep, narrow chasm where I walked.

I walked a footpath beside the raging waters. Since the Khan came by a secluded lane over and down the ridge, it must have been worn by deer and other folk of the woods. Yet they too must traverse it in pricked-eared wonder, their wild hearts clamoring from intimations forbidden to me and to even the great Khan. I half saw, half divined, a scene of unworldly beauty. Its accompaniment was the river's roar as Miranda's singing had accompanied the beauty of her face and flowing hands. The walls of the canyon steeped as the river's tumult grew. Their dark cedars stood one and one instead of close and thick as in the upper world; perhaps only a few of the most valiant could take root among the crags. Perhaps here was a great kingdom enchanted into this small space. Maybe it was a scene from a Land of Faery transported here by the arts of the Khan's magicians.

No, it was only a natural wonder that a traveler in a wild and lonely land had chanced on and reported to the Khan. The romantic scene about me was but part of it, and likely a small part. The place where the Khan vanished and stayed long, the most holy on all the earth in his subject's sight, was still ahead of me;

and I surmised it to be the birthplace of the stream at the head of the canyon. When very he had laid eyes on it, had he decreed it the secret shrine of a great pleasure ground, where would stand his summer palace?

Below my musings I had kept loose track of my steps. When I had taken about three hundred, the moon gave me a glimpse of Miranda on the deer path. When I came near she smiled and, leaning toward me, spoke in my ear—else I could not have heard her above the multitoned thunder of the waters.

"Let's go to the source," she said. "I'll lead the way."

So we walked on. When there was no room to walk between the stream and the canyon walls, the path wound upward, seeking ledges and projections on the face of the cliff and clinging there like a living thing—but it had been made by living things, deer and suchlike who had business up the canyon and had found their way there. So their fawns could follow them, they had picked unerringly the safest route, for not even the wide-horned stags could survive a fall into the rock-bound cataracts, and only the highborn otters, to whom had been given dominion over wild, white floods, dared plunge and play. Thus Miranda and I, young, strong, good walkers, and with nerves steadied from many adventures, could follow in their steps.

When the path dipped to the water's edge, I caught her hand and stopped her and spoke in her ear.

"Perhaps we're the only people alive who've ever walked this path."

"No, there are others who believe that God is greater than the Khan and who came here to affirm it. There are those whose souls are as haughty as his and came here at their command. And there must be those who had to come because of eager eyes and itching feet."

"What did they find?"

"I think all of them found grace."

I thought she might say "strength" instead of "grace." I could not think through her meaning but I knew she spoke the truth. She was very pale and her eyes were big and soft and many intimations were being given her.

"Will I find it?"

"Yes, a little, unless you're a demon, not a man."

"How could I be a demon?"

"It's very easy to become one, I think—although most who do are not recognized by real people and perhaps often not by themselves. All you'd have to do would be to get rid of your soul. I don't mean to sell it. You hear of that, but I've thought it over, and who is there to buy it? Not the Devil. What would he do with it? I think you only have to stop wanting it and it dies."

Spray from the surges flinging in my face stung like snow crystals. "This water is ice-cold," I said, not in the least uneasy over changing the subject.

"Yet it doesn't freeze in the bitterest winters. I suppose it's too violent for frost to get hold of it. Did you know it chills the river for more than a mile below its mouth?"

"No."

"The old *gibbaleen* told me."

In the slow-swirling pools under the cascades it appeared milky-white, making me think of some of the glacier streams in the High Pamir. And now the air became intensely cold and only our exercise kept us warm. There was no longer any vegetation close to the brim.

We went on, farther and higher, and both of us became greatly afraid. But we had drawn so close that each of us recognized the other's fear as the same, and it was one that Nature put into us, for our protection, not terror from a false god. Its main cause was the roar of the river between the rock walls in concatenation with a continuous explosion not far ahead. The path narrowed and steepened.

We followed it still and it led us to the canyon rim. The sound, though enormous, was not so terrible now that we had escaped from its reverberations on the rock walls; and we advanced through a cedar wood, walking hand in hand. And then we came to the birthplace of the river.

At least, this was its borning into the upper world, lit by the sun, moon, and stars, although it had had a dark fetal life in the womb of the mountain. We stood near the mouth of a cave whose breath was deathly cold. From its upper jaw hung a row of dragon teeth, long and sharp, and the lower was set with what looked like broken, blunt snags, but they shimmered in the weak moonlight, and I did not believe that they were limestone stalactites and stalagmites; nor did the portal itself look like stone. In a moment I guessed the truth. It was a cave of ice.

Now we saw other caves, many of them half-hidden by the crags, overhanging more than half of the inner rim of a bowl hewn by a giant stonecutter out of the solid rock. And in the bowl was as strange a spring as ever flowed.

The water did not well up continuously but burst up with enormous force at such rapid intervals that the ear could hardly distinguish the separate explosions. No doubt gushings and splashings and the continuous and compound echoes from the rocks and the ice caves almost filled the fleeting silences between the claps, to cause an undulating roar. But to the eye the ejaculations were distinct, and their effect on the mind was awesome in the extreme. They did not take the form of upbursting geysers, instead they lifted the whole body of water in the bowl in the shape of a giant mushroom that constantly overtowered the rim and which swelled out, rose several feet, and diminished again with each pulsation. Only a small fraction poured out to form the stream. And the underground river heaved up by the earth's convulsions must be abysmally deep, for the rocks throbbed in time with the bursts, and we felt that their terrible central sound rose from far below us.

We walked nearer and took our stand on a crag from which we could look down into the crater. Its walls had been scoured and polished by the upheaving flood, and now we could hear another sound under or running through the terrific undulation. It was of stone bounding against stone. The only explanation I could conceive was that boulders and rock fragments were hurled up by the exploding waters and struck against the crater walls.

And now Miranda's sharp eyes made a strange and thrilling discovery. Farther around on the crater rim was a seat carved out of solid rock, affording an open view of the heaving waters and their plunge into the chasm. Its lofty position and its shape of grandeur told us both in the same instant that it was a throne.

Miranda said something I could not hear. Smiling strangely then, she took my hand, and together we walked the short distance, and climbed the little rise that brought us to it. And here the uproar ceased to hurt the ears and stultify the brain, I did not know why unless, striking an adjacent cliff, it ricocheted in the form of echoes.

I knew it was not bravado, or even Miranda's expectations, that caused me to sit on the throne. When I did so, she nodded her head slightly, and I realized the beauty in her face.

"Will you sit here?" I asked when, after a moment, I had risen.

"I don't need to."

"Do you think I'm the only one except the Khan who ever sat there?"

"Of course not. Kublai Khan didn't carve it himself. The sculptor he'd appointed tried it plenty of times."

"I think he had the sculptor strangled."

"He may have, but that didn't change it. And squirrels have climbed into the seat, and birds have lighted there."

"Why did you have me meet you in the ravine?"

"I thought it would help you in what you intend to do."

"Have you any idea what it is?"

"I've tried not to think. But Nicolo told me last night that you'd been seen in the old clothes market and you were trying to raise money for a journey. I think if the journey is to be only a mile from the market, it is going to be difficult and dangerous."

"You still haven't fully answered my question. You said you thought it would help me but you didn't say why you wanted to help me—why you did help me."

"Because when you were in desperate need of money, you didn't sell Sheba."

"No, I didn't." I spoke only because she stood waiting.

"Will you tell me why?"

"No, I can't, because I don't know. All I know is, I'm going to make the trial—take the journey you spoke of—without selling her, or not at all."

"Not even as a last resort?"

"No."

"Did you succeed in raising money any other way?"

"I had a little over twenty dinars and Pietro lent me five more." And she returned my smile.

"Yet you're going to make the trial?" she asked.

"Yes, the best I can."

"Marco, do you remember when you took me from the house of Simon ben Reuben, he gave me a mezusah? That was a little gold shell to wear around my neck, containing the promises of his God."

"I remember it well."

"He got it himself just before I left, then spoke to me in a low voice. If ever I was in great need, I was to open it and get something out of it. Once I did open it. It was not when you were about to sell me—that was on your soul, not mine—but long after that, in the city of Bukhara. I saw what it was and put it back. I thought of the old Jew and all he stood for and I decided my need wasn't as great as I had believed. I believed that someday there would come a greater one."

I did not speak and only bent my head.

"I was right. It came when I lay awake in the middle of the night. So I opened the mezusah and took out what he'd given me. Cup your hand."

I did so. She laid in it a diamond of the worth of two hundred dinars. The dying moon made it cast an inch-long luster on my palm.

CHAPTER 12

THE COURT OF KUBLAI KHAN

BEFORE SUNDOWN OF THE DAY PRECEDING THE EVENT, CROWDS began to gather on the causeways allotted to them. By midnight something like fifty thousand crammed the outer galleries of the great hall while thousands more, hopeless of any glimpse of the glory, lined the avenues kept open by the guards down which would walk princes, barons, and ambassadors on their way to their posts of honor. There was almost no sound. The people were grave of face and manner as though gathered in the temples of their gods.

Not long after sunrise I took a stand behind one of the lines, and since the people were mainly of less stature, I could peer over their heads with little danger of being observed. Over a gorgeous robe of dark-red brocade decorated with golden tigers hunting silver cattle, I wore a barracan of light, rough wool. Under my headcloth, my hair was dressed in the Venetian fashion. I had shaped my mustache to resemble Nicolo's and shaved my beard.

Back of me, Sheba, in white trousers and sleeveless jellick, watched over a bundle roughly triangular in shape, with six-foot sides.

It was the rule of the Court that when the Khan held durbar, even princes must dispense with their trains except for slaves bearing gifts. So when Nicolo and Maffeo came from the guest-house, they had only four attendants. One was a tall Indian in handsome array belonging to Nicolo; he carried a bundle wrapped in silk that no doubt contained the fire-walker's suit. Two Persian slaves of Maffeo's bore cloth of gold and silver, Samarkand silk, and a rolled rug, a marvel of the rugmaker's art said to be five hundred years old, that he had bought in faraway Kashgar. Wearing Chinese dress of profuse embroidery, Miranda brought up the rear. In her hand was a golden bowl covered with the identical piece of embroidery that the Arghum girl Araxie had given Nicolo for a place in our caravan, and which he had had in his saddlebag during our flight from ambush. The pattern of that story was as strange, I thought, as that of the needlework.

Despite their modest trains, the two ambassadors greatly impressed the watchers. The red, richly decorated robe of one set off the blue robe, fully as gorgeous, of the other; both towered over the nobles before and behind them and walked with a kingly stride no squat Tatar could attain; the like of their countenances had never been seen by most of the people; and the whisper sped like a rustle of wind that they were ambassadors from Frankistan, beyond the setting sun.

I waited until almost the last of the great folk having a rightful place in the hall were about to pass by. Catching my signal, Sheba removed the covering from Iskander's horns and lifted them on her shoulder; I shed my barracan and headcloth. Then I fell in behind a Mongol lord and his gift-bearing slaves, and myself took stately strides. Sheba, long-legged as her kind and with a swinging gait inimitable this side of Africa, walked in my footsteps. She was raised to carry a jar of water weighing eighty pounds on her high-held head, so she made light of her burden, holding it with one hand.

Whatever admiration we succeeded in winning from the crowd, certainly we aroused more curiosity than the wildest bearded sheik from Kurdistan.

An usher met me at the door. I spoke in the Jagatai Mongol; and my voice was steadier than I had ever hoped.

"I am Marco-po, bringing a gift to the Khan. I wish to stand nigh to Nico-lo-po and Maffeo-lo-po, ambassadors from Frankistan."

The usher bowed low and led the way into the vast hall. The horns towered high under even this lofty roof, but not one of the immense, silent, motionless throng turned his head an inch. On a carpet so deep and soft that I did not have to tread lightly to make no sound, I walked up an aisle through the throng for at least a hundred paces and was posted within ten paces of the base of a many-storied dais. On the lower floors sat the Khan's brothers and sons and kinsmen on chairs of silver and enamel; on the next to the highest a woman of fifty or more, fat and no longer comely, occupied a silver-and-ivory chair amid a blaze of jewels. At the very top, at least twenty feet above the throng, an empty chair awaited an occupant. It was not so large as to dwarf a man of ordinary size, but it was of gold, inlaid with ivory, pearl, and jade, and studded with an uncountable number of diamonds, rubies, and emeralds in fabulous design.

The merest roll of my eyes disclosed Nicolo and Maffeo on my right hand. They too stood like statues, but they had not failed to see me and identify me. Maffeo appeared bewildered. Nicolo had turned white with fury. I was glad of its intensity, because no man can think straight and act with discretion when torn by such passion. I could not look at Miranda without turning my head, but I was deeply aware of a golden haze that was her hair.

Ghosts gathering in the Halls of Death, awaiting the entrance of their terrible king, could not have stood more motionless and mute. The silence held for a period difficult to estimate—I thought it was fifteen minutes but perhaps it was not even five—and was at once thrilling and agonizing. Then the notes of a hidden flute floated into it and lightly breached the silence as a waking bird's first call breaks the profound hush of dawn.

Other flutes began to sound in harmony with the first, and then massed zithers, harps, dulcimers, and violins from behind a long fretwork in alabaster. It must be that our hearts swelled with the swelling music, for every face I saw was strangely lighted; and as the trumpets came in with their mounting peal of exultation, louder and louder blaring of triumph beyond measure, the hair lifted on my head and my flesh turned to ice and fire.

Then, underneath the wild and savage symphony, we heard the low beat of kettledrums. Slowly they gave more voice to their cruel pride; they were the stirrers of men's blood, the inciters to kill. Soldiers marched and horses charged to their reverberant beat; they were a mighty echo to the pulse of fury throbbing in warriors' veins; they boomed forth the final glory, the glory of battle.

It is by battle that I conquered and my sires conquered before me. It is by battle that all these softer glories light on my head and shine forth unto you. I am Kublai, the grandson of Genghis, the brother of Mangu, and I hold by the sword.

For me the world was made.

The paean was rising to a terrible crescendo when a door behind the throne opened, and onto the dais came a being too effulgent to be a mortal man. While no one breathed, he seated himself in his golden, bejeweled chair, placed his scepter on a stand at his knees, and laid his hands, one on top of the other, on his breast.

He had only one follower—a Siberian tiger, with rich fur and heavy ruff, big as an ox. He yawned, showed his big fangs and red gullet to the crowd, then dropped down at his master's feet.

The paean ended with a crashing chord. Then there came a voice as though from Heaven, filling the vast room.

"Bow and adore!"

All subjects and sojourners to the Khan's Court—the queen and the princes and every human being in the room except slaves that were counted as chattels and whose very lives were prostrate—dropped to their knees and smote their heads four times upon the floor.

2

Head down with the rest, so reduced from man's heights and so lost among the swarm of suppliants that I was hidden from enemy eyes and need not fear making any mistake or attracting the least dangerous attention, I took some bearings as though I had an astrolabe in my hand. I could see no immovable stars, but I thought of Mustapha . . . Miranda . . . Simon ben Reuben . . . Sheba. I remembered a throne of stone where I had sat last night that would outlast the wonderwork of gold and jewels before which we bowed down. When I rose again, I felt in my right mind.

Still I must not look to the right or the left, but it was not against the Khan's law to look at the Khan. The glitter and gleam and godlike luster that played about him was the effect of a long coat of gold with collar, cuffs, frontpiece, and hand-breadth belt of square-cut, close-set jewels, diamond buttons, low-brimmed hat covered and ablaze with rubies, pearls, and diamonds, set off by the painted wall behind him and the throne of massive gold with its fabulous adornment. It must be that the blue Chinese lamps were so placed that they set fire to all the jewels—each burning with its separate flame to make a multicolored conflagration dazzling the eyes and putting the mind in shadow, because the big tiger crouching at his feet looked gaudy beyond nature. Under all this was a man. He was a man as surely as I was one, and as Sheba was a woman and as red Roxana that I had ridden had been a mare. He was a man of medium height, over sixty years old, rather stout, with a big, rather coarse nose, heavy jowls, and slanted, narrow, magnetic eyes. Genghis Khan and most of his sons had had blue eyes and fair skins and fairly heavy beards. Kublai was brown-skinned and wore only a wisp of beard.

Presently he spoke in Jagatai Mongol in a clear, warm, quite pleasant voice. I had heard that sounding boards had been built into the room and did not doubt that it carried to the inner galleries.

"I am returned to my beloved Xanadu Keibung, and I greet you all."

No voice bade us prostrate ourselves, so we all stood still.

"There is one here who is about to undertake a long journey in my name—even unto the city of Budapest, which my cousin Batu razed to the ground thirty years ago, and whose king pays tribute to Toghon Khan, my viceroy and kinsman, lord of the Krim Tatars. Although there are many here of greater office, he has served me well, and since he will be gone from me for many a moon, it is fitting that I greet him before all the rest. Caidu of Wanchuan, you are welcome here."

I heard his greeting to the grizzled Tatar in only the shell of my ear. I need take no hints as to the procedure of acknowledgment and gift-giving, as I heard it discussed all the way from Koko-Khotan. An inkling of what would come next made the blood rush to my head. . . . Now the royal stewards were taking Caidu's offerings from the hands of his slaves and he was prostrating himself with tears rolling down his cheeks. . . . Now the Khan was speaking again.

"This day of departure of my ambassador to my Western kingdoms is the day of return of my ambassadors from beyond my Western kingdoms—even from the Court of the Christian Pope, Lord of Frankistan. They have been gone for nigh ten years. They have crossed and recrossed the whole habitable world. It comes to me they have served me faithfully, whether or not their mission was crowned with success. Although there are many here of greater name and place, it is fitting that I greet them only next to my departing servant Caidu. Maffeo and Nicolo, the older and younger brothers Polo, I make you welcome."

Nicolo and Maffeo took one pace forward. I heard the Khan ask them in turn of their missions, and listened to their studied replies. This was a mere formality—the letters they had brought from the Pope and other ambassadorial business would be taken to the Imperial Council. Then in respect to Maffeo's seniority, the Khan addressed to him first the imperial utterance that told the main business of the durbar.

"My servant Maffeo, you have my leave to make offerings to the Khan."

"Great Khan, they are only tokens of my fealty," Maffeo answered, "and I lay them humbly at your feet."

The polite procedure was for Maffeo's slaves to continue to hold the gifts until the Khan dismissed him, whereupon the stewards took charge of them. In this case, the Khan asked to see the antique rug and admired it. I did not think his interest in it was more than lightly passing. I believed he was far more interested in Nicolo and the gifts he brought. When his *Chiah*, an exalted secretary in Mongol courts, had informed him of the ambassadors' return, likely he had forgotten Maffeo but remembered Nicolo. He was the kind of strong, cunning, intensely ambitious man who took a king's eye. . . .

It was coming now. The chessmen were set out, the players had disposed of lesser matters, the contest was about to begin. It was Nicolo's move.

"My servant Nicolo, you have my leave to make offerings to your Khan."

"Great Khan, the only considerable gift I bring is a token of fealty from the King of Kerman, entrusted to my hands for delivery to you. With it lie some trifles that are beneath your attention but which I hoped would set off the king's offering for the greater pleasure of your sublime eyes."

"The slave girl may walk to the foot of the dais so I may see the gifts."

It was the slave girl that he wanted to see, for her pale golden hair was more beautiful and more precious than all the cloths of gold in the whole pageant. It was the slave girl that he looked at mostly as she came and stood at the foot of the dais—and he must be an epicure beyond any in the world, for he had seen and sorted over thousands of the most beautiful girls that had ever breathed. Yet he took a cursory glance into the golden bowl.

"Your slave may return to her place. And truly the balas ruby is a handsome jewel, well set off by the smaller rubies, turquoises, and jade." He moved his arm slightly, and the sleeve with its cuff of close-set diamonds, rubies, and emeralds fell back to reveal a diamond bracelet crowned with a ruby like a coal of fire. It was of the hue called pigeon-blood and as big as a pigeon's egg.

"In this bundle are garments of a strange nature and use," Nicolo said. "They consist of helmet, a robe, mittens, and boots, and their wearer can walk unharmed through fire or stand in fire until his breath gives out. They were given to me for a service done the priests of the Swasti at your Imperial Highness's city of Suchow."

"Of what are they made?" the Khan asked after a brief pause.

I had already observed the band of fifty tattered foul-faced magicians squatted on the floor to the left of the dais—very plainly a mighty power in the Court. Now I turned my gaze from the Khan's countenance to glance at them again. They had straightened their bent backs a little with the effect of so many cobras towering to strike. When Nicolo spoke, I had no doubt that he had flicked his eyes in the same direction.

"Great Khan, the wise doctors in Frankistan would believe that they are made of the skins of salamanders, which reptiles are said to be immune to fire. The magicians of the Swasti give out that they are the skins of dragons killed by sorcery. I will not gainsay them, although time may reveal them to be of some other substance."

"I've never seen a dragon, unless I count the great crocodiles of Hind worthy of that name," the Khan remarked. "I believe the garments to be made of a noncombustible fiber found in my High Altai, and which my couriers use as packets for most precious writings, lest they be destroyed by fire."

Nicolo did not move except to catch his breath. He had been compromised by his own blunder in the opening, but he kept his countenance and his air of loyal subjection to the King of Kings.

"Doubtless that is so. I would wish that a portion of this offering be used to make a packet for carrying a pronouncement of overlordship and protection from the Great Khan to the kings of Frankistan. Now I plead to make one more trifling offering. It is of the slave girl Linda who was just now at the foot of your sublime throne. She comes from England, an island at the outer rim of the habitable world, and there she would be counted of noble blood. It is my fond hope that since not many maidens of her sort have ever been seen in these portions of your realm, you will accept her, if only as a curiosity, to keep or dispose of at your pleasure."

A change came over the Khan. Every soul in the great hall perceived it. The advantage that I had not earned, that I had not foreseen in my fondest dreams, had been short-lived.

"From England, say you. My brother Mangu Khan spoke to me of England as the birthplace of the great Richard. Is it near to Budapest?"

"Near according to the expanses of your imperial realm, somewhat far by the thinking of Christian kings. But there is trade by way of Germany between the countries, and their kings exchange envoys."

"I consider the maiden Linda very personable and I accept her with pleasure. And now I believe you have another petition to make to me. If it is what I think—to present a young man in whom you take pride—I grant it before it is asked."

There fell a brief pause in the smooth, unhurried flow of events. Everyone sensed it, and perhaps no few sensed more than that, and perhaps there were hearts other than Nicolo's, Miranda's, Sheba's, and mine that stood still.

"No, Great Khan, I have no petition to make now," Nicolo answered in a clear voice.

"You have not?"

"No, Great Khan."

"My servant Maffeo, have you?"

"No, Great Khan."

A puzzled line appeared between the Khan's brows.

"No subject or sojourner in my realm is denied the right to make offerings at my open durbar, and it comes to me that the slave girl of the young man standing near you has been long burdened by a heavy gift." The Khan turned his eyes on mine. "What is your name and abode?"

"I am Marco Polo of Venice," I answered in Jagatai Mongol, taking one step forward.

The Khan noted the use of the courtly tongue, not commonly learned by sojourners.

"Are the great horns held by your slave an offering to me?"

"Yes, Great Khan."

"What are they? I have never seen their like."

"They are the horns of the wild sheep called argali, found in your Imperial Majesty's most high realm, the Great Pamir. This pair is the largest I or the people of the country have ever seen."

"How did you come by them?"

"I followed the ram to his high ramparts and slew him with bow and arrow."

"Why, that was good hunting! But perhaps the ram was burdened from carrying such heavy horns."

"No, they were his crown, in which he took great pride. He bounded over crevices and climbed cliffs that to the eye looked sheer, his ewes and their lambs behind him."

"The lambs could follow their mothers to the heaven-jutting crags of the Pamir?"

"Yes, Great Khan. They are born there, and on their first day they must follow where their mothers lead."

"Now that is a wonder. To what use do the rams put their great horns?"

"To no use, Great Khan, except to butt rival rams. They are an endowment from God to show their sovereignty of the cliffs and crags and snows of the High Pamir."

"I am pleased with the offering and the instruction." He cast his narrow imperious eyes on Nicolo. "There is a curiosity in my mind which I wish to relieve. How came this young man to be at your side?"

"No doubt he asked the usher to post him there, although against my will."

"Why against your will? He bears the same family name as you and your brother Maffeo, and he is a Venetian. Isn't he of your blood?"

"No, Great Khan. He is the bastard son of my wife by a wandering jongleur. I suffered him to join our caravan until he desecrated the temple of the Swasti in your city of Suchow."

The squatting magicians had listened until now with blank faces and empty eyes. At this last they turned their red-rimmed eyes on me with ineffable malevolence. But they were very strangely and wonderfully rebuked. The tiger lying at the Khan's feet raised his immense ruffed head, so beautifully adorned to be so terrible, fixed his green eyes on the magicians, and uttered an ominous growl.

Only for a few seconds did I give way to the fond belief that my saints or very Providence had moved in my behalf. Such believing would comfort my heart but dull the edge of my mind. I wanted no comfort now, only the clearest eyes and the most powerful thought of all my days. Realizing this, it came to me instantly that the tiger had smelled rage and hatred on the magicians, which he took to be dangerous to his master.

"In what way did he desecrate it?" the Khan asked in deep gravity.

"By stealing a suit of fire-walkers' garments."

"Was he punished?"

"Too lightly, Great Khan. He paid a fine of nine times the head magician's valuation of the garments."

"What was that valuation?"

"Five hundred dinars, which many thought much too low."

"It is a very strange story, but you are my accredited ambassador, and our time grows short."

He looked to a mighty lord in a richly bejeweled gown—a South

Chinese, I thought—standing among the nearest to the dais with six slaves loaded with gifts. But before he spoke, I raised my hand.

The Khan saw it. He looked from me to Nicolo with searching eyes and back to me. The arrest of a thousand breaths was like a silence that lies under all the silences we know, and the tiger sprang to his feet. And then when I thought that I would not be acknowledged and the scarf would be put about my throat and my eyes darkened, the Khan slowly raised his scepter and leveled it at my breast.

3

"Great Khan, I seek justice at your hands and in your sight."

"What is your complaint?"

"My name and honor have been defamed in your hearing and the hearing of this company. I was conceived by Lucia, the noble wife of Nicolo Polo, at a time when they cohabited; and by the law of Venice and in the judgment of all men who look fairly upon our faces, I am his son."

The Khan raised his head a little and spoke to the multitude.

"It is the law of the Mongol that if a charge of bastardy is made by a husband against his wife's child, and the child or the wife contests the charge, the burden of proof is on its maker. If it can be shown that the husband and wife cohabited later than twelve months prior to the child's birth, the husband must produce unimpeachable evidence of the adultery, or the charge is dismissed. For the women of the Mongol are not chattels, but keepers of the houses and the mothers of warriors."

A long gasp filled the hall like the vagrant wind.

"Such a charge has been made in my very hearing and refuted there. So the truth must be established before any other business is done." The Khan turned to me.

"Can you prove that Nicolo and your mother Lucia cohabited in the period specified?"

"Not in this Court, Great Khan. Those who had personal knowledge of it are far away. But the charge of bastardy was not made until Nicolo returned from his first journey here with sons by a later wife. No one in Venice had ever doubted that I was his son. And before your eyes there is a maiden, once my slave in Venice, and lately Nicolo's slave, who has heard folk speak of him as my father."

"By the law of the Mongol, even a slave may give testimony. Linda, did you hear such report?"

Miranda stood tall and answered in a clear voice, for she was Marian Redvers, daughter of Sir Hugh Redvers of England.

"Sire, the noble Jews who had care of me before I became Marco Polo's slave never doubted that he was Nicolo Polo's son."

"Then the only evidence so far given that might point to bastardy was Marco's committing a crime unnatural in a man of high birth. Marco, what was your purpose in stealing the fire-walkers' robes?"

"Great Khan, I intended to bring them to you. My mother's uncle, Friar Johannes Carpini, who came to the Court of Kuyuk Khan, brought back a piece of the mineral fabric and left a letter telling its origin in the High Altai. If your Imperial Highness had not heard of it, I thought that it would be useful to your person and your subjects for fire protection."

"Marco, did Nicolo know it was a mineral substance, not dragon or salamander skin?"

"He read the letter at my trial, Great Khan."

"Nicolo, is that true?"

"Yes, Great Khan, but I was not altogether convinced."

The Khan's magicians did not look at him or at me, only crouched down with dead eyes.

"Marco Polo, the redress you made of forty-five hundred dinars was described by Nicolo as too light. Were you allowed to keep the garments?"

"No, Great Khan. They were taken from me by the magicians and given to Nicolo, who today gave them to you."

"Why did the priests give them to Nicolo?"

"Because, they said, he had not entreated a reduction of my penalty, although I was a kinsman, a fellow Christian, and a Venetian."

"How near did the fine come to taking your all?"

"I retained one camel, poor raiment, the ram's horns, and my slave girl Sheba."

"Not even a horse?"

"No, Great Khan."

"Why did you not sell the slave girl and buy one?"

"I had sold my slave girl Miranda, known to you as Linda, to pay for my transport in Nicolo's caravan, and I walked from Suchow to Xanadu in penance."

"Yet you came to my durbar in handsome dress."

"Miranda gave me a diamond that she had saved for bitter need. I sold it to buy this robe."

"Marco, isn't it true that you chose a robe that would call attention to your resemblance to Nicolo Polo?"

"Yes, Great Khan."

"Then you knew he would deny you in my hearing?"

"I thought he would do so."

"You wished that he would, believing that his denial would not be believed?"

"Yes, Great Khan."

"You were right. My eyes and my mind and my heart declare you his son. It is my conviction that he lied to you, a great sin, or to himself, a great frailty." The Khan raised his eyes to sweep the hall. "The charge of bastardy made by Nicolo Polo against Marco Polo remains unproven."

Perhaps it was the little stir that moved through the throng, eloquent of their thrilling joy, that roused up the tiger. But his great emerald eyes fixed on Nicolo as though he again smelled hate. If so, it was impotent, and he dropped down again and licked his painted shoulder.

"Marco Polo, you are entitled to redress," spoke the Great Khan. "I will not levy on my late ambassador, for he may be guilty only of an error in judgment in saying what he cannot prove. And since there have been passages between you and the slave girl Miranda that ill fit her as my slave, I now present her to you."

"Great Khan, I am rich beyond my dreams and bound to your service in deathless gratitude, and I pray your leave to speak to my slave girl Miranda and receive her reply."

"It is given, and I doubt not we will listen with cocked ears."

"Miranda, I hereby set you free, and if it is your wish, I will beg that you be given passage in the caravan of Caidu, the Khan's ambassador to Budapest, whereafter you may make your way to England."

"Marco, I accept freedom as the price of my diamond," Miranda answered instantly, "but instead of returning to England I wish to remain with you."

"Then so be it," the Khan declared in a resonant voice. "Marco Polo, I accept your service and will appoint you a task ere long." With that he raised his hand to dismiss me from his attention.

I dropped on my knees and knocked my head four times upon the floor in the full kowtow to Kublai Khan, as though indeed for him the world was made. For I was Marco Polo, an adventurer from Venice, for whom no grain of corn or dust was made, but who by the same token must get on in the world, and who loved it with great passion. And beyond all this, he was a man of middle height, past sixty, stout, with a gross nose, who had sighed a little as he parted with his new slave girl; so I could not withhold my tears.

I saw him reach for the wine cup that stood on his stand. Then the notes of a hidden flute floated into the silence and lightly breached it as a waking bird's first warble breaks the mysterious hush of dawn.

HISTORICAL NOTES

BOOK ONE

1. The legend of Prester John is still told and believed in remote areas of Central Asia. Marco Polo repeated it with tongue in cheek for reasons unknown.

2. This simple formula for invisible writing must have been known to the skilled Arabian chemists long before Marco Polo's time.

3. We cannot help wondering over the effect on history if Kublai Khan's plan of importing one hundred learned Christian priests to spread Christianity throughout Asia had been carried out. It may be that the greatest opportunity that ever came to any man came to Pope Gregory X (1271–1276). For reasons even now unknown, he let it pass.

4. The hypothesis of hatred between Nicolo Polo and his son Marco Polo underlying the plot of this novel derives from evidence that Nicolo left his wife before Marco was born to live in Constantinople, did not return at her death, and did not lay eyes on Marco until he was in his sixteenth year. If this were deliberate abandonment, which I believe, Marco obtained poetic revenge when he dictated the account of his travels that has come down to us. After brief mention of Nicolo's earlier journey, he abandons him to oblivion. Not merely pushed into the background, he is barely mentioned throughout the long chronicle.

5. The Jews were well advised. However, the rebellion of Kublai's cousin Nayan was put down in four years of costly war. "He was wrapt in a carpet, and tossed to and fro so mercilessly that he died."

6. In spite of the culture, gaiety, humor, and spotty piety of the Venetian people in Marco Polo's time, they were ferocious as wolves in punishing criminals.

7. The fact that the world was a sphere was as well known to savants in 1270 as the existence of island universes to astronomers of the present day.

8. Hypnotism was employed by mystics in India for psychoanalysis (by whatever name) long before the Christian era.

9. Even Albertus Magnus tried to make out that asbestos was salamander wool or plumage. Actually the ancients knew what it was, but never put it to general use. The piece that covered the napkin of Saint Veronica was found in a pagan tomb of the Appian Way.

10. The earliest authority on chess was Masudi, an Arab writing three hundred years before Marco Polo, and the game was ancient even then. The Italians probably learned it from the Byzantians a century before Marco Polo. Carlyle believed that King Canute of England was a chess player.

11. Eratosthenes of Alexandria, who knew perfectly well that the world was round and something like 25,000 miles in circumference, lived seventeen hundred years before Columbus.

BOOK TWO

1. Mount Ararat, nearly 17,000 feet high, stands in these cold highlands.

2. The Polos came to Hormuz with apparently every intention of taking ship on the Arabian Sea and going by sea to Cathay. Why they changed their minds and retraced their steps and journeyed overland, no historian can tell. So it is fair for a novelist to guess.

3. Marco's mention of having "lost his whole company except seven persons" to the murderous slave-catching Karaunas near the village of Konsalmi is one of the very few references to personal experiences in the whole body of his work. He tells no more than this, but the trick that the bandits played in this novel is a time-honored one among their ilk to the present day.

4. The descendants of the Old Man of the Mountains have reigned over their sect from then until now. One of the later Imams, Aga Khan I, won the favor of the British and died in 1881. The heir to the present Imam married and was divorced by an American movie star, Rita Hayworth.

5. The custom of permitting temporary marriages between travelers and the girls of the oasis was widespread in Central Asia. In Kashgar the girls were known as *chaukans* until very recently.

6. In Marco's day, lions were fairly common in Asia from Arabia to the western foot of the Pamir. However, he used the word "lion" to mean the tiger as well, and occasionally described the latter as having black stripes. Small, pale-colored tigers are found today in Persia, but it was the black-maned lion of the desert that captured the imagination of royal hunters, sculptors, architects, and poets of that region and time.

7. The author has seen a lion launch a charge so violently that he could not instantly obtain traction—his legs driving at such a pace that he literally tore the turf from under his own feet.

8. Marco Polo's description of the great wild sheep of the Pamir is the first known reference to the animal in Western literature. As a result it has been officially named *Ovis Poli*—the Marco Polo sheep. Kermit Roosevelt wrote me that he considered this sheep the finest big-game trophy he had ever taken.

9. Such tales are still told of the dread Takla Makan.

10. It is not at all unlikely that the learned physicians of the Mohammedan capitals had learned the use of escharotics.

11. On his return to Venice at long last, Marco Polo owned a slave named Pietro. By the ups and downs of Kismet, was he Zurficar the Tatar?

12. The worship of the mystic cross Swasti was widespread in the great highlands bordering the Gobi. Its worshipers were called the Swastika, which word came to mean the jointed cross itself.

13. Unlike Kublai's great palace in Peking, well described by Marco Polo, his pleasure palace Xanadu (Chandu) Keibung is not portrayed in any contemporary writing that we know. But Marco gives us a few paragraphs about the park, and a great poet dreamed about it to the whole world's gratitude.

14. The striped hunting lions Marco Polo described were patently tigers. The tigers to which Kublai's trainers had the most access were the huge, long-furred tigers of Korea and Eastern Siberia.